The Charmed Library

ALSO BY JENNIFER MOORMAN

The Magic All Around

The Vanishing of Josephine Reynolds

THE MYSTIC WATER NOVELS

Average April

A Slice of Courage Quiche

The Necessity of Lavender Tea

The Baker's Man

RETELLINGS OF FOLKLORE, MYTH, AND MAGIC

Diana and the Milky Way

Nina, the Bear's Child

Praise for Jennifer Moorman

"*The Charmed Library* is a page-turning tale of renewal, redemption, and the powerful healing magic of books, community, and love. Jennifer Moorman's lyrical style and imaginative, surprising plot charmed me from the first page to the final chapter."

—MARIE BOSTWICK, *NEW YORK TIMES* AND
USA TODAY BESTSELLING AUTHOR OF
THE BOOK CLUB FOR TROUBLESOME WOMEN

"*The Charmed Library* is a reader's dream come true. With favorite classic characters come to life, book boyfriends made real, and intrigue around the corner of each enchanted bookshelf, Moorman has woven a satisfying tale of family secrets, lifelong friendships, and the joy of new beginnings. For anyone who has ever been swept away by the magical power of words."

—LYNDA COHEN LOIGMAN, *USA TODAY* BESTSELLING
AUTHOR OF *THE LOVE ELIXIR OF AUGUSTA STERN*
AND *THE MATCHMAKER'S GIFT*

"A whimsical, heartfelt escape that honors the emotional power of great stories—not just how they begin, but how they must end."

—SUSAN MEISSNER, *USA TODAY* BESTSELLING AUTHOR
OF *A MAP TO PARADISE*, FOR *THE CHARMED LIBRARY*

"*The Charmed Library* absolutely charmed me—a love letter to the magic found in libraries, to the words of our favorite books that open up whole worlds, to the power of love to heal. From the first page, I was enraptured by Stella's story. What book lover hasn't wished they could meet their fictional friends and crushes in the real world? But woven into the wonder of literary characters coming to life is a journey of self-discovery and the realization of how instrumental books are to a community and to a woman trying to find her way. This is Moorman's best book yet!"

—JOY CALLAWAY, INTERNATIONAL BESTSELLING AUTHOR OF THE STAR OF CAMP GREENE

"*The Charmed Library* is a wish come true—a love letter passed from book to reader and back again. Jennifer Moorman invites us into a world both timeless and fresh, reminding us to savor each moment, delight in the magic hiding in plain sight, and challenge the impossible. Like its author, this story sparkles and is destined to charm readers everywhere."

—MELISSA R. COLLINGS, AWARD-WINNING AUTHOR OF THE FALSE FLAT

"This twisty, intriguing tale is brimming with atmosphere, heartbreak, magic, and ultimately a bright spark of hope!"

—RACHEL LINDEN, BESTSELLING AUTHOR OF THE MAGIC OF LEMON DROP PIE, FOR THE VANISHING OF JOSEPHINE REYNOLDS

"In *The Vanishing of Josephine Reynolds*, Moorman deftly weaves her trademark everyday magic into a tale of time travel, mystery, and romance. At the heart of the story is Josephine, a young woman so stricken by grief that she wishes to no longer exist. Transported to the 1920s when she passes through a magical door, Josephine has one last chance at life—if she can find the courage to live and love again."

—KERRY ANNE KING, BESTSELLING AUTHOR OF IMPROBABLY YOURS

"An ancestral home holds stories, secrets, and maybe even the ability to rewrite history in Jennifer Moorman's latest enthralling must-read.

The Vanishing of Josephine Reynolds seamlessly blends the present day with 1927—and a splash of Moorman's signature magic—in a moving, unputdownable race against time. A testament to family ties, the power of love, and the indomitable human spirit, Moorman's latest proves that, sometimes, the impossible can become possible. I was hooked from the very first enchanting page."

—KRISTY WOODSON HARVEY, *NEW YORK TIMES* BESTSELLING AUTHOR OF *A HAPPIER LIFE*

"*The Vanishing of Josephine Reynolds* drips with lush Jazz Age detail, a vivid cast of characters, and a protagonist whose future literally depends on her ability to navigate the past. In one novel, Jennifer Moorman gives us a time-bending tale of both suspense and self-discovery and a heroine we can't help but cheer as she learns what she's truly made of—and perhaps, how to love again."

—BARBARA DAVIS, BESTSELLING AUTHOR OF *THE ECHO OF OLD BOOKS*

"*The Vanishing of Josephine Reynolds* is absolutely mesmerizing! Jennifer Moorman expertly weaves a story of time travel, suspense, love, and the 1920s into a book with twists and turns and an ending I never saw coming. I stayed up *way* too late for too many nights simply because I couldn't put it down. It's magnificent!"

—MADDIE DAWSON, BESTSELLING AUTHOR OF *LET'S PRETEND THIS WILL WORK*

"*The Magic All Around* is brimming with lyrical Southern beauty, page-turning mystery, and delightful magic. With a house built of enchanted wood, a mother-daughter bond that changes a life, a family saga that brings you home, and a captivating love story, *The Magic All Around* is a work of storytelling-art. For readers of Sara

Addison Allen and Lauren K. Denton, this is your next captivating read. If we have eyes to see and ears to hear, Jennifer Moorman is here to remind us that there really is magic all around."

—PATTI CALLAHAN HENRY, *NEW YORK TIMES* BESTSELLING AUTHOR OF *THE SECRET BOOK OF FLORA LEA*

"Brimming with love and crackling with magic, this story will feel like home on a page—whether it's the home you miss or the home you're hoping to find."

—NATALIE LLOYD, BESTSELLING AUTHOR OF *A SNICKER OF MAGIC*, FOR *THE MAGIC ALL AROUND*

"Combine four parts love, two parts excitement, a dash of humor, and a pinch of magic, and you have Jennifer Moorman's delightful *The Baker's Man*. Moorman's sweet, heartfelt confection will please anyone looking for a charming, witty, utterly delectable read!"

—LAUREN K. DENTON, *USA TODAY* BESTSELLING AUTHOR OF *THE HIDEAWAY* AND *A PLACE TO LAND*

"Jennifer Moorman's *The Baker's Man* is a teaspoon of love, a dash of magic, and a whole heaping cup of Southern charm. Anna's legacy of unconventional romance and luscious baked goods is a treat from start to finish. Perfect for fans of Amy E. Reichert and Jenny Colgan."

—AIMIE K. RUNYAN, BESTSELLING AUTHOR OF *THE SCHOOL FOR GERMAN BRIDES* AND *THE MEMORY OF LAVENDER AND SAGE*

"*The Baker's Man* is a charming recipe of magic, romance, friendship, and the importance of staying true to yourself."

—HEATHER WEBBER, *USA TODAY* BESTSELLING AUTHOR OF *MIDNIGHT AT THE BLACKBIRD CAFÉ*

The Charmed Library

A Novel

JENNIFER MOORMAN

HARPER MUSE

The Charmed Library

Copyright © 2026 by Jennifer Moorman

All rights reserved. Printed in the United Kingdom. No portion of this book may be reproduced, stored in a retrieval system, or transmitted in any form or by any means—electronic, mechanical, photocopy, recording, scanning, or other—except for brief quotations in critical reviews or articles, without the prior written permission of the publisher.

Published by Harper Muse, an imprint of HarperCollins Focus LLC, 501 Nelson Place, Nashville, TN 37214, USA.

HarperCollins Publishers, Macken House, 39/40 Mayor Street Upper, Dublin 1, D01 C9W8, Ireland (https://www.harpercollins.com)

This book is a work of fiction. The characters, incidents, and dialogue are drawn from the author's imagination and are not to be construed as real. Any resemblance to actual events or persons, living or dead, is entirely coincidental.

Any internet addresses (websites, blogs, etc.) in this book are offered as a resource. They are not intended in any way to be or imply an endorsement by HarperCollins Focus LLC, nor does HarperCollins Focus LLC vouch for the content of these sites for the life of this book.

Without limiting the exclusive rights of any author, contributor or the publisher of this publication, any unauthorized use of this publication to train generative artificial intelligence (AI) technologies is expressly prohibited. HarperCollins also exercise their rights under Article 4(3) of the Digital Single Market Directive 2019/790 and expressly reserve this publication from the text and data mining exception.

Library of Congress Cataloging-in-Publication Data
Names: Moorman, Jennifer, 1978- author
Title: The charmed library : a novel / Jennifer Moorman.

ISBN: 9781400259007

Art Direction: Halie Cotton
Cover Design: Lindy Kasler
Interior Design: Chloe Foster

25 26 27 28 CPI 10 9 8 7 6 5 4 3 2 1

MIX
Paper | Supporting
responsible forestry
FSC® C013604

To you, the one who's always wanted to have a slumber party in the library and magic your favorite fictional character out of a book. I'll bring the snacks.

I almost wish I hadn't gone down that rabbit-hole—
and yet—and yet—it's rather curious, you know, this
sort of life!

   —Alice in *Alice's Adventures in Wonderland*

The only thing that you absolutely have to know,
is the location of the library.

           —Albert Einstein

Prologue

Stella Parker had never burned a book in her life. Had never once thrown pages of text—much less handwritten love letters and poetry—into a fire. Yet there she was, purposefully setting fire to one of the most precious things in her life: words.

Wisps of smoke and ashes floated from the ancient flue on a blistering Saturday early evening breeze. The haze rounded corners, spiraled up tree trunks along the Main Street sidewalk, and lingered in pockets of shadow. The townsfolk in Blue Sky Valley, North Carolina, stumbled into the ashy air unexpectedly and were overcome with longing. Many were compelled to hurry home and hug someone or to buy a journal and write down their thoughts. Some wandered out into the mature pine forest until the soothing sounds of birds and the soft green blanket of grass beneath their feet helped lessen the ache. None were aware of *why* they felt the unusual emotions or that their peace came at the cost of Stella's heartache.

Deep inside the town's library, where dust mites danced in the slanted light and the walls hummed with the energy of a million stories, the words Stella sacrificed did not simply vanish—they would always belong to this town, to its magic, to the unseen force that wove Blue Sky Valley together. As the ashes faded into the dusk, the library listened, waiting, knowing that every story—especially the ones set free—would find its way home.

Chapter 1

*B*rilliant orange flames separated inside the decades-old furnace as Stella stared, mesmerized. The fire burned hot at its core, blackening the edges of the paper and ravenously consuming everything within its steel walls. Stella, frustrated and tired of her own heartache, waited for the pressure to release from her solar plexus—that spot just below her rib cage that ached every time something was *wrong*. But so far, the discomfort had only intensified.

Even as she watched her journal burn, along with every word she'd written over the past few months, her fingers itched to record this event, to detail the way the ink-stained pages writhed in the flames, the way flecks of paper lifted on pops of air and danced before shriveling.

Guilt planted a seed deep in her belly and started to grow something thorny and tangled. Her stomach clenched when three golden, shimmering words rose from the flames and slid out the open mouth of the furnace. They glittered against the black metal like stars in a midnight sky. **Surrender. Anew. Forgiveness.**

Was the journal forgiving her? Or were the words telling her she needed to extend forgiveness? But to whom? Not *him*. No way did he deserve her forgiveness. The lines between Stella's brows deepened. Didn't surrender mean *giving up*? What was left to give up? As if life hadn't asked her to give up too much already. The glowing words dissipated into the darkness of the basement.

There would always be another journal to fill. Because there would never be enough paper, enough *space*, to release all the words clawing, springing, secreting their way out of her. There would never be an end to smears of ink on her fingers or the phrases that trailed up the walls. She would forever see words slinking across floors and slipping into her room at night like best friends intent on keeping her company.

For as long as she could remember, Stella had seen words the same way someone might spot a bird or watch a dragonfly zipping through cattails. She saw words everywhere. Ever since she'd received her first pack of crayons, she'd been crowding white spaces with all the words pressing in on her heart. Stella captured words and poems and cataloged them in journals. She drew word maps in colored ink in her diaries and added special captions to photographs when words floated over images in a family album. She jotted down people's names and the words that followed them like beloved pets. She made notes about places around town and all the words living there, even the haunted ones she sometimes saw ghosting around. Words like *eerie*, *bewitched*, and *phantasmic*.

When Stella was a child, her mother had encouraged her to share the words, insisting her talent was a fantastical gift that would guide Stella toward her dreams. Desiring the special attention and wanting to please her mother, Stella kept, wrote, and cherished the words. But after her mother was gone, the idea that the words could lead Stella to her dreams seemed like a terrible joke. In what dreams did mothers leave? She tried to ignore the words. She wanted to refuse their neediness to be caught and loved.

But Stella quickly realized she didn't have a choice. She couldn't neglect the words. She couldn't stop their appearance or keep them housed inside her. Some days the words felt like a swarm of agitated bees living in her body, and to release their fury, she had to write. She worried she might implode if she didn't free them, if she didn't give them new life on the page. What if she kept them trapped inside and then suffocated beneath their creative weight?

Some days the words were delicate and soft like goose feathers floating through her. On those days she felt light and joyful, and her pen flowed across the pages like water easing down a river. She learned to pay just enough attention to the words to catalog them with the hope that they would eventually stop showing up when she grew up.

That had yet to happen, and today irritation stung her. Why hadn't setting fire to her past—literally—soothed her? Why couldn't she burn the words, the *emotions*, as easily as the flames destroyed the paper?

Maybe she was being dramatic. That was what her older brother, Percy, would say in his easy teasing way, but there was probably a whole lot of truth laced through his jokes. Where Stella was emotional, Percy was even-keeled. Where she was paralyzed some days by the frantic beating of her own heart, Percy appeared perpetually calm and peaceful.

The fire crackled, and Wade Haynes's smiling face lurked in her mind. Her jaw clenched. The last time she'd seen him was when he walked out of her apartment six months ago, leaving behind a stifling feeling of failure, a fast-food receipt stained with the greasy fingerprints of his children, and two simple, charred-black words: **passing time**. She'd been all-in with that relationship, believing they were both in love. But his walking away and never contacting her again proved she couldn't have been more wrong. The truth that he'd simply been *passing time* with her filled her with shame and fury.

The rejection still pricked like she'd eaten stinging nettles. Stella had filled a journal full of letters and poems she would never send, *couldn't* send to Wade. Now, months later, on the anniversary of their first date, two cups of overly sweet coffee churned in her belly. She knelt in front of the wood-burning furnace in the library's basement and tested Ray Bradbury's temperature hypothesis. Did paper catch fire at 451 degrees Fahrenheit? How could she even prove the author's statement? The antique thermometer gauge didn't register above 250 degrees. The more important hypothesis was: Would setting fire to words inspired by Wade set her free?

The answer was no.

She wanted to burn Wade's memory from her heart, turn it all to ashes she could sweep up and dump into the garbage. But instead, a memory of Wade and her laughing surfaced. Followed by the memory of the afternoon she met him at the state park and he'd taken her in his arms and spun her around. Then the day he'd tried to waltz with her in the art gallery and they'd almost knocked over a porcelain vase. Next, the time they went to the movies, sat in the back row like teenagers, and he couldn't stop kissing her. Then the day he'd texted her ten different haikus about his love for her and how they'd be connected forever.

"Enough!" she spat and squeezed her eyes closed as if that would stop the barrage. Her shoulders slumped. She and Wade had been happy. *Really* happy—until they weren't.

Stella glanced at the furnace. Words and books were some of the few things that understood her. How many times had she wished to disappear into a novel? Would the thousands of books in the library above her now chant *murderer*? Would she walk the gauntlet of their disapproval, their condemnation? Warm tears of frustration left wet tracks on her cheeks. Tears heavy with sorrow splattered on the floor, and the ground trembled beneath her feet, sending out waves of disappointment.

"I'm sorry," she whispered as the thin journal cover shriveled in the furnace.

A sheet of paper, charred and brittle around the edges, lifted on a wave of heat and floated out of the furnace opening. Stella pinched it between two fingers. Burns like bullet holes marred some of the words, but she had memorized the poem.

The sky was endless,
the silence deep.
The sun dropped into the trees
and I never once tried to stop it,
only watched and shivered
in the wind,
in the absence of you.
I love you with a love
that wounds.
Reckless, stubborn, willful.
I hug my ribs,
thank them for caging my heart
or else I'd never have control of it,
if I ever do.
I love you with a love
that overcomes me
like the tide,
rushing away,
stealing everything from my grasp,
even you.

Stella sighed. Blackened paper crumbled around the edges and fell toward the floor like dying butterflies. She knelt in front of the furnace, sailed the poem back into the flames, and watched it burn to ash.

The basement door at the top of the stairs opened, sending golden light down the steps, highlighting the worn treads. "Stella?"

She jumped to her feet, swiped at her wet cheeks, and slammed the furnace door shut, singeing the skin on her fingertips. The fire hissed and swelled inside its metal cage. She shook out her hand, trying to cool her fingers, and winced. "Be right up," she called.

The first few steps creaked as Arnold Cohen, the head librarian, descended halfway. "Should I ask why you're using the furnace? Don't look so shocked. A few of the windows are open, and it looks like I have a fog machine going upstairs in the historical stacks."

Stella glanced over her shoulder at the furnace before meeting Arnie at the staircase. She cleared her throat. "I was testing hypotheses."

His thick, graying eyebrows lifted. "And?"

Stella gripped the handrail and tugged herself up the first few steps. The old wood groaned in resonance with her heart. "The results are disappointing."

Behind his glasses, Arnie's dark, deep-set eyes watched her, studied her. "You can't burn away the past."

She squeezed the railing harder. The nape of her neck tingled as though embers clung to her skin. Her exhalation shuddered in the space between them, rippling through the air. "I wish I had a shovel to dig it out then."

"If you could have taken the easy way, what would you have learned? Nothing."

Stella scowled. "And what have I learned, Arnie?"

"How to handle your heart differently next time." Arnie turned and ascended the stairs. "It didn't escape me that you carried your journal down here and yet you're not returning with it. I assume you want me to keep it a secret from the books upstairs that you tossed one of their brethren to the flames."

Stella followed him up and switched off the basement light. A flickering glow quivered across the darkened concrete floor and caught her attention. Words formed in the cavorting shadows. **Goodbye. Forget. Next time.** There would be no *next time* for how to handle her heart; as far as she was concerned, her heart was a dead, useless thing taking up space in her chest. She closed and locked the basement door.

✦ ✦ ✦

STELLA HAD OPENED the Blue Sky Valley Public Library that morning, having no idea that she'd sneak away that afternoon to burn her journal. Just after lunch, a visitor had wandered in.

The older woman, probably in her mid-sixties, had approached Stella at the circulation desk. She was looking for a self-help book, specifically one covering the topic of releasing the past. When they arrived at the section, Stella pointed out a few books that might be of interest, but the woman didn't say anything for a moment.

"Is there anything else I can help you with?" Stella asked, sensing the woman's hesitation.

Her tears surprised Stella, but not as much as her words. "Don't do what I did."

Such a broad declaration that included a world of options. The woman could be encouraging Stella not to wear orange lipstick as much as she could mean don't rob the local bank.

She continued, "Don't spend your life re-creating the past. He ran out on me twenty years ago for 'the love of his life,' and do you know how I've spent those same twenty years?" Stella shook her head. "Angry, bitter, you name it. Now look at me!" Her voice rose above an acceptable library level. "Shriveled, that's what I am."

She wiped at her tears and forced a smile that looked more pained than natural. She pulled one of the self-help books from the shelf and smoothed her hand across its cover. "I'm on a road trip to find myself. I didn't realize until an hour ago that I had been taking him with me everywhere, holding what he did to me inside my body like a terrible disease. Reliving my past over and over again. He's been riding in the passenger seat this whole time. Metaphorically, of course."

The woman patted Stella's arm. "Listen to me, going on like I've lost it. Well, I plan to lose *him*, which is why I'm here and why I'm going to start with this book." She held out the choice to Stella. "Don't do what I did. Don't hold on to things that hurt you."

The woman's words echoed through Stella's mind long after she'd checked out the book and left the library. It wasn't until late afternoon that Stella consciously realized she had the journal in her purse, which forced her to admit that she'd been carrying the memory of Wade around with her *for months*. Like an albatross around her neck.

Would she still be hung up on Wade twenty years from now? That question fueled her to burn the journal and attempt to burn Wade's memory along with it. She'd only half succeeded and was left with a growing sense of remorse.

There was no reason to stay until the library closed tonight. Arnie tried to send her home early. Only two people had come in during the late afternoon, and each stayed less than an hour. With no special activities happening that evening, Arnie could have handled the closing routine alone, but Stella wasn't in the mood to go home and sit.

Because she wouldn't just sit; she'd fret about why she hadn't been able to incinerate Wade's memory from her heart. Next the guilt, possibly coupled with regret, would creep in about the burned journal. No, she'd rather go home after staying at the library as long as possible and then face-plant on her bed without thinking at all.

She'd worked alongside Arnie as his library assistant for the past four years, so the few nighttime procedures went quickly. At nine p.m. Stella said good night to Arnie, grabbed an armful of books she planned to read during the next two weeks, and carried them to the rear parking lot. A creature of habit, Stella parked her car in the same spot every day. First row, fourth space, to the right of the library's exit.

Thanks to a hundred-year-old oak tree, this spot was covered in afternoon shade that kept her leather car seats from feeling like molten lava after sitting outside all day in the Southern heat. Years ago, the local Lions Club championed for the mature tree not to be harmed when the city paved the library's parking lot. The grand oak now grew out of an open circle in the black asphalt, and over time its enormous roots had buckled and cracked the pavement like an overcooked hot dog, creating natural speed bumps throughout the lot.

As she walked to her car, Stella hopped over words that slipped out of the pavement's cracks. **Uno, due, tre, quattro, cinque.** She glanced at the book on top of her stack, an English–Italian dictionary. Her newest quest was to learn enough Italian that she could read Michelangelo's *Rime* in its original language. So far, she could count to ten, say a few casual greetings, and order *gelato al pistacchio*. Basically a vocabulary far outmatched by an Italian preschooler.

She placed the books in the passenger seat and drove in silence through downtown. Not much had changed in Blue Sky Valley since she was a kid, and tonight, its predictable routine comforted her. Many of the town's lights winked out one by one as she drove.

Some shop owners put their businesses to bed for the night, flipping around Closed signs and switching off interior lamps. Other businesses turned on lights, calling forth those interested in the nightlife, which was far from wild in a small town like this. There wasn't much to do in the historic downtown area other than find consolation in the corner pub or dine at Bruno's Café.

Just on the edge of the town center was the theater that had room enough to show two movies only. Currently it was playing flashbacks—*Grease* and *Jaws*—and selling double feature tickets for those who wanted to enjoy the summer nights with romance followed up with a dose of terror at the thought of swimming in the ocean.

Stella pulled into the shadowed driveway of her childhood home and pressed a button on the garage door opener attached to the visor. The aluminum door groaned as it lifted and revealed the almost-empty interior meant for two cars. She parked in the middle and then shuffled to the mailbox. All of today's mail was junk, but three different Realtor postcards were part of the stack. One had a note scribbled on it in blue ink. *Stella, Percy said you were ready to sell. Call me! Anita.*

Stella ripped the postcard in half and then dumped all the mail into the outside trash bin. She was tempted to call Percy and tell him to back off, but that would require a conversation she didn't have the energy for. She lowered the garage door behind her. Leaning into her open car door, she wrangled the stack of books from the passenger seat.

As she unlocked the house-to-garage door, she wondered for the umpteenth time why she bothered to lock a door that was secured behind a garage door no human could manually open from the outside. She knew this to be true because during a power outage last month, her car had been trapped in the garage. Not even YouTube how-to videos could help her figure out how to lift the metal door

10

when the pull cord was stuck. She hadn't been strong enough to tug it free, and since she lived alone, there was no one to help her. A peal of loneliness echoed through her now.

Stella dropped the books on the kitchen counter. "Hello, house," she said as she flipped on the hallway light. Her cell phone dinged, alerting her to a message from her best friend, Ariel. She grabbed a pencil from the kitchen counter, twirled her dark curls into a messy bun, and stabbed the pencil into her hair to hold it in place.

Ariel had moved to Blue Sky Valley, just down the street from Stella on Magnolia Drive, when they were in fourth grade. Ariel introduced herself that very first day, and Stella knew they'd be fast friends. With airy words like **hope**, **enchantment**, and **stardust** floating around Ariel like confetti, how could anyone not gravitate toward her? Stella certainly had.

She grabbed the library books and carried them into the living room and debated whether she should tell Ariel about burning the journal. Just thinking about it caused her stomach to ache. But if anyone would understand, it was Ariel, who'd been by Stella's side through every celebration and every heartache since they were nine years old.

Stella opened Ariel's text: The first customer of the morning asked if I could dye her poodle red and cut her to look like Elmo. How do you cut a poodle to look like Elmo, I ask. She shows me a YouTube video that I can't unsee. How was your day? What's on the schedule tomorrow?

Stella smiled for the first time in hours, then texted: Tell me you said yes. Send photos. I'm about a solid 6 today on the scale of life. What would it be like to be a ten on life's enjoyment scale? What would she give to be free of the heaviness, to find her way to *real* love and joy? She continued: Tomorrow's library events include adventure club and maybe the knitting club. What's on tomorrow's agenda for you? Dogs groomed like dromedary camels?

Ariel replied: I did not agree to Elmo. That would have been a total dog-tastrophe. Nor would I agree to camels, although I could be bribed with the right gift. When are you gonna learn to knit so I can sell dog sweaters on the side? Breakfast tomorrow? I can pick you up in my sweet ride.

Stella laughed. The veterinary hospital had invested in a mobile dog grooming unit, and Ariel, the local dog groomer, drove it all over town and the surrounding towns six days a week. It put smiles on faces to see the neon-pink Fur Real Dog Grooming van drive by. The horn even sounded like a dog bark. Stella texted that she'd love to have breakfast, and they set a time for Ariel to swing by the library and pick her up.

Stella placed her phone on the counter, but it dinged again. Ariel again. Want to talk about why you're a 6 today? I've been told I'm THE BEST listener.

Just knowing Ariel cared and wanted to listen eased the ache inside Stella, but she didn't know how to articulate what she was feeling, so she replied: Thanks, but we can chat tomorrow. 🦄

Stella opened the refrigerator, which was shockingly bare, and what little it did have wasn't snack-worthy. Suddenly, a burning sensation started in her heart, like a sparkler shoved straight through her chest. She released the refrigerator door and sidestepped, pressing a hand to her heart and leaning over in pain. Was this horrendous heartburn? A heart attack? A vision of the burning journal flared to life in her mind. In a panic, she thought, *Is this because I burned the words? Am I being punished?* The intensity scalded her insides and pushed "Dear Lord" from her lips.

In a moment that could have been ripped from a *Ghostbusters* movie, what looked like violet fluid struggled to rise from a kitchen tile, but once it fully emerged, it formed a group of words. Pulsating letters, dark plum in the center and pale lavender toward the edges. Undulating tendrils, like the roots of a plant, hung from the letters as if they'd been dug out of a magical garden. The words trembled across the floor near her feet.

"'I fell in,'" she muttered, and instantly the burning in her chest subsided. Stella inhaled a deep breath and stood straight. The words rushed across the floor, up the bottom row of kitchen cabinets, and over the countertop until they wrapped around a purple pen near one of her half-used journals and then disappeared.

Stunned and slightly frightened, Stella stared at the pen and massaged her fingers into her chest. The words had never been so demanding, never so forceful. She'd also never seen words appear that way before. These were different, more alive, more substantial than they'd ever been.

Stella walked to the purple pen and opened the journal to a blank page. She didn't need to question what the words wanted. They *wanted* to be written down. But why? What did the words mean? At the top of a clean page, she wrote, *I fell in*.

Fell in what? Stella thought of a dozen things she'd fallen into over the past year. Despair, hopelessness, faux love. She'd also fallen into books, into fits of laughter with Ariel, and into silence at the sight of a sunset.

She stared at the purple words on the page, a crease forming between her brows. A shiver ran up her arms as she closed the journal. Part of her wanted to shrug off this new experience with her beloved words, to say it was no big deal. But she placed a hand over her heart and knew they were no ordinary words. They had an agenda . . . one that might burn a hole right through her.

Chapter 2

Sleeping peacefully wasn't in the scope of possibilities for Stella, not after the blistering eruption of purple words demanded her attention in a way that frightened her. When she was younger, Stella saw words every day, especially when her mother was still with them. As she'd grown, they slowed to appear a few times a week. But never, in all her years of word spotting, had *any* of them felt like last night. She desperately wished the purple-words experience was an anomaly, a freak occurrence.

But she had doubts—a truckload of them. Mainly because the words *I fell in* meant nothing to her, which led her to believe there was more . . . More what? She didn't know. The idea of more words accompanied by more pain bred trepidation within her.

At ten the next morning Stella dragged herself down the wide, concrete library entrance stairs, masking a yawn behind her hand. A pink van idled at the curb. Ariel waved at her through the window. A group of kids walking up the sidewalk made hand signals for

Ariel to press the horn. She obliged, and the kids burst into laughter at the artificial dog woofing. Oh to be young, rested, and joyful.

Stella opened the passenger door and hauled herself up into the cab. This month Ariel had a stripe of fuchsia dye ribboning through her blond ponytail. Last month it was sherbet orange, and the month before had been aqua, but only the hair underneath the top layer. Ariel's fresh face was makeup free with a tinted sunscreen to protect her fair complexion. A scattering of tan freckles connecting on the bridge of her button nose trailed along both cheeks. She looked rested, an obvious contrast to Stella's exhausted state.

"Thanks for picking me up." Stella wrinkled her nose at the smell of shampoo and cooked pork. "Why does it smell like—"

"Bacon? Delicious buttery biscuits?" Ariel finished. She reached behind her head to a built-in metal shelf and retrieved an oversize white paper sack. She handed the bag to Stella. The bottom was still warm.

"I swung by the diner and grabbed breakfast for us. You know how packed it is on Sundays, so I thought we could drive to the park but dine in so we can enjoy the AC. At first I considered a quick morning picnic, but—"

"It's June and definitely too hot?" Stella said.

"Like swampy hot," Ariel agreed. "You should see the line at Frost Bites."

Stella buckled her seat belt. "It's probably a mile long."

"At least two miles, and it's not even lunchtime." Ariel shifted the van into Drive. "Can you imagine what July and August will feel like?"

Stella nodded. "Like walking on the sun."

"Barefoot." Ariel slipped on a pair of oversize silver sunglasses and turned up the radio. "Under the Boardwalk" blasted on the oldies station, and Ariel belted out the tune as the van wound its way through town toward the city park. She glanced over at Stella. "You're not singing. Why aren't you singing? We love this song."

Stella yawned again and shrugged. "You take the solo today."

Once they were parked and gazing out over a vibrant-green swath of grass and mature oak trees, Stella unpacked the bag on the dashboard. There was an egg white, kale, and tomato biscuit for Ariel and a bacon, egg, and cheese biscuit for Stella. Ariel had also ordered extra biscuits to share. Stella divided the wad of flimsy brown napkins and unwrapped her biscuit.

"I didn't think to ask for plates," Ariel said, folding down the paper wrapped around her biscuit.

Stella waved off the idea that they needed a fancier setup. "Just more trash to bother with. How's your morning been? Any outrageous requests?"

Ariel covered her mouth and half chewed, half laughed. "Pretty tame morning. I had an early wash and trim first thing over in Willow Lake, and after this little break with you, my day is jam-packed. I'm counting on this breakfast to hold me over through the afternoon."

"You need me to bring you lunch?" Stella asked. "I don't mind, and Arnie won't care if I cut out for a bit."

Ariel shook her head, and her moonstone earrings swayed. "Nah, but thanks. I'd rather push through and then take a longer dinner break to eat without stressing about running behind."

They ate in silence for a few beats. Stella's mind drifted to last night's words, and she rubbed a ghost ache from her collarbone. She couldn't work out what any of it meant by overthinking, but that didn't stop her brain from darting all over in an attempt to solve the mystery.

As she bit into the biscuit, her mind refocused on breakfast. The local diner, Grits & Gravy, baked the absolute best biscuits in the world, and Stella would debate this with anyone, knowing she'd win. Unlike stereotype diners that were grease pits, Grits & Gravy was anything but a sloppy, grease-filled locale. The food was an unusual combination of comforting and sophisticated. The menu was filled with homey favorites, but all the ingredients were fresh and food was cooked to order, elevating the usual diner fare.

The buttery biscuit had a crunch on the bottom with a soft, pillowy, layered center, and Stella couldn't imagine anything more perfect to sandwich between it than her favorite breakfast combo: bacon, eggs, and melted American cheese.

"These biscuits are everything," she said.

Ariel nodded. "Divinely inspired."

"Mind-blowing."

Ariel lifted her hand and waved it through the air. "Miraculous."

Stella laughed. "You win."

Ariel poked the last bite into her mouth. "These biscuits win."

Stella glanced out the passenger-side window. A young man tossed an orange Frisbee to an overly eager border collie. A jogger ran by on the trail that wound through the park. Just thinking about going for a run exaggerated Stella's fatigue. She reached for a napkin and wiped a blob of cheese from the corner of her mouth.

Ariel cleared her throat and turned down the radio's volume. "Maybe I'm wrong, but you seem a bit off today. I'm also interested in why you were a six yesterday. Does it have something to do with why you're giving off a muddy vibe today?"

Stella paused, confused by the statement and wondering if somehow Ariel knew about the purple words. Then she remembered their texts last night. "Oh . . . it's nothing worth talking about."

Ariel pointed at Stella's face. "You have the worst poker face.

Actually, you have *no* poker face. As you said the words, your facial expression drooped and you got sad eyes."

Stella tried to look offended, but she wasn't. Ariel knew all of her expressions and diversion tactics. Stella finished her biscuit, then took a slow inhale. "Muddy vibe? Sounds gross, which is probably accurate. I didn't sleep well."

"Any particular reason?"

Stella nodded. Multiple reasons, but she wasn't ready to talk about the words yet. "I burned a journal yesterday."

Ariel's eyebrows rose dramatically. "Like some kind of ritual? I know people burn candles and papers with messages on them to release bad energy or to cut energy cords, but you? You burned a *book*? You don't even dog-ear the pages." Ariel glanced out the window. "Have we slipped into an alternate universe? What was in the journal? Symbolic writings?"

Stella held up a hand, her buttery fingertips reflecting the sunlight. "Whoa, that got real woo-woo real fast. A ritual, seriously? What kind of ritual would *I* be doing? No, it was everything I'd been writing for and about Wade during the past six months. I'm over it. I'm tired of feeling connected to him, so I burned the journal in the library's furnace."

Ariel twisted off the cap on her water bottle and took a long drink before responding. "That's kinda like a ritual. You were hoping to sever your connection by burning everything you wrote about him."

Stella shrugged and wiped her fingers on a napkin. "All those words . . . burned." *Lost forever.* And yet she still felt every one of the words vibrating inside her. Burning the journal hadn't erased what happened from her heart. She thought of the golden words that slipped out of the furnace. **Surrender. Anew. Forgiveness.**

Maybe she should start a new journal, write those three words at the top of a clean page. But that didn't *feel* like what she was supposed to glean from them. Understanding what the words meant and how they were connected to her life had never been as confusing as the past two days.

"How do you feel now?"

"Confused," Stella admitted.

"Should I assume by you being a six last night that it didn't go as planned?" Ariel asked.

Stella opened her own water bottle and took a drink. "Why can't I get over him?"

Ariel cut her gaze over to Stella and pursed her lips. Then she toyed with the turquoise pendant hanging from her necklace. "Because you don't want to."

Stella choked when she tried to swallow. Drops of water dribbled from her mouth. "What?" she squawked. "Why would you say that?" She wiped her mouth with a thin napkin, tearing it in her roughness.

Ariel inhaled a slow breath and then pinned her Caribbean-blue eyes on Stella. "Now, don't get mad, but if you wanted to let it go, you would. There might be a bit of bitterness lingering inside you. I can help you get it out—"

Stella bristled. "I'm not bitter!" Then she immediately flushed with embarrassment and sagged against the seat. She thought about the older woman visiting the library yesterday—she'd been bitter for twenty years. "I'm sorry. I shouldn't yell at you. I didn't sleep much last night."

Ariel's understanding smile sent a wash of guilt over Stella. "For what it's worth, I think burning the journal was brave. It shows you're *trying* to let go, and that's something. You've been through a lot in the past four years. Leaving Memphis, losing your dad, moving home, and then spending a year with Wade, hoping he'd come through, only to realize he was . . ."

"Stringing me along the whole time? Using me and lying to me? Making me believe love was real?"

Ariel gazed out at the park as sunlight glinted off the hood of the van. "I wouldn't describe it exactly that way, but yeah. It's no wonder you've been angry and clutching reasons to stay that way."

Was she holding on to Wade . . . on purpose? The idea made her insides squirm. Being with Wade had made Stella feel alive and seen. While he hadn't been as interested in books, he'd willingly listened to her prattle on about them. He'd also praised Stella's creativity and encouraged her to write, not just in her journals, but poetry and short stories. He'd even written poetry for her. It was lousy, for sure, but it had charmed her.

The memories shot heat into her cheeks, followed by a burst of anger. Why had he bothered showering her with so much love and attention if he never planned to follow through with his promises? Stella had tucked those stupid poems into the journal, which was now a pile of ash.

Desperately needing to divert her thoughts from her ex, she glanced over at Ariel and noticed flower-shaped words spiraling around her best friend's throat like a daisy-chain necklace. **Intrigued. Romantic pursuits. Ask me out.** "Are you dating someone?"

Ariel shot a look at Stella, and her eyes narrowed. "Are you using your word magic on me?"

Stella laughed. "Are you admitting I'm right?"

Ariel sighed dramatically. "No, but I'd like to be. He's a client, though, so I don't know how it would work."

Stella's mouth dropped open. "Wait, you'd like to be dating one of your dogs?"

Ariel realized her mistake and giggled. "Wrong word. He's a *customer*. He brings in his German shepherd, Scout. He named her after a character from one of his favorite books."

"*To Kill a Mockingbird?*"

Ariel nodded.

"You should probably marry him. A book nerd is a solid choice."

Ariel scrunched her face. "Marry him? I'm not even sure we can make a date happen. He's really cute and nice, and he's not wearing a wedding band, but I have no idea if he's dating anyone. Plus, some married men don't wear rings. And it's not like I can slide that in without being awkward. 'Hey, a regular shampoo and cut for Scout, and are you single?' There's just not a way to segue there."

"You have his name and number," Stella said with a sly smile. "You could call him and ask him out."

Ariel gasped. "Not happening. I'd prefer it to be more organic and not force it."

Stella smirked. "You mean you'd prefer he do the asking."

Ariel reached for another biscuit. "Exactly. Want half?"

Stella nodded, and Ariel split the biscuit down the middle, handing the larger half to Stella. They sat in silence for a few moments eating.

Stella replayed tossing the journal into the fire with hope that it would free her from the connection with Wade, but if anything, she felt worse. Then she thought of the violet words that ripped an ache through her chest last night: *I fell in.* Did the words have something to do with Wade?

"You know what I love most about fairy tales?" Stella asked.

"The jewels? The crowns? Having your own princess castle?"

Stella chuckled. "All great guesses, but I love how you always know who the bad guy is in fairy tales. He's easy to recognize because he's probably wearing black or a wild cape or has arched eyebrows and an evil gleam in his eyes. But here in our world, the bad guy sometimes looks like Prince Charming, and he's charismatic, intelligent, funny, and has the perfect smile. Sometimes you think you've found the prince, but he's actually the villain." She paused. "Do you really think I'm the problem here with Wade?"

Ariel finished her half of the biscuit and wiped her mouth. "Honest thoughts?"

Stella braced herself and nodded.

"I'm not saying he didn't have bad vibes and that he's not at fault. He didn't treat you well, that's obvious. And the way he left you was cruel in my opinion. But now after all these months, we can see that him being gone and not contacting you is an indicator that you don't need his kind of energy in your life. So it's a gift, really, and if you're still angry about it or still feeling mopey about losing him, then maybe it's because you want to keep holding on and being angry and sad."

Stella frowned. "Why would anyone want that?"

Sadness drifted across Ariel's face. "That's a good question."

THE REST OF the day at the library passed slower than chilled cane syrup. On incredibly slow days, Stella normally dusted books, trying not to inhale the filth and microscopic debris collecting in crevices, which wasn't as easy as it sounded. Breathing in at the wrong time could mean you sucked in a throatful of dank, dusty particles and spent the rest of the day sneezing with watery eyes.

Instead, she ran a report to see which books hadn't been checked out recently. Sometimes books hid amid the library shelves and weren't checked out for years. Last week she found a book that hadn't left the library since February 1988. Books like that had to be weeded out, a twinging liberation. Stella cringed at the idea of getting rid of books, but space in the library was precious, and how could they make room for new books if they never weeded out the ones that had frozen in place?

Thankfully she and Arnie had creative ways of finding homes for the weeded titles. They advertised for people to come pick through the free books or sold books at fundraisers for the library and other local activities. It amazed Stella how a book could have sat on a shelf for a year with no interest, yet it might be the first one snagged in a giveaway. She imagined the rehomed books trembling with excitement on their way to being loved and enjoyed again after feeling forgotten for so long.

After a few hours of weeding, Stella leaned her head against the edge of a shelf. When she closed her eyes, Ariel's voice sounded in her mind. Discomfort spread an ache to her chest area, giving her a feeling of indigestion. Could heartburn *literally* make her heart ache? Or was it just the bacon from this morning?

After all these months, how was it possible that she still had heart spasms because of Wade? Their time together was limited, with his demanding job and caring for his kids, and every time they'd seen each other had felt exciting. The way he hugged her like he never wanted to let go. The way they snickered like there was always a secret they couldn't wait to share. She *missed* feeling buoyant, missed the anticipation of the next kiss. Why was it easier to remember the heart-lifting moments and ignore the truth?

Shame burned through her. Wade was long gone and the only thing stopping her from truly letting him go was her. She rubbed her fingers against her breastbone. Ariel would say that Stella's heart chakra was out of alignment or needed to be "cleansed." A defibrillator box hung on a nearby wall. Could the paddles shock all the gunk from her heart, including stubborn emotions that she may or may not be allowing to linger? She could hear Ariel's voice in her head: *That is most definitely not the proper way to cleanse your heart.*

Fire hadn't worked. Lightning wasn't going to fix her. So what would? Ariel would say to try meditating and breathing. Breathing she could do, but Stella meditated about as well as she spoke Italian. In fits and starts. Poorly.

"Hey, kiddo," Arnie said, startling her from her thoughts. "The knitting club rescheduled. Why don't you call it a night? You look beat."

"Thanks, Arnie," Stella said with a sigh. "Just what a girl wants to hear."

"I thought women wanted honesty," he teased.

"Pfft," she said. "Who told you that nonsense?" He slipped his arm around her shoulders and gave her a squeeze. "I know what you mean. I do feel a bit worn down. I'll take you up on that offer and head home"—she glanced at her cell phone—"half an hour early. You sure you can close up without me?"

His expression said, *Are you kidding me?* "Is a heffalump pink?"

"Does a woozle leave tracks in the snow?" she countered.

Arnie smiled at her. "I'll see you tomorrow."

Stella grabbed her keys from the counter where she'd tossed them earlier and walked to her car parked behind the library in the first row, fourth space, to the right of the library's exit. Same as always. She drove through town with a persistent burn in her chest and wondered if she had any antacids at home. After pulling into the garage, she grabbed for her purse, but it wasn't there.

She stared in confusion for a moment, then checked the floorboard and the narrow area between the passenger seat and the car door—as if it would even fit there. Her searching fingers found a pen, a rubber band, and a lonely, fragile cheese puff. She climbed out of the car to give herself a different vantage point and fisted her hands on her hips. Nothing but cracking leather seats. She retraced her steps in her mind and saw her purse sitting beneath the circulation desk. It would take her less than fifteen minutes to drive back across town and grab it.

She called Arnie as she drove. Thankfully she kept her cell phone with her while she worked. When he didn't answer, she left a message. Even though the library's rear parking lot was empty when she returned, Stella parked in her usual spot.

On the lot beside the library sat a bungalow where most of the head librarians had taken residence since it was built in the early 1900s. Arnie had convinced the town to let him purchase the home, and for as long as Stella could remember, it had been his.

Arnie's most extravagant possession in an otherwise humble life was parked in front of his cottage—an inherited 1955 silver BMW 503 convertible.

All the lights were off inside. Arnie never went to bed before midnight, and most evenings he stayed up well into the wee hours. There was no way he was sleeping already. He must still be inside the library. Stella jingled the keys on her key ring until she found the fat-headed gold key that unlocked the back door.

Her assumption that Arnie was still inside was validated when the beeping of the alarm didn't start as soon as she opened the door. The only light still illuminating the library dangled high above the circulation desk, spotlighting the circular space like an actor in a play, leaving the rest of the stage in darkness.

"Arnie?" His name echoed through the empty library, returned to her, and circled around her shoulders.

She squatted behind the desk and reached for her purse. It seemed to jump into her hands, saying, *I thought you'd left me here!* She shouldered the bag and stood. The burning sensation in her chest intensified, and Stella gripped the edge of the counter. A small pool of liquid, a vivid purple, rose through the desktop as though a fountain had burst inside the wood. Just as they had last night, letters emerged from the glowing goo, forming words. Violet roots stretched out from the words and wrapped around objects on the desktop as the fire in her blood intensified. Her hands became clammy, and Stella swayed with nausea.

The words **love once** undulated on the desk, and as soon as Stella spoke them aloud, the blistering in her chest lessened. She steadied herself and swallowed, thankful she hadn't barfed on the desk. She lifted a trembling hand to her forehead and inhaled a slow, deep breath.

The journal was at home. Would the pain return if she didn't write down the words immediately? She quickly said, "I'll write you down when I get home, I promise." Seeming to understand, the words unwrapped their purple tendrils and skittered off the countertop, disappearing into the dark library.

Stella drew in another breath and rubbed her fingertips across the left side of her chest. What was happening to her?

Laughter drifted across the foyer. She glanced toward the vault door on the opposite side of the room. The door to the antiquities archives stood ajar, and more laughter—no, *giggling*—tumbled out the open doorway. Stella started walking toward the sound but hesitated. Arnie *never* giggled, and it was a woman's voice.

Chapter 3

Blue Sky Valley boasted a history dating back past the American Revolution, and many unusual, historical, and unique items and books had been tucked into a spacious, separated, and sealed section beneath part of the library. Built into the limestone, the solid walls had withstood several natural disasters over the years, and the archives remained a fortress of knowledge and artifacts.

Stella followed the sound of laughter and voices toward the vault door, which was partially open at the top of the stairs, but it shouldn't have been unless Arnie was down there. She tugged on the door's metal handwheel, opening it wider. She stood, listening, but silence greeted her. Had she imagined the laughter?

"Arnie?" she called in a voice quieted by the unease swelling inside her. Smoky-gray words poofed out of the open space: **Apprehension. Fear. Anxiety.**

Were the words a warning? Was there a reason to be uneasy about the archives tonight?

Stella tiptoed down the stairs, breathing in the scents of earth, old parchment, and tanned leather. At the bottom of the staircase, she saw a lamp burning at the far end of the room. Was Arnie researching? She took two steps into the dimly lit archives and shivered. Laughter swept down the nearest aisle. But it wasn't Arnie's laugh. It belonged to a female. Had Arnie invited a *lady friend* into the archives? She froze, wondering if she should turn around and pretend she never found Arnie in an awkward situation, but curiosity propelled her forward.

Glowing typewriter-font words slipped out of the shadows and floated across the shelves, then across a World War II uniform hanging in a display case. **Borrowed Time. Temporary. Please stay.** The last phrase tightened Stella's throat. More voices drifted out and quivered around her.

"Arnie?" she whispered.

The pool of lamplight touched the tip of her tennis shoe. She gripped the edge of the nearest bookcase and peered around it. A young boy wearing an outfit made of brittle autumn leaves grinned and leaped onto a study table. He wiggled his bare toes and winked at Stella. A woman, sitting with her back to Stella, laughed; her long blond hair gleamed in the soft light. A dreadfully thin man with a nose like a toucan's beak walked toward the table as his deep voice resonated against the shelves. His white shirt ballooned around his narrow frame as he walked, and the bend-snap, bend-snap of his loping gait reminded Stella of a flamingo. Was he reciting a psalm?

The man's steady gaze stretched past the table and landed on Stella's face. Her back straightened as though she'd been electrocuted. The man stopped speaking, tucked a worn Bible against his chest, and bowed his head toward Stella, causing the blond woman to turn in her chair. The impossibly beautiful woman's skin glowed as though she'd eaten handfuls of stars. Stella had never seen anyone lovelier, and she had trouble looking directly at the woman's face. Her eyes burned the way they did when she stared at the midday sun.

"*Ya su. Kalispèra,*" the woman said in a voice smoother than poured ink.

Is that . . . Greek? Stella's brain struggled to translate. She and Arnie hadn't practiced Greek in months. "Good evening?" she mumbled.

The young boy leaped from the table, leaving a glittering comet trail behind him. Stella jerked backward, tripped over her own feet, and fell, knocking her head hard on a shelf. Her vision blurred, and she crumpled against the bookcase, sliding down until she plopped on the floor like a rag doll.

A thin face dominated by an overly large nose leaned into her swirling vision. His green, glassy eyes studied her face. "My dear lady, are you quite all right?" He turned his beaked nose away from her and called to someone over his shoulder. "Arnie, I do believe one of your characters has lost her way."

Arnie? Stella's vision tunneled, and then everything disappeared.

✦ ✦ ✦

"STELLA?" ARNIE SAID as he lifted her into a sitting position. The faint glow from the lamp highlighted the creases of concern on his lined face. "Come on, kiddo. Don't you know better than to scare an old man?"

Stella blinked. He lifted her slowly and propped her upright against a bookshelf. She touched the back of her head and winced.

"Probably gonna have a real goose egg back there. What were you doing down here? You left almost half an hour ago."

"I forgot my purse. I found it under the front desk, but then I heard voices. Yours, I thought, and I noticed the archives door was open, so I came down here looking for you, but I saw . . ." A cold sensation on her leg distracted her for a moment. She bent her right leg toward her and patted the back of her capris. The fabric was wet from knee to cuff. "Why are my pants wet?"

"My chamomile tea," Arnie said. "Let's try to stand. Slowly, now. Slowly."

Stella grabbed Arnie's outstretched hand, and with his help, she eased to her feet, swaying for a few seconds before her equilibrium righted itself. The book spines in her line of vision undulated like underwater kelp until she blinked a few times and refocused. A throbbing ache pounded inside her skull. "Why is your tea on my pants?"

Arnie tugged on his earlobe, looking apologetic. "I spilled it when I tried to pull a book from the shelf, and when I returned to clean it up, you were sprawled on the floor. I'm assuming you slipped on it and fell."

Stella noticed a mop propped against the study table. She didn't remember slipping on the wet floor. What she remembered was seeing three strangers in the archives. She peered around Arnie's shoulder.

He glanced behind him before turning back to her. "How're you feeling?"

"I feel like Wile E. Coyote after an anvil has fallen on his head."

"Let me drive you home," Arnie said as he hooked his hand around her elbow. He slid her purse over her shoulder and led her up the aisle away from the study table.

Stella sighed but leaned into him. "I'm fine, Arnie. I have a headache, but I can drive." In truth, her head throbbed so intensely that nausea surged. First the purple words and now this.

"Maybe I should take you to the ER to see if you have a concussion. Or keep you awake all night with coffee and lousy jokes."

Stella stopped walking, forcing Arnie to stop. She inhaled a few slow breaths and peered behind them. "A few aspirin will help, but I thought I saw— There were people down here."

Arnie frowned, causing his thick eyebrows to form an unruly bridge over his nose. "This morning? Do you mean the Wallaces? Weren't they researching Libby's genealogy?"

Stella shook her head, which caused her to feel like she'd been twirling round and round. She closed her eyes and swallowed another swell of nausea. When it was safe to open her mouth, she said, "No. Tonight. When I came looking for you, I saw—a boy dressed like Peter Pan. He was standing on the table, and then he jumped at me."

Arnie's laugh startled her. It burst out down the aisle, and the books shivered on their shelves. An antique bell in a display case vibrated, sending a low hum into the room. "You knocked yourself silly."

She started to argue with him, but what if she'd actually fallen, knocked herself out, and created the entire scenario in her dreaming mind? Still, the brief interaction had seemed real. And what about the words she'd seen when she entered the archives? **Apprehension. Fear. Anxiety.** Were they meant to caution her regarding the people? But she and Arnie were very much alone in the archives now. If she pushed the issue about the people, she'd have to admit the words she'd seen, and that wasn't a secret she wanted to share with Arnie.

He urged her forward out of the antiquities section and led her up the staircase to the main floor. They passed through the unlit spaces until Arnie stood at the back door and set the alarm.

He stepped onto the back stoop with her, pulled out his keys, and locked the door. "I'd feel better if you'd let me drive you home."

The humid night air smelled of blooming magnolias and cut grass. "I'm not gonna risk barfing in your car, but thanks." She dug her car keys out of her pocket and adjusted her purse on her shoulder.

"You call me if you need anything, you hear me?"

"Yes, sir." She waved over her shoulder as she shuffled to her car. Arnie stood and watched her reverse out of the parking space and drive away. As she turned onto the main street and glanced into the rearview mirror, she saw him descend the stairs and cross the grassy lot toward his cottage.

Stella gripped the steering wheel with both hands and cranked the air-conditioning to help ease the queasiness from the pounding in her skull. *Don't barf. Don't barf. Don't barf*, she repeated as a mantra in her mind.

A half hour later when she crawled into her bed in the quiet house, she closed her heavy eyelids. Crickets chirped outside her bedroom window. Her mind created an image of a man's bulbous green eyes staring at her, calling her one of Arnie's characters. That image was followed by a young boy leaping off a table, leaving a sparkling golden trail behind him. A woman whispered words in Greek, and Stella marveled at her own imagination before she drifted off to sleep.

Chapter 4

Monday morning Stella awoke feeling hungover, reminiscent of someone who'd reveled all night at the Mad Hatter's tea party where the tea had been spiked and the party was full of madness. She hadn't had a legit hangover since the night before she left Memphis to come home because of her father's heart attack, and that was almost four years ago now.

The scalding shower water soothed the pounding in her skull until she faced away from the spray and the water assaulted her bruised head like a hailstorm. She wrapped a towel around herself and wiped her feet on the flatter-than-a-johnnycake bathmat. Glancing up, she noticed the outdated jewel-toned wallpaper peeled away from one corner.

As with most things in her life, it was past time for an update. Everything—house included—needed a refresh. Her childhood home was trapped in a thirty-year-old design style chosen by her flippant mother and her acquiescent father. She had the inheritance money to make changes, but she hadn't removed a single item from the house for no other reason than she, too, was chained to the past.

Stella cried out when her comb grazed over the golf ball–size lump on the back of her head. She smoothed styling gel through her curls and decided to let her hair air dry. Back in her room, she pulled on a pair of linen shorts and a yellow cotton blouse. Out of nothing but habit, she clasped a daisy pendant necklace around her neck. It had been a gift from her mother on her sixth birthday—a goodbye gift, even though no one in the family knew she was leaving yet. Stella recalled how long the necklace chain had been at the time, more suited for an adult than a child. Her mother said she'd grow into it. Had she also expected Stella to grow into the acceptance that her mother had left their family?

Stella didn't know why she still wore the necklace like a talisman that might somehow call her mother back to her. So far, it was nothing but an infrequent reminder that her mother had better things to do than raise a family.

In the kitchen, she chased two aspirin with a large glass of water. While the single-cup coffee maker started to brew, she sagged onto the sofa. Barely a minute later, the coffee maker released a hiss of steam and plopped the last few dark drops into her cup. She grabbed it and dumped in two sugar packets and a splash of milk before returning to the sofa.

Summer heat pressed against the window, causing the air conditioner to create condensation like pearls of sparkling dew across the lower half of the panes. A mental image of the strangers in the archives triggered a memory of the vivid purple words rising through the circulation desk. Her chest spasmed, and Stella jolted upright on the couch, nearly spilling her coffee.

"The words," she blurted. She'd come home half out of it because of the headache and had completely forgotten.

Stella found her journal and purple pen where she'd left them on the kitchen counter. She took a quick sip of her coffee and flipped to the page with the words *I fell in*. She hesitated, remembering the words she needed to add, and then frowned. She uncapped the pen and wrote *love once*.

"I fell in love once," she said to no one, and the lines on her forehead deepened. "And it was a mess." She slammed the journal shut. "Thanks for the brutal reminder. As if I needed it."

She stood in the kitchen drinking her coffee, not wanting to relax on the couch because she wouldn't relax. Not with her mind annoyingly zigzagging between the weird night with Arnie in the archives and the painful purple words that appeared without warning and without clarity. What did they want? What message was she obviously missing?

Toss in the burned journal full of words of love, despair, and loneliness, combined with the realization that she was still hung up on her ex *on purpose*, and could a day start any worse?

Her cell phone dinged with a text from an unknown number. Hi! I heard you were in the market to sell your house. I know we can fetch a great price. Call or text me at this number, and let's make a deal! Carla

Stella gritted her teeth. Percy. He had to be behind these Realtors sharking around her, intent on selling their home. Why didn't he care about where they grew up? Why was he so willing to get rid of their memories? *How* was it so easy for him to move on?

She glanced around the outdated kitchen. If she closed her eyes, she could picture her dad sitting at the table, drinking coffee and reading yesterday's paper, giving her the highlights she wasn't the least bit interested in at the time. Now she'd sell her first edition of *Gone with the Wind* just to hear his voice again. Loneliness expanded around her, nearly swallowing her. She pressed her hands against her chest, her lungs protesting when she inhaled.

She dumped out her coffee and put the mug in the dishwasher. Then she dropped a few handfuls of Froot Loops into a zip-top plastic bag. She grabbed her purse and noticed her worn copy of *Beyond the Southern Horizon* on the counter. Just seeing it swelled her heart again with longing for her dad. It was one of his favorite historical fiction WWII books, and he must have read it a hundred times.

She picked up the book and pressed it against her chest, hugging it because she couldn't hug her dad. He used to tell Percy and Stella the heroic tale of Jack Mathis as though the American soldier had been a family member. Because of the way her dad described Jack and his achievements, Stella had grown up having a crush on a fictional man. The grainy black-and-white photos of Jack included in the pages to add a more realistic flair to the novel had only cemented her adoration because Jack was undeniably handsome, and he had set the bar for the kind of man Stella was searching for. An impossible hunt so far.

Jack Mathis's fictional story had been inspired by a real-life, local war hero born in 1919 in Blue Sky Valley who died in the Second World War during the Battle of the Bulge. The real soldier was said to have been named Johnny Moore, and he had sacrificed himself to save four soldiers in his unit when they were attacked by a German spy hiding in their ranks.

The author of *Beyond the Southern Horizon* had taken quite a bit of creative license with his version of the events. Jack Mathis had cataloged his squad's journey, written about their highs and lows, detailed their loves and fears, and penned his own poetry in journals while he was stationed overseas. The story went that after Jack's untimely death, one of his men retrieved his journals and took them back to the States upon his return. Afterward, a historian happened upon the journals and crafted a detailed novel about a hero he never wanted forgotten.

Stella understood that the few photographs inside the book weren't authentic and were most likely of a model dressed in period garb. But to Stella, the soldier in the photos was the ideal man, a swoon-worthy hero. Jack watched the world with his steady gaze and pale eyes, and Stella had often daydreamed about his eyes looking toward her.

She flipped open the book to a photograph and rubbed her thumb over the image. When had she stopped believing that finding a man like Jack was realistic? Years ago, probably. Long before Wade. Even though it presently annoyed her, she couldn't deny there was still a tiny whisper of hope that real love could be found. The stack of happily-ever-after novels on her TBR proved she hadn't quite given up. Could she find a man like Jack one day? Someone who would make promises and keep them?

Stella could blame her dad for introducing her to a fictional man with no equal in the real world, but loving *Beyond the Southern Horizon* and Jack connected her with her dad, and that bond was life-giving. She slipped the book into her purse and grabbed the half-filled journal and pen before she drove across town to the library.

Blue Sky Valley bustled with early morning activity. Kids dressed in brightly colored bathing suits leaped in and out of a lawn sprinkler that waved through the air like a rainbow of water. She envied their freedom, their laughter. When was the last time she laughed so easily, the last time she didn't feel weighed down by her own heaviness? Frost Bites, the downtown ice cream shop, turned on its neon-pink Open sign, and Beau Anderson stepped out on the sidewalk to roll out the blue-and-white-striped awning. The temperature already soared above ninety degrees, and the shop would be full of patrons by midmorning.

Once she arrived at the library, Stella tossed her purse into a bottom drawer tucked beneath the circulation desk. She willed herself out of the lingering funk. This pattern of dragging herself through life, living the same day on repeat with Eeyore-worthy gloom always threatening, was tiresome.

A wholly more interesting way to spend the day was to start figuring out what was going on. She wondered if there would be an opening to talk to Arnie about what happened last night in the archives. Even though he insisted she'd knocked herself silly, the "vision" seemed too real, too authentic to be a hallucination or dream. As Stella walked the main floor, popping Froot Loops into her mouth, she found Arnie in the folk and fairy tales section near the front of the library.

His blue button-down shirt was neatly pressed and tucked into gray slacks. His gray-white hair was neatly combed and parted, and his black glasses matched his polished shoes that shone in the morning light. Arnie dressed like a man better suited for a lawyer's office or a corporate job. He had told Stella on numerous occasions that one secret to not looking like a frail old man was not to dress like one. No one would call Arnie frail or old. For a sixty-eight-year-old head librarian, Arnie looked anything but worn out and feeble, and he was the best-dressed man she knew. He was also the most intelligent.

He shelved an oversize copy of Edith Hamilton's *Mythology* bound in navy-blue leather. "Morning, sunshine. How's the concussion?" He cocked his head at her as if daring her to lie about how she really felt.

Stella shrugged and avoided his steady gaze. "I've had worse days, but it hurts like the dickens." She motioned toward the back of her head.

"No permanent damage, I hope?"

She pushed her damp hair behind her shoulders and rubbed the back of her neck. "We'll have to wait and see."

"How's the heart?" he asked, his voice gentle and wrapped in kindness.

So much for avoiding conversations that rekindled the sadness. Arnie's concern was sincere and valid. Her heart had taken more of a beating than the cracking she'd given her skull. "Still there, but wishing it was shriveled and charred and lifeless."

Arnie shelved another book. "To give the Grinch a run for his money?"

Stella straightened a book on a nearby shelf, lining up its spine evenly with the ones on each side. "I'd totally beat him."

Arnie chuckled. "Because if you're anything, it's heartless and cruel, especially to children."

Arnie had a way of pulling out her smile even when she didn't feel like ever smiling again. "Anyone been in yet?" she asked.

He shook his head, and they walked toward the circulation desk. A slow, quiet library day could often be excruciatingly boring, but a peaceful start to the morning was one of Stella's favorite things. It felt like inhaling a deep breath or standing barefoot in a grassy meadow. Libraries in the mornings felt like endless possibilities, endless stories that could take a person anywhere. Stella grabbed the baggie of Froot Loops. "Did you finish all the morning tasks? Clear the book drop? Run the hold slips? Reboot the computers?"

"Are you testing me to see if I can still perform my duties efficiently?" He pointed toward a rickety cart that Stella thought had been built at the same time as the library—a millennium ago. The right back wheel lagged as though caught on bubble gum, and the left front wheel squeaked to high heaven. "As my minion, I'm going to command you to shelve the rest of those. You might want to oil that front wheel again. WD-40 is in the desk drawer."

Stella caught sight of a flyer taped to the end of a bookshelf. Blue

Sky Valley's annual festival was that weekend. "What about festival duties? Do you need me to call anyone or follow up on anything?"

Arnie shook his head. "All moving along like clockwork. The town's committee is even more organized than last year. They'll start setting up Friday, and I have our list of duties already, but no reason to worry about that right now. Do you have everything ready for the care packages and donations?"

Stella nodded. "We have an overflow already, and I suspect we'll get even more donations during the festival."

"Your dad would be proud," Arnie said. "You've grown what he started. Every year it's gotten bigger." He glanced over his shoulder. "That reminds me. I have another box of book donations for you."

She smiled, thinking about the program her dad started years ago. Being a navy veteran, he'd wanted to honor others in the military, so he'd started creating care packages for those actively serving. He used the festival every year as a big push to gather supplies and donations for the boxes. She'd taken over after his passing, and it had been her idea to add books to the care packages.

"Thank you for the extras."

Arnie slid back the cuff of his blue shirtsleeve and checked his watch. The silver face was so large that even from a distance Stella could tell the time. "Margot should be here in half an hour. She'll want to set up in the story time room before the kids start crowding in. I told her she could bring cookies again, but she'd have to keep an eye on little Brendan Brannigan. He likes to shove extras into his pockets."

Stella's lips twitched in one corner. "And his mama sure didn't like sending those extra cookies through the wash."

Arnie exhaled and rubbed his ear. "I got an earful."

"Two earfuls."

Arnie's dark eyes searched her face, and his expression reminded

Stella of when she was young and her dad would lift her up in his arms as though she was a prize at the fair, smiling up at her with such pride and love.

"You sure you're okay?" Arnie asked. "Work half a day, and if you're not up for the afternoon, take off." He tossed his thumb over his shoulder as he walked off. "I mean it, kiddo."

She popped the last of the Froot Loops into her mouth. "Arnie, I'm *fine*."

"That's what women say when they're anything but," he said as he headed toward the main staircase leading to the second floor.

She walked over to the library cart. Its three shelves were loaded with children's books—picture books, board books, read-alongs, easy readers, and chapter books—all needing to be returned to their homes on the main floor.

"Arnie, I wanted to ask you about—" Three glossy brochures sat on top of the children's books. She picked them up and waved them in the air. "What are these?" she shouted loud enough for Arnie to hear.

She pinched the papers between her forefinger and thumb and held them away from her body the way someone might hold soiled towels. Serif words, blocky and bold, slipped out from between the pressed pages. **Revive. New faces. Matriculation.**

Arnie turned and looked at her. His smile lifted his cheeks. "Three great colleges with outstanding English programs. Two close by and one a thousand miles away in case you need a change of scenery."

Exasperation throbbed in her head. "College? I have a master's degree in accounting."

Arnie stopped smiling. He closed the space between them, his shoes clicking against the polished tiles. Stella's back straightened as she prepared for a lecture.

"You could still go back to school. Get a degree in something you actually enjoy," he said.

"I don't need a degree to be your assistant. Besides, I'm too old to go back to school."

Arnie laughed. "You're never too old to start something new. It would take you less than two years for another degree, even less time if you only want certifications. If you don't want to go back to the university, that's okay, but you need to consider a higher-paying job. You're too smart to be someone's assistant forever. Your father would want more for you, and so does Percy. I assume he's said as much."

Stella slapped the college brochures on the countertop. Arnie wasn't the big baddie lording over her, but his questioning made her doubt her life choices *again*, and that peeved her. Why? Because she didn't want to look deep enough to discover the heart of the issue. She knew Percy wanted more for her, and her dad would, too, if he were still alive. As if either of them truly knew what "more" was. How could they when Stella didn't even know?

"If you need me, I'll be putting away books." She pointed to the brochures. "You can add those to the ashes in the furnace." She skipped the grease needed to ease the cart's front wheel and squeaked and shoved her way toward the children's section.

She heard Percy's voice in her head: *Just the two of us against the world*. Stella and Percy had no family left except an aunt living in Rhode Island. She didn't count their mother, who had been nonexistent in their lives for more than twenty years. Stella didn't even know if the woman was still alive. Percy had always looked out for her and was grateful he didn't have to shoulder the burden of sorting through their dad's final arrangements alone, but he certainly hadn't wanted Stella to quit her accounting job in Memphis and move back to Blue Sky Valley.

Aside from telling her she needed to *Get a better job* or return to accounting, Percy had also been nagging her to sell the family home they'd both inherited, but Stella refused. When Percy pressed her for a reason, she'd said, *It's our home.*

He'd corrected her: *It was our home, and just because a thing once was something doesn't mean it always has to be. We can change our minds, start over, try something new.*

Starting over and trying something new was easy for Percy. He had a temperament built for adventure and taking life just as it was. *Percy knows how to hold up his hands on a roller coaster and enjoy it*, their dad used to say. *And what about me?* Stella had asked. *You're a lot more like me*, he'd said, and she had shined at the compliment until he added, *You like to hold on too long, too tightly. I wish I'd held up my hands and enjoyed the ride more.* Her dad had never confirmed if holding on was good or bad, but at the time she'd suspected that holding on wasn't the best option. These days *holding on* for Stella was the same as *being stuck*.

Now Percy lived on the west coast of Florida, enjoying the beach life he'd dreamed about. He worked as a financial advisor in a successful firm, and every time he talked to Stella, he pestered her about going back to *a real job*.

Stella sometimes thought about looking for a job in finance again, but imagining sitting through years of crunching numbers and balancing someone else's spreadsheet made her eyes glaze over. As a kid, she had believed a more magical life was possible—one where words came to her, books were portals to other worlds, and her mother cherished her. But after her mom left, life didn't feel magical anymore, and the only thing that was left of the magic were the words and books. Suddenly her ability with words had seemed too weird, and she wanted to be normal-ish. *Normal* equated to boring, safe, and practical. Growing up and pursuing a career in finance made sense, but she never loved it and certainly wasn't happy doing it.

Returning to Big Sky Valley and working in the library was a bit of an escape, and she loved how books made people happy, how they made people think about and question reality. Mostly she cherished how she could disappear into a book and not have to engage in the world unless she wanted to. After four years, she had settled into a life here, and the idea that she should or even could change her life path sounded unsafe. And exhausting.

She shelved books up and down the aisles in an annoyed huff until she heard Margot Marshall call out to her from the foyer.

Stella stepped out from the stacks, and Margot lifted one hand in a wave. She carried a plastic container of cookies in her other hand. Her dark braids draped over her shoulders.

"Morning, Mrs. Marshall. Excited for story time? Can I help you get ready?" Stella asked, thankful for the distraction from her frustration.

Margot thanked her as she handed over the container and a stack of napkins. Stella breathed in the scent of warm chocolate chip cookies as she followed Margot into the story time room. Once inside she placed the cookies and napkins on the far table.

Margot dug through her worn canvas bag of books and removed a hardback copy of Washington Irving's short stories. "I checked this out last week, and I need to return it. Television and movies have skewed my students' knowledge of the *real* Ichabod Crane, and I needed to set them straight. I was satisfied in knowing they enjoyed Irving's original story just as much as all of the copycats. It's so mysterious and open-ended." She passed the book to Stella.

The book warmed in Stella's hands, radiating heat like a lava rock. Slanted cursive words rippled out of the book like circular waves leaving an epicenter. **Green eyes. Pontificating. Bible.**

Stella looked up at Margot, a shiver quivering up her spine. "Did—did Ichabod Crane have green eyes?"

Margot tapped a scarlet fingernail against her matching cherry lips and then nodded. "Most people remember the description of his skinny body and smallish head, the opposite of a bobblehead, I would imagine. But yes, I think he did. Glassy green. Why do you ask?"

A gentle buzzing filled Stella's head like the distant hum of white noise. She lowered the book, causing the words to dissipate. "Just an image I remember. We arranged the bean bags and chairs in here last night, although most of the kids want to sit on the floor—"

"Or lay on the floor," Margot said with a chuckle.

"Don't you wish adults would allow themselves to get as cozy and attend a story time? I'd be up for lying around all day listening to someone read books."

Margot's laugh filled the room. "Sign me up for that!"

Stella smiled. "I'll add it to the suggestion box. Anything else you need?"

Margot turned in a full circle, her knee-length polka-dot skirt twirling out like an opening umbrella as she studied the room. "Not at the moment. Thanks, Stella. I'll holler if I need you."

Stella carried Washington Irving's short stories to the circulation desk. She tapped her finger against the front cover of the book. The world was full of coincidences, but her fingers tingled, so she grabbed her notebook and jotted down her thoughts, a haiku this time.

My Ichabod Crane, Lover of she who did not, You were never found.

Then she closed her notebook and returned to the book cart. As she shelved the last children's book, the story time children began pushing through the front doors with their parents in tow. Half the parents stayed with their kids, and the other half dropped them off as though the library were a temporary day care. Tiny voices and whispered giggles filled the downstairs until the kids were safely snuggled in the room with Margot. The sounds of the library soothed Stella, and she found herself relaxing somewhat.

At the circulation desk, she opened one of the side drawers and pulled out her mug, which said *Librarian Because Book Wizard Isn't an Official Job Title*. Arnie had given it to her last Christmas. She wasn't officially a librarian because she lacked the proper schooling and license, but he didn't care, and she liked thinking of herself as a book wizard.

She wanted coffee, but Arnie would probably encourage her to have at least two cups of green tea before she imbibed high levels of caffeine again. Green tea tasted like drinking earth, which was probably the point, but Stella preferred her dessert-style coffees.

One of the mothers slipped out of the children's room and walked toward her. The mother waved a book before placing it on the counter. "Arnie suggested this book last week for Tyler. He said all young boys love it, and he was right. Downside is that Tyler has been jumping off everything. It started with his bed, and this morning he asked if I thought there was an easy way to get on the roof. Lord, have mercy—the *roof*." She rolled her hazel eyes as she shook her head. Tiny words marched up the woman's forearm: **Resilient. Thankful. Youthful.**

"Boys. God love them, but they just grow up to be men while still holding on to their little boy spirits, right? What do we do with them?"

"Not fall in love with complicated ones, that's for sure," Stella mumbled.

"What's that?" the woman asked, leaning closer.

"Nothing," Stella said with a hesitant smile. Crimson words resembling caterpillars crawled out of her notebook as though creeping, not wanting to be seen: **Inferior. Misleading. Abscond.**

A testament to her last relationship? Stella refocused on the mother and glanced at the returned book. *Peter Pan* was printed in gold letters across the glossy paperback. She thought of the young boy she'd imagined leaping toward her in the antiquities archives. She fluttered the pages with her fingers and out slipped a few winged words. **Come away with me. Never grow up. Always believe.** Stella slapped her hand on the book, and the words rushed off the desk. She looked up at the mother.

"Is Arnie around? I wanted to thank him," she said.

Stella nodded and pointed toward the stairs. "He's up there somewhere. I'll get this returned for you."

The mother smiled and nodded. "I'll see if I can catch him after story time."

Stella stared down at J. M. Barrie's novel. So many words today. They hadn't been this active in years. Something odd was definitely happening.

She stacked *Peter Pan* on top of Washington Irving's stories while her fingertips burned. She heard Arnie's designer shoes approaching her from behind, and she whirled around.

Arnie lumbered across the way with an armful of books and a stack of folders. He raised his eyebrows at her in question.

"Someone returned a book with "The Legend of Sleepy Hollow" in it, and then *Peter Pan* was just turned in," Stella said.

Arnie dropped the books on the desk. "And I had scrambled eggs for breakfast with two biscuits."

Stella frowned. "I'm serious, Arnie."

"So am I. I shouldn't have had two, but I couldn't stop myself this morning." He patted his rotund belly and shrugged. "But I'm an old man. Shouldn't I enjoy the simple things in life, like buttermilk biscuits?"

"Arnie," Stella said and sighed. "Those are characters from the vision—the *dream* I had."

Arnie placed the stack of folders next to the books as the front door opened again. "Stella, you work all day, nearly every day, in books. You'll dream about them now and again."

"No, I'm talking about last night when I was downstairs in the archives, and I . . . Well, I guess I fell, but I thought I saw Peter Pan and a super-skinny man. He was reciting psalms, and he had green eyes. And there was a blond woman. Beautiful, like a fairytale queen or something."

Arnie stepped toward the front of the desk. "Sounds like a woman *I'd* like to dream about. Do you think she can cook?" He sidestepped Stella. "Good morning, Mrs. Little. How can I help you?"

"Good morning, Arnie," Mrs. Little said. "I almost hate to return this one."

Stella turned to face the tall, middle-aged patron just as she heaved a heavy book onto the high counter. Stella tilted her head and read the spine. *Greek Mythology*.

Mrs. Little propped her arms on the desk and leaned toward Arnie. Her glossy maroon lipstick shone in the fluorescent lighting. A smile stretched across her rosy face and dimpled her cherub cheeks. "Can you imagine being so beautiful that people would go to war over you? Just to have your love?"

Arnie chuckled. "Not in the least. Did you enjoy your reading?"

"Very much. I need another suggestion. Something mysterious, I think."

Arnie walked out of the desk area and led Mrs. Little toward the staircase where adult fiction lived on the second floor. As they walked up the steps, Stella heard her ask, "Do you really think Helen of Troy was that beautiful?"

"Stunning," Arnie said. "Breathtakingly stunning."

Stella stared at the returned mythology book, and very slowly, she reached out and touched it. The hardcover heated beneath her fingertips. A woman's laugh, followed by the echo of Greek words, drifted through the library. Stella thought of a woman whose voice was as smooth as honey, whose face she could not look upon directly. *Helen of Troy*.

Stella glanced toward the vault door leading to the antiquities archives. "What in the world is going on?"

Chapter 5

Later that afternoon Arnie shooed Stella out of the library, forcing her to take off early. "The cozy-mystery group rescheduled," he said. "One of the members inherited a fortune and has mysteriously disappeared, leaving no note and not responding to texts or phone calls. When they went to her house to check on her, they found evidence of a break-in and two untouched glasses of wine on the dining room table. The group let me know that the game is afoot."

Stella snorted a laugh. "You just made that up."

"I did, but not about them rescheduling." He motioned around the library. "There are two people on the computers, someone reading yesterday's newspaper, and one kid researching how to build a floating maglev train. I'd bet you lunch tomorrow that the evening stretch will be duller than last night's dishwater."

"It's not as though I have anything else to do." Other than what she'd been doing all day: allowing the conversation with Ariel yesterday, the mysterious words, the returned books combined with the archives incident, and Arnie's college brochure surprise to run on a loop in her mind. Stella hesitated. She hadn't broached the archives subject again yet. Maybe now was the best time. "About last night in the archives, can we talk about what I saw—"

The library phone rang, and Arnie snatched at the receiver as though it could be an emergency. He talked for a minute and then pressed the hold button. He handed Stella her purse. "Spend this free afternoon engaging in entertaining activities or hang out with friends."

With the exception of Ariel, Stella didn't have anyone she considered a close friend. She knew lots of people in town because of her job, but she spent most of her time in the library, at home reading, or hanging out with Ariel when they weren't working. "Is that a joke?"

Arnie's smile dimmed. "Stella, you're too young not to be enjoying yourself with others your age. You can't busy your life away."

"I can't?" she asked. "So far my strategy is working."

"Is it, though?" Arnie asked, his bushy eyebrows lifting and creating furrows across his forehead. "When it slows down here, which should be in the next hour, I plan to research more in the archives."

Stella's curiosity returned. "About the archives—"

He pointed dramatically to the phone in his hand. "I need to get back to this call."

Not ready to give up, she asked, "What are you researching? Anything I can help with?"

He hesitated just long enough to stir up her suspicion. "Nope. Nothing of interest to you." He pointed toward the door. "Out with you, and I don't want to see your face until tomorrow."

Stella huffed. Her questions would have to wait because Arnie wasn't cooperating.

He pasted on a winning smile. "Have fun. Try it out."

While Stella drove home, she wondered if Arnie was being evasive on purpose. But why? What could he possibly have to hide in the archives?

In the kitchen, she took two aspirin and filled a glass with cold water from the fridge. She drank half the glass and stared down at the linoleum. Colored in earth tones, mostly mustard and tan, the octagonal designs alternated with diamonds. The stain-resistant flooring had been laid when the house was built. It had probably been modern and popular once, but now the dated pattern froze the house in time. And it wasn't just the kitchen that had halted. The entire house could be a model home from thirty years ago.

Brittle-edged words, quivering like a tremor, moved across the linoleum. **Stagnant. Enervate. Misplaced.** The words shuddered out of the kitchen. Stella followed them into the living room and then down the hallway toward her parents' bedroom, where her steps slowed on the worn carpet.

The irony of still thinking of the room as her parents' bedroom wasn't lost on her. They hadn't shared that room together in more than twenty years. Yet it hadn't changed. Had her dad left everything the same in case his wife returned? Had he hoped if she saw the bedroom was still hers she might decide this was, in fact, where she belonged? If that had been his tactic, it had failed. Magnificently. Heartbreakingly. The thought made her want to hug her dad tight, squeeze him until all the sadness he must have carried for years released. Because one thing Stella and her dad shared was the understanding of heartbreak.

Knowing he'd frozen time in this room and it hadn't worked, why hadn't Stella changed anything since he died? His clothes still hung in the closet and crowded the dresser drawers. The last book he'd been reading, *Fahrenheit 451*, sat collecting dust on the bedside table. In all these years, she could have updated the room and moved her own things into the larger space. But she hadn't. She'd done exactly what he had—left the bedroom as a museum piece, showcasing "life as we hoped it might be . . . but wasn't."

Why was she still sleeping in her childhood bedroom with the frilly dust ruffle and poofy white comforter with the eyelets frayed and torn from years of washing? The faded, pale pink wallpaper her mother had chosen years ago still plastered the walls. The hope chest at the foot of her bed was stuffed full of her childhood drawings, dreams, and diaries—a testament to her hope and a reminder of its disappearance.

She had also left Percy's room exactly the same, as though he might show up one day, still fascinated by his basketball bedspread or high school trophies and blue ribbon awards. His small desk held the same dinosaur lamp and pencil sharpener, neither used in the last fifteen years.

The halting words moved over her parents' floral-patterned mauve comforter, a gaudy design that, in Stella's opinion, had always been hideous. **Stagnant. Enervate. Misplaced.**

As the words shuddered and disappeared, she felt them sink deep into her bones, causing a tremor to move through her. She was living in a time capsule—stagnant as roadside ditchwater.

Stella walked out of the bedroom. Ariel was right. Her inability to let go of things was her own doing, and not just with Wade. Proof of her stalled-out life was everywhere. She slumped onto the couch. Her dad was also right. On the roller coaster of life, she held on with a grip so tight, she'd never be free or truly happy. She'd never have open hands to receive anything else. Unless she let go.

Could she be more like Percy, riding through life with his hands waving in the air like fangirls at a Taylor Swift concert? Her cell phone lit up on the coffee table, and she leaned forward to see

Percy's name and image on the screen. She debated sending him to voicemail, but then he'd text and call back within a day.

"Hey," she said, trying to sound peppier than she felt. "I was just thinking about you."

"I figured you'd ghost me," Percy joked.

She sagged back against the cushions and propped her feet on the table, even as she heard an echo of her dad telling her to keep her feet on the floor. "I thought about it."

"I bet you did," Percy said. "I'd just text and call back tomorrow."

"Which is why I answered," she said. "Saves us both the trouble. Listen, about the Realtors—"

"You heard from them?" Percy asked, his voice buzzing with excitement. "Great! Have you discussed options yet?"

Stella pinched the bridge of her nose. "What would it take for you to lay off about the house?"

"What would it take for you to consider the idea of moving forward?" Frustration tinged his words.

Stella noticed a thread fraying on the throw pillow. She worried it between her fingers. How could two truths exist inside her at once? The house trapped her in the past, and the house connected her to people she loved. "I'm not ready yet."

"Yet?" Percy asked. "So there's a maybe in there somewhere?"

She sighed and smoothed her hand across the couch cushion. Maybe she could loosen her grip on the past. Maybe she could *ease* into changing some things.

Percy's voice was gentle when he said, "Hey, we can talk about that later. Today I'm calling for a good reason."

"You make it sound like you usually call for bad ones. Did you get a raise? Find another great job? Buy a house on the beach? Charter a yacht?" She grimaced at the hint of jealousy in her voice.

"As a matter of fact, I did find a job, but not for me," Percy said. "For you! I just got off the phone with a client who works down in Miami, and they're looking for someone with your qualifications."

Stella sat up. "Miami? That's almost eight hundred miles from here." Definitely not a change she was ready for.

"You do know there are multiple forms of transportation these days, right?" Percy shot back.

"What's the job?"

"It's a posh accounting firm that handles only wealthy clientele," he said.

She barely contained a groan in response. "Why would I want to move to Miami?"

Percy went on, ignoring her question. "They'd start you out with a six-figure salary, and the benefits are—"

"Percy, listen," Stella interrupted, "I appreciate your eagerness to share this with me, but it's not for me."

"Why not?" he asked, not masking his irritation. "You haven't even given it any thought. Give me one good reason."

It was true, she hadn't given it more than ten seconds of thought because her immediate response had been a knee-jerk no. "I don't want it?" The idea of moving *again*, and to a town she had no interest in, instantly caused a twinge in her solar plexus. She rubbed her hand against her stomach.

"That's not a good reason, Stella," Percy countered. "You can't spend the rest of your life not doing anything. You're shelving books in our hometown library, for Pete's sake. That's not a real job. It's a . . . it's a . . ."

Now it was Stella's turn to fire up her annoyance. "It's a what, Percy?"

His sigh pushed through the phone, and his voice carried years of disappointment. "A job for a kid, and, Stella, you're not a kid anymore. You're thirty years old."

"That's offensive to every fantastic librarian or library assistant on the planet. If there are other libraries in the universe, then you've offended them too. This is a perfectly respectful, enlightening job, and plenty of good comes from those who help people find the perfect books. What if this is exactly what I want to do with my life? What if I'm happy just as I am? Why can't you support me?"

Percy didn't say anything for a few seconds, and she wondered if she'd been too harsh. But she was sick of Percy telling her how to live her life.

Finally he asked, "Are you happy, Stella? 'Cause I don't think you are. Just think about the offer, okay? I'll email you the details. It's a great opportunity."

Stella clenched and unclenched her jaw. She couldn't picture herself living in Miami and definitely not working for upscale clients. But Percy was correct about one thing: She wasn't exactly happy. "I'll think about it."

"You will?" So much relief filled his words.

The phone beeped in her ear, and she pulled it away from her face to see that Ariel was calling. "Hey, that's Ariel. We'll talk later."

"Think about it!" Percy said. "Don't make me come up there."

"Wow, Percy," she said dryly. "That's such a threat. I'd love to see you, but I gotta go. I love you. Bye!"

"Love you too."

She switched the call. "Ariel, you still there?"

Music played in the background. "I was about to hang up and text instead."

Stella groaned. "Percy called. He wants me to take a job in Miami."

"Miami!" Ariel gasped. The background music lowered. "That's in another state! No way, you're not leaving me here. I won't let you. I mean, unless it's your dream, but please say it's not your dream. I'd miss you, and it's Miami! That's totally not your vibe."

Stella laughed. "And what *is* my vibe?"

Ariel paused. "Small-town cozy book nerd with extraordinary writing skills?"

Stella stopped smiling. "You think I have extraordinary writing skills?" As she repeated Ariel's statement, words popped out of the ashes in the fireplace, smoky gray and wispy. They waved like echoes of flames and slid out of the hearth and across the floor toward the windows. **Imagination. Tell me. Pages of you.**

"Not that you've let me read much, but, Stella—and we've never really talked about this—you have *a gift* with words. You know what I'm saying? It's not like regular people. You can't possibly have that gift and not be meant to use it."

Other than her mother, Ariel was the only person Stella had ever told about her ability to see words and how they came to her. She trusted Ariel with her secret because she had always embraced Stella, oddities and all. Stella had no interest in opening the door to the warmth and excitement of magic she'd shared with her mother, but Ariel saw Stella's gift as celebratory and sensational. Even so, Stella had never felt safe enough to tell anyone else about it, never wanted to give the words more attention than necessary.

"Hey, are you still with me?" Ariel said.

"Yeah, yeah, I'm here," Stella said. "It's just that I . . . Well, I've never thought of my words as something I could use for anything. Other than for myself, of course."

"Maybe it's time you start thinking about it," Ariel said. "How about over Chinese takeout tonight. My treat? I can bring it over."

"Order my usual?" Stella said.

"You got it! I'll see you around six."

Ariel disconnected, and Stella walked to the living room windows. She stared out at the backyard. She'd spent her whole life filling notebooks with words and stories and maps and colors and hadn't thought there could be something more to it, not since her mother left. She had been trying so hard to be normal and ignore that the words carried more meaning for her life. Was that why they were coming so frequently now, why the violet ones were so aggressive and fierce? Was something inside her ready to be unleashed?

Stella hugged her arms around her middle. It didn't seem to matter if she was ready for what was coming or not. It was coming regardless.

STELLA AND ARIEL sat on the living room floor on one side of the coffee table. An assortment of Chinese to-go boxes were situated on top of magazines to keep from making a mess on the table. For the hundredth time eating like this with Ariel, Stella was reminded she should buy place mats, but for now, the dated magazines would suffice.

Using her chopsticks like she'd been using them her whole life, Ariel scooped vegetable fried rice out of a container without dropping a single grain in her lap. Stella, on the other hand, fumbled her chicken and broccoli like she was playing with her food. At this rate, she'd still be eating at midnight.

Ariel put down her container and stabbed her chopsticks into the rice. "Hold them like this," she said, adjusting the position of Stella's chopsticks between her fingers. "Yes, like that. Now open and close them."

Stella copied Ariel's finger motion and groaned. "Why is this so difficult for me?"

"Tonight in particular?" Ariel asked. "You're giving off a weird vibe tonight. You've got something else on your mind. What is it? Percy and the job? Or are you still upset about the journal and Wade?"

Stella's exhale fluttered the pages of the closest magazine. "All of the above. It's been a strange few days," she admitted, thinking about the happenings at the library combined with the feeling that her foundation was shifting sands beneath her, forcing her to re-evaluate her life.

"Tell me about it," Ariel said, looking at Stella with large blue eyes.

Stella picked up an egg roll and took a huge bite. She chewed slowly, debating what to tell Ariel and what to leave out. As she swallowed, she decided to share it all, even the things that didn't make sense.

"I've been thinking about what you said about Wade and how *I'm* the one keeping him around in my thoughts, which stunned me because you're right. I've been carrying around anger and hurt because I *wanted* to, even though I said I didn't, which kinda depresses me. I've been blaming him, and yet . . . it's me.

"Percy thinks I should take a job in Miami, and I don't want to because, well, I don't *want* to, and Arnie thinks I should go back to college to get another degree or at the very least a certification. Both of them believe I'm settling for my library job, that I should be doing more."

Ariel took a bite from her egg roll and chewed slowly. She sipped her water and then asked, "What do *you* think? Are you settling for the library?"

"Yes and no," Stella answered honestly. "I love being there. I love the books and the words and helping people find what they're looking for, but Arnie and Percy aren't wrong exactly. I'm not trying to do anything more."

"Are you interested in doing more?" Ariel asked.

"I haven't been," Stella said. Then she looked around the living room, at the dated throw pillows and fading wallpaper. She brushed her hand against the flattened carpet that should have been replaced years ago. "But I'm starting to believe it's time for more. Last night I forgot my purse after we closed the library. I went back to get it, and I heard voices coming from the archives, so I went down there to see what Arnie was doing because I heard a woman—"

Ariel gasped. "Oh, please don't tell me you caught him getting frisky!"

Stella laughed and grimaced. "Yikes, but thankfully no. There were three strangers down there—a boy, a man, and a woman. They looked like they were wearing costumes, and it startled me. I slipped and knocked myself out—"

"Say what? Why am I just hearing about you being knocked out?"

Stella gingerly touched the back of her head. "I'm fine. It left a knot, but that's not the interesting part. When I came to, Arnie was there, but the people were gone, and he said there was no one else in the library." She stopped talking and waited for Ariel to comment.

Confusion moved across her friend's face. "What does that mean? The people had already left by the time you came to?"

Stella shook her head. "Arnie said there hadn't been anyone there, so maybe I . . . dreamed it?"

"Dreamed it?" Ariel's face scrunched. "How could you have dreamed people being there if that's the reason you fell?"

Stella shrugged. She'd asked herself the same question. "It's not like I could prove there were people there. But they *seemed* real to me, and when I tried to ask Arnie about it again today, he diverted."

Ariel reached for her stir-fried veggies and ate with rapt attention. "You think he's hiding something?"

"Maybe. Then there's the words."

"What about the words?"

Stella frowned, wondering how to explain the heightened frequency and intensity of how the words interacted with her. "There's a lot more of them recently. Ever since I burned the journal." Her chest tightened, and her eyes widened. "What if this is happening to me because I"—her voice quieted—"*murdered* the words?"

Ariel choked on a slice of glazed carrot. After drinking a huge gulp of water, she cleared her throat. "You didn't *murder* anything. But you might be on to something about this happening after the journal." She put her container on the table and wiped her hands on a napkin. "Change usually comes after a rock-bottom moment, and I think burning the journal was you hitting bottom and making a decision to change. Maybe the words are trying to tell you something."

Stella leaned back on her hands and stared up at the fan blades spinning above them. "Trying to tell me what?"

"Maybe it's time you use them for more than your journals?" Ariel asked.

Something akin to inspiration quivered in her chest. "Percy would laugh me out of town if I told him I wanted to be a writer." The realization stunned her. *Did* she want to be a writer? She'd never thought of herself that way, but she'd filled hundreds of pages and not just with random words. She'd written poetry and short stories and even a few novel-length ideas she'd started but never finished.

Ariel rolled her eyes. "Who cares what Percy thinks? He loves you, but he has no clue what kind of life is best for you. If he thinks you should be sitting behind a desk crunching numbers and balancing spreadsheets *in Miami*, then he doesn't know diddly-squat about you. There's *no way* that's your life path."

Stella picked up her container of chicken and broccoli. She poked the chopsticks around the pieces of meat. "I did work as an accountant for a while, though."

Ariel huffed. "We've all done things *for a while*, but that doesn't mean it's what we're supposed to keep doing. Do you want to be an accountant?"

Stella's stomach rolled. "No."

"That was easy," Ariel said. "You've never said anything before about being a writer, but do you want to be one?"

Stella slowly chewed a piece of chicken. "Maybe," she said. "I never thought it was a possibility."

Ariel nodded. "If it *were* a possibility, would you be interested?"

Tingles spread over Stella's skin so quickly that she shivered. Could she gather together thousands and thousands of words and form a story? It was a daunting idea, moving from writing down phrases here and there, creating colorful art in her journal with words, to writing a complete novel.

"Possibly," she said. She put down her take-out container. "My mother used to tell me that my words were a glorious gift that would guide me toward my dreams."

"You never told me that," Ariel said.

Which wasn't a surprise since Stella rarely spoke about her mother, the topic too awful for discussion. "Do you think my words are a gift?"

Ariel nodded. "I don't *think*. I *know*."

Stella often saw words around people, even patrons in the library. She'd never thought about deciphering their meanings and using them to assist somehow. "Aside from writing, maybe I should be using my words to help people."

Ariel's expression shifted to surprise. "The other day in the van, you knew I was interested in dating before I said anything. That was because of the words, right?" Stella nodded. "Can you hone that kind of focus on other people?"

Stella grabbed her take-out container again. She stabbed a piece of chicken and popped it into her mouth. "I don't call forth the words. They normally just show up."

"Have you ever tried to call them?"

Stella stared at Ariel and blinked a few times in the silence. "No, not intentionally."

Ariel scooted to face Stella. "Let's try it. I'll be the test subject."

Stella put down her food. "I have no idea how to call them forth." She situated herself to face Ariel like they were about to play a game of patty-cake and inhaled a deep breath. "Let's just focus on books. Think about something you'd like to feel or learn about, but don't tell me, and I'll see if words show up and I can pair them with a book."

Ariel nodded and closed her eyes. After a few seconds, she said, "I'm ready. Read my words, Stella."

Stella laughed and then tried to clear her mind, which was cluttered with everything from self-doubt to a grocery list of items she needed to buy this week. But she focused on Ariel and thought, *Come on, words, please show up. I'd like to know if I'm supposed to use this ability for something more.* In a moment, shimmering blue letters arose from Ariel's hands. Stella was so startled, she inhaled sharply.

Ariel's eyes flew open. "What is it?"

The words floated from Ariel's pale skin, and Stella whispered, "It's working." She tilted her head as the words rose vertically into the air. **Deep blue. Ruins. Atlantis. Sea monsters.** Stella scrunched her brow. "You want to read a book about sea monsters?"

Ariel looked taken aback. "How . . . Wait, are you judging me?"

Stella shook her head quickly, and the words dissipated among the spinning fan blades. "Of course not, I'm just surprised. I wouldn't have thought you'd be interested in an ocean adventure, but let's see . . ." The image of a book appeared in her mind. "You should read *Twenty Thousand Leagues Under the Sea*. It's classic sci-fi with underwater ruins, deep-sea exploration, a futuristic submarine, and 'sea monsters,' some of which are giant squids."

"Wow, Stella," Ariel said with a huge smile. "I think you just proved you *can* call the words and use them to help people. Think about how you could use that for writing!"

Stella mirrored her best friend's expression. "I can't believe that worked." She leaned her elbow on the coffee table and rested her cheek against her palm. "I'm a little stunned. All these years I never knew that I had any control over the words—"

Without warning, a searing sensation burst inside her chest like she'd swallowed a ghost pepper. Stella folded forward and moaned, pressing both hands to her chest. Her insides burned like a wildfire, and tears filled her eyes. She heard Ariel calling her name, but it was muffled and sounded far away.

Violet liquid pushed up from the low-pile, worn carpet, and once it fully emerged, Stella saw the familiar pulsating words with their dark center and paler edges. Long tendrils spiderwebbed out from the letters, wriggling like a creature dug from the earth. The words slid across the floor and circled near the fireplace.

Stella knew she must speak them aloud, so in a raspy, strained voice, she said, "'Did I ever.'" Immediately the inferno raging through her body lessened.

Ariel was in panic mode and gripping Stella's arm and shaking her. Stella inhaled another breath. The words flew across the living room and up the hallway where they disappeared. Stella could guess where they'd gone—to the journal.

"Stella!" Ariel's shrill voice filled the room.

"I'm okay," Stella said, then cleared her throat. "I'm okay."

Ariel dropped back onto her bottom and exhaled loudly. "What happened? I thought you were having a heart attack or choking. You scared me to death."

Stella stared down the hallway. "I'm sorry I scared you, but that's not the first time this has happened. There's something I haven't told you—"

"If you tell me you're dying of heart failure, I won't be able to handle it," Ariel said.

Stella shook her head. "It's not about my health. It's the words. A new kind started showing up, and they . . . Well, you saw what happens."

Ariel's mouth dropped open. "*That* was because of words? What did you see?"

Stella stood and stretched, then rubbed her fingers across her chest. "I'll show you."

Ariel followed her into the kitchen. Stella picked up a pen and opened the journal beside it. She flipped to the page where she'd written down the previous words so far. She jotted down the newest ones and then showed the page to Ariel.

Ariel read aloud, "'I fell in love once. Did I ever.'" She looked up at Stella. "What does this mean?"

Stella shrugged. "I have no idea, and before you ask, no, I also have no idea why this is happening."

Ariel wrapped her fingers around the black moonstone amulet hanging from her necklace. "Something is changing."

Goose bumps rose on Stella's skin.

"I *feel* it," Ariel said as she gazed back down at the written words. "Don't you? You said yourself that you feel like it's time for more."

Stella nodded. "But I don't want anything to change. I want

everything to stay exactly how it is. I'm comfortable and happy and everything is just fine."

Ariel gave Stella a look that said she wasn't fooled. "Do you really believe that?"

Stella huffed but didn't respond, because they both knew the truth.

"If what's coming is anything like what just happened," Ariel said, "then I don't think you have much choice but to go with it."

"What if I don't want to go with it?" Stella slammed the journal shut, and the pen rolled across the counter.

"What if it's somewhere better than where you are right now? Are you happy? Truly happy?"

Stella sighed. "Is anyone?"

Ariel nodded. "Yes. I mean, no one is happy 24-7, but yes, I do believe there are people who are genuinely happy, but those people keep evolving and trying new things and keep living. And maybe you . . . Well, maybe you haven't—"

Stella held up her hand to stop Ariel, who pressed her lips together and looked apologetic. "I know what you're about to say. You're going to tell me that maybe I've stopped living. And you know what? You're right. I'm definitely stuck." She motioned to the space around her. "This entire place is a testament to how 'stuck' I am. I know I have to do something. I could uproot my life. Change my career. Follow the trail of these words that are spelling out who knows what." She wrapped her arms around herself. "But I'm kinda terrified."

Ariel nodded. "You don't have to do all of that at once, but I know you're curious about those words." She pointed at the closed journal. "Don't you want to know what they're trying to tell you?"

"Yes. Do I want them to feel like they're burning holes in my body? No, but maybe that's the only way I would pay attention to them."

Ariel touched Stella's arm. "Come on, let's finish dinner and celebrate that you can tug out words to help people find books. That's a start to something bigger, and it's worth celebrating, right?"

Stella chuckled. "Always looking for the silver lining." She followed Ariel into the living room, casting one more glance over her shoulder at the journal and its mystifying words.

Chapter 6

*T*uesday at half past noon, Arnie returned from the local sandwich shop with brown paper sacks. Blobs of grease smeared the bottom of one bag, looking as though someone with hands coated in oil had carried it for him. He plopped the splotched bag on the circulation desk, and Stella closed her copy of *Beyond the Southern Horizon*.

"Lunch is served," Arnie said, walking around the desk. "I have Vicki's too. Where is she?"

A smile of surprise curved Stella's lips. "You bought me lunch? You didn't have to do that, but thank you." She pointed to the second floor. "She's reshelving titles in adult fiction."

Arnie's bushy eyebrows rose. He removed a folded handkerchief from his back pocket and swiped it across his forehead. "Did you bring something for lunch today?"

It was no secret that Stella's food choices at home consisted of mostly prepackaged goods, and if anything needed to be cooked, it was microwave friendly. Ariel joked that Stella could survive on cheese crackers, kids' cereals, and Hot Pockets without her body rebelling. Maybe one of these days she'd mature into cooking meals that required the stove or an oven, but then, maybe she wouldn't. "Well, no. But I have a box of Lucky Charms in the kitchenette."

Arnie made a dismissive noise in his throat. "Your diet is atrocious."

Stella shrugged. "Or adventurous. Who knows what chemicals are in my food. Every day is a risk."

Arnie opened his paper sack. "I'm not sure that's anything to brag about."

Stella pointed toward the greasy bag. "What's with the overabundance of grease? Did you ask them to empty out the fryer's goodness into my bag? I sure hope so," she teased.

Arnie's smile emerged, causing the glasses on the bridge of his nose to rise on his cheekbones. "Based on your current eating habits, I bought the worst thing on the menu for you. Philly cheesesteak with extra goo."

The scents of melted cheese, cooked steak, and toasted bread wafted out of the bag as soon as she opened it. "Arnie, you're my hero."

"Don't you know it," he said. "Take a break. I'll cover the desk while you eat. Take Vicki's to the break room, too, please. I'll let her know lunch is here."

The front door opened and a man walked in, bringing rays of light with him like a cape of sunshine attached to his shoulders. He scanned the high ceilings in the lobby as though he'd never been inside the building before. When his gaze lowered, his eyes locked on Stella's. He strode toward her with purpose, keeping his focus on her. She took in his features as quickly as possible: average height and a toned, athletic body. He moved effortlessly, like he was used to being in constant motion, like he enjoyed exercising. His sun-bleached blond hair and friendly face with Cupid's bow lips made him look like a model for polo shirts or Nike gear. As he neared, his mouth lifted into a smile, and small lines crinkled out from the corners of his eyes. Neon-yellow words, thin and stretched, slipped out of his shorts pocket. **Possibility. Welcome. Summer wind.**

Stella slid her lunch bag across the counter, leaving a thin grease track. Arnie pulled a tissue from its box and wiped it across the desk.

"Good afternoon," Stella said after clearing her throat, aware that Arnie was lingering just over her shoulder. "Can we help you find anything?"

The man's boyish grin combined with his laugh lines was utterly charming. "I'm new in town. I just accepted a job at the middle school for the coming fall, and I'm looking for information on soccer plays for kids and how to coach them. I've recklessly signed up to help lead a bunch of boys for a summer league, and I've never been a coach." He laughed, sounding unsure but excited. "I know *how* to play, but I'm not sure how to *teach* what I know to kids. Make sense?"

Stella pursed her lips in thought. "Why would you sign up for something you don't know how to do?" The question slipped out before she could stop it. She'd never agree to do something she wasn't sure she had the skills for.

He leaned forward over the desk. "Sometimes you have to take a chance, right? It's a new adventure."

His intense gaze drew her in like a magnet, so she leaned away. Quick-paced, crowded words skittered out from beneath his hands on the desk. **Come on. Give it a try. Take a chance.**

"No," Stella blurted, and the man's expression changed to one of confusion. She whirled around to Arnie. "I mean, um, Arnie here is your guy. He knows exactly what you need, don't you, Arnie? He knows where all the soccer books are kept."

Arnie tilted his head, and his eyebrows crawled toward the center of his brow. "As do you."

"But *you* know where the best ones are. I'll just take a quick lunch break while you help out Mr. Soccer Coach here." Stella turned back toward the man. Why did he look disappointed? "Seriously, Arnie is your guy. Good luck," she said, grabbing her book and the lunch bags, then scurrying toward the library's kitchenette.

When she glanced over her shoulder, wispy, bright blue words followed her like an airplane's condensation trail. **Adventure. Carefree. Risk.** Stella glared at the words before taking one last look at Arnie speaking with the man, and then she disappeared around the corner.

Fifteen minutes later, as Stella folded the sandwich paper around the other half of her cheesesteak, Arnie stepped into the doorway of the kitchenette. She stood, opened the '70s gold refrigerator door, and shoved her sandwich inside.

"Hey, kiddo," Arnie said. "How're you feeling?"

Stella stared at the contents of the refrigerator for a long pause before closing the door. He wasn't asking about her changing life path or the strange ways words were showing up. So she responded with, "The headache is finally gone, and now my stomach is full, thanks to you."

Arnie stepped into the kitchenette. "Want to tell me what that was about?"

Stella stared at the aging black-and-white tile floor and processed her choices: play dumb or admit the truth. She brought her gaze up to meet his. "To what are you referring?" she asked innocently.

Arnie's exasperation was evident in his knowing stare. Stella heaved a sigh that could have lifted kites into the sky. She dropped back onto one of the vintage chrome and red vinyl chairs that had been donated years ago by the local diner when they remodeled. When she leaned back, air whooshed out of a crack in the vinyl.

Stella laced her fingers together in her lap. "I'm no good with guys."

Arnie walked to a cabinet and pulled down a tall, decorative tin full of loose-leaf green tea. "Certainly not if you scurry away like a mouse every time one of them shows any interest."

Stella fought the urge to roll her eyes. "He *wasn't* showing interest. He was looking for a book."

Arnie filled the electric kettle with hot water and plugged it in. Then he sat down at the diner table across from her. He folded his hands together on the black laminate tabletop. "I saw the way he was looking at you, all googly-eyed. I believe he would have taken a book *and* you out to dinner. I think he'd prefer the latter more than the book, but you snuffed him out without giving him a chance."

Stella's chest tightened at the idea of going out with a man again. The image of Mr. Soccer Coach, all sunshine and ease, coasted through her mind. Then she saw an image of herself beating those thoughts of him with a fly swatter until they were scattered pieces blowing away. "I don't want to give him a chance."

"Or any man."

Stella's temples started to throb, and she clenched her jaw. "I don't *need* a man," she said, knowing she sounded like a brat. But she truly didn't. Especially not until she figured out how to *stop* holding on to the memories of Wade. She didn't even have any good examples in her life of what a healthy, loving relationship looked like. Her parents had crashed and burned. Arnie had been single for as long as she'd known him. Percy dated like it was part of his profession. Ariel was *waiting* for a guy to realize she was a dream catch and ask her out.

"Maybe the perfect guy for me doesn't exist," she said. Her throat squeezed as though protesting the words.

"You don't believe that," Arnie said.

Stella stood abruptly from the table, wanting to end the conversation before it became sentimental and hopeful, before some shred of romance tried to wheedle its way into her heart, which was currently a confusing mesh of *Love is a train wreck* and *Happily ever after exists*.

When she tried to walk past Arnie, he reached out and grabbed her arm in a relaxed grip. "Hey." His voice was gentle enough to cause her throat to close up. "You don't need a man. You're right about that. I'm not implying you do. I just think you might eventually like to have a partner, someone fun to hang out with and enjoy similar activities with. Not every man will be like Wade."

"What about the half dozen other guys I've tried dating? They all ended the same way. Failures." She picked up her copy of *Beyond the Southern Horizon*. "Don't suppose you have a clone of Jack Mathis somewhere, do you?"

Arnie shifted in his seat, and his gaze drifted toward the doorway. "Jack Mathis?"

Stella sighed. "He checks all the boxes for me." Then she rolled her eyes. "But alas, he's fictional. And even if he *were* here, I'm not ready."

Arnie said, "You'll know when you are."

The kettle whistled, sounding like a voice of mourning. Arnie's sigh followed her out of the kitchenette, pushing against her back like a rush of understanding.

✦ ✦ ✦

STELLA WAS SHELVING returned books on the first floor when Dana Cannon, a high school history teacher, walked through the front doors. She wore gardening khakis and a lightweight, button-up aqua shirt that enhanced her startling light green eyes. Her wavy dusty-brown hair—streaked with silver that reflected light like tinsel on a Christmas tree—was tucked behind her ears. Stella placed the books in her arms back on the cart and walked toward Dana, wondering what kind of book she might be searching for.

As if called to action, green, grasslike words lifted from Dana's shirt and circled around her body. **Blossoming friendship. Folksy. Secret murder from an unfolding past.** The image of a Fannie Flagg novel rose in Stella's mind. The connection surprised her, but it was similar to how she'd felt when she tested her gift on Ariel last night. How could she share what she'd seen with Dana without coming across as incredibly odd? Beat around the bush or be direct? What if she was wrong?

"Good afternoon, Dana," Stella said. Opting for a combination of evasive and direct, she continued, "It's a good day for a Fannie Flagg novel, don't you think? Something like *Fried Green Tomatoes at the Whistle Stop Cafe*?"

Dana's slow smile added to her surprised expression. "I was just thinking about that book. I haven't read it in years, but I loved it."

"Really?" Stella said, exaggerating her surprise while her own confidence soared. "I could have it ready for you at the front."

"I'd like that," Dana agreed. "It does seem like a good day to read it again."

Arnie stepped out from between a row of shelves, seemingly caught off guard by Dana's presence. She smiled, and Arnie stood stock-still as though he'd completely forgotten which way he had been heading. Stella watched, puzzled by his behavior.

"Good afternoon, Mr. Cohen," Dana said. "I was hoping to find you here today."

Arnie's lips parted. "You were?" He rubbed one hand down the back of his head.

Dana pulled a folded sheet of paper from her front pocket. "I had a specific question about Wildflower Hill and its connection to the Revolutionary War, and I hoped to find a book on the subject. Next month my students are preparing reports on both the American Revolution and the happenings in Blue Sky Valley during the same time. I'm sure you've heard the stories of the hauntings and other nonsense. But I'm looking for authentic information, the *facts*. Clyde Johnson said you were something of an expert—"

"Arnie," he interrupted.

Dana looked up from her paper, blinking her light eyes in the silence. "Pardon me?"

"Call me Arnie."

Stella leaned against the archway and grinned. *Is Arnie nervous?* As if in answer to her question, silvery, glittery words slipped out from beneath Arnie's shoes. **Magical. Green eyes. Yes yes yes.**

"Arnie," Dana said. She handed him the piece of paper. "I've made some preliminary notes about all the information I could find on the internet, but the facts are seriously lacking, and ghost stories meant to scare children can't be considered reliable sources, regardless of what the town swears to be the truth. Do you think you can guide me to a place to start?"

Arnie stared at the sheet of paper as though she'd handed him a love note. Then he looked up and caught Stella's gaze. His eyes pleaded with her, but she didn't understand his expression. He held out the paper for Stella, so she walked toward him.

"Stella, Ms. Cannon needs—"

"Dana," she said. Pale sunlight stretched down from the windows and pooled around her feet.

Arnie's gaze strayed to Dana's face and lingered there. "Dana," he said in a voice that had gone all soft and comfortable around the edges like a naptime blanket.

Stella cleared her throat. "How can I help?"

Arnie shoved the yellow legal pad paper into Stella's hands, and she struggled not to crumple the page. "I have a book I was supposed to order for Yvette Camden this morning, and it's somewhat of an emergency book. You can handle this." Then he hurried off, his dress shoes clacking against the tiles in rapid beats. Stella and Dana stared at his back as he scrambled up the main staircase.

Stella refocused on Dana. "I think I can lead you to the proper section. Arnie is more of the expert on Wildflower Hill, but if you have any questions later, I'm sure he'd be willing to help out . . . once he orders that emergency book, of course."

"Of course," Dana repeated. Her gaze lingered on where Arnie had disappeared up the staircase. "Let's grab Fannie Flagg, too, while we're at it."

After Stella helped Dana locate two books that contained the most information about Wildflower Hill along with Fannie Flagg's classic, she went looking for Arnie. She found him standing in the poetry section, tapping his fingers in a repeating rhythm against the spines. Stella recognized the pattern as Morse code. *SOS.*

"Sending a distress signal? Do you want to be the pot or the kettle?" she asked.

Arnie stilled his fingers and then pulled a book from the shelf before returning it almost as quickly. He turned toward her. His gray hair was ruffled around the edges, and his gaze seemed to reach out into some far, unseen distance. When he spoke, his speech was slow and thoughtful. "Sometimes you meet people, and you know you can handle yourself with them. You know you'll never lose control or give too much of yourself away. There is an amount of comfort in that feeling. Your heart is safe in that not-all-of-me space.

"Other times you meet someone and everything stops and brings that person into complete focus. Colors and sounds are muted as though that person is in a spotlight. And all you want to do is stay *right there*." Arnie sighed. "I can't think when Dana is around. At all. Complete doofus. I'm terrified I'm going to babble or blubber or both. It's like I revert to an awkward teenager. It's better if I make myself scarce when she's around."

Although Stella had never been cautious enough with her heart and had lost control of her emotions too many times, she had never felt what Arnie described—the dreamy feeling when time slowed as it intensified the connection to someone else. Arnie was one of the most capable, independent people Stella had ever known. He possessed equal amounts of composure and finesse. She couldn't imagine anyone making him feel tongue-tied or clumsy.

"Arnie, have you ever thought about asking Dana out? Starting small, like taking her out for coffee or tea?"

His face paled, and then he laughed—a deep belly laugh that rippled out and pressed against the library windows. "Can you imagine? I'd be all thumbs and left feet with her."

"I'm no expert on Arnold Cohen, but I've *never* seen you go all dewy-eyed for a woman before. I'm not sure missing out on this is worth your fear about being a doofus."

Arnie walked toward Stella and slipped his arm around her shoulders, guiding her toward the staircase. "Let's circle back. Do you want to be the pot or the kettle?"

✦ ✦ ✦

AT THE END of her shift, Stella told Arnie goodbye and headed toward her house. The late-afternoon sun filled the inside of her car with stifling summer heat. She rolled down the windows but found little relief from the outside air as it circulated inside the car, turning the interior into a convection oven.

Waya Lake shriveled from its banks in the intense heat, and teenagers hung out in the shade rather than sunbathing on the shore. Kids stood in line at the shaved-ice stand ordering treats in a rainbow of colors and racing to shovel them down before they melted.

The asphalt shimmered like a desert mirage as Stella drove to the pharmacy. She needed to buy another bottle of aspirin and a Pepsi from Mr. Jordan, Blue Sky Valley's pharmacist for the past forty-five years.

"Where are your helpers?" Stella asked him as he rang up her purchases.

"Sent them home an hour ago. The air-conditioning is having a time keeping up with this heat, and the girls were sweating like sinners in church, and boy, were they complaining. Another hour of that, and I would have lost *my* cool. Figuratively, of course, since this place has already literally lost its cool."

Stella nodded. "Air conditioners should know better than to give out during summer in the South. How's a person supposed to survive?"

As soon as she sat back down in her car, sweating through her clothes and sticking to the cracked leather seat, she opened the Pepsi, and it burned a dark pathway down her throat. Then she drove home, thinking about how she'd helped Dana find the perfect book. Excitement lit her up for the first time in months. The possibility of using her words to help library patrons thrilled her. What else would she be able to do with the words? How else could she call them forth to help her with people, with her own life? Would it be possible to actually write a book, to become a novelist?

When Stella parked in the garage and got out of her car, she noticed flat, mud-brown words squeeze out from beneath the weather stripping on the sides of the house-to-garage door. **Heat. Stale. Heavy.** "That's not a good sign," she said. When she opened the door, a wave of hot air billowed out.

After walking into the house, she inhaled sticky, dense air. She checked the thermostat, which read eighty-five degrees. Stella pulled out her cell phone and searched for the local HVAC company, then dialed their number. An energetic employee answered and asked if Stella was having issues.

"It feels like Death Valley in my house," Stella complained, thinking about the girls who had been working at the pharmacy today. At least that place was cooler than hers.

The bubbly voice on the other end of the line apologized, but Stella could hear the faint whir of cool air pumping into their office and the sound of ice cubes swirling around in a glass. The young woman's concern only stretched so far because she wasn't sweating pools on the floor.

"Let's see, I can get someone out there tomorrow afternoon. Will that work for you?" the woman said.

"Tomorrow? I could sweat to death by then," Stella said, then apologized. "Yes, of course. Thank you." They scheduled a time for tomorrow afternoon when a technician would come by the house and check the system. Stella ended the call and then repeated her earlier question to herself. "How's a person supposed to survive?"

She walked through the house and tested opening windows in the living room. Her optimism for a breeze dissipated within an hour, and her hopes that it would cool down when the sun set were laughable when she realized the interior temperature didn't drop a single degree as the sun plunged behind the trees.

She walked into her bedroom and opened the closet door to find something cooler to wear—perhaps a swimming suit—and something snapped beneath her foot. Stella bent over and picked up a purple crayon broken in half. Where had this come from?

Her gaze landed on an unassuming cardboard box sitting on the top shelf. There was only one word on the box, written in purple crayon years ago by Stella.

The word *Why?* slanted downward, and the wobbly letters looked like they were written with a trembling hand. Stella remembered writing the word and then tossing the crayon inside the box. She hadn't touched that box since she was a kid.

She hesitated before reaching up and pulling it from the shelf. Closed inside were Maria Parker's most prized possessions—or what Stella's dad had decided to keep: a shoebox full of her jewelry, all costume and rhinestones; a few tubes of half-used lipstick and eyeshadow so retro it was probably back in style; a pair of red heels; and a sweater stitched with a bunny. Stacked on top of the assortment was a single photo album that still trapped a faint scent of women's perfume. This was the only album Stella owned that included the whole family, when they were living as though everything was okay and everyone was still together. A sense of loss, familiar and profound, crept into her chest, almost as overpowering as the heat.

Stella remembered only scattered, mostly broken memories of her mother, like a video montage that wouldn't make sense to anyone else watching and barely made sense to her. She doubted she would recognize Maria's laugh or even her voice since she hadn't heard it in more than twenty years. What she remembered most vividly was how beautiful Maria had been, with curly black hair—like Stella's now—and her wide, infectious smile that showed all her teeth. But did Stella remember that because of the photos? Without these few photographs as proof, Maria might never have existed in their lives at all. She was more like a footnote in a term paper, one of those throwaway extras that no one reads and is easily overlooked as an unimportant fact.

Maria left when Stella was six years old. It was an ordinary day in the middle of fall, just when the leaves had started to change and litter the sidewalks. Maria had dropped off Percy and Stella at school with their heavy backpacks and sack lunches. She'd waved and blown them a kiss, then she'd driven off on a route that should have taken her straight to work. Except Maria never showed up at work, and she never showed up at the house again either.

Stella thought back to that night when their dad had to tell them the news—that their mother needed a break from her family, needed to go *find herself*, as though it was something she had dropped off somewhere but couldn't remember where. Turned out "finding herself" meant Maria moved to New York City to pursue her dream of becoming an actress. Stella had never told anyone that strangling truth, not even Ariel, because it sounded like a tragic plot in a novel that no one would believe. A mother of two leaves her adorable children to be raised by a single parent so she can have a 0.1 percent chance of making it on Broadway. Not exactly Hallmark movie material or going to win Maria a Mom of the Year award.

Stella never told anyone not only because it was dreadful but because of the shame and disbelief attached to Maria's decision. Had she and Percy not been good enough to stick around for? Had they been so disappointing that Maria hadn't bothered to send them birthday cards or holiday greetings? How could she have erased them so completely from her life? What did Maria tell people if they asked if she had children? Did she say no? Stella's chest ached just thinking about it.

She couldn't imagine how horrible that conversation must have been for her dad. How much he must have struggled to help two kids understand such devastating news, the same news he, too, had to try to make sense of.

As far as Stella knew, no one had ever heard from Maria again. She'd disappeared into the world as though she'd never existed. Some nights when Stella couldn't sleep, she wondered if she might try to find Maria again, just to ask her *why*. But Stella was more afraid of finding the woman than hearing the answer. What if the answer was more heartbreaking than telling herself that Maria was a negligent parent and Stella was better off without her?

The heat in the closet pressed in all around her, and a line of sweat slid down Stella's back. She blinked away the thoughts of Maria, and another idea tumbled through her mind.

She grabbed her phone and called Arnie. He didn't answer, so she left him a message, telling him she was planning to have a slumber party for one at the library. There was no way she would be able to sleep in her miserable, hotter-than-Hades house. And at least in the library she wouldn't be alone—there were half a million books to keep her company.

✦ ✦ ✦

A SCATTERING OF cars still sat in the parking lot when Stella arrived with her slumber party accessories—one small bag of clothes, toiletries, her copy of *Beyond the Southern Horizon*, and her journal; a sleeping bag and a pillow; and snacks. Once inside, she dropped her stuff beneath the circulation desk and searched for Arnie. He leaned over the second-floor railing near the fiction section and called down to her in a stage whisper.

"What are you doing back here?"

Stella craned her neck back. "I left you a message. My house feels like Arrakis. The AC gave up, and they can't come to check it until tomorrow afternoon. Can I sleep here?"

Arnie laughed. "You're the kind of person who would make up that story just so she could spend the night in a library. Where's Ariel?"

Stella shrugged. "I didn't want to bother her, and she's house-sitting four dogs, which is too full of a house for me."

"This could be considered special treatment," Arnie said.

Stella smirked. "I'm going to take that as a yes."

"I would never agree to let Vicki, Dan, or Melanie sleep here overnight."

"They're all part-timers," Stella said. "Plus, they wouldn't want to spend the night in a big, dark library alone. *And* none of them bring your favorite cookies." Stella pointed toward the circulation desk. A local bakery box waited for him.

Arnie's gaze followed her finger. "Bribery? Is there no end to your corruption?"

Stella held open her hands, palms facing up. "I do what needs to be done. Half a dozen white chocolate macadamia nut should do the trick."

"Sure, kiddo," he said. "Stay as long as you like. I would suggest sleeping in the fairy-tale section. There's a better view of the stars coming through the windows. I'm going to be doing late-night research in the archives tonight, but I'll keep it down."

Stella's interest roused. They still hadn't discussed the night she hit her head. "Doing research . . . alone?"

Arnie's eyes narrowed. "Of course. Nothing that would interest you . . . yet."

"Yet?" she asked.

Arnie straightened the spectacles on his nose. "I'll let you know when things get good."

His words sent a zing of electricity up her spine. He moved away from the balcony, but glistening words the color of ripe grapes slipped out from beneath his shoes and tumbled from the second-floor ledge toward Stella. **Mystery. Concealed. Encounter.** They landed at her feet, circled her three times, and then faded into the tiles. What was Arnie researching in the archives? Why was he being so secretive? Stella still wasn't convinced she'd dreamed the vision of the people the other night, but without proof, there was nothing to reveal otherwise. If he said he was alone, then she had to believe him, but something felt off.

Although she was off the clock, she helped Arnie go through the closing routines, and once everyone was gone for the evening, Arnie wished her good night and headed into the archives, saying he'd set the alarm once he was finished but wouldn't bother her again in case she was already sleeping. She didn't press him for more details, but perhaps she'd sneak down to the archives in a bit, just to check up on him. Until then, Stella grabbed a copy of *The Wonderful Wizard of Oz* and her stuff from home and found a spot in the fairy-tale section near the windows.

She stretched out on her sleeping bag to read and assumed she'd be awake for a while, giving Arnie enough time to settle in before she dropped in on him. She nestled into her sleeping bag and opened the book to her favorite chapter.

✦ ✦ ✦

STELLA'S EYES POPPED open, and her heart jumped like someone had shocked her with a defibrillator. Moonlight streamed through the glass and cast silver stripes across her chest and legs. Something—a noise, a nearby movement—had woken her. She pushed herself up on her elbows, reached for her cell phone, and checked the time: *1:15 a.m.* The sound of stifled laughter caused the hair on the back of her neck to stand. She stayed perfectly still until she heard the shuffling of multiple sets of feet down an aisle near her.

She scrambled out of the sleeping bag as though she'd discovered snakes at the bottom of it. Then she crouched and tried to scan through openings on the shelves while her heart thundered. Stella crept barefoot down the aisle, but the intruders' movements stopped. Her pulse throbbed hard against her temples, and she held her breath. At the end of the aisle, two shadows stepped into the moonlight. Their silhouettes shimmered, and their white teeth were visible against their darkened faces. One appeared to be wearing clothes a few sizes too big for him. *Two teenage boys.*

Stella inhaled a deep breath so she could either release a scream or demand that they get out immediately, but one of the boys burst out laughing. Then he shoved the boy beside him, and they both ran off down the adjacent aisle.

She wasn't thinking properly when she snatched a book—a spontaneous weapon—from the closest shelf and chased after them. A door slammed somewhere, echoing through the cavernous foyer, but by the time she entered the main foyer, the library was silent except for her own labored breathing. Her body stayed rigid for another minute, her senses heightened and searching. But no one was moving anywhere near her.

Stella stood in the middle of the empty foyer for a few more minutes, listening, waiting, training her ears for anything. Soon her heartbeat slowed, and she wondered if she'd imagined the boys. Had she been dreaming? Still she walked through the library checking all the doors and windows. On her last pass through the foyer, she tugged on the vault door leading to the archives. It was closed and secure. Arnie had obviously finished his research and gone home.

She shuffled back to her sleeping bag, taking the aisle where the boys had been hiding when she'd first heard them. She was looking for out-of-place books or vandalism. Then she noticed something in front of her that shimmered in the moonlight. Her eyes couldn't focus on what it was, but it reminded her of peering through a waterfall. She hurried straight ahead and slammed into something.

Her brain immediately computed the *something* as a giant spider-web. Stella's scream was muffled by plastic sticking to her face. The book she'd planned to use as a makeshift weapon bounced out of her hand and slid across the floor behind her. She lurched backward and ran her hands over her face as if to check for damage or spiders.

Then she stepped forward with caution and reached out both hands. Her fingertips grazed bands of plastic that had been stretched horizontally from one bookshelf to the other. Plastic wrap. Stella snatched the plastic from the shelves and crushed it together until she had a hard, plastic ball in her palm.

She stomped around the library again calling out, "I know you're in here!" "Come out, come out, wherever you are," "Show your faces," and "Real funny trick," but she saw no one, and no one came out of hiding to admit to the prank. Where were they hiding? How had they gotten into a locked library? Should she call Arnie or the police? Getting kids into serious trouble didn't seem like a fair punishment for pulling a prank in the library. But knowing all the windows and doors were locked also made the likelihood of kids being able to break in extremely slim. Would the police assume she was making up a wild story?

But was she? She'd *seen* something, and she'd definitely run into the plastic-wrap wall. Stella performed another search of the library, but after half an hour, she gave up and returned to her sleeping bag. She called Arnie, but his phone went straight to voicemail. Nothing could be done until tomorrow anyway.

"Here's to hoping they don't burn the place down."

She dropped the plastic-wrap ball beside her and grabbed *The Wonderful Wizard of Oz*. She thought it would take a while before she could fall back asleep, but when she laid her head on her pillow and closed her eyes for a moment, exhaustion crept in. The book slipped from her relaxed fingers. As she dozed off, she thought she heard voices and someone whispering the name Huck.

Chapter 7

"Rise and shine, buttercup."

Arnie's voice drifted into Stella's mind, and she blinked in the pale yellow morning sunlight. She experienced that moment of *where am I?* followed by the memory of moonlight, laughter, and an impact with a wall of plastic wrap. Arnie stood at her feet, dressed in black slacks and a charcoal-gray button-down. He held a cup of coffee that released spirals of steam toward the high ceiling.

She stretched and yawned before sitting up and rubbing her lower back. The sleeping bag bunched around her waist. "What day is it?"

Arnie laughed and held out the mug for her. "Wednesday."

Stella was about to take the mug and tell Arnie what happened last night, but when she looked around for the ball of plastic from the prank, she didn't see it anywhere. Creamy-white words formed from the steam rising from the hot liquid. **Fiction. Disappear. Out of time.**

Goose bumps rose on her arms. What had happened to the plastic wrap? She *knew* she hadn't dreamed walking around the library chasing possible vandals, and she hadn't dreamed running into the plastic wrap.

"You called me last night?" Arnie asked, still holding out the mug. "Everything okay?"

"I might be hallucinating, but I don't think so," she said, then reached for the mug of coffee and thanked him. "In the middle of the night, I'm pretty sure I saw two teenagers lurking around the stacks, and they set up a booby trap for me."

A crease formed between Arnie's eyebrows. "I'm not sure if you're being serious or not."

Stella cupped her hands around the warm mug and heard a crinkling noise. Instead of smooth ceramic, the mug felt papery. She pulled off a folded college brochure that had been wrapped around and taped to the mug. She shook the paper in the space between them before dropping it on the sleeping bag.

"You and Percy . . . Are you two working together to plan my life? He's trying to get me to take a job in Florida, and you're going on about extended education. Will you ever stop nagging me?"

"Anything is possible," Arnie said. "What's this about a job in Florida?"

Stella sipped more coffee. The hot liquid slid down her throat and sent tendrils of warmth through her, waking up her sluggish body. "Don't get me started on Florida, but I'm serious about the possibility of library vandals. They stretched plastic wrap across the bookshelves, and I ran into it. I took it down and wadded it up, and the ball of plastic was right here when I went to sleep." She pointed at an empty spot on the floor. "I don't know how they got out. You set the alarm when you left, didn't you?"

"Of course." Arnie frowned. "Are you sure you weren't dreaming?"

She'd never "dreamed" so much in her life and certainly not dreams that were so vivid, so corporeal. Last night hadn't felt like a dream at all. Stella touched her face as she thought about the wall of plastic. "Two teenagers, I think. Laughing, seemingly up to no good, but when I chased after them, they disappeared."

Arnie crossed his arms over his chest. Stella placed the mug beside her and shimmied out of the sleeping bag. She glanced over her shoulder to where she'd seen the boys and their shadows stretching across the cartoonish train track rug.

She stood and walked toward the rug and stared down at the curving railroad track. Bright red words wiggled out from between the carpet fibers. **Believe. Childhood. Wonder.** "I don't remember seeing any boys in here when we were closing down last night," she said. "But maybe they were hiding out somewhere. In a closet or in the bathroom."

Arnie removed his glasses. He polished the lenses on his shirt-sleeve and cast a look of doubt in her direction.

Stella glanced away from his searching gaze. "I walked around and checked all of the doors and windows. Nothing appeared tampered with." She returned and grabbed her coffee. "Even the vault was closed up. So . . . now I'm wondering, what if I wasn't dreaming?"

A rush of thoughts surged through her like a storm wind. All of this started after she burned the journal. Had that triggered some kind of avalanche of, dare she think, *magic*? The words were popping up triple time, plus the agonizing ones sprang out without warning and seared her from the inside with a message she didn't understand yet. Now she was seeing people in the library who supposedly weren't really there? First Peter Pan, Helen of Troy, and Ichabod Crane in the archives, now these two teenagers.

Arnie walked toward her. "Hey, kiddo, you look stressed." He slipped on his glasses. "Maybe you weren't dreaming. Some people believe the library is haunted. I'm not one to discount unusual sightings."

Ghosts? Was he serious? Although that was a better explanation than Stella believing she'd caused some sort of chain reaction of magical doom. Her forehead scrunched. "By prankster teenagers?"

Arnie laughed and shook his head. "I don't know that I've heard anything quite *that* specific, but who's to say it's not?"

She pulled her fingers through her unruly hair. "You're just trying to make me feel better about losing my marbles."

Arnie slid back his shirtsleeve and checked his watch. "Library opens in an hour. Clean up your party scene here, and you can shower at my house. Use your key. I've already set out clean towels. There's also a pan of biscuits staying warm in the oven. Jelly's in the fridge."

Stella's chest warmed, and not because of the coffee mug cradled in her hands. Even if she were losing control of her life, she wouldn't lose Arnie. Along with Percy and Ariel, Arnie had been one of the remaining constants in her life for as long as she could remember. "You're too good to me."

"Not possible," he said, making a shooing motion with his hands before walking off.

BY MIDMORNING A constant crackle of energy, like an electrical undercurrent, slowly built beneath Stella's feet, causing a tingle to zing up and down her spine. She felt anxious in her skin, like she had an itch out of reach and below the surface.

As she shelved books, more than a dozen buzzing, quivering words akin to a swarm of bees waited for her on an empty shelf in the self-help section. Like winged insects, they flew toward one another and formed sentences. Stella's body flooded with the familiar ache of needing to write. These words wouldn't be satisfied with being seen. They craved to be inked on a page.

A library patron had left behind a brown paper napkin emblazoned with the logo from the coffee shop up the street, so Stella grabbed it and pulled a pen out of her back pocket. The words buzzed around the shelf, levitating in an undulating motion. She wrote them down.

> *Meet me in the dark,*
> *when the world has fallen still.*
> *Our love will burn bright.*

Stella didn't understand why she'd needed to write these particular words, as she had no desire to meet anyone offering love to her in the dark. But she folded the napkin and slipped it into her back pocket with her pen.

Maybe her restlessness today, the jittery unease, could be blamed on her second cup of coffee or on the summer heat slipping inside. But the air in the library felt out of sync with how it should be, like a thunderstorm brewing indoors, and Stella had an inkling as to why.

After a lifetime of seeing the words, she couldn't deny that her unique magic was real. However, admitting there was *more* enchantment in the world alarmed her. She'd been trying so hard to live a normal life after her mom left. She could entertain the possibility of using her talents to start redirecting her life. But accepting the possibility that extraordinary, wilder magic existed threatened to upend her grip on normal, and the strangeness in the library unnerved her.

Stella returned to the circulation desk just as a redheaded woman walked into the library. The woman carried an armful of books, and she smiled as soon as she made eye contact with Stella.

"Good morning," Stella said. "Looks like you've been busy."

The woman nodded. "Mostly for my boys, but I'll be honest, I stayed up all night finishing this one." She pulled *The Adventures of Tom Sawyer* out of the stack and slid it closer to Stella. "I told myself I'd only read until nine and then it was ten. Then before I knew it, it was three a.m., and I don't even care that I look like I stayed up all night. I couldn't put it down. It's probably hard to believe I've never read this classic before now." She tugged on her fiery-red, shoulder-length hair. "I also read through this one." She slid *Adventures of Huckleberry Finn* out of the stack.

Stella's smile wavered as watery letters leaked out of the pages. They formed puddles on the desk and then collected into words. **Teenagers. Shenanigans. Superstitions.** A queasy feeling wormed through her, and she experienced a surrealistic moment like Alice must have felt when she tumbled down the rabbit hole.

Stella nodded absently. "Those two boys certainly got into some wayward escapades."

The woman leaned forward and whispered, "I'm a bit relieved my boys aren't like these two. They're bighearted and well-meaning, but with Tom skipping school and getting into fights—not the kind of friend I want my boys to have, but I bet they were fun too."

The two boys silhouetted by moonlight flashed into her memory. Stella reached for the remainder of the returned books. "Is there something else you want to check out while you're here? Can I help you find anything?"

"Since we're on the subject of troublemakers, I think I'll start the Harry Potter series. I heard there are twins who get into a lot of mischief," she said. "But I know where to find those books. I'll be back." She scurried off toward the children's section, humming "Every Little Thing She Does Is Magic."

Stella stared at the books. She rubbed her fingertip against the embossed title of *The Adventures of Tom Sawyer*.

"Ichabod Crane, Peter Pan, Helen of Troy, and now Tom and Huck." There was a definite connection between the library books and the character sightings—if she could call them that. What was actually happening here?

Stella dug through her overnight bag and retrieved Jack Mathis's novel. She flipped through the pages and stopped on one of the photographs. "Now if *you* were coming to life . . ." She smiled at the absurdity of the idea, knowing if Jack showed his face, she might hightail it the other way. She and relationships with men did not mix well together, like gasoline and stupidity. "Best if you *don't* show up, Jack."

STELLA LEFT THE library during the afternoon to run home and meet the HVAC guy. He was able to repair the air-conditioning unit with ease and said within three to four hours, the house should feel pleasant again. Returning to the library and its cool air was a relief until the temperature in the house cooled from ninety degrees to a tolerable seventy-two.

That evening when Stella and Melanie finished the closing routine, Stella found Arnie sitting at the circulation desk. He flipped through the accordion file that was stuffed with paperwork for the festival. Sweat beaded across his forehead, and he rubbed one hand up and down his jaw and then against the back of his neck.

Stella draped her arms over the desk and studied him. "You don't look so hot."

Arnie cut his eyes over at her but continued to look through the files. "Says the woman who slept on the library floor last night."

"Hey," Stella joked, "there's no reason to cut so low. I thought I was looking pretty good for sleeping on the floor and being haunted by teenagers. But really, are you feeling okay?"

Arnie pulled his handkerchief from his back pocket and wiped it across his forehead and then down both sides of his neck. "It's hot as blue blazes outside, and it's creeping indoors. I'll be fine when the autumn gets here. How's the head, kiddo?"

"When are you going to stop asking about my head?" She plucked an ink pen out of a mug on the counter and twirled it through her fingers.

"When you give me an honest answer. Still seeing ghosts?"

The pen slipped through her fingers, and Stella shivered. "Not in the last few hours." She picked up the pen and dropped it back into the cup. Flimsy words poofed out of the mug like dust. **On the edge. Stirring. Unexpected.** They wriggled toward Arnie and disappeared up his shirtsleeve.

Arnie wiped his handkerchief across his forehead once more before he tucked it back into his pocket. He reached for a bottle of water, and his hand trembled against the plastic. He seemed to be having trouble catching his breath for a few seconds before he twisted off the cap and gulped down half of the water in the bottle.

Stella slid around the desk and propped her hip against the counter beside him. "Seriously, are you okay?"

Arnie pushed away from the desk in the rolling chair. He rubbed his left shoulder and nodded. "I'm starting to think that maybe I stretched my tuna salad one day too many." He reached over and patted Stella's hand. "Don't worry about me. I've been worse. Is the AC fixed in the house?"

Stella nodded. "I'm heading home. You sure you don't need anything? What about for the festival? Is there anything you need me to help with? Last-minute location or vendor changes?"

Arnie placed his hands on his stomach. "I assure you, it's all organized and prepped like a well-oiled machine. We have very little to take charge of this year, except your care packages."

"A few people on the committee were kind enough to volunteer to help me, so that's all organized too."

Arnie closed his eyes for a moment. "I don't foresee any hiccups at this point. There's bound to be *something* unexpected, but that's what makes life interesting. I think we'll be smooth sailing."

Stella crossed her arms over her chest. "Don't overwork yourself then. The festival is always a success because of all the overtime and hard work you and the committee put into planning, so take it easy these last few days. I'm going to call you later and check to see how you're feeling, and if you don't answer, I'm going to come back here. Answer your phone when I call. That's an order."

Arnie tossed his thumb over his shoulder. "Yes, ma'am. Now get out of here, go home, and relax. *That's* an order."

Stella shoved her Jack Mathis book and her notepad into her purse and then slung the bag onto her shoulder. She grabbed her duffel and sleeping bag and saluted Arnie.

"You need to work on your salute, soldier." He opened a drawer and pointed at his cell phone. "Call me tonight. I promise to answer."

✦ ✦ ✦

My love for you swells
against the cage of my heart.
This time, stay with me.

Stella tucked the pen behind her ear and sighed, closing her eyes as she sank back onto the worn couch cushions. *Ugh, why am I writing love poems today?* For one indulgent moment, she allowed herself to recall the memory of what it felt like to be held, to offer her heart in exchange for nothing. The familiar thrill of her hand entwined with another's drew an extra sigh from her lips. But the ache of loss followed closely behind.

Words arced across the living room wall, an explosion of rippling colors, like an aurora borealis made of letters. It was as though the words and emotions had been plucked straight out of her heart and splashed across the wall. Stella picked up her pen and wrote.

> It's not as though I remember every moment clearly. My memories of you often come unbidden, in the colors of the sunrise, in the lightning bugs weaving through the trees, in the black-and-white pages of a book. My first instinct is to push them away, but sometimes I linger for a moment, standing in the center of those memories with closed eyes and open arms, and I remember you when we were us, when we were in love.

The AC blew a steady breeze across her face, and she breathed in the artificially cold air that smelled faintly of rubber and heated metal. She reached over for her cell phone and called Arnie. His voicemail picked up, so she left a message.

She cooked a premade cup of macaroni and cheese in the microwave and ate it standing in the kitchen. After a dessert of two peanut butter cups, Arnie still hadn't returned her call. Unease trickled into her mind. She grabbed her phone to call him again, but it rang in her hand. Her relief that it was Arnie quickly vanished.

"Percy," she said on a sigh.

"Well, hello to you too," he said.

"I thought you were Arnie," she admitted.

"Sorry to disappoint," Percy said, sounding slightly put out.

She glanced at the time on the clock. Why *hadn't* Arnie called her yet? "What's up?"

"Given any more thought to Miami?"

Stella didn't bother hiding her irritation. "No."

Percy echoed her frustration. "This is a *huge* opportunity."

"So you take it," she argued.

"Stella—"

"Listen, Percy, I said I'd think about it, and I will. Right now I need to call Arnie."

"Don't wait too long," Percy said. "This opportunity won't be around forever."

"Noted," she said with an eye roll he couldn't appreciate. She said goodbye and then called Arnie immediately. The call went unanswered.

"Come on, Arnie," she said to his voicemail. "Pick up. Call me back."

Another fifteen minutes passed, and Stella sat on the couch flipping through the English–Italian dictionary, looking up the Italian word for *mistake*. She glanced up at her car keys sitting on the coffee table. Words tangled around the key ring. She tilted her head and squinted. **Darkness. Panic. Pain.** Stella tossed the book aside, jumped up from the couch, grabbed her cell phone and keys, slipped on her tennis shoes, and ran out of the house.

✦ ✦ ✦

THE CHARMED LIBRARY

STELLA PARKED IN the lot, rushing into her usual spot. As soon as she unlocked the library door and ran inside, the air felt electrified and anxious. Words, stretched thin and nearly transparent, scampered across the shadowy floor like an army of bug-shaped letters. Stella had difficulty focusing on any of them long enough to read them.

The single light above the circulation desk spotlighted a tall man whose hands were buried in his dark brown hair. He wore an expression of complete frustration. Stella stopped moving, unsure of how to process the vision of a stranger standing in the deserted library. The back door clicked shut behind her.

The man's attire was enough to cause her to pause and stare. His handsome features were half in shadow, but he was dressed like a gentleman from the Regency era. He wore a high-collared white shirt covered by a white vest, both tucked into black trousers. His long black dress coat hung low, brushing against the backs of his thighs. He grabbed the receiver of the telephone in one hand, pressed it to his ear, and shifted it away again. His fist closed over something in his other hand. He sensed her presence finally and turned to look at her. His polished black boots shone in the light.

He bowed his head slightly to her and then extended the receiver in her direction. "I do not understand this strange invention," he said in a British accent. He opened his fist, revealing a cell phone. "Nor this. Are you . . . Stella? Your likeness and name have been flashing on this peculiar torch. Arnie needs medical aid."

Stella's shock disappeared, and she rushed toward the man. "What do you mean, Arnie needs medical aid? Where is he?" Stella recognized Arnie's cell phone in the man's hand. "Did you steal that?"

The man looked offended and gazed at her with disdain. "I beg your pardon? I have no need to steal. My wealth is quite well known."

Stella waved her hands in the air. "Never mind. Where's Arnie?"

The man pointed toward the open vault door. "He needs a doctor—"

Stella ran for the archives, shouting for Arnie as she hurried down the stairs. She found him at the far end of the archives surrounded by three people who also wore costumes.

Arnie was flat on his back with his face contorted in pain. Stella grabbed her phone and dialed 911, then dropped to her knees between two people she'd never seen before—a man and a woman, both dressed in period costumes. Stella grabbed Arnie's hand, which was sweaty and trembling. The two people beside her stood and backed away, moving near the study table.

The 911 operator answered and immediately asked questions. Stella answered the first few quickly, but the question "What is happening?" wasn't easy to answer. Sweat soaked through Arnie's dress shirt, and his breaths came in short bursts.

"Arnie, what's wrong? Talk to me," Stella begged.

The operator continued to engage Stella in conversation, and when Arnie opened his eyes, Stella said, "He's conscious!"

He squeezed her hand. "Kiddo? Where did you come from?" His left arm jerked, and the man dressed as a soldier and kneeling across from Stella grabbed it and pressed it back to the floor. Arnie's eyes rolled back in his head.

"Could be a heart attack," the soldier said. "We sent Darcy up to call for help."

"Ma'am, is Arnie having a heart attack?" the operator asked.

"I don't know. Maybe. Please just send someone to the library! I'll be here." Intense fear gripped her like talons. "Arnie, what is going on? Arnie, look at me. *Please.*"

He shuddered, but his eyes opened. "Kiddo," he breathed out. Then his eyes closed, and his head lolled to the side.

"Arnie!" Stella shouted. "Don't you dare die on me!"

The soldier touched his fingers to Arnie's neck. "There's a pulse."

Stella's entire body trembled. She held Arnie's hand and told him over and over again that he was going to be okay, that everything was going to be fine. Gray, cloudlike words drifted around Arnie's head—**Final. Stop. Let go.**—and Stella continuously waved them away because they terrified her.

When the paramedics arrived, Stella experienced a modicum of relief, although seeing Arnie on a stretcher challenged her strength to hold it together. She stood off to the side and chewed on her thumbnail. They'd given him an aspirin and put a small tablet beneath his tongue. One of the paramedics—whom Stella recognized as Niall Wiley—strapped a blood pressure cuff onto Arnie's arm and listened to his heartbeat with a stethoscope, while his partner started an IV line in Arnie's other arm. Niall put an oxygen mask over Arnie's nose and mouth.

"Stella?" Niall called and motioned for her.

She hurried toward the stretcher, pressing her hands against the starched, disposable sheet pulled tight across the thin cushion. Arnie's gaze focused on her, and he opened one of his hands. Stella slipped her hand into his.

"Arnie," she said, feeling the sting of tears.

"Take care of them," he said.

Stella wrinkled her brow. "What?"

"My friends . . . They're not from around here . . . Keep them in here, okay? In the library. Take care of them. Come see me tomorrow. I'll tell you everything. It's temporary. Jack—I wanted to tell you about him."

Stella shook her head, not understanding in the least. "Who's Jack? What do you mean?"

Arnie's eyes closed again, and he didn't respond.

Stella looked up at Niall. "Is he drugged?"

Niall shook his head. "No, but it's common for disorientation to occur. Terrible this happened during your party."

"Party?" Stella asked.

Niall nodded toward the small gathering of costumed people. This wasn't a party Stella had been invited to.

"We need to go," Niall said.

Arnie squeezed Stella's fingers, and his eyes opened. "Remember what I said."

"Wait, should I go with you?" Stella asked.

Niall rested his hand on Stella's shoulder, and she felt ripples of comfort radiating down her arm. "We'll get him stabilized. Grab some things for him, if you want, and bring them to the hospital. I'll make sure you can get in to see him."

Stella nodded her thanks and let go of Arnie's hand as they wheeled him away. She clenched her hands together in front of her lips, holding her breath. As they disappeared up the stairs, someone stepped up beside her.

"Are you okay?" the soldier asked.

Stella looked at him. "No. He's like a second father to me." She swiped at the tears on her cheeks and looked around at the four strangers gathered in the archives with her.

The tall, handsome Englishman from upstairs stood with his arms crossed over his chest. Was he the one the soldier called Darcy? A tickle started in the back of Stella's brain until it became a full-blown irrational wave of thought. Fitzwilliam Darcy? As in Jane Austen's Fitzwilliam Darcy? Had Arnie been hosting some kind of Regency-era party?

But that couldn't be, because the others didn't fit in. The woman was dressed in an elaborate blue dress embellished with embroidered white flowers, and her chocolate-brown hair was braided. She gripped a book in her arms and watched them with an anxious expression. She spoke French to the man beside her, who was dressed like medieval royalty. He nodded and slipped his arm around her shoulders, pulling her against him.

The soldier shifted his steady gaze toward Stella. His face—the familiar angles of it, the fullness of his lips, the way the lamplight reflected in his pale eyes—she felt as though she knew him.

"I'm Jack," he said. "If there's anything I can do . . ."

The sluggish cogs in Stella's brain clicked into place one by one, until the hairs on top of her head stood on end. The man beside her—she had stared at his face for years. He'd often been the hero in her daydreams, the man whose eyes saw straight into her soul. She looked at him. "Jack . . . Mathis?"

He nodded once. "Yes, ma'am."

Her knees wobbled. "As in Jack Mathis from *Beyond the Southern Horizon*?"

Jack nodded.

"Is this a joke?" Stella asked.

"Is that rhetorical?" Jack asked.

"This can't be happening."

Jack stepped closer to her. "I assure you, it is."

Chapter 8

*J*ack Mathis? No way was that possible. How could it be? Stella shook her head and walked toward the stairs leading up into the library. "I can't do this right now. *Whatever* this is."

"Hey," Jack called.

Curiosity and heat zinged through her body on a current of electricity. Stella wanted to keep walking away, but her body halted her, causing her tennis shoes to squeak against the floor. She glanced at Jack, the soldier from her dreams. Not to mention a soldier *from a novel*.

"Where are you going?" he asked.

"I want to grab some things for Arnie and take them to the hospital." She started up the staircase. "I'm not hanging out with you, Jack Mathis, and Mr. Darcy and whoever the French couple is. I wasn't invited to this costume party. In fact"—she stopped halfway up the staircase—"what am I thinking? You need to go home." She turned around and descended the stairs.

Arnie's voice drifted into her mind. *Keep them in here, okay? In the library. Take care of them.* What did that even mean? Who were these people in the archives? Was there a chance they *were* characters from books?

Jack shoved his hands into his pockets and pursed his lips while he rocked on his boot heels. "Stella, right?" He didn't wait for her to answer. "I don't want you to freak out, but this is our home for now."

Stella's thoughts stuttered. "I'm sorry, what? This is most definitely *not* your home. This is a library and we're closed." She rubbed her temples. Everything in this moment felt like complete madness. Arnie was in an ambulance on his way to the hospital, and she was stuck dealing with . . . "I'm supposed to believe that you're Jack Mathis? And that man in the black coat . . . he can't be Fitzwilliam Darcy—"

"I beg your pardon," Mr. Darcy spoke up from behind Jack, stepping out into full view. "I most certainly *am*—"

"No!" Stella yelled at him, cringing at the shrill tone of her voice. She looked sheepishly at Mr. Darcy. "You're exactly as I imagined you'd be, but this is ridiculous, right? Arnie might have put this party together, but I'm ending it."

Jack stepped toward her, and she temporarily lost her grip on her anger. "You're upset. You and Arnie are close, and you're scared and confused, and I know this sounds cockeyed." He pressed a hand to his heart. "I *am* Jack Henry Mathis. I have no reason to lie to you, Stella."

His words resonated in her chest, flowed through her like steaming coffee, warming her all the way to her toes. He pulled his other hand out of his pocket, and three words, pastel pink and fluttery, drifted out as though caught on a breeze and floated straight toward her. **You. Me. Please.** Stella watched the words as they coasted toward her. Without thinking about what she was doing, she opened her hands. The words landed on her palms and melted into her skin, leaving behind an imprint of warmth.

"Jack Mathis is from a book, one of my dad's favorites," Stella babbled. "It's impossible. People don't walk out of books. Who would believe that? Sure, what book nerd hasn't dreamed about a fictional boyfriend being real or seeing Mr. Darcy?"

Mr. Darcy's shoulders straightened, and he inclined his head. "I cannot argue with her logic."

Jack pointed toward a study table. "Perhaps you should sit down. Arnie didn't want you to find out this way, but he's been keeping secrets from you."

Arnie *was* keeping secrets. But why? Jack pulled out a chair, and Stella walked to the table and dropped into it, feeling the cold, unforgiving wood press against her bones. The back of her head throbbed. *I wish I had an aspirin, a Pepsi, and a do-over for the past few days—no, years.*

The French couple lingered near a bookshelf, watching her. Stella remembered all the French lessons she and Arnie had done together. She asked, *"Parlez-vous français?"*

The woman nodded, which loosened strands of dark hair from her braid. She smoothed her hands down her dress before wringing her hands together in front of her.

"Êtes-vous ici pour une fête?" Stella asked.

The woman glanced at the nobleman beside her. His shoulders stiffened, but he nodded as though encouraging the woman to answer. She replied, *"Non."*

Jack sounded surprised when he said, "You speak French."

Stella nodded. "And a few other languages. A fun thing Arnie and I have done together for years. He knows I love words." She pressed her palms against the cold tabletop. "The French couple says they're not here for a party. And they're not the first strange characters— emphasis on the word *characters*—I've seen roaming around the library."

Jack sat on the edge of the table and looked at her. "You have an idea about what's happening, don't you?"

She glanced up at his handsome face, studying the lines of his eyes and mouth. "An idea that I'm not ready to accept." Looking at him felt like a dream. In fact, the last few days were playing out like a strange waking dream sequence. Could this actually be happening?

"Go get the things for Arnie," Jack said. "I'll keep everyone down here in the archives tonight."

Stella's logical brain kicked in. She thought of the cash box, which held very little money, and the priceless antiques and artifacts in the archives. An image of the costumed strangers pilfering Blue Sky Valley's precious history formed in her mind. She shook her head.

"I can't leave people in the library. That's against the rules."

Jack touched her arm, and she stared at his fingers against her skin. She wanted to reach up and place her hand on his, just to feel his skin and see if her fingertips would tingle at the touch, to see if he was actually real.

"Lock us in. We'll be fine."

She *wanted* to believe him, but what he was saying wasn't reasonable. Arnie trusted her to be responsible with the library and its holdings, but he'd also told her to keep these people in the library. What if logic had nothing to do with what was going on? Could she sincerely be standing *in the flesh* with her biggest crush? Her gaze drifted over Jack, taking in the real-life version of him.

Jack's World War II uniform consisted of a drab olive-green, long-sleeve jacket with copper-colored buttons and two front pockets. A tan tie and matching olive-green shirt were tucked behind the jacket. Patches, pins, and stripes of color decorated the jacket, and if her dad had been there, he would have known what each item represented. Stella, on the other hand, was completely distracted by his hazel eyes.

"You can trust me, Stella," Jack said, interrupting her thoughts.

The weird part was, she *did* feel like she could trust him. "This is outrageous, but okay."

When Jack smiled at her response, Stella's lips parted. For years she had wondered what Jack Mathis looked like when he smiled; now she knew, which made her need to see it over and over again.

"Go see Arnie. I'll see you tomorrow," Jack said, his words sounding like an enchantment in her ears.

Stella nodded. "I'm not locking you in the archives. That would be barbaric, but I'll lock up the library like usual. I'm assuming you know how to get out if you need to, but just know you'll set off the alarm if you open the outside doors."

Jack nodded, repeating himself. "I'll see you tomorrow."

✦ ✦ ✦

STELLA LEFT JACK and the others in the library, closing them up in the archives. Although this entire night felt like an out-of-body experience, an awareness of powerful magic hummed through her. The words had sent her to Arnie's aid tonight. She had so many questions, but all she could handle was putting one foot in front of the other.

In the darkness, she crossed the lot between the library and Arnie's cottage. Using her spare key, she let herself into his place. He would want a change of clothes—his own clothes—rather than the open-back gown and skid-proof socks that were the normal standard issue at the hospital.

Stella had never been in Arnie's bedroom before, so she flipped on the light and stood in the doorway, hesitating and trying to shake off the feeling of being an intruder. *This is for Arnie and his sanity. He needs his own things,* she told herself. She stepped into his room and went straight for the closet. There was an overnight bag on the top shelf, so she pulled it down and packed a couple shirts and a pair of pants, along with a belt, two pairs of socks, and underwear. Then she added some miscellaneous toiletries, not knowing what he could live without or what he might actually want. Because he *would* only be gone a few days at most, and then he could have whatever he needed. Arnie was coming home; she wouldn't accept—couldn't accept—any other scenario.

When she arrived at the hospital, she tried to remain calm, but all she wanted to do was run as fast as she could to the nurses' station. Skinny, trembling words crowded together on the sterile white tile in the hallway, but they parted like the Red Sea as she hurried past. Worry tightened her chest.

Lisa Danforth sat behind the circular desk, blew a pink bubble with her gum, and popped it before smiling at Stella.

"Hey, honey," Lisa said with a voice so gentle it could subdue a wild animal. "I've been waiting for you to get here. He's in ICU room 79."

Stella clutched the rounded edge of the desk. "ICU? Why? Is he . . . is he worse? Is it that serious? I mean, I know it's serious, but the ICU—"

Lisa reached up and gently pried Stella's fingers from the edge of the desk. "It's customary to put most heart attack patients in the ICU. Yes, it's serious, but he's stable."

Lisa had lived next door to Stella's family and was a young nurse just starting out at Blue Sky Valley's hospital when Stella was born. A few years later, when Maria ran off to New York, Lisa came over to their house often to check on her and Percy. On Saturdays, which was usually Lisa's day off, she'd bring over baked goods and spend time with them.

Lisa had been at the hospital when Stella's dad was admitted after his heart attack and never released. During those couple of days, Lisa had brought Stella and Percy gallons of coffee in Styrofoam cups and a never-ending supply of snacks from the vending machine. They'd spent Lisa's breaks talking about which books they were reading, debating which ones were worth reading and which should be used as doorstops. No one had seen as many of Stella's tears as Lisa had—with the exception of Ariel and Arnie—and seeing Lisa now felt like being wrapped up in a wool blanket, toasty and familiar.

"Stable, as in he's going to be okay?"

Lisa nodded. "He's uncomfortable, but they've given him something for the pain. Definitely a heart attack, though, and not a stroke. He's lucky you were there. I hate to think about what would have happened if he'd been alone."

Oh, he wasn't alone. He was hosting a party with an invite list that included my childhood crush.

Lisa reached across the counter and squeezed Stella's hand. "Go on," she said.

Down the hallway, Stella pushed open the door to room 79. Arnie lay inside, hooked to machines that seemed to be keeping track of every part of him, constantly assessing his vital signs. A breathing machine pushed oxygen into his lungs, and the steady, rhythmic whoosh of air was almost soothing. Medication given intravenously dripped slowly from an IV bag with a long, snaking tube that stretched from the bag to his hand. Arnie wasn't awake, and he didn't stir when she approached. Stella looked down at him, wishing his visage didn't recall images of her dad in a similar position.

She dropped the overnight bag in a chair and then stood next to Arnie's bed and exhaled. "I'm not sure what you think you're doing, but you are *not* allowed to leave me, especially not like this, not with all of these questions. I know there's something going on. Something's not right, Arnie.

"What were you doing tonight? Why are there people in the archives? I don't know how or why, but I have a feeling *you* know something big you're not telling me." She rubbed her temples.

"This is a lot to handle in one day. Finding you on the floor and meeting that man calling himself Jack in the library. What did you mean when you said you *wanted to tell me about him*? And I left the people in there, Arnie. Strangers. In the library, because you asked me to. I don't know what we'll find tomorrow, but I'm trying to trust that you know what you're doing. And we've never talked about my words before, but they might be what saved you tonight, and the purple ones . . ." Stella inhaled a shuddering breath.

"You'd better heal fast because I have questions, and I'm expecting answers." She pressed her cold fingers against the warm skin of his hand. Her heart squeezed just as a machine beeped. "You get some rest and come back home. That's an order."

A nurse opened the door and pushed in a cart loaded with smaller machines. "Need to check a few things."

Stella nodded and slid out through the open door, clicking it shut behind her. She stopped by the nurses' station and had a quick conversation with Lisa before driving home. Once she was home, Stella pulled up the library schedule. Melanie was on vacation for a couple days, so she called Vicki and Dan to ask if they could come in on their day off tomorrow to help since Stella wasn't sure when Arnie would be able to return to work.

Then she texted Ariel. Arnie had a heart attack. I found him tonight in the archives. He's at the hospital and stable. Call me tomorrow?

Ariel texted back almost immediately. Do you want to talk now? Should I come over? I'm so sorry, Stella.

Stella wrote: No, I'm exhausted, but thank you. Tomorrow?

Ariel responded: Of course. Get some rest.

Stella wanted to mention the people in the archives, specifically Jack Mathis, but she was afraid Ariel would think she'd lost her mind or was so overcome with worry that she was batty. Besides, Stella wasn't even sure what would happen tomorrow. Would she find the archives empty?

She sat on the edge of her bed and stared at her empty hands, remembering the day she lost her dad, which made her think of the weeks following her mother's absence, and more recently of Wade walking out of her life like it was the easiest thing he'd ever done. She glanced at the lamp on her end table and remembered a day when Wade called her his "lighthouse," saying she was like a light in the darkness, giving him hope. Turquoise words tumbled through her room like waves rolling onto the shore. She reached for her notepad and wrote.

When the ocean was not blue
but a wild, relentless fury,
when it caught you,
tossed you, pushed you under,
when you knew you were lost,
I stood waiting, welcoming,
high above the spray
and the violence,
lighting a path to safety,
to rest, to peace,
to my arms
when you needed that more
than you needed air,
I was your lighthouse, your love.

Stella reread the poem. Every relationship, every experience, every heartbreak had given her words. Words that reminded her of the past but also words that healed.

She closed the notebook, turned off the light, and lay back on her bed. She pulled the sheets up to her chin and gripped the soft fabric in her fingers, closing her eyes. Without meaning to, she found her thoughts drifting to Jack, which caused a stirring in her chest that crept down to rouse a long-sleeping emotion inside her. What if Jack Mathis was in the archives tomorrow when she got there? Could it be possible to have an actual conversation with him? What would she even say to a fictional man she'd adored for years? Her heart rate elevated as her stomach filled with jitters. The wobbly ceiling fan blew paper-thin, illuminated orange words around her room. **Devotion. Different. Desire.**

Her thoughts shifted. She imagined Arnie lying in the hospital bed, and tears pooled behind her closed eyelids. When she rolled over, the tears leaked down her face and onto the pillow. She opened her eyes and saw more words curled up on the faded carpet beside her bed. **Uncontrollable. Hearts. Safe.** Past relationships had taught Stella that when it came to love, the heart was *never* safe. Why did those words cuddled up together make her think of Jack Mathis?

Chapter 9

Stella's cell phone alarm buzzed early Thursday morning. She blinked open her eyes, focused on the pale pink wallpaper, and experienced a moment of forgetfulness. For a few seconds she drifted back to childhood, thinking her dad would be awake in the kitchen, drinking black coffee and heating up blueberry Pop Tarts for her and Percy's rushed breakfast before school. Percy would already be in the bathroom fixing his hair as though his teenage years depended on the perfect hairstyle.

Then reality settled in. No one was in the house with her. Not her dad, not Percy. A weight pressed on her chest, making her breaths labored. Stella remembered Arnie was in the ICU. She pushed herself into a seated position and battled lightheadedness. After kicking off the covers, she padded into the bathroom to shower and prepare for a day she wasn't sure she could handle.

She'd never been in charge of the library full-time without Arnie. It wasn't as though managing it was too complex for her, but the idea of being there without Arnie for who knew how long felt all wrong.

What was the library without Arnie? Less enjoyable for one thing. Lonelier for another. But she wouldn't be alone today because both Vicki and Dan had agreed to come in.

She'd received no calls or texts during the night alerting her that someone had set off the library alarm. Did that mean the people in the archives hadn't left? Or had Arnie given them the alarm code? Would he share something as private as that with people Stella had never met before? And what about that Jack Mathis guy?

Stella's thoughts whirled so badly she felt dizzy in the shower. Once out of the hot water, she twisted her wild curls into a messy bun on top of her head. She dressed in a white blouse and flowy knee-length skirt. Instead of her usual sneakers, she strapped on a pair of sandals. Then, before she realized what she was doing, she performed a slow twirl in front of the mirror.

After a complete turn, she stopped and gawked at her reflection. "*What* are you doing?" It dawned on her then that she was dressing up for a potential encounter with Jack. She rolled her eyes at her reflection. "Clearly you're sleep deprived." Nothing else could explain why she would waste an ounce of energy on her appearance given everything else that was going on.

Stella stomped into the kitchen, annoyed with her ability to get sidetracked so easily by a handsome face. Her annoyance increased when she realized she was out of instant coffee pods. She snatched a half-full box of Cheez-Its and drove to the library, leaving a dusty trail of frustration behind her car.

As she drove, Stella called the hospital. Lisa was back at the nurses' desk and bent the rules enough to tell Stella that Arnie had experienced a setback during the night—difficulty breathing and spiking blood pressure. They had adjusted his medication in order to get his system back in control, and he needed to remain on the oxygen machine. The doctor didn't want to risk the chance that

Arnie's heart was not yet strong enough to pump oxygen properly to the rest of his body. He was doing a little better this morning, and he'd been lucid enough to speak with the doctor and his nurses until he'd fallen asleep again. His stay in the ICU would be for at least a few more days, and he'd remain under observation for possibly a week, depending on his recovery. Stella asked Lisa to keep her updated if anything changed.

Blue Sky Valley could never be called a sleepy town. The sun shone down on people walking through the park at the end of Main Street. Small groups sat outside at the coffee shop's wrought iron tables, most of them sipping iced beverages in the rising heat. Families snuggled into Grits & Gravy to fill up on stuffed French toast and pancakes covered with sweet, sticky syrup. It was an odd juxtaposition to see the townsfolk going about their day like normal when Stella had experienced anything but a normal evening. Shouldn't everything be tilted out of alignment, not just *her* life?

When she arrived at the library, the alarm was still set. Either no one left last night after her, or Arnie's guests knew the code. Both options unsettled her. She checked the archives almost as soon as she arrived. The heavy vault door was still closed and unlocked, but when she walked through the aisles, she found no one. She felt silly doing it, but she called out to Mr. Darcy and Jack, even wished good morning in French to the couple, but no one responded. Where were they? The most logical explanation was that Arnie had given them the code, and one of them reset the alarm after they left. If that was the case, then they were just regular folks. And Jack Mathis wasn't a character from a book, but someone *pretending* to be him?

With no one there to offer answers, Stella went through the process of opening the library for the day, clicking around the tiles on her sandaled feet. Vicki and Dan would be in within the next hour, but without Arnie, the building was oddly quiet. Even when they weren't in the same room, Stella felt Arnie's presence and was comforted by the fact that he was around somewhere. But now, alone in the library, she felt the silence intensifying his absence and her worry.

It also didn't help her mood that around every corner she kept imagining running into Jack. Disappointment darkened her temperament. Shouldn't she be relieved that the partygoers from the night before were gone and the library was still in working order? That they hadn't burned it to the ground or stolen what little money there was or robbed the archives?

"What did you expect, Stella?" she asked herself, sounding as irritated as she felt. "Jack Mathis showing up with coffee, asking you how your night was?"

"You must have read my mind."

Stella gasped and spun around so quickly that she had to steady herself against the circulation desk. Jack Mathis stood in front of her, tall and striking, wearing a pair of shorts, a navy-blue T-shirt with a New York Yankees logo, and white tennis shoes. He held two mugs, steam rising from both.

"Good morning," Jack said. He extended a mug toward her and smiled. "Cup of joe? If you don't mind me saying so, you're looking lovely today. How was your evening? Were you able to rest?"

Stella stared at him and pressed her hands against the waistband of her skirt. "You . . . your clothes."

Jack glanced down as if surveying himself. "More suitable than my uniform, yes?"

Stella's thoughts shifted to slo-mo. Jack Mathis was just as handsome in street clothes, if not considerably more unsettling for appearing so normal. At least when he wore the uniform and said he was a man from a book, her brain attempted to accept it. Now

Jack Mathis looked like a regular guy, albeit a distractingly good-looking one, which immediately put Stella on the defensive. Was he just a regular guy? Someone Arnie "brought out" for her to have a chat with?

Jack extended the mug farther. Stella reached out and wrapped her hands around the warm ceramic. "Yes," she finally said. "You look more suitable. Thanks for the coffee."

Jack sipped from his mug and watched her. "Did you rest?"

Stella stared at the steaming liquid. Was she really going to have a normal conversation with this guy? Neither of them mentioning how bizarre it was for him to still be here? "Not the greatest night's sleep I've ever had. I didn't really think you'd be here today."

"I don't expect so," Jack said.

"How did you get out of the library without setting off the alarm?" Stella asked. "Did Arnie give you the code? How did you get back inside this morning?"

"I didn't leave last night," Jack said simply.

Stella exhaled and put her mug on the desk. "Seriously? You expect me to believe you spent the night in here?"

"Do you have a minute? Let's sit." He walked around the desk and slid out a chair for her. He waited for her to sit down before he sat in the rolling chair near her and scooted his chair closer. "Let's start with the easier question. How's Arnie?"

She crossed her legs at the ankles and lifted her mug only to set it down again. "The nurse said he was resting better now, but he experienced shortness of breath last night, and his blood pressure was high. They adjusted his medications, and they're leaving him on the breathing machine for now. The medication adjustment and the oxygen seem to help. She said he might be in there for as long as a week. I know Arnie, and he'll follow their directions to a T. I bet he'll be out of there sooner. I know he wants to come home."

Jack's smile sent a rush of comfort toward Stella. "Hearing that he's resting well and aiming to come home soon is the best news I've heard all day."

"All day? Been up long?" Stella asked, unable to stop her smile. "It's only seven."

"I've been up for hours," he said, then drank more coffee. "Waiting for you."

Stella straightened in the chair. "Why?"

Jack put down his coffee. "There's no reason to be scared of me."

A nervous laugh bubbled up her throat. "I'm not scared."

"Your expression says otherwise."

Stella tried to relax her face. "I just don't know if you're a creep or not."

Jack's laugh charmed her. "A creep? I've been waiting for you to get here because I assumed you'd have questions."

Goose bumps rose on Stella's arms. "I do have questions, but none of them seem like they'll cover the entirety of this situation's strangeness. I'm having trouble accepting what's happening here. None of this makes any sense."

Jack nodded. "That's a fair response."

But even as she shared her disbelieving thoughts, she also knew there had been other odd things happening in the library during the last week, things she couldn't explain and Arnie had shrugged off. Like the people in the archives the night she fell and the teenage boys teasing her the night she slept in the library. What about the books people returned that seemed connected to the library sightings? Could all of it be part of something extraordinary?

What if the man before her really was Jack Mathis? Quick, delicate flutterings, like leaves rustling in a breeze, shivered through her. She remembered the initial excitement she'd felt when she and Wade had first stumbled into a relationship. The bubble of anticipation rising within her now was similar. How many times had she daydreamed about Jack? Embarrassment flushed her cheeks. Hundreds, probably thousands of moments. She might have swooned if she wasn't so hesitant to believe this could all be true, that some sort of *magic* existed in the library. The kind of magic that brought dreams to life.

Her palms started to sweat. With one more lurch toward reality, she asked, "Who are you? I mean, *really*. Did Arnie find you somewhere and ask you to dress up? To pretend to be from one of my favorite novels? You can be honest with me. I don't know how much he's paid you, but I'll keep it a secret. I don't want you to be out the money, but this charade doesn't have to keep going."

Jack leaned back in the chair and slid his palms down his thighs. "You want this situation to be logical. You want all the answers to fall into place and *make sense*, but why? What are you afraid of, Stella?"

"I'm not afraid," she said defensively. Insecurity stabbed at her solar plexus. She closed her eyes, trying to find a place of safety within herself but hearing only the echo of her dishonest words. "*Afraid* isn't the right word."

Jack sat up straighter and waited for her to continue.

"Yes, I want this to be logical, and yes, I want this to make sense, because those things are safe and ordinary."

Jack's gaze focused on her. "And you want ordinary because that's what you are?"

"Yes!" she said and immediately added, "Well, no." A small smile tugged her lips when their eyes met. She glanced at the floor. "My own weirdness I can handle. I'm not sure I'm ready to accept that some kind of great big magic exists."

"But wouldn't it be fun if you did?" Jack asked. His smile unknotted some of the tension in her muscles. "What if it's time you stretch your willingness to believe in the extraordinary?"

Stella turned toward the desk, away from his piercing gaze, and cupped her hands around her coffee mug. Her sweaty hands felt slick against the ceramic. "You want me to accept that you and the other people I've seen in the archives have stepped out of books? That people from fiction are here and alive, just walking around the *real* world?"

"It's temporary, but yes."

Stella shot a glance at him. "What do you mean by *temporary*?"

"We're not here permanently," Jack said, pushing one hand through his dark brown hair. "We're not able to come and go as we want whenever we want. There's a process, and it's a temporary one."

Her chest felt as though it were being buried beneath a pile of reference books. If she *wanted* to believe Jack Mathis was real, now he was telling her he was only here temporarily? Long enough to raise her hopes and then smother them? A red flag rose quickly in her mind, whipping in the windstorm of her thoughts. "How long are you here?"

"Two weeks. But I've already been here eleven days."

Two weeks? Only three days left. Fuchsia words, appearing in an ever-widening spiral, emerged over his shoulder and drifted down his arm. **Hold on. Enjoy the moment. Be here with me.** Jack glanced down at his arm and then back at her. Could he feel their presence?

Stella looked away and fiddled with the mug's handle. "And then what happens? *Poof?* You turn to ashes in sunlight?"

Jack laughed quietly. "We're not vampires, Stella. But I don't know what happens exactly when my time is up. It feels like being filled with sunlight and warmth and air, like every part of my body becomes wind and light. I've never asked Arnie what it looks like to him."

The front doors of the library whooshed open, and Ariel rushed into the small entry alcove. She caught sight of Stella behind the circulation desk as she hurried across the main floor. Ariel's blond hair was parted in the middle and braided down both sides, with the left side striped in bright pink. She lifted one hand in a wave and then pointed toward a white to-go bag.

"Stella!" she said, sounding out of breath. "I've been texting you."

Stella stood and looked around for her cell phone. "You have?" She found her phone hidden beneath a stack of books she needed to check in. As soon as she lit up the screen, she saw she'd missed a series of texts. "Sorry."

Ariel plopped the bag on the counter. "I brought breakfast. I was worried. How's Arnie? Oh—hello," she said, noticing Jack, who stood beside Stella.

"Good morning," Jack said.

Ariel looked him up and down and passed a questioning glance toward Stella.

Stella motioned between the two of them. "Ariel, this is Jack. Jack, this is my best friend, Ariel."

"New hire?" Ariel asked.

"No," Stella and Jack said simultaneously.

Jack tried to mask a chuckle by clearing his throat. "I'm only visiting."

Total understatement. According to Jack, he would only be "visiting" for three more days, and then what? He would sparkle his way back into his book?

"He's a friend of Arnie's," Stella clarified. "Thank you for breakfast and for checking in." She relayed what she'd learned about Arnie's condition. "Vicki and Dan are coming in soon, and when everything is settled here, I'd like to head back to the hospital to catch visiting hours."

Ariel pressed her hand against the garnet pendant hanging from her necklace. "I'm so sorry, Stella, but the good news is that it sounds like he's stable. If there's anything I can do, please let me know." Her gaze drifted to Jack. "Where are you visiting from?"

Out of nowhere a red-hot sensation exploded in Stella's chest and expanded so quickly that it stole her breath. She wobbled sideways, buckling against the desk and gripping the edge to keep from falling over. She heard herself moan, but it sounded like it came from somewhere deep in the earth. Jack and Ariel both called her name.

Two Jacks stepped into view, then bright violet liquid pushed out of his shorts pocket, like goo squishing from the fabric. Pulsating letters the color of ripe plums and outlined in lavender wriggled down his leg. Tendrils dragged behind the letters and circled the floor at Jack's feet like a creature from a fantasy novel.

Stella croaked the words, "'Tell you that?'" Instantly the burning in her body stopped. She inhaled a shaky breath and straightened. Jack's hand was on her arm.

Ariel's panicked voice asked, "Stella? Are you okay? Is this that word thing again? What's happening?"

The intense purple words rushed into the bottom drawer of the desk where Stella's purse and notebook were stashed. She moved away from Jack, wondering briefly why the words had come out of him. Then she pulled open the drawer, grabbed her notebook, and flipped to the page where she'd been cataloging these particular words. Including the new additions, the page now read: *I fell in love once. Did I ever tell you that?*

Stella slid the notebook toward Ariel while shaking her head and rubbing one hand across her chest. "I don't know how much more

I can stand. If these words are supposed to mean something to me, I'm failing at knowing what."

Ariel frowned. "Maybe it's a story."

"Nothing I've ever read," Stella said.

"You've read thousands of books," Ariel said. "What if it's one you've forgotten? They have to mean something, like clues."

"Clues to what?" Stella asked.

"I've never seen words like that before," Jack interrupted, startling the women.

Stella gaped at him. "What do you mean?"

Jack shoved his hand into his pocket as though making sure nothing else was in there. Then he pointed to the notebook. "The purple words."

"You can *see* them?" Ariel blurted.

"Can't you?" he asked. "Stella's always had words around her."

Stella gasped. *What does he mean by* always? She leaned her hip heavily against the edge of the desk. Unsteady and shaken by Jack's awareness, she pressed her hand to her forehead. Was she going to faint?

"No," Ariel said.

Jack touched Stella's arm again. "Why do those words hurt you?"

Stella met his gaze. "I don't know. But how . . . how can you see my words?"

Jack looked momentarily confused. "I just thought it was part of *you*. I've seen them for years."

"Years?" Ariel asked, her voice pitching higher than normal. "I thought you were visiting Arnie. Have you met Stella before?"

"No," Stella and Jack said together.

"Not formally," Jack added.

"Not in person," Stella said.

A cell phone alarm went off in Ariel's bag. She plucked it out and silenced the alarm. "I gotta get to work, but are you going to be okay? I feel weird leaving you here alone."

"She's not alone," Jack said.

Ariel glanced at him and bit her bottom lip. "That's not helping. No offense, but something eerie is happening, and I don't know you from Adam. You're giving off a vibe I can't describe, but it's making my tummy feel funny, and, you"—she pointed at Stella—"I don't know what you're—"

Stella lifted a hand to stop Ariel's flow of words. "I'll be okay. I'll text you later. Vicki and Dan are coming in, remember? They'll be here soon. Wait, why is Jack's vibe making your stomach feel off?"

Jack looked above and around him. "Vibe?"

"You're hiding something," Ariel said plainly to Stella. "That's what I'm feeling about *you*. Want to elaborate?" She pointed at Jack. "Figured it out. Your vibe means you're a love interest—"

"Say what?" Stella asked, feeling her heart rate escalate to a rapid pace. "I'm not hiding, well, not exactly— Listen, I'll text you later. I promise. Right now, there's a lot going on here, and I need to get my head straight."

"You text me 911 if you need me for anything," Ariel said as she dug through her shoulder bag. She placed a milky-white stick of selenite on the counter. "This absorbs bad energy, just in case."

Jack smiled. "Am I the bad energy?"

"Or Stella," Ariel said with a one-shoulder shrug. "It's not biased."

Stella sensed her best friend's increasing worry, so she said, "Ariel, I promise I'll text. Get to work."

"Carry that with you," Ariel said, picking up the selenite and handing it to Stella. "It works." She looked pointedly at Jack and then rushed out of the library.

Once they were alone, Stella looked at Jack. Why did Ariel think he was a love interest? Or was she picking up on Stella's infatuation with the fictional Jack? Just the idea made her feel unstable. She placed the selenite on the desk out of sight from anyone.

"What did you mean when you said you've seen my words for years?"

Jack's hazel eyes never left her face, and he gave no indication of deceit when he said, "This isn't the first time I've visited the library. Arnie's brought me here before."

"How many times?" Stella asked, surprised by how dry her mouth had gone.

"Ten to twelve, probably. Not every year, and I didn't always see you when I was here, but I think you were eight or nine when I first saw you."

Chapter 10

Stella stared at Jack. Doubt and shock plumed inside her. Words tumbled through her mind, none of them forming quickly into sentences.

"This must surprise you," Jack said, ending the silent stretch of awkwardness.

"Let's swap *surprise* for *flabbergast* and agree that it's still not equal to what I'm feeling right now. You expect me to believe you've known me since I was a kid? You look about my age—"

"I'm twenty-seven," Jack said.

Stella's harsh laugh echoed through the main room, bouncing off the tiles and flying back toward them. "I'm older than *you*? Yet somehow you've known me since I was eight or nine." A tremble started in her core and spanned out through her limbs. One more shake and she just might fall apart. "I think . . . I think you should leave. Arnie would have told me. It's too much, you pretending to know me—"

"You and Percy used to come here every Saturday when you were kids," Jack said. "And Arnie acted like he didn't know you were the ones building forts out of books and paper towels taken from the restroom."

Stella stopped breathing, and her back went as rigid as a bookshelf. Her jaw clenched.

Jack pointed toward the east wing of the library. "In the poetry section because you thought no one ever used those books, beneath the table nearest the supply closet."

A chill shot through her. "How could you possibly know that? Did Arnie tell you?"

Jack continued, "I know Percy liked to pretend he was a knight with a sword made from cardboard. You humored him and pretended you needed to be rescued at least every other time. When Percy was a teenager and brought his first girlfriend to the library to show her around, you felt left out and sulked in the fairy-tale section until Arnie brought you a Dilly Bar and his favorite book.

"Arnie told me a lot of stories about you. That he made scavenger hunts for you after school and on the weekends while your father worked. I know that after your mother left, Arnie was especially worried about you. He liked having you around for multiple reasons, but he wanted to keep you close because he didn't want to lose you to your sorrow.

"I saw your words even when you were little, but Arnie never mentioned them. Eventually I asked him about it. He can't see them. But I knew—I *saw*—how the words appeared and how you'd light up. They kept you company and filled your mind with hope."

Stella could hear the faraway echoes of Percy's laughter in the foyer, around the shelves, and drifting down from the second floor. She imagined their tennis shoes slapping against the tiles as they raced for the staircase in search of the next scavenger hunt clue. She thought of all the books she'd read in an attempt to disappear into those worlds when living in her own became too challenging, too dark.

"Stop," she said. "I don't know how you know these things—"

Jack held out his arms, palms up and facing her, a sign of surrender, of peace. "Because I've been here, Stella. Arnie brought me here for two weeks every few years, and sometimes I'd see you and Percy. But there were years when I didn't see either of you, so Arnie would update me. And now . . . now you're all grown up and sadder than I've ever seen you."

Stella inhaled sharply, feeling vulnerable, her heart too exposed. "I'm not sad. I'm . . ." What was she? Lost? Confused? Stuck? All of the above.

"You're what? You used to be bursting with life and hopefulness. It was contagious." He stepped toward her. "Arnie planned to tell you about me and all of this one day, but he kept putting it off. Now he can't."

Stella fiddled with a pearlescent button on her blouse, then caught Jack's gaze. "What was he waiting for?"

Jack shrugged. "The right time?"

"Which is now only because he had a heart attack." She pressed a hand to her stomach. "If you've been coming here for years, why haven't I seen you?"

"It's all part of the way this plays out. We get good at hiding or blending in. Would you have noticed me without my uniform?"

"You're hard to miss," she said without thinking.

He grinned. "Am I?"

His eyes lit with interest, and the flutters returned. "Let's assume I believe your story. You're not the only character from a book Arnie has brought out?"

Jack shook his head.

"A bunch of fictional characters have been wandering around the library for at least thirty years?"

Jack shook his head again. "Oh, much longer than thirty years."

Stella's mouth dropped open. "Seriously? *How* is that possible?"

Jack looked around as though checking to ensure they were alone. Then he whispered, "I'll show you."

"Stella!" a voice called from behind them.

Vicki had come in through the back door, and Dan was close behind. Vicki's unruly red hair hung around her round cherub face. The summer heat reddened her cheeks, and her green eyes were bright and alert. Her blue cat's-eye glasses matched her skirt, and her white sleeveless top was dotted with tiny strawberries. She hurried toward Stella and waved good morning as she crossed the foyer. Dan, with his sensible ironed slacks, polo shirt, and dress shoes, hustled to keep up with Vicki's quick pace. A leather satchel was slung over his square shoulders, and a pair of glasses bounced against his collar as he hurried along.

"How's Arnie?" Vicki asked.

"I tried to call him," Dan said, "but I guess he doesn't have his phone."

Vicki scrunched up her face at him. "Of course he doesn't have his phone. He's in the *ICU*," she said slowly as though the idea of Arnie feeling up to using the phone was ridiculous.

Dan shrugged. "My sister had a baby and was texting and posting Instagram photos a couple hours later." Vicki looked astonished.

Stella gave them the same update she'd given Ariel and finished with, "Once you two get settled, I'll probably head to the hospital to check in."

"Of course, of course," Vicki said. "We'll be a-okay here. Nothing to worry about, right, Dan?"

"Right," Dan agreed. He reached out his hand toward Jack. "Hey, I'm Dan."

Jack shook his hand. "I'm Jack. Nice to meet you."

Vicki waved. "I'm Vicki. Are you Stella's boyfriend?"

Stella made a choking sound in her throat. Jack patted her on the back and chuckled. "No, I'm a friend of Arnie's."

"A friend of Arnie's is a friend of ours. Where are you from?" Vicki asked.

"Ohh-kay, Vicki, Dan," Stella interrupted, "thank you both for coming in. Let's walk through what I've already done today and then distribute tasks. Sound good?"

"Walk with us to the kitchenette and talk," Vicki said. "I need to drop off my things and put my lunch in the fridge. Nice to meet you, Jack! Dan, come with us." Dan obliged.

"I'll be right back," Stella said to Jack and he nodded.

A few minutes later, after Vicki and Dan dispersed into the library with their task lists, Stella returned to the circulation desk where Jack waited. "You wanted to show me something?"

He hesitated. "Any chance Vicki or Dan is going to pop over?"

Stella's eyebrows lifted. "Are you about to show me something they can't see?"

Jack straightened. "This is Arnie's secret and his responsibility. It's above my pay grade, so to speak, so I shouldn't even be telling you, but after everything that's happened, you deserve to know. It isn't meant for everyone, but I know Arnie trusts you."

"Evidently not enough to tell me himself," Stella grumbled.

"He was going to. I don't know why he kept waiting." Jack opened a bottom drawer of the circulation desk. It was a drawer Stella had opened hundreds of times, but the only thing Arnie stored in it were old library files.

Jack grabbed a few flimsy files, stacked them on the counter, and then knocked on a metal piece that wasn't the bottom of the drawer but made it appear as though the drawer was empty.

"What's that?" Stella asked.

Jack detached the metal divider, revealing hidden items stored beneath it. Stella held her breath and peered over his shoulder.

Jack lifted out a wooden box with swirling patterns engraved on the top. He flipped open the lid and removed an old-fashioned library date stamp and an ink pad, then reached back into the drawer and withdrew a stack of retro library due date cards, the kind that used to be in the back of every library book but had been replaced by electronics and high-tech practices. Then he pulled out two final things from the drawer, a copy of *Beyond the Southern Horizon* and an emerald-green fabric-covered book.

He handed *Beyond the Southern Horizon* to Stella. She pointed at the green book. "What's that one?"

Jack hesitated but held the book so Stella could read the title. *The Unraveling of Mrs. Russo*.

"I've never seen it before," Stella said. "Why does Arnie keep it there?"

Jack deposited the book back into the bottom of the drawer. "You'll have to ask Arnie."

"My list of questions for Arnie is extensive." Stella flipped through *Beyond the Southern Horizon*. Adhered to the inside back cover was a library due date card slid into its sleeve. Stella scanned the dates on the card. For more than thirty years, dates had been stamped. The second most recent date was last year, and beneath that a stamp from less than two weeks ago was the last entry.

"That's Arnie's personal copy," Jack said. He pointed to the date stamp and ink pad on the counter. "That's what makes everything possible."

He lifted the hinged lid on the ink pad and revealed blue ink that twinkled as though the ink had been mixed with glitter. Stella stepped forward and leaned over for a closer inspection.

"Why is it sparkling?" she asked.

"Touch it," Jack said.

Stella poked her index finger into the ink. A jolt of electricity shot up her arm and ricocheted inside her chest, making her temples throb and reminding her of the bright purple words that had started appearing to her. She yanked back her hand and looked at her finger just in time to see the ink absorb into her skin, sending tiny sparks of fire into her hand, up her arm, and pulsing in her chest before dissolving.

"What was that?" she whispered, feeling a prick of terror that trembled her voice.

Jack reached out for her hand and enclosed it with his. "This ink, coupled with sunlight, is what brings us here. Arnie adds the library due date cards to the chosen books, then stamps them with *this* stamp and ink. He exposes the stamp to sunlight, speaks the character's name he wants to appear, and somehow, we become possible." He released her hand.

Carefully, he closed the ink pad and returned both it and the date stamp to the box. Then he slid the box back into its spot in the bottom drawer. He placed his book on top and then replaced the metal divider to hide what Arnie didn't want anyone to find. Once Jack returned the folders to their spot, the drawer resembled nothing more than a messy filing system.

"How can a stamp and ink possibly do this?" Stella asked. "It sounds like *I've* stumbled into a fictional story."

Jack shook his head. "I don't know *how* it works. I just know that it does. That's the magic of it. Arnie knows things he hasn't told me, and now you can ask him."

Stella rubbed her fingers back and forth across her collarbone as her heart beat erratically. "How can this kind of magic be real?"

The idea of book characters coming to life and walking around

Blue Sky Valley seemed *too* fantastical. What if it wasn't, though? She'd never told anyone but Ariel about her gift for words because she feared people would think she was delusional. Yet here she was acting as though Jack's explanation was too outrageous to be true.

Stella glanced down at her fingertip. "Why wouldn't Arnie have told me? Of all the people in the world who would have believed this insane possibility, shouldn't I have been the one person he could have told?"

Jack pushed his hands into his pockets. "Yet you're having trouble believing it from me. What would make him telling you any different, any more convincing?"

Stella shrugged. "Because I *know* him. I trust him. Or I *did*." She shook her head. "I can't believe he didn't think he could tell me years ago. I would have believed him. I would have wanted him to *show* me, of course, but I would have given him the opportunity. And instead, he kept it from me for years."

Jack pushed away from the desk and stepped toward her. "I could be wrong, but you haven't told Arnie about the words you see, have you?"

She didn't respond.

"Maybe you're being too hard on him," Jack said. "This isn't the kind of secret you can drop into someone's lap. It's an exceptionally difficult one to tell just anyone."

Stella frowned. "Since when have I been 'just anyone' to Arnie?"

Jack countered, "Since when has *he* been just anyone to you?"

Her cell phone rang. She grabbed it off the counter and answered. "Hello?"

"Stella? Hey, honey, this is Belinda in the ICU. I'm on call today, and Arnie is awake and in stable condition. He's been asking for you. You're welcome to come on by for a visit. We just ask that you don't bring any drama, not that you would, but what Arnie needs is peaceful, low-key visits, so that's all we'll tolerate."

"Yes, ma'am, of course," Stella said. "I would never jeopardize Arnie's recovery." Which was true, but as soon as she saw him, she was going to demand he tell her the truth about everything. As tempting as it was to believe Jack, she needed to hear it from Arnie. She ended the call and put her phone on the counter.

Stella's gaze drifted to the bottom drawer where the box and two books were hidden. An idea sparked and within seconds it was burning as hot as blue flames. She opened the drawer, even as Jack protested. She removed the files and the metal divider and pulled out the box with the mysterious ink pad and stamp.

"What are you doing?" Jack asked, his voice pinched with concern.

"Testing a hypothesis."

Chapter 11

Stella placed the carved box on the counter and flipped open the lid. Then she closed her eyes and concentrated on a book. But not just *any* book. On the book that *wanted* to be found by her. Her chest tingled as though she stood in a beam of sunshine, and she opened her eyes.

Shamrock-green words twirled and leaped across the counter. **Free-spirited. Mischievous young boy. Ageless.** Jack stared at them. It unsettled her that he could see the words too. The letters danced into the air as Stella left the circulation desk and headed toward the children's section.

"Where are you going?" Jack asked, following her across the foyer and stopping halfway.

"I'll be back," she said, shooing him away. "Guard the precious stamp and ink pad!" Her voice held a teasing tone, and Jack frowned.

In the children's section, Stella scanned the titles until she found *Peter Pan*. Had she really been looking at Peter Pan in the archives the other night? An image of the young boy leaping off the table appeared in her mind. She flipped to the back of the book and saw there was already a due date card tucked inside its sleeve. She slid out the card. The most recent date was from a little longer than two weeks ago. Stella pressed the book against her chest.

The idea that she could bring fictional characters to life felt intoxicating. What book nerd hadn't dreamed of such a possibility? But what would having this kind of magic—this kind of *power*—mean? How could it be contained, controlled? Or would it be unwieldy? The bigger question was: Would it work if she tested it?

A prickling started behind her eyes and fireworked into her head. Brown, stiff-moving words appeared from a shelf and plummeted to the floor. **Sailor. Castaway. Tropical island.** Then an image of the book cover of *Robinson Crusoe* appeared in her mind. Stella quickly detoured to the fiction section and searched for a copy. This book, too, already had a library due date card in the back. How many characters had Arnie brought to life over the years?

Stella returned to the circulation desk where Jack stood waiting with his arms crossed over his chest, an expression of impatience marring his handsome face. She placed both books on the desk.

"Remind me how this works," she said.

Jack's scowl deepened. "This isn't a good idea. You should talk to Arnie first."

She flipped open the ink pad and picked up the stamp. She rotated the dials on the bottom of the rubber stamp so the date was two weeks from today, and then she looked at Jack.

"Arnie was going to tell me about this anyway, so what's the harm in testing it? Tell me how this works. *Please*," she added in hopes of convincing him.

Jack reached for the stamp, but Stella stretched her hand as far away from him as she could.

"This isn't a joke, Stella."

A line creased between his brows, and she felt an urge to rub it away with her thumb. She gripped the stamp tighter instead. "Who's joking?" she asked. "If Arnie's done this before, and clearly he has"—she pointed at Jack—"then it can't be that bad. Besides, what if it doesn't even work for me? What if you have to be the head librarian or some other magical rule nonsense?"

"There are other things you don't know about," Jack said.

"Like what?"

"I don't know everything, but Arnie does. At least talk to him before you do this," Jack said, his voice pleading.

"Hey," Vicki called as she entered the foyer from the children's section. "The festival this weekend takes place in the library, too, right? Arnie hasn't told me anything." She caught sight of the stamp in Stella's hand. "What have you got there?" She leaned over the counter and peered down at the ink pad. "Is that a vintage library stamp? Cool, can I see it?"

"No," Stella and Jack said together.

Vicki looked surprised and leaned away from the counter. "Are you sticking around for a particular reason?" she asked Jack. "It's probably visiting hours at the hospital. Don't you want to go see your friend?"

"Speaking of Arnie," Stella said, "I'm going to head that way soon. Are you and Dan okay for a while without me?"

"Of course," Vicki said. "The festival?"

"Yes, sorry. There will be some activities set up in here like last year. I don't know all the specifics either, but I'll ask Arnie today. He's awake and alert, so I'll get all the details."

Vicki eyed the stamp and ink pad again. "I'll find Dan and have him handle the circulation desk while you're gone. He's better with people." Vicki turned on her heel and walked off.

Once she was out of sight, Stella flipped *Peter Pan* to the back cover where the library card was snuggled into the pocket. Should she listen to Jack and wait until she talked to Arnie? But what if he continued to deflect? She realized *this* was why he'd been so secretive about the archives. Would he refuse to tell her the truth about the ink pad and stamp? Another thought creeped into her mind.

"What if Arnie hasn't told me yet because he doesn't think I can handle this kind of magic?" Could she? Accepting the words she saw was one thing, but embracing enchanted magic and fictional characters walking around unleashed the unknown. What else might exist in her world that she had yet to see? "Do you think I can handle knowing the truth about the library?"

Jack paused and then nodded. "I do."

She slipped out the card and stamped the ink pad. There was still the chance that this test would fail.

Jack held out his hand. "Stella, give me the stamp. You have no idea what you're doing."

"You said you believe I can handle it." He reached for the stamp, but she pressed it to *Peter Pan*'s card before he could stop her. "Now what? Find sunlight?" She glanced at the back door and saw rays of yellow light pouring through the windows. She rushed toward the door with the sounds of Jack following her. She shoved open the back door and held the book out into the light as though extending an offering to a sun god. The ink date glittered and shivered on the paper. "What happens now? Do I say something like, I wish Peter Pan was—"

"Stop!" Jack demanded. The back of Stella's neck tingled as though she stood too near exposed electricity. "You can't bring him back. He was just here."

"What?" she asked.

"You can only bring out characters once a year," Jack said.

"So . . . you can only be here for two weeks *once a year*? Who made up these rules?" Why did that cramp her heart?

Jack reached slowly for the book. "That's right."

She slid *Peter Pan* from Jack's reach and asked, "What about Captain Hook?" She stared at the date stamped in blue ink. The ink darkened to an obsidian color. She waited but nothing happened.

Had she gotten the process out of order? Maybe she should try again. Even though an uneasy feeling skirted beneath her skin, she returned to the circulation desk and tossed *Peter Pan* onto the counter. She grabbed *Robinson Crusoe*, propped it open, and slipped out the library card.

"Any other ridiculous rules you care to share before I test again?"

Jack stood behind her and shoved his hands into his pockets. "I should stop you, but some lessons you need to learn the hard way. Go ahead and invite another friend. You're going to have quite a mess at the end of the day."

Stella stamped *Robinson Crusoe*'s library card and carried the book to the back door. She held it in the sunlight. "Robinson Crusoe, do you want to be my friend?" The ink shimmered and deepened in color. Again, nothing happened.

As she returned to the circulation desk, she turned in a full circle and saw no fictional characters wandering around, no mysterious people lurking near the bookshelves. There was some relief in knowing that there were limits to what was possible.

But a small part of her had wanted to believe in Jack's crazy story about a magical ink pad and stamp. She wanted to believe that she could bring the fantastical into her own world. Arnie had obviously done it, hadn't he? Maybe she lacked the ability or the capacity to use the magic.

Her face heated with embarrassment. She must look like a naive nitwit to Jack. She went back to the circulation desk and dropped

Robinson Crusoe on top of *Peter Pan* with a sinking feeling weighing on her. She slammed the ink pad shut and shoved the library cards back into the books. After tossing the library stamp into its box along with the ink pad, she roughly returned everything to the bottom drawer and out of sight.

"For a second, I believed your story about the hocus-pocus ink pad. Maybe Arnie is good enough to do something special, but, big surprise, I'm not."

Jack gripped the back of his neck. "Just wait, Stella. You'll see what you've done. And Arnie won't be here to help you."

She held open her hands and motioned to the library around her. "There's so much chaos in here right now." As soon as she said the words, the hairs lifted from the back of her neck and on her scalp. She darted her gaze around the library, but nothing—other than her heartbeat—had changed.

"Your sarcasm is not amusing," Jack said. "You'll be eating crow before you know it."

Unease slinked around her, and Stella smoothed her hands down her skirt. "I'm going to go see Arnie." She grabbed her purse. Beneath her sandals, aqua words rose up from between the floor tiles like water pushing up from an underground spring. **Attraction. Hope. Anticipation.** Her eyes widened. Would the embarrassment never end? She lifted her gaze to Jack's face. He appeared as flustered by the words as she was.

She blurted, "I have no idea what those words mean."

"I have an idea," he said quietly.

Stella clenched her jaw. "Maybe it would be best if you aren't here when I get back."

Jack's wounded expression created a swift desire to retract her words.

"And where should I go, Stella? You know I can't leave the library."

The aqua words waved across the floor between them and crashed onto Jack's shoes before disappearing.

"Can't you go back into your book?" Was that what she really wanted? After all these years of dreaming about Jack Mathis and finally being able to talk to him, she was telling him to leave? Maybe it would be better if he left since she'd made a fool of herself. He'd *have* to leave soon anyway.

"It's not that easy," Jack said. Then he walked away from the circulation desk.

"Is anything?" she mumbled.

Jack stopped and glanced at her over his shoulder. "Attraction. Hope. Anticipation. For you? All easy." His half grin was enough to cause her pulse to beat thick and hot.

✦ ✦ ✦

STELLA KNOCKED LIGHTLY on the hospital door as she pressed the cold silver handle against her palm and the door clicked open. Sunlight slanted through the partially open blinds and striped the tile floor. The room smelled like soap and blooming lilies, but she also caught the faint lingering scent of astringent cleaners.

Vases of carnations, lilies, roses, and daisies had colorful ribbons tied around them attaching Get Well Soon and Thinking of You balloons to their shiny glass. An assortment of greeting cards had been propped open to display their illustrated fronts toward Arnie. The gifts weighed down the small square end table beside Arnie's bed and the round dining table near the windows. Stella had been so distracted with her own issues that she hadn't thought to send anything, but word had obviously spread quickly through town. He'd been in the hospital for less than a day, and already there wasn't much room for more well-wishes.

An attractive news reporter with a bouffant hairdo and flawless makeup beamed from the TV screen mounted high on the wall opposite the bed.

Arnie's gaze found Stella's, and he lifted the TV remote and pressed the Mute button, then pushed himself up into a more seated position, straightening his back and adjusting his nasal cannula.

Seeing him alert sent an avalanche of relief through her. She released a trembling breath. "Easy now, tiger." She dropped her purse in a chair that looked like it had been in style in 1960. There was a concave depression in the burnt-orange bottom cushion that made Stella think it had likely been in the room since the sixties as well.

Arnie smiled. "Aren't you a sight for sore eyes?"

She crossed the small room and leaned against the bed, careful not to tangle herself in the tubes and wires coming from the machines. "I want to scold you for doing this to me, but it's *so* good to see you. I prefer you in the library rather than a hospital room, but I'll take seeing you anywhere for now."

Arnie reached for her hand, and she let him take it. He squeezed lightly. "Sorry for the scare, kiddo."

Stella swallowed past the tightness in her throat. She dropped a brown paper sack on the rolling overbed table pushed against the wall. "I picked up healthy breakfast muffins from the coffee shop. These were made especially for you with bark and twigs and hippie love."

Arnie chuckled. "I've been pestering the nurses to call you for hours."

"I had to get the library settled before I could leave Vicki and Dan alone." She paused to consider if she should mention Jack straightaway, but she opted to ease into that drama. "Vicki is completely capable of handling it, but she likes a to-do list, and she isn't as good with the patrons, so Dan is working at the circulation desk while I'm gone. They both said to tell you that they're thinking about you, and they hope you'll be back soon."

Arnie shifted, and his gaze drifted toward the window. "I appreciate them coming in to help out. Thanks for keeping an eye out, kiddo. And thanks for the change of clothes. The gown was a bit breezy, if you know what I mean."

Stella walked over to the window so she could open the blinds more. "Better?" she asked. "Seems a shame to block out so much of the light. Percy hated it when the nurses closed Dad's blinds when the sun was out, saying Dad needed to rest. He argued that Dad could rest while still admiring the sunlight. If he couldn't be out in it, then Percy wanted him to at least know it was there." But her dad had never walked out of the hospital, had never stepped into the sunlight again.

She went back to the bed and hopped up to sit near Arnie's feet, tucking one leg beneath her. "You're welcome for the clothes, and we're handling the library."

Arnie cleared his throat. Weariness rolled his shoulders forward as he exhaled in rhythm with the machine. Seeing him wearing a plain white T-shirt, rather than his usual sharp attire, seemed to intensify his tiredness. He stared down at his hands when he asked, "How *is* everything at the library?"

Stella had come to see Arnie with the intention of a peaceful conversation, possibly peppered with a few questions, but her need for answers burned like coals in her stomach. Like the words that often came to her, she couldn't keep her questions inside for long. She decided not to mention using the ink pad. First she wanted to hear his version of the truth. She inhaled a slow breath before catching his gaze. "Arnie, I need you to be honest with me."

Arnie's brows pushed together, but he said nothing.

"You want to talk about the library?" she asked. "Then I need you to tell me what's going on. Tell me about the people who were with you in the archives last night. Who are they?"

Arnie looked away as though thinking, possibly debating what to say. He rubbed over the spot on the top of his hand where the IV was placed. "Last night? I think it was Darcy, right? And Belle and the prince and Jack. It's a little hazy at this point, but I know Jack was there."

Stella's heart gave an unexpected squeeze. She clasped her hands together in her lap. "Arnie . . . this morning the others were gone, but *Jack* is still there."

"Darcy should still be there too," Arnie said.

Stella shook her head. "Not that I saw."

"He wouldn't leave," Arnie mumbled, looking fretful. "He wouldn't."

Stella tapped Arnie's hand with one finger. "Arnie, focus for a minute, please. Jack told me he's from *Beyond the Southern Horizon*. He said he's been coming to the library for years. And he showed me your hiding spot in the bottom drawer, the one with the stamp and ink pad—"

"He did?" Arnie asked, sounding alarmed. His heart monitor rhythm increased, creating taller spikes in the lines, and a beeping noise increased in speed.

Stella reached for his hand, and Arnie's eyes met hers. "Hey, it's okay. Deep breaths."

"No, it's not okay," Arnie said. Another rush of spiking heart rate lines appeared. "He shouldn't have done that. It wasn't his place."

"Arnie, you have to take some breaths and slow down your heart rate or the nurses will be in here stat."

His gaze darted to the monitor, and he inhaled and exhaled a few times, slowly decreasing the annoying beeps and calming the heart rate line.

When Stella felt it was safe, she said, "Arnie, the magic . . . It's real? That ink pad and stamp can bring characters"—she lowered her voice—"to life?"

Arnie nodded and closed his eyes. Stella's breath caught. Why hadn't it worked for her?

"You should have told me."

He inhaled slowly, held his breath for a moment, then exhaled. "I didn't want to tell you. Not yet."

A jagged shard of hurt pierced her. "Why not?"

Arnie opened his eyes. "Go get a cup of coffee, Stella, and let's dig into that bag of goodies you brought. Then we can talk."

Ten minutes later, Stella rolled the overbed table into place and set her Styrofoam cup of coffee on it, then arranged two plates and set a muffin on each one. She picked at her muffin, causing it to crumble, as she waited for Arnie to talk.

He popped half of his muffin into his mouth, chewed, and swallowed. "I didn't intend to be the keeper of the magic—"

Stella had taken a sip of coffee and choked slightly. "Seriously? Is that your title? The keeper of the magic?"

"Am I telling this story?" he asked sternly.

She waved a hand at him. "Proceed."

"This wasn't something I set out to do, but once I took hold of the magic, there was no turning back for me. No alternate path. It was my duty to keep this knowledge within the library. From one angle, it looks like I didn't have a choice with my life, but from a different view, I can look at it like a perk, a chance to meet book characters I've loved or been curious about.

"When I was a kid, my grandparents were always taking in overnight guests, people passing through town who needed a warm meal and a place to stay. One night a woman came to stay with them, and I was there that day. She was from Ireland, which sounded exotic and worlds away from here. She carried a steamer trunk that looked like a relic from medieval times. That night she found me reading and asked if I wanted to see her antique books. Even as a kid I was fascinated by books, so of course I said yes.

"Her books were remarkable and peculiar. Like nothing I'd ever seen. Her trunk was also full of other oddities. Jars and apothecary bottles, dark blues and greens and clouded glass. One particular bottle caught my eye. The liquid inside was cobalt blue and sparkled and stirred like it was alive. The label read *anáil na beatha*."

"Is that Irish Gaelic?" Stella asked. "What does it mean?"

"The breath of life," Arnie answered. "She saw my interest, and that was where it all began. Because of my grandparents' kindness offering a place to stay and food to eat, she gave me this special bottle in return. She explained how to use the magic to bring fictional characters to life, to let them walk with me for a short time. Only fictional characters. It doesn't work for real-life people mentioned in books."

"So no bringing Cleopatra to Blue Sky Valley?"

Arnie frowned. "Absolutely not. Can you imagine?"

Stella clasped her hands together. "I'm having trouble imagining most of this, but continue."

"The woman also expressed the seriousness of the responsibility along with dire warnings. I was too scared to use it for years. Not until college when I worked in the university library, and feeling overly bold one afternoon, I tested it."

Stella had finished her muffin while Arnie talked. His story captivated her in the way fantasy novels enchanted her. When he didn't elaborate, she asked, "You tested it. What does that mean?"

Arnie reached for a glass of water and sipped slowly. "I poured a little bit of liquid onto a stamp pad and used an ordinary date stamp. The rest of the bottle is stashed away in the archives. A little bit goes a long way. That afternoon I found a copy of *Little Women* and stamped the due date, two weeks from that afternoon. Then I held it in a ray of sunshine, and said, 'Jo March.' A bit later, she showed up, and my life has never been the same."

Apprehension gripped Stella. "A bit later? How much later?"

Arnie shrugged. "Five minutes, maybe. But as the keeper of this knowledge, and the protector in a way, I knew being a librarian was to be my calling. It's not what I first intended for my life. I wanted to be a surgeon, but that all changed the day I met Jo March."

"You wanted to be a surgeon?" Stella interrupted. "I can't picture that at all."

"How could you? You've only known me as Arnie, head librarian," he said with a small smile. "But I lived a lot of life before you came along."

"Let's say I believe in this sparkly 'breath of life' ink. What's it like when you bring out characters?"

"After Jo, I wasn't sure what to expect," Arnie said. "She was so strong-willed and vocal. Not offensive, but forthright in a way I should have expected from reading the book. Meeting characters in person adds layers of complexity that you don't expect. After her I was very deliberate about choosing the most interesting characters I could think of. When they show up here, they have knowledge of where they're from—of their own stories—but they're also aware that they are with you in a special place, that they are *out of their element* temporarily."

Stella clasped her hands together, her mind still circling back to Arnie's earlier comment. "You said Jo appeared five minutes after you stamped the book and put the ink into sunlight, right?" It had taken Stella longer than five minutes to leave the library after stamping the books, and no one had appeared. "If someone doesn't appear in five minutes, does that mean the magic didn't work?"

Arnie shook his head. "The time it takes differs every time. If you follow the process, it always works, no matter how long it takes a character to arrive."

A shiver rippled over Stella's body.

Arnie continued, "If you bring out more than one, they interact with one another, and let me tell you, they don't always get along. Captain Ahab is a challenging man with a singular focus, and Elizabeth Bennet couldn't stand him at all. His arrogance nearly undid her good manners on multiple occasions. At the same time, I'd also brought out Sherlock Holmes, James Bond, Scarlett O'Hara, and Atticus Finch."

Stella blurted, "What were you thinking?"

Arnie almost laughed. "That was probably the most complicated two weeks I've ever had with a group of characters. I could have sent someone back early, but that's an unpleasant choice. After that, I decided I would bring no more than four here at a time. Much more and they're difficult to control. But I've also brought out only one at a time, depending on who it is and how much one-on-one time I want."

Stella closed her eyes and pinched the bridge of her nose. Was it possible she'd released characters into the library today?

"Listen, kiddo, I *know* how it sounds. Like maybe they have me on too many meds. I get it. This is partly why I never told you."

Were Captain Hook and Robinson Crusoe roaming the library right now? With unsuspecting Vicki and Dan alone with them?

"Jack!" Stella said, remembering how she'd told him to leave. Would he, *could he*, leave?

Not understanding her sudden alarm, Arnie nodded. "I suggested *Beyond the Southern Horizon* to your dad. Did you know that? I always loved that story. Your dad enjoyed some military fiction, which was why I suggested the book to him, but I didn't know he'd pass that love on to you and Percy. I can't remember the first year I brought Jack out, but we bonded. That doesn't happen with all the characters, but Jack and I formed a friendship. He has a special interest in Blue Sky Valley, since it's his birthplace, and of course, I talked about you and Percy a lot.

"From the first time he arrived, Jack was taken with you and Percy. I thought, in time, I might share the library secrets with both of you, and Percy could meet one of his heroes. I knew you had a crush on Jack, but what young person doesn't have a fictional girlfriend or boyfriend? You were too young for any of that nonsense for years, but the other day you mentioned wishing there was a clone of Jack, which was oddly coincidental since I'd brought him out a few days before. I thought maybe it was time to tell you the truth and you could meet him."

Stella lifted her cup of coffee with a trembling hand. The liquid had gone cold, and the bitterness sat on her tongue before she swallowed. Her pulse quickened at her temples. When she spoke, her voice was a whisper. "This is . . . a lot."

Arnie's features softened for a moment and he nodded. "Stella, I'm not making up fairy tales here. As unbelievable as it all sounds, it's still true. The world is full of the impossible. You know what Roald Dahl said."

Stella stood from the bed and walked over to the window. "Yeah, yeah, if we don't believe in magic, we'll never find it." She stared down at a long stretch of asphalt rippling in the summer heat. Her heart filled with a tickle of hope. After a couple of years of heartache and loss, she *wanted* to believe the world might hold a little bit of wild magic.

Stella looked at Arnie. "Why have you waited all these years to tell me?"

"Kiddo," he said, "I'm sorry I haven't been honest with you about all of this, but I wasn't sure you'd want this life. Once I realized what was possible with books, all other paths for me evaporated. I felt responsible to the magic, to the library." Arnie sat up straighter. "There are warnings. Consequences when things go wrong."

Stella sensed a shift in Arnie's mood. "Like what?"

"I *could* have used the magic anywhere, and I did. But being in the library allows me the ability to keep the characters safe," Arnie explained.

Stella's mouth went dry. "Safe from what?"

"The world," Arnie said. "Do you know why I asked you to keep them in the library?" Stella shook her head. "If they get out in the world, they could get lost or hurt or worse. They can die."

Stella's forehead wrinkled. "After two weeks, wouldn't they just disappear back into their books?"

Arnie's shoulders sagged. "No. They can't get too far from the source of the magic."

Stella returned to the bed and sat on the edge. Arnie's distress filled the air with a suffocating heaviness. "What happens if they do?"

"If they die, they're gone. Forever," he said. "They disappear forever from every book, every article, every piece of history. Except"—he tapped his fingertip against the side of his head—"from in here. People hold on to the memory of that character for as long as they have it, but it feels like a dream, and no one in the future will ever be able to know those characters or love them. Even the authors who wrote the characters are forever separated from their creation. It's terrible."

Stella hesitated before saying, "You sound like you've experienced it."

He met her gaze. "Do you remember *The Treasure of Ruby Lou*?"

"Yes!" Stella said immediately, and then a cloudy sensation pulsed through her brain. "Well . . . I think so. Two best friends went on a treasure hunt in an enchanted forest, or was it a quest for a wishing well?" The harder Stella tried to remember, the more evasive the memory became.

"Remember the author?" Arnie asked.

Stella shook her head. "No." Her chest tightened. It wasn't like her to forget books or authors.

"One day I brought out Ruby Lou and her best friend, Pearl," Arnie said. An expression of immense guilt tugged his features downward. "They were witty and adventurous . . . and rebellious. They snuck out of the library, and I searched for them all over town for days. I never found them, Stella. I hoped they were living somewhere, happy and unharmed, but a few days after the two-week mark, their book disappeared from the library. After an extensive internet search, I realized they had vanished from existence. Their book never written."

The truth of Arnie's devastation was still evident on his face. Stella's skin prickled. All of this was true. The magical potion from Ireland, the glittering ink pad and library stamp, and the ability to breathe life into fictional characters.

Stella's stomach dropped. She'd told Jack it would be better if he wasn't there when she returned. What if he'd changed his mind and left the library? What if he got lost? What if her stamping *had* worked?

Panic pounded her heart. She stood from the bed as a chill swept down her body. "When the characters arrive, are you there to give them instructions?"

"Stella, are you okay?"

Her entire body started to tremble. "Are there rules you have to give them? So they know what *not* to do?" Like leave the library.

Arnie said, "It's important they know my rules while in the library, but yes, I'm there to instruct any new characters." He reached out his hand for her, and she instinctively grabbed it. "Stella, what's wrong?" His heart rate increased. "Just know that I didn't tell you sooner because I didn't want to trap you in a life you didn't want."

Stella's anxiety spiked. "Can more than one person use the stamp, or is one of the rules that only one person can use it at a time?"

Arnie frowned. "I'm not sure. Why?"

"I need to get back to the library. I've left Vicki and Dan long enough." Possibly left them in a complicated situation with fictional characters. "I'll check in later."

"Hey, kiddo, you sure you're okay?" Arnie asked.

Stella shook her head. "No, there's a lot happening, and I need to get back."

"I'm here if you want to talk it out," Arnie said. "And be kind to Jack, okay? He's a good friend and a good man."

Remorse wriggled through her. What if he ended up like Ruby Lou and Pearl? She would *never* forgive herself. Stella grabbed her bag and pulled out her cell phone and turned on the ringer.

"Call me if you need anything." Then she ran out of the hospital to her car and drove to the library like someone trying to break the speed of sound.

Chapter 12

On the drive back to the library, Stella's emotions ping-ponged between irrational fear at what she might have left behind and guilt over how she'd treated Jack before she left. Those feelings were compounded by Arnie's admission of the magic and what the ink pad and stamp were capable of.

The library parking lot was full of cars when Stella drove by on her way to her spot in the back lot. As soon as she turned off the ignition, dark gray words swirling like tornadoes flew out of the air vents and around her head. She swatted at them, causing them to twist around the steering wheel. **Escape. Warning. Panic mode.** The words rushed toward the car's ceiling and then dive-bombed the dashboard, smashing into pieces. The trembling letters rejoined into broken words and limped across the lower portion of the windshield.

Stella's cell phone rang and startled her. She dug in her purse as she opened the car door, and a wave of summer heat stole her breath. She withdrew the phone and answered. "Ariel, hey—"

"Finally! I've been texting you! Are you okay?"

"I was at the hospital with Arnie, and I didn't check my phone before I left. Listen, I can't talk right now, but I'll call later."

Squeals erupted from the lawn area just off to the side of the library's back steps. Stella walked around a parked car to get a better look at who was squealing.

"What's going on?" Ariel asked. "Talk to me. My stomach feels all weird and unsettled."

Stella squinted in the bright sunlight, shielding her eyes from the blaze. "What did you eat?"

"Stella," Ariel said, sounding exasperated, "it's not food. It's *you*. What's going on with you and that guy at the library?"

As Stella speed walked toward the back door, she saw a group of young women dancing in a lopsided circle with unbridled excitement. Their giggles and high-pitched voices bounced toward Stella.

A man wearing a top hat and riding attire stood on the back steps, looking slightly embarrassed by the surrounding women. Sunlight beamed off his striking face, casting light in every direction. His baritone rumbled, and the young women seemed hypnotized.

Stella's skin tingled in an entirely unpleasant way. *Is that Darcy? Outside the library?* "Ariel, I have to go." She disconnected the call as she heard the start of Ariel's protest. Stella's brain and legs kicked into gear and she sprinted across the parking lot.

The idea that Fitzwilliam Darcy could be lost to readers everywhere sent her into full-blown panic mode. Where had he come from? She hadn't seen him earlier that day, but now he had groupies mesmerized by his dashing smile and British accent. She wheezed as she leaped onto the steps and gripped his arm.

Darcy released an *oomph* as Stella slammed into him and jerked his arm toward the library doors.

"I beg your pardon," he said as he snatched his arm out of her grip. His tall shadow cast an imposing silhouette. "That is no way for a lady to behave." He straightened his coat.

Stella struggled to catch her breath. "You can't be outside the library. Get back inside."

He tilted his head and studied her. "I don't recall being asked to obey the whims of a young woman. And if you can't see for yourself, I have guests assembled. It would be rude to leave them when they have specifically asked for my attendance."

Stella glanced at the women on the grass. More than half of them cradled books and notepads in their arms. *The Jane Austen Readers.*

"Perfect timing," she grumbled as she recognized the women who enjoyed meeting every other week to discuss their love and devotion to all things Jane Austen.

"Stella," Carrie Lincoln said, stepping forward from the group. "I can't believe you and Arnie came up with this idea."

"What idea?"

Carrie pointed at Darcy, her cheeks flushed with delight. Her eyes had gone all dewy, and her dilated pupils seemed to pull sunbeams toward her face. Carrie sighed audibly as she twirled a lock of her long blond hair around her finger.

Darcy straightened his shoulders. "The pleasure is all mine, I assure you."

Stella narrowed her eyes. "Turn it off for a second, will you?"

"Turn what off?" he asked. "I don't understand your meaning."

Stella looked at Carrie as her mind quickly created plausible explanations. "You mean the look-alike?"

Carrie and the rest of the group nodded like bobblehead dolls. "He's superb. It was such a fun surprise for us this morning, even though he didn't show up until the end of our meeting, just as we decided to go to the coffee shop. Then—*poof*—he was there, and we *had* to ask him to join us."

"Oh no, you don't," Stella said, shaking her head and grabbing Darcy's arm again. "I'm sorry to disappoint you, Carrie, but that's not going to happen. Mr. Darcy has to stay here with me because . . . we have other plans."

Darcy looked at Stella, questioning her with his expression. She squeezed her fingers tighter on his arm. When she spoke, her voice was a whispered warning. "Mr. Darcy, get back inside the library or I am going to lose it."

"Going to?" he asked with a raised eyebrow. "I think you've already gone round that bend, Miss Parker."

Stella clenched her jaw, and Darcy relented. He removed his hat and bowed gracefully to the women.

"I do hope you'll accept my sincerest apologies, but it appears I have a previous engagement that I cannot miss."

The women swooned like dandelions bending in the breeze, and Stella groaned. But then she remembered what it felt like to feel weak in the knees at seeing a man's smile.

"Thanks for understanding, Carrie. We really appreciate y'all being a part of the library. Next time we'll make sure Mr. Darcy shows up on time for your meeting."

The smiles on the women's faces reminded Stella of a dental commercial. Bright yellow words fluttered around their feet like butterflies surfing over the blades of grass. **Next time. Dreams do come true. Single.**

As Stella dragged Darcy back into the library, Carrie called out, "Thanks, Stella! We'll see you both next time. We can't wait!" The door clicked closed and shut out the rest of Carrie's excited, hopeful words.

Stella pulled Darcy down a deserted aisle before she released her grip on him. "What are you doing? Are you trying to get us all thrown into the loony bin? You can't just walk around Blue Sky

Valley. You don't exactly blend in with the townsfolk, and you know you're not supposed to leave the library. You do know that, don't you?"

Did he know the rules? How did Arnie handle characters when they arrived? Did he explain the rules of their short-term stay? Stella wondered if there was a how-to manual somewhere.

Darcy's cheek dimpled. "I had no intention of going with them."

Stella tilted her head. "You didn't?"

"Certainly not," he said. "Conversing easily with those I have never seen before is not a talent I possess." He gripped the breast of his coat.

"You seemed to be handling it well," Stella said. "They were enamored."

Darcy spun his hat around in his fingers. "They quickly would have realized that I am not the most enjoyable company. I do not have the ability to appear interested in their conversation, which I fear would have been intensely focused on me."

Stella laughed. "Most definitely. So you know about Arnie's rules?"

He nodded.

Stella felt her shoulders relaxing from her ears. She softened her tone. "We can't lose you."

"Do I sense affection in your voice?" he asked.

Stella's cell phone dinged with a text and startled both of them. "It's Vicki. She typed *Emergency 911* in all caps." Darcy met Stella's gaze before slipping down an aisle. Stella hurried toward the circulation desk, trying to calm her rapidly beating heart. Vicki stood at the desk with a frantic expression, shoving papers around on the countertop and opening and closing drawers at random. Stella called out to her, and Vicki's head popped up.

"Oh, Stella, finally! I can't do this without you," Vicki said, running straight at her. Anxiety filled her wide eyes. "Dan had to leave unexpectedly. His cat got loose, and the neighbor was having trouble catching it, and Dan was having a fit to get home. He may or may not come back."

Stella hesitated before asking, "Is that all?"

"No! It's a circus here," Vicki said, tugging her unruly frizz into a ponytail at the nape of her neck. "I've been looking for a note, a memo, *anything* that would let me know what's going on because this is definitely not on the calendar. There are no emails about it and no one called ahead to confirm the appearances. I wanted to call Arnie, but I didn't want to bother him. I knew you'd be back soon and could handle it, but then you took longer than I thought, and I'm freaking out. I have no idea what to do, but one of the guys is a real weirdo. Frankly, he scares the bejesus outa me."

Stella blinked a few times, struggling to understand. "Pause. Go back, please. None of that makes any sense."

"I know!" Vicki said in exasperation. "It's a complete mess. I have no idea what to do."

"Let's start at the beginning. What appearances?" Stella asked. *Please don't say Captain Hook and Robinson Crusoe.*

"The impersonators," Vicki said. "There is a man who looks like he washed ashore a hundred years ago, a charming Englishman, and a man I'm pretty sure is a pirate."

Stella's knees wobbled, and the blueberry muffin she'd eaten with Arnie churned in her stomach. She tried to focus.

Jack rushed down the main stairs accompanied by a man wearing ragged clothing and a coiled rope looped over his neck and hooked under one arm. Stella felt a surge of relief that Jack hadn't listened to her and left.

"Jack," Vicki said as she stepped toward him. "Did you find him? He was really terrifying the children *and* me."

Stella passed a glance between Jack and Vicki. "You didn't leave, and . . . you're helping Vicki? Who's terrifying the children?"

"We didn't find him," Jack said to Vicki, "but Mr. Crusoe and I will be ready when he reappears."

Stella's stomach performed a somersault. "Mr. Crusoe?"

The man with Jack turned his tanned face to Stella and lifted his thick eyebrows in response. "Yes?" Unraveling, threadlike words uncoiled from his rope and dropped to the ground like sand falling through an hourglass. **Orinoco. Wooden cross. Friday.**

"This is really happening," Stella said, looking at Jack.

His hazel-eyed gaze found hers. "No one else for you to pass the buck to."

Stella's thoughts felt as though they were pushing through pine tar. Words drifted past her line of vision like leaves caught in a swirling wind. **Ink pad. Breath of life. Sunlight.**

Jack stepped into her personal space. Rather than backing away from him, Stella didn't move. She could smell the scent of the forest on him—Douglas fir and winter with an earthy undertone. She blinked the haze from her eyes.

"Captain Hook, courtesy of your irresponsibility, is running amok in the library."

Stella laughed because that was the only response her brain could produce. She covered her mouth, but more hysterical laughter pushed through her fingers.

"It's not funny," Vicki said. "He's really intimidating. I mean, he's playing the part really well—a little too well. Jack was nice enough to try to help me find him and tell him we won't be needing his services today or any other day. Arnie wouldn't approve. You should have heard the children screaming."

Stella's laughter stopped abruptly. The realization of what she'd done caused stomach acid to bubble up her throat. "I think I'm going to throw up."

Vicki dragged Stella to the circulation desk and pushed her into the desk chair. The metal trash can scraped over the tiles as Vicki slid it toward her and told Stella to lean over it.

"I'll get some cold towels from the bathroom. Stay here," Vicki said as she hurried off.

A shadow fell over Stella's body. She cut her gaze up to see Jack standing near her.

He placed his hand on her back and rubbed small circles between her shoulder blades. His touch comforted her for a couple of seconds, and then it sent warmth traveling from her spine to radiate through her body. Her head throbbed.

Jack shook his head. "This isn't the worst situation I've seen, but Captain Hook? Really, Stella? Of all the jerks you could have brought here, why him?"

She hung her head. "I wasn't thinking about what would happen if it worked. Can we return Hook to his book before the two weeks are up?"

"There are ways to return characters early," Jack answered, hesitation in his voice.

Stella gazed past him to the shipwrecked man, who stood looking around the foyer, apparently on high alert for a rogue pirate. Arnie had mentioned that sending characters back before the two weeks were over was an unpleasant choice. What did that mean? "What ways?"

Jack shook his head. "Nothing we need to discuss now. We have bigger issues."

She made a mental note to ask again later. "And that's Robinson Crusoe?"

"At least he's accommodating," Jack said.

Stella remembered the pull to grab *Robinson Crusoe* from the shelf. Had something inside her known they'd need his help?

Jack rubbed the back of his neck. "It's a good thing you didn't invite any other troublemakers."

"Did you know the book club invited Darcy to go into town and have coffee with them? He was outside on the back steps."

Jack's skin paled for a moment. "I've been too busy trying to find Hook. Darcy wouldn't have gone. He doesn't like crowds, but he knows better anyway. We *all* do. Well, the good ones of us."

Stella nodded. "Arnie told me everything. About the magic, the warnings about what happens if we lose characters, and about you."

Jack touched her shoulder and then stepped aside as Vicki approached. Under his breath, he said, "We'll discuss that later."

Vicki returned with a wad of wet paper towels. She pressed them against Stella's neck, and Stella thanked her.

"Should we tell Arnie?" Vicki asked.

"No!" Jack and Stella said together, surprising Vicki.

"We've got this under control," Jack said.

"We do?" Vicki asked. "You don't even know where the crazy pirate is."

Stella stood and wiped the cold, wet paper towels over her face before tossing them into the trash can. "We'll find him," she said, sounding more confident than she felt. "Vicki, you stay here at the desk in case anyone needs you. Jack, Mr. Crusoe, and I will split up and search the library. He has to be here somewhere, right?"

Vicki looked relieved to stay in relative safety behind the circulation desk.

Was Hook still in the library? What if he slipped out when they weren't looking? What would happen to Peter Pan's world if Captain Hook never existed? Stella realized Arnie had been right not to tell her the truth sooner. She was too irresponsible to handle it. Look what havoc she had already caused.

Stella walked away from the circulation desk with Jack and Mr. Crusoe. "What's the plan?"

A line creased between Jack's dark brows. "I don't think we should split up. Hook isn't the most reputable character. He's not the cartoon version you're imagining."

Stella narrowed her gaze. "How do you know what I'm imagining?"

"Because I'd bet you're thinking about Disney's Captain Hook."

"How do you even *know* about that version of Captain Hook?" Stella asked.

"Arnie and I have often discussed various iterations of characters," he said. "This is *not* that older, wig-wearing guy looking for a crocodile."

"So he's not a vain, evil coward with a childish temper who periodically cries out in terror?" Jack shook his head. "What about Barrie's blue-eyed man with a handsome countenance and elegant diction, who wasn't actually murderous?"

Jack shook his head again.

"Whose heinous version *is* Hook then?" Stella made a shooing motion with her hand. "This will go a whole lot faster if we split up. I'll shout if I see him, and then you two can come and help if needed."

Jack's voice was flat when he echoed, "If needed." He slipped a knife sheathed in a narrow holster out of his pocket and removed the knife from its case. "Take this."

Stella handled the knife as though it were a snake. "Unless this is an extreme way for me to open the mail, I'd rather not."

Jack closed Stella's fingers over the hilt and held his hand over hers. "It will at least surprise him long enough for you to scream for help."

Stella's eyes widened, and her pulse quickened. "How scary *is* this version?"

"He's a low-life pirate willing to do whatever is necessary to get what he wants," Mr. Crusoe said. "And he'll likely try to take you captive, looking the way you do. But we'll keep you and the children safe from the devil's army."

Stella glanced at Jack. "Looking the way I do? The devil's army?" She eyed the knife in her hand and held it awkwardly by her thigh. "I'll take the second-floor historical section."

"I advise against splitting up," Jack said again.

"Noted. Let's do this fast. The quicker we find him, the quicker we can make sure nothing else bad happens," she said as she walked up the main staircase, holding the knife away from her body and praying she didn't fall and cut herself. She headed toward the historical section, where she peered around bookshelves and glanced under tables. *It's not like he would hide under there,* she thought after she'd leaned over and looked beneath a third study table.

On a final sweep of the historical section, she glanced at the far corner and gasped. A lean, well-built man stood with his back to her. He wore a black leather duster jacket over fitted black pants and black boots that came up to his knees. His close-cropped hair matched the color of his clothing, and he stood with one hand pressed against the tall glass window that showed a view of the grassy lawn behind the library. His other arm hung at his side, ending with a sharpened, gleaming silver hook.

He turned at the sound of her inhale. With his strikingly light eyes and scarred, smirking face, this Captain Hook was definitely *not* Disney's or Barrie's version.

Chapter 13

Stella gaped at the pirate. Hook's five o'clock shadow looked like a permanent fixture, as though he would never grow a beard and he'd never be clean-shaven. Heavy, dark brows shadowed his forget-me-not blue eyes. She was most taken aback by the fact that he was so attractive, although in a frightening way—like the way a dragon is mesmerizing in its splendor but also dangerous and deadly.

"Hello, love," Hook said in a thick British accent. His gaze drifted toward the knife she held loosely. "Come to do me in, have you? I don't fancy you the type."

Stella opened her mouth to agree with him, but Hook moved quickly toward her and snatched the knife from her hand before she could react. He tossed it aside. The knife skittered across the floor until it bounced off a bookshelf and disappeared under a table. Then he looped his arm around Stella's waist, and she stumbled forward as he pressed her against him.

She struggled and squirmed before his hook came into her peripheral vision. She stopped as sunlight glinted off the silver.

"It's lonely at sea," he said, his breath stinking of rum and cloves.

"You might consider a toothbrush on your voyages," she said, trying to breathe as his grip tightened on her waist.

Hook rubbed his scruffy face against her cheek like a cat brushing against its owner's leg. Stella scrunched her eyes closed. Under different circumstances, it might have been somewhat thrilling to be held close by a roguish pirate, but the hook was too terrifying, especially since he was sliding it through her hair at the moment.

"You smell like caramel," he whispered against her neck.

If she screamed, would Hook stab her? He shoved her back against the wall. Her panicked gaze followed the trail of a thin vertical scar that stretched from his lower left eye to the corner of his lip.

"You sure are a lovely thing."

Hook pressed his mouth to hers, and she nearly choked on her own breath. He kissed her like a man completely starved for physical contact, like a man who needed her breath to survive the next few seconds.

Then a loud *thunk* sounded, and Hook released his grip on her. His body crumpled like a rag doll to the floor. Stella stared at his leather-clad body lying in a heap at her feet, her heart nearly leaping out of her chest.

Jack stood in front of her with a book in his hands. "*War and Peace.*" He turned the book over so she could see the spine.

"I've just . . . He . . ." Stella swiped the back of her hand across her lips.

Jack dropped the book on the nearest table. Then he leaned down, hooked his arms beneath the pirate's armpits, and dragged Hook away from Stella's feet. "Mr. Crusoe!" he called. He returned to Stella and put his hand on her arm. "Are you okay?"

Stella tried to pull her trembling fingers through her hair, but they caught on her curls. "*Okay* is not how I would describe myself at the moment." She pressed her hands to her chest as if that would calm her heartbeat. "You gave me a knife, and you attacked with a book? Isn't that the opposite of what should have happened?"

When Crusoe appeared, Jack said, "Will you take Hook down to the archives and tie him to a chair? Make sure he can't get free. And take his sword. We don't want him armed."

Mr. Crusoe lifted Hook onto his back, draping the pirate's arms over his shoulders, and carried him away. What would the people in the library think? Could they be convinced this was part of a play or reenactment?

"This has gotten *so* out of hand," Stella said. She wiped her mouth again. "And unexpectedly scary. No wonder the kids were terrified. The appeal of pirate romance has completely evaporated for me."

Jack walked over to the table, picked up *War and Peace*, and returned it to its shelf. "At least we caught him. Sorry it wasn't before he . . ."

Stella touched her lips again. "Thanks for rescuing me."

Jack nodded. "The chaos should be over now."

Finally, her heartbeat settled into a more peaceful rhythm. Knowing Hook couldn't cause any more mayhem offered major relief. "This is probably where I should say that you were right."

Although Stella had never imagined what kind of kisser Hook would be, she was sorry she now knew. Desperate, air-sucking, forced kisses were as far from what she dreamed about as possible. But she had wondered what kind of kisser Jack would be. While he didn't seem like the shy, nervous type, he also didn't seem like he'd be as aggressive as Hook, trying to suck all the life from her body like a dementor from Azkaban. Would he be passionate and direct without being forceful?

Her brain quickly created a list of Jane Austen's leading men—so many swoon-worthy characters whose kisses changed lives and captured hearts. She scratched through Fitzwilliam Darcy's name immediately. Then she cleared her throat when she felt her cheeks warm. What was she doing? Making a list of men who might kiss like Jack after just being kissed by a merciless pirate?

Stella rubbed her fingers across her forehead. "I'm sorry about all of this. I should have listened to you. This is a mess."

Jack nodded and pushed off from the bookshelf. "It's mostly sorted."

"Will we be able to keep Hook tied up for two weeks?" she asked.

"I don't see why not."

Stella's mind whirred. "What about food and water? We can't starve him. Or . . . do you eat?" She'd seen Jack drink coffee, but was that for show?

Jack laughed unexpectedly. "I can eat, yes, but do I need to? No."

"Whoa, that's weird. You can stay here for two weeks and never eat? What about sleeping?"

"I can sleep," Jack said, "but it's much the same. I don't need it. Because I guess in a way, I'm not real in this world."

His mouth turned down at the corners, and he looked away from her. Did that bother him? Stella felt compelled to reach out and touch him. When she grabbed his hand, he looked at her.

"But you *are* real," she said. "In your story, I mean. You lived in Blue Sky Valley and had a life and a family. Maybe it's easier not having to worry about food and sleeping when you're here now. You can enjoy yourself twenty-four hours a day."

He squeezed her hand. "It is odd—or weird, as you say—that I *feel* very real, but I know that in this world I'm not."

Stella released his hand. "Honestly, Jack, this whole situation is weird. Not just *you* but all of it. The library, the magical ink, the idea that characters can disappear from books forever. You, in particular, are less odd to me, because I've been reading about you for so many years. But . . ." She hesitated, doubting her ability to say the words rising within her.

Jack stepped toward her. "But what?"

His hazel eyes stared into hers, and for a moment, Stella felt a lightness in her body like she hadn't experienced in a long time. She was reminded of the girl she was before her heart had broken. "I've dreamed about having a conversation with you for years."

Jack's features shifted, and she could swear she saw desire in his expression. "We're having a conversation now."

"We are." Stella smiled shyly. "You've always felt like a real person to me, and I had all kinds of questions I wanted answers to."

"Ask me anything."

Stella felt herself leaning toward him, and almost instantly an alarm went off in her head. What was she doing, looking at Jack with puppy dog eyes? Could this day be any more insane? She'd been kissed by Hook, and now she was standing inches away from her childhood crush, acting like she might swoon?

She cleared her throat, stepped away from Jack, and broke the moment they'd been sharing. "What about Hook? You think it's okay to leave him tied up for two weeks?"

Jack sensed the shift in her energy, and his shoulders straightened, his expression unreadable. "We certainly can't let him wander around, no matter what kinds of promises he makes. I suspect he'll try to woo someone into untying him, so don't fall for that. He's not a good guy."

Stella shook her head. "He's too intense for me. Totally not my type." She headed toward the main staircase, leaving Jack to catch up.

When he was by her side, he asked, "What is your type?"

She nearly blurted, "You," but managed to press her lips closed.

Jack paused at the top of the stairs and looked at her. "Everyone has a type."

Stella continued walking. Her skin itched below the surface, and the back of her neck prickled with heat. Silvery, shiny words drifted across the steps, and she stopped moving. **Come out, come out. You can't hide forever. Open up.** She narrowed her eyes at the words, and they skittered into the shadowed corners. She caught Jack watching her, knowing he'd seen the words. "I'm not interested in having a type."

Jack didn't speak again until they were halfway down the main staircase. "What's his name?"

Stella's chest tightened. Could Jack see into her soul, see all the secrets she kept there, the ones she wanted to bury for all time? "Whose name?" she asked, hoping to divert him.

"The name of the guy who hurt you bad enough to make you want to give up. Did you ever bring him to the library?"

Stella clenched her jaw. "He wouldn't have come to the library. He didn't even like to read." Speaking that truth out loud struck her as funny. She'd spent a year with someone who didn't like books? How was that even possible? "He didn't *make* me do anything. It was my choice to stop wanting anything other than what I have right now. Why is everyone always telling me to do something different with my life? Go to school, take a new job in Miami, go on a date. I'm perfectly fine—"

Stella's lungs squeezed painfully, blurring her vision with black dots and shooting stars. Her body seized, and she tilted sideways. A fire burned at her core and sweat beaded on her forehead.

"Stella!" Jack said, catching her in his arms before she tumbled headfirst down the staircase.

Brilliant violet liquid spilled over the nearest step like a waterfall of neon. Vibrating letters formed from the liquid, rising like magic. Tendrils writhed from the letters, reminding Stella of jellyfish. The words grabbed her sandals and then slinked up her leg as shivers wracked her body.

Jack squeezed her in his arms. "Stella, I don't know what to do. Tell me how to help."

She had to speak the words aloud. Her teeth chattered so violently that her voice came out in staccato bursts. "'He was excruciatingly handsome and no ordinary man.'" Within seconds, the shaking and the burning stopped, and Stella sagged in Jack's arms.

After a moment, he sat her up beside him on the step. "What is happening, Stella?"

She swiped her hand across her sweaty forehead and then rubbed her hands up and down her arms. "That's a good question."

"Is this something medical?" he asked.

Worry deepened the lines on his face. Without thinking, Stella reached up and touched his cheek, trying to smooth away the concern. "Are you asking if I have a brain issue?" She lowered her hand. "I don't know. It just started happening a few days ago. How can *you* see the words when no one else can?"

"I'm not sure." Jack placed his hand on hers. "Are you okay?"

Stella nodded. "It's intense but passes quickly, as soon as I acknowledge the words out loud."

Jack rubbed his thumb across the top of her hand. "I'm curious about this excruciatingly handsome man. Is he the guy you don't want to talk about?"

"Wade? Ha, no," Stella said with a sarcastic laugh. "He was attractive, sure, but not excruciatingly handsome. That's too high level for him." She stood with Jack's help and thought of her journal tucked into her purse. "I need to write down those words. I don't know what they'll eventually reveal, but I know they mean something."

"Wade," Jack said, repeating the name. "Are you still in love with him?"

Stella stopped on the bottom step. "In love? No. Absolutely not. It's been done for months, and I'm over it." The lie stung Stella's tongue and throat, making her feel like she'd eaten a ghost pepper. "The truth is, I'm *getting* over it. I've been dragging around my broken heart like a trophy, but not anymore. I'm making some changes."

Jack looked like he wanted to say more, but he only nodded.

Vicki rushed over and met them. "I saw Mr. Crusoe drag the pirate down into the archives. Is that okay? Is that legal, to hold someone hostage in the library? Are the police going to come pick him up?"

"Vicki," Stella said, shifting gears quickly, "we aren't holding him hostage. He's . . . intoxicated, so we're subduing him until his employer can come get him."

Vicki's eyes widened. "Are you serious? I hope word doesn't get out that we had a drunken pirate impersonator in the library."

Stella leaned forward and whispered, "Just keep a lid on it, and no one will find out. I don't plan on telling anyone. Do you?"

Vicki shook her head. "It's about time for me to end my shift, but I don't really want to leave you here alone during the evening."

Stella glanced at the large antique clock hanging on the wall. "Your shift is technically over already, so I'll take it from here. Thanks for coming in and helping out. I'm sorry everything got so out of hand. It's been one of those days, but I'll be fine to close down tonight."

Vicki glanced over her shoulder as though someone might round an aisle and sneak up on her. "What about the other impersonator? I didn't see the Englishman leave. The tattered guy who dragged the pirate downstairs hasn't left either as far as I know. They certainly didn't stop by to tell me they were leaving."

Stella rubbed the tense muscles at the back of her neck. "I'll get it all back in order." When Vicki looked skeptical, Stella added, "I promise. I have Jack here to help me."

As they returned to the circulation desk, Vicki smiled at Jack.

"You're a godsend. You knew exactly what to do. Do you live around here—"

Stella cleared her throat. "Thanks, Vicki. You're okay to come back tomorrow?"

"Of course." Vicki gazed a few seconds longer at Jack and then sighed softly before gathering her phone and purse from the circulation desk. "It was really nice to meet you, Jack. Don't be a stranger. You can always stop by."

"The pleasure is all mine, Vicki," Jack said, holding out his hand to shake hers.

Vicki looked disappointed that he offered a handshake rather than a hug or something more involved, something that would cause their arms to be tangled around each other. She slid her gaze away from Jack and toward Stella. "Don't forget the book club will be here at six thirty," Vicki said. "Arnie usually handles that, but I guess it will fall on you now."

Stella nodded. "Shouldn't be a problem."

Vicki said goodbye and left out the back door. Stella reached into her purse and removed her journal. She wrote down the new words, so now the page included: *I fell in love once. Did I ever tell you that? He was excruciatingly handsome and no ordinary man.* She closed the journal. Was she writing a diary entry or the beginning of a romance story? Was it her voice telling the story or someone else's?

"Tonight should be easy, right? No more issues," she said to Jack. But as soon as she spoke, the hairs on the back of her neck stood, and three muddy-yellow words skated across the tiles near them. **Chaos and books. Get loose. Stop-your-breath kisses.**

Jack watched the words whiz by, and his eyebrows rose. His gaze locked with Stella's.

"I don't know about you, but I'm really interested in stop-your-breath kisses."

Chapter 14

At six thirty sharp, Stella had the book club attendees settled into their usual space on the first floor, sandwiched between the biographies and the reference books with their chairs in a horseshoe shape. Jack stood beside the circulation desk flipping through a shiny trifold pamphlet. She recognized it as one of the college brochures Arnie had tried to force on her. Jack glanced up when he heard her approach.

"Yours?" he asked.

Stella rolled her eyes. "Arnie wants me to go back to college and get a different degree or certification."

"You were an accountant, right?" Jack said. "But you've been working in the library instead."

Stella nodded. "Accounting was practical, but I know without a doubt it's *not* the job for me." She reached for the brochure and flipped through it for the first time. "I can't imagine going back to school for another degree, but if I did, I'd probably study English or creative writing."

Jack's eyebrows lifted. "Now *that* actually fits you."

Stella smiled. "It does." She leaned her hip against the desk. "If I'm honest, Jack, after losing my dad and the relationship catastrophe with Wade, all I really wanted was to disappear, and I could do that here in the library. I could be like a book on the shelf, something that's noticed sometimes but not messed with otherwise. But recently so much is changing—"

"Like those words?" Jack interrupted. "You said they only recently started showing up. They're different from the others."

"Very different," Stella agreed. "Violent in a way. Words have always shown up whenever they wanted to. But the other night with Ariel, I tried commanding the words to come to see if I could figure out what book she wanted to read."

Jack straightened. "Did it work?"

Stella smiled again. "It did. I didn't know I could do that, and it made me realize my life should be more about the words and writing and helping people find other people's writings. I know Arnie and Percy want something more for me—an advanced degree or a posh accounting firm in Miami—but what if I'm *supposed* to be here? I could be doing something with purpose, something I already love." Her cheeks had grown warm with the confession. "I'm still trying to figure it out. Arnie's enchanted library surprise feels connected somehow, but I can't quite piece it all together."

"I can't picture you living in Miami," Jack said.

Stella fiddled with the brochure. "That's what Ariel said too."

His smile faltered. "I'd possibly never see you again if you moved to Miami, even if Arnie brought me back."

The awareness struck Stella as if she'd stepped off a curb without meaning to. Jack seemed saddened by the idea of never seeing her again. Did he feel a connection between them too? She'd finally met him in real life, and the experience hadn't aligned with any of her daydreams. She'd envisioned flirting, hand-holding, and looks of longing passing between them. Instead, their time together had been riddled with complications and mishaps, and she'd ended up being kissed by a stinky pirate.

In her silence, he continued, "It's not like I saw you every year, but it's nice to finally be able to talk with you."

She barely knew anything about Jack—other than what was included in his book, and reading that story for years didn't count as truly knowing him. But she *wanted* to know more about him while they had time left, which emboldened her.

"When I daydreamed about talking with you, I imagined it going differently."

Jack chuckled. "The dreams didn't include dastardly pirates and screaming children?"

"Only a few," she teased. Did she even remember how to flirt with a guy?

"You said you had questions." He took the colorful brochure from her and returned it to the counter.

"So many," she said. "That's the trouble with books. There are always so many things I'm curious about, little pieces of information that aren't included because how can an author possibly include everything? Such as, before the war, what was your life plan?"

Jack's lips lifted in one corner. "Going straight for the big ones. I planned to study medicine."

"I already know that," Stella said, remembering what one of the Battle of the Bulge survivors from Jack's unit revealed in his storyline. "Donald Langan said you were brilliant, could have been a successful surgeon. He said you loved talking about science and medicine and that you were always looking out for the guys."

Jack didn't respond for a few seconds, but finally asked, "Is this how you felt when I recalled to you what you and Percy had done growing up? A not quite uncomfortable but still peculiar feeling that someone knows about your personal life when you haven't told them about it?"

Stella's smile reflected on Jack's face. "It's probably comparable. It's just that I've— Well, to say I've read your book a lot doesn't suffice. It's probably more accurate to say I've almost memorized it, which sounds *so* creepy when I say it out loud." She laughed nervously. "Makes me sound obsessed."

Jack chuckled. "I can't rag you about that. I've been watching you off and on for years. What's that level of creepy?"

Stella burst out laughing, the sound echoing strangely—but familiarly—in her ears, like a long-lost friend who had finally returned. She pressed her hands to her chest as more flowed out of her. The reappearance of her laughter felt delightful.

"Why were you so curious about Percy and me?" she asked.

Jack paused in thought. "At first because Arnie talked about you two all the time. I felt like I knew you as well. Then later . . ." Jack's cheeks darkened and he looked away.

Stella shifted on her feet, sensing the air around them fluctuating, warming. "Later?"

His hazel eyes found hers. "Later you grew up, and when you got closer to my age, I could see you as my peer and someone I would have wanted to ask out on a date. To a neighborhood dance."

Is this for real? My fictional boyfriend crush has wanted to take me on a date? Before she could stop herself, she blurted, "I'm a terrible dancer."

Jack stepped closer to her. "Is that a no?"

"No!" she said quickly. "I mean, no, it's *not* a no, but yes, I'm not someone you'd want to take to a dance." Was she seriously talking him out of wanting to take her on a date?

"I could show you a few moves," he said.

Stella's mouth went dry and then her stomach growled so loudly that it echoed in the foyer. She and Jack both busted out laughing.

"So, food?" he said lightheartedly. "If I remember correctly, you have a deep love for pizza."

Stella placed her hands on her stomach as another growl sounded. "But you said you don't get hungry. Is it too weird to eat?"

Jack laughed. "I'm not a ghost, Stella. I can eat and act like a regular man with needs."

Stella's eyebrows rose, and laughter rushed out of her again.

Jack cleared his throat. "I meant *physical needs* like eating."

Stella's giggles continued. A carefree feeling rose up in her, easy and comfortable, and she couldn't remember the last time she'd felt that way.

"Sure you did." She pulled out her cell phone and winced. Several unread texts from Ariel filled the screen. She'd forgotten she hung up on her best friend earlier in the day. With everything that had been going on, she'd completely forgotten to call or text her back. She'd have to do that soon. But first she searched for the local pizza place. "According to your *physical needs*, do you want pepperoni or supreme? That wasn't in your book."

"Surprise me," Jack said.

Stella ordered the pizza and tossed in an order of cheesy bread as a bonus. Then she read Ariel's texts while guilt bloomed in her chest. "Excuse me for a minute," she told Jack. "I'm going to call Ariel real quick. Can you keep an eye out?"

He nodded, and Stella walked into the children's section and dialed Ariel's number. Her best friend picked up on the first ring.

"Where in heaven's name have you been? I was just about to drive to the library!"

"I am *so sorry*," Stella said sincerely. "It's been a madhouse today. We had . . . visitors and so many people. Vicki was shorthanded for a bit because Dan left, and there was a lot to organize. The book club is here tonight, and I lost track of time. I'm sorry to worry you."

"And Jack?" Ariel asked.

Her question stunned Stella into silence for a few seconds. "Jack? What about him?"

Ariel huffed. "Is *he* still there?"

Stella's heartbeat quickened. "What does he have to do with anything?"

"Why aren't you answering the question?" Ariel asked.

"Yes, he's still here," Stella admitted. "He's been helping out."

A few seconds passed and no one spoke. Had Ariel hung up? Stella pulled the phone away from her ear and saw the call was still live.

"Are you going to tell me what's going on or not?" Ariel said. "And don't give me some baloney response about the library being super busy today. I drove by this afternoon on my way to an appointment, and the whole outside of the building felt like it was pulsing with energy."

Stella pressed one hand against her heart. "What does that mean?"

"Stella Parker, you're my best friend, and I *know* you," Ariel said. "I know when you're being shady, when you're trying *not* to tell me something. Whatever it is that you're not saying is sitting in my stomach like a ball of thorns. *Something* is going on with you and the library, which is why I'm getting such an out-of-control vibe about the place."

Stella exhaled. She *couldn't* tell Ariel the truth. "I'm sorry, Ariel. It's not that easy, and it's not my secret to share."

"So you're admitting there's something," Ariel said. "That's progress. Whose secret is it? Arnie's? And I'm going out on a limb here, but Jack's involved, isn't he? And if Jack knows, then I'd say it's okay for me to know, wouldn't you?"

Stella started to protest. "Ariel, I don't think—"

"I have a client call coming in," Ariel said. "Let me call you back."

Ariel hung up. Crisis averted. She was persistent, so she wouldn't give up, but at least Stella had more time to figure out what wild story to tell her best friend to prevent her from learning the truth.

✦ ✦ ✦

STELLA PLACED HER third piece of pepperoni pizza on a paper towel, then she slid the half-empty pizza box back toward Jack. He wiped his mouth and grabbed another slice. They drank Pepsi out of two mismatched plastic cups she'd found in the kitchenette cabinets.

She could almost pretend they were two regular people, enjoying pizza together, possibly having a date. "The clothes," she said. "Does Arnie keep a stash around here somewhere? A magic closet?"

Jack smiled around his cup, took a sip, and then placed it down. "If by *magic* you mean, does he stock it with our preferred options, then yes."

"But Darcy's wearing exactly what I'd expect," Stella said, biting into her slice.

Jack cocked an eyebrow. "Darcy wouldn't suffer himself to be a drip."

Stella agreed. "I can't imagine him in regular clothes." She pointed at Jack's T-shirt. "Why the Yankees?"

He looked affronted. "*Why* the Yankees? They're only the winningest team in history with twenty-seven world titles. They've been to the World Series forty times. Then there's Babe Ruth, Mickey Mantle, Lou Gehrig, Joe DiMaggio, Yogi Berra—should I keep going?"

"Superfan," Stella said. "I had no idea. What other gold nuggets can I dig up?"

Jack playfully rubbed his chin as though thinking. "My favorite song is 'I'm Stepping Out with a Memory Tonight.'"

Stella shook her head. "I don't know that one."

Jack's shock caused her to laugh. "But it's a perfect dancing song."

Stella took another bite of her pizza. "A good reason I don't know it."

He pointed to her cell phone. "Arnie's told me about technology wonders. Can you find the song and play it on your phone?"

Stella wiped her hands on a napkin and searched a music streaming site. She lowered the volume on her phone, tapped Play, and the song filled the space around them. It transported her to the 1940s, and when she closed her eyes, she could see couples slow dancing across a gymnasium floor. She'd read Jack's book repeatedly. His fictional journals in the book didn't include these little details.

Another curious thing was the author's lack of mentioning Jack having a wife or girlfriend. In 1945 a man his age would have been married already. Fictional Jack had a richer backstory than she knew, proven by his love of the Yankees and Jimmy Dorsey. What else hadn't the author included in the published novel?

"Did you have a girlfriend?" What kind of woman was Jack Mathis's type? Would she be intelligent and beautiful and know how to cook? Would she be classy and always put together? Stella doubted Jack's type would eat kids' cereal or premade macaroni and cheese while standing up in the kitchen.

Jack chewed slowly and swallowed. "When?"

"When you left for war. Was there someone you left behind?" Stella put down her half-eaten slice. "The author, well, he didn't include anything like that in the book, so I wondered . . ." It would have been so easy to fall in love with a man like Jack. She'd be surprised if other women hadn't felt the same way.

He took a drink before answering. "There's always more than what appears in the printed book. More to the stories captured within the pages. I didn't have a girlfriend when I left. A few weeks before, yes. Ellen." He said her name like it still unsettled something inside him, and he didn't elaborate.

Stella's curiosity flared. "What happened?"

He glanced down at the floor. "You can't just leave it there?"

Stella made a scoffing noise. "Could you?"

He smiled at her. "I actually thought Ellen and I would get married. It made sense," he said. "We dated for two years, and she was a good girl. Capable and kind. I figured we'd settle down and have two or three kids. She liked flowers, so I wanted land outside the city to give her a garden. Then the Selective Training and Service Act of 1940 went into practice. Four years later, my district was selected, and given that I was classified as a 1-A, I was called into action."

"Two years was a long courtship for that time, wasn't it? Didn't girls get married when they were barely adults?"

Jack studied the pizza box. "When we met, she was seventeen. Her parents weren't in a rush to marry her off. When we found out I was going to join the war, she said she cared a lot about me, but she didn't have 'that feeling.'"

"What feeling?"

He met Stella's gaze. "That feeling that she wanted to wait for me to come back. So she broke it off."

Stella gaped at him. "*She* broke up with *you*? After two years?"

He chuckled. "You say that like it's an impossible idea."

Stella wanted to say, *Have you seen you? You're gorgeous and thoughtful and well-mannered, and did I mention gorgeous? How could anyone spend two years with Jack Mathis and decide he wasn't worth waiting for?*

They sat quietly for a few minutes while Stella created images of Ellen and Jack together—in her mind they were dancing on a polished floor while Jack spun her around and Ellen laughed. Then they were sitting on a picnic blanket in the park, eating grapes and cheese on crackers. Then they were strolling beneath the moonlight—

Jack interrupted her thoughts. "I wanted to get married."

"I'm sorry Ellen broke it off," Stella said. "It seems kinda heartless to do that to a man going off to war."

Jack lifted one shoulder. "Better before I left than after I got back."

But Jack had never returned from the war.

"I wouldn't have wanted to come home, thinking I'd finally be able to get my life back on track, only to have my girl ditch me," he said. "*If* I'd come home."

"If you had, do you think you would have eventually gotten married?"

A small smile lifted his lips. "I'd like to think so. I wanted a family. A home. All that jazz."

Stella stared at him. "I wish you could have had it all."

Jack's gaze lingered on her. "You said you aren't in love with Wade anymore, but were you?"

Stella reached for her slice of pizza and stopped. A door opened in her mind. She pictured Wade leaning against the doorjamb with his boyish smile, arms crossed over his chest, asking her if she was coming in to join him or not. A small part of her ached to go back to those days with him when he'd made her feel special, but the much larger part of her was so not interested in his half-hearted romance. "I thought I was."

Jack propped an elbow on the desk and watched her. "Tell me about him, about the two of you together."

Stella pinched the bridge of her nose. "I can't possibly prepare you for the ugliness."

"I've seen some pretty bad stuff, Stella."

Passages from *Beyond the Southern Horizon* flashed through her mind—his two closest comrades killed by a mortar shell explosion a few yards from where he stood loading the gun on a tank, raging blizzards and freezing rain, and wounded soldiers freezing to death while Jack slept in a foxhole wrapped in a coat he took off a deceased German soldier.

He'd definitely seen worse than her busted-up relationship saga. "Wade was one of Percy's friends. He was older by a few years, but we'd known each other almost our whole lives. When we had Dad's funeral, Wade was there, and we reconnected. We chatted off and on for a couple years before anything started happening. He was married— Well, he was separated and had been for more than a year. But he wasn't officially divorced."

Jack sat up straighter in his chair. "You dated a married man?"

"Don't look so surprised," Stella said, even as the words filled her with a sickening shame. "It's not like I'm the first woman to make a bad decision. He and his wife weren't living together. I'm not saying that makes it okay, but it made it *seem* more okay. They were co-parenting their three children, so the kids lived with her full-time, but Wade was basically with them all the time at her house. His kids were—no, *are*—his life. That part of his situation was always clear to me. He would do anything for them. A trait of his I admired."

"Do you have a picture?" Jack asked.

"One," she admitted and wondered why she hadn't deleted it yet. "I ditched the rest. I couldn't stand seeing them on my phone." She scrolled through the photo album on her phone until she found the last remaining photograph of Wade—one she'd taken while they were having lunch a month before he left her. She held out the phone to Jack.

"Decent-looking guy, obviously older than you, but I can see why you were attracted to him."

Stella shook her head. "I was so desperate for love and comfort that I probably would have been attracted to a mannequin if it had shown interest."

Jack laughed but then stopped abruptly. "Sorry. I know that wasn't an easy time for you."

She waved her hand dismissively. "No, it was meant to be funny. Self-deprecating humor, but it still carries a lot of truth." She pocketed her cell phone. "After my dad died, I was in a vulnerable, needy state of mind. Wade and I started talking on the phone and sending emails, then that evolved into lunches here and there, then a couple dinners. Eventually we were talking every day and sneaking off to do all sorts of things."

"Sneaking?"

"Is there a better word for what we were doing?"

Jack frowned. "I suppose not. Continue."

"At first, we had a lot of fun together. We went to movies, museums, and concerts. We went on a few weekend getaways. We laughed a lot, and when we were together, Wade seemed freer. Uninhibited by all the responsibilities of work and homelife." It suddenly struck her that she was an escape for Wade, a way for him to release his regular life and have a pretend one with her. She also questioned if she'd really been happy with him or if he'd also been a temporary escape from her pain and loneliness.

"I guess we fell into *something*. At the time, I thought I loved him, but after a while, I felt restless with what we were. I wanted to be with him, but he wasn't mine to want, not really. Our future together wasn't something we talked about often, but when it came up, it was always him talking about it. How we'd be together, how he was excited for me to eventually meet his kids. It sounds so dim-witted to me now, but I actually thought we'd be a family one day—me, him, the kids."

Jack nodded. "That sounds like a natural progression. Why weren't Wade and his wife divorced?"

Stella rolled her eyes. "That's a great question. His kids weren't little anymore. His oldest was already driving. Not that it's ever a good time to get divorced, but it *feels* worse to me if the kids are small. The easy answer is they weren't divorced because they didn't *want* to be. I also didn't understand why, at the time, he spent most of his free time with her and the kids when he could have spent more of it with me."

"Did you ask him why or tell him you wanted to be clear about your future together?" Jack asked.

Stella sighed. Reliving the past with Jack highlighted even more how she and Wade weren't ever going to work. "I asked him if we could start spending more time together, if we could take our relationship to the next level. And if there were plans for him and his wife to divorce."

Jack leaned forward, caught up in her story. "What did he say?"

"He said I wanted too much," she answered. "He said I didn't understand what he was going through, how difficult it was for him to make time for me. He had his children to think about, to provide for, to be present for. I understood that, but didn't I deserve to be present for too?" Stella shrugged.

"I realize how pathetic that sounds. I was settling for a subpar relationship. He said I was living in a dream world. I didn't understand how gritty and imperfect life was. I should have understood that what he was giving me was good enough. He had to think of his kids first, and a full-time relationship with me wasn't possible. After *all those months* he finally admitted he'd never seen a future with us in it."

Stella folded her paper towel into a square and then into a smaller square, and then into an even smaller square. The anger and heartbreak she'd grown accustomed to didn't emerge. When was the last time she'd thought about Wade without feeling suffocated? Now, the sense of freedom was like a thunderbolt.

"How could that relationship have been good enough for anyone?" Jack said quietly.

Stella looked at him and knew he'd never be the kind of man to do what Wade did. "He left my house that day, and we never spoke again. He didn't call or text. After two weeks, in a moment of complete weakness and probably too much caffeine, I called him. He didn't answer. So I texted him, asking if we could talk about what happened. But he never responded."

"Did you want him back?" Jack asked, his expression revealing his disbelief.

Stella groaned. "I realize it was pathetic, but at the time, my heart was broken. How could someone who supposedly cared about me ghost me? I wanted anything to make my heart feel better."

"And you thought it could be him?"

"At the time, he seemed like the obvious solution," Stella said, "but I can finally see how flawed that thinking was."

Jack leaned back and crossed his arms over his chest. "Did it ever occur to you that Wade was wrong? Did you ever think the way he treated you was a reflection on how he felt about himself and wasn't about you at all? What if he was *wrong* about everything, Stella? Especially about you?"

Stella rubbed her fingers across her collarbone. "I made so many mistakes with him. I saw it as admirable that he was willing to give up everything for his kids."

Jack locked eyes with her. "He didn't give up everything. It sounds like he kept his life exactly the way *he* wanted, with the exception of you. I'd bet he would've kept you around for as long as you would have stayed. Until you finally decided he wasn't good enough for *you*."

Jack's words resonated within her. "I mishandled a lot, especially my heart."

"Everyone makes mistakes," Jack said with a small smile. "Maybe falling for a man who wasn't single wasn't the best idea, but I bet you were good to him. I bet you made him feel special and important. Love is complicated, and we all make a mess of it at some point."

Stella picked up her cold pizza crust and pointed it at Jack. "Says the hero." She took one last bite.

Jack shook his head. "I'm just one guy who made a good decision. Anyone can be a hero if they want to be. This is *your* story. You get to write it. I think it's time you stop writing yourself as the loner or the aimless heroine."

"What about the bitter crone?" Stella teased. She unfolded her paper towel, wiped her hands on it, and stood. "In the chapter with Wade, I'm pretty sure I was the pathetic nobody."

Jack pushed away from the desk and stood. "Says who?" His anger startled her. "Says the guy who was resentful about what he couldn't give you? The guy who wouldn't make time for you because he had a list of excuses? The guy who shined a light on what he thought were your shortcomings? It sounds to me like he wanted it all—you, the kids, his wife—and he expected you to agree that your life together would always be on *his* terms. It doesn't sound like what you wanted mattered a great deal to him. That's not love. That's selfishness. He did you a favor by disappearing, even though it hurt you. But he's not the verdict on your worthiness, Stella. Look at you. You're smart and kind and weird and funny . . . and beautiful." Jack closed the distance between them.

His intensity and willingness to defend her astonished her. Stella hadn't been called beautiful since Wade whispered it one night in his car. Jack reached for her and twined their hands together. The contact stole her breath.

"If he failed to see and appreciate you and treat you as worthy of so much love and respect, then he never deserved you. Only a fool would take for granted and gamble with something as precious and rare as love. I've known you for a scattering of moments, and I can see who you are."

His hands sent warmth through hers and radiated up her arms. "What do you see?" she asked.

"I can see how lucky any man would be to stand in your light. I see how deserving you are of love."

Her heart fluttered wildly. Jack was so close to her, so close she could see the dark blue flecks in his hazel eyes.

"Have you ever been kissed by a character from a book? Other than Hook?"

"No," she said as he came closer. "But I've daydreamed about it lots of times."

Jack grinned. "I bet you have." He leaned down to kiss her.

"Stella Parker!" Wearing bright pink scrubs that matched the strand of dye in her blond hair, Ariel looked like a streak of color as she rushed across the foyer toward the circulation desk.

Jack and Stella jumped apart quickly. Lightheaded and filled with yearning, Stella reached out to the desk to steady herself.

"Ariel," Stella said, surprised at how breathless she sounded.

Ariel laid her arms on the high top of the desk and shifted her gaze from Stella to Jack and then back to Stella.

"You two are as lit up as a pair of sparklers. What is going on here?"

"Nothing!" Jack and Stella said together.

Then someone screamed.

Chapter 15

Ariel flinched, and Stella turned toward the screaming. Shouts peppered the air, sounding like kids on a roller-coaster ride. Although the voices didn't sound terrified, the chill ripping through Stella's body told her they weren't screams of excitement either. Firecracker words whizzed through the air, blowing the grease-stained paper towels off the desk. **On the run. Bottles of rum. Surprise.**

Thunder rumbled outside the library, and a bolt of lightning illuminated the nearest window, shooting white light inside the building and flashing off the polished bookshelves.

"Tell me that's part of some group activity you have going on tonight," Ariel said, her voice uncertain.

"The book club," Stella said.

"Come on," Jack said, grabbing Stella's hand and pulling her through the library.

Ariel followed them. "What's going on?"

They ran to the spot where Stella had left the book club attendees. Chaos had overtaken the space. Overturned chairs disrupted the neat horseshoe arrangement. A few books had been tossed around, some lying face up and staring at the scene, while others were face down with crumpled, distressed pages. An uncapped blue ink pen rolled across the center of the area as though trying to escape.

One woman sprinted past them with her purse clutched to her chest like a precious child. Four women were huddled together near a bookshelf, holding on to one another's arms like a broken game of red rover. Another woman sat with her feet propped on the chair next to her. She watched the scene unfold while eating a cookie. She made eye contact with Stella and shrugged.

Vicki rushed toward Stella and clutched her arm. "Stella, I am so sorry."

"Vicki!" Stella said. "What are you doing here? I thought you went home for the evening." How had Vicki returned without Stella knowing? Had she been that absorbed in Jack?

"I did, but I forgot I needed a book from the archives for a research paper I'm working on," Vicki said quickly. "Arnie lets me take some of the historic books home. When I went down there tonight, that man was *still* tied up."

"There was a man tied up in the archives?" Ariel interrupted, looking at Stella in disbelief.

Vicki continued, "You said someone was going to come pick him up, so why was he still down there? He begged me to help him, and he was so pitiful. I couldn't just leave him there. It's *wrong*, Stella. But once I untied him, he knocked me out of the way and ran off. I tried to follow him, and then I heard a lot of commotion coming from up here. I think he's still intoxicated. Should I call the police?"

"There's a drunk in here?" Ariel asked, her eyes continually widening.

Stella's body felt blasted by an arctic freeze. "Hook," she whispered. She pried Vicki's fingers from her arm. "Give me a second, okay? Try to calm everyone down. See if anyone needs assistance."

"Hook what?" Ariel asked. "Stella, this is out of control. What in heaven's name is happening? This place feels like chaos, fear, and deception have fused."

"We'll explain later," Jack said to Ariel.

The only man in the book club stared down an aisle with his closed umbrella in his hand, pointing it at someone just out of sight. Thunder boomed.

"Let her go," the man demanded.

"I don't think so, mate," another man responded in a thick accent.

"Hook," Stella repeated with dread.

Hook continued, "I'm not holding her against her will. It's obvious she needs a bit of fun."

"She's my *wife*," the man argued. "Marsha, get back here."

"Tim," Marsha answered from down the aisle, her voice pinched and nasally. "You see the *hook*, right?"

Tim's hand squeezed on the umbrella handle, and he lifted it higher. "Don't make me use this."

"Planning to teach me a lesson with that useless weapon, are you?" Hook's laugh raised the hairs on Stella's arms.

"Ariel, stay here," Stella said. "Help Vicki if you can. I promise we'll explain everything."

Stella and Jack hurried over to the end of the aisle to stand beside Tim. Hook stood with one arm looped around Marsha, who appeared somehow less frightened than she should have been. The way she gazed up at Hook made Stella worry that Marsha wasn't interested in fighting her way out of the pirate's embrace. Hook tilted back a plastic water bottle and gulped down the contents. He grimaced and dropped the bottle on the floor. Water spilled out in an arc across the tiles.

"Couldn't afford the good stuff, mate?" Hook asked. He squeezed Marsha closer to him and buried his face in her teased, oversprayed hair. "I only have the best on my ship."

"Is there really *good stuff* when it comes to bottled water?" Stella asked.

"That's not water," Tim said. "It's rum. Or it was. And it's not cheap."

Stella gaped at Tim. "You brought alcohol into the library? That's against the rules."

"Are you seriously reprimanding me about library rules when a psychopath has my wife?" Tim asked.

"She doesn't exactly look like a damsel in distress," Stella said.

"Love," Hook called, turning his sly-eyed gaze on Stella, "there's no reason to fight over me. There's room enough for both of you." Using his hook, he motioned Stella toward him.

A cannon blast of thunder sounded, rattling books on the shelves, followed by a streak of lightning that illuminated Hook from behind.

"What should we—" Stella asked Jack, but when she turned to look at him, he wasn't beside her. "Jack?"

The woman sitting in the chair pointed down the next aisle, and Stella's eyes widened. Thunder boomed again as the storm approached, and Stella returned her attention to Hook. A shadow stretched behind him as Jack appeared around the bookshelf.

"Let her go, Hook," Jack demanded.

Hook's back stiffened, but he recovered quickly. He spun around with Marsha still pressed against his side. Hook shoved Marsha away from him. She gasped and stumbled toward the bookshelf and then to her knees.

A blade glinted in Jack's right hand. "Wasn't last time enough to make you want to stay tied up? For your own safety, of course."

Blackened words squeezed out from between books on the shelves before dropping to the floor and circling Hook's boots. **Sneak. Ashes. Swept away.**

Hook's eyes narrowed, and he repositioned his hand to where his sword should have been sheathed, but thankfully Crusoe had taken it. "I have fitting plans for you, mate, but not tonight."

Hook sprinted toward Jack and knocked him out of the way. His heavy boots slapped against the tiles until he was gone. Marsha pushed herself up off the floor and gawked at them. Jack met Stella's gaze, and then he ran off, shouting at Hook.

Ariel appeared at Stella's side and gripped her best friend's hand. "Did Jack have a knife?" she whispered.

"Wh-where did he go?" Marsha stuttered.

Stella and Ariel hurried down the aisle and helped Marsha to her feet as she wobbled on her heeled sandals.

"Where did that man go?" Marsha asked again. "Why would the library let someone like that in?"

"I'm sorry, Marsha," Stella said. "This is a public building, and we're not allowed to turn people away. However, we can report troublemakers. That man was here earlier as . . . an impersonator, but he has a drinking problem, so we asked him to leave. I guess he came back because he was angry. I'm so sorry he manhandled you. Are you okay? Did he hurt you?"

Marsha shook her head. "Drinking problem. I understand that." Her gaze traveled to her husband, who scowled and walked toward them. "He's awful good-looking, though. Such a waste of a good face. You think he could work through his issues with some counseling?"

Stella's brow wrinkled. "I suppose." Did Marsha sound hopeful, as though she could have a future with Hook?

"Marsha," Tim said, reaching for his wife. "Are you okay?" He pulled her into his arms and crushed her against his chest. "Where did that man go? We need to call the police. He could have hurt someone."

Stella jabbed her thumb over her shoulder. "My friend went to catch him. I was telling your wife that he's a disgruntled impersonator we hired earlier to entertain the children, but it didn't work out. I'm sorry for all the trouble. I hope this won't tarnish your devotion to book club."

Tim released his grip on Marsha so he could look at her face. "You sure you're okay? Let's get you home." He smoothed his hands down her stiff hair, which sounded like he was petting prickly grass. Then he slipped his arm around Marsha's shoulders. "You can't control everyone," he said to Stella. "It's not your fault, but I hope you'll follow the proper procedures and let the police know about this. He's not the kind of man who should be wandering around town."

Stella puffed out her cheeks and exhaled. "Definitely not. And next time you come to the library, you leave the booze at home."

Tim's eyebrows lifted, and Marsha snorted into his shoulder. "Understood," he said as he and his wife walked away.

Stella wanted to rush after Jack, but surely he could handle himself. The library meeting space was a mess. "I need to clean this up. You don't have to stay, Ariel. I can call you later."

"No can do," Ariel said. "You're not getting rid of me until I know what's going on here, and why would I leave you to clean up this mess alone?"

"Vicki's here—"

"I found everyone and apologized," Vicki said, "except for the people who were already spinning their tires speeding out of the parking lot." Her red hair was wilder than ever and her expression showcased her exhaustion. "We'll need to do damage control for the ones who got away."

"Why don't you go home, Vicki?" Stella said. "I'll handle cleaning up."

"You'll call the police, right?" Vicki persisted. "I saw Jack run off after that man."

"Outside the library?" Stella's concern returned.

Vicki shook her head. "Down in the archives, but the police, yes? You'll call them and have them apprehend the Hook impersonator?"

Stella nodded, even though she had no intention of calling the police. "I'll get the library put back together, and I'll find out who was at tonight's meeting and reach out to them personally. You go on home."

Vicki shuffled her blue flats against the tiles. "I'm really sorry about tonight. I don't agree with you keeping him tied up in the archives, but I can see why you did. I wish his employer had come sooner. You'd think they would have taken you seriously and picked him up already."

"If only," Stella said.

Vicki patted at her unruly hair. "See you tomorrow."

"Good night, Vicki."

The rain continued to batter the library as the thunder and lightning storm settled over Blue Sky Valley. Rough winds whipped around the edges of the building, and the trees bent and groaned. Stella and Ariel worked in silence as they cleaned up the meeting area. Every few minutes, Stella glanced over her shoulder, expecting Hook to return, but he never did. She tried not to worry about Jack and where he'd gone.

With the last chair righted, Ariel said, "If I'm understanding all of this, a Captain Hook impersonator with a drinking problem showed up earlier today, you tied him up in the archives until his employer could get him, Vicki found him hours later and untied him, he returned with revenge on his mind and wrecked the book club, and Jack was going to duel him with a knife. Did I miss anything? Oh, perhaps the real story about Jack, a *friend* of Arnie's who has been spending all day with *you* instead. Just a good citizen helping out at the library?"

Stella closed her eyes and sighed. "It's all complete madness right now." She opened her eyes and looked at Ariel. "If I tell you the truth, you're not going to believe it."

Ariel fisted her hands on her hips. "I believe in *way* more outrageous things than you do."

"You have a point," Stella said. "And I would have agreed with that until today."

"So tell me this truth that you don't think I'll believe," Ariel said. "I'm your best friend, and I have a feeling Jack already knows."

"Jack is a big part of it," Stella agreed. "There's something Arnie hadn't told me about the library, something *big*—"

Jack returned and interrupted Stella's explanation. "No sign of Hook anywhere. Crusoe said that one second he was in the chair, and the next second, he was gone. But Crusoe admitted that he took a nap. Vicki must have freed Hook during that time. Darcy hasn't seen him either."

Stella squeezed her fingers around the back of a chair. "Arnie is going to lose it when he finds out what I've done. This is a small town. You think they won't talk about this? They certainly will. Then word will get back to Arnie lickety-split, and he'll think I've become incompetent. Letting drunkards into the library. Not that I actually let a drunk man in . . . but it's also a public place, and if someone intoxicated shows up, I can't tell people no. Maybe I can spin it that way. I absolutely don't want to tell him that I used the ink and brought Hook out of *Peter Pan*."

Jack walked over and touched Stella's arm. "Hey, breathe for a minute, will you? We're going to figure this out."

"Will we?" Stella asked. "Because I don't see how. A supervillain is loose in the library, and we can't find him."

"I'm sorry, what?" Ariel interjected. "I'm not following the ink and the bringing him out of *Peter Pan* thing. Is this about the impersonator?"

Stella sighed. "He's not really an impersonator."

Jack leaned his hip against a bookshelf. "And I don't think he's quite the supervillain. Now if you'd brought out Voldemort, maybe."

Stella's mouth dropped open. "How do you know about him?"

"You don't think I like to read too?" Jack asked. "Anyway, Hook's a rogue pirate, but he's mostly interested in women and rum and fighting the Lost Boys, who aren't here."

"What about him leaving the library?" Stella asked. "What if he's already gone? How would we ever find him?"

Jack placed both hands on her arms. "Breathe, Stella. Most of us *don't* leave. Even the really nasty ones."

Stella tried to inhale a slow, deep breath but failed when her lungs constricted. "What about the nobleman and Belle, was it? I completely forgot about them until now. I haven't seen them since Arnie's heart attack."

Jack nodded. "That was their last evening."

Anxiety's vise grip on Stella's chest lessened. "So everyone is accounted for. Except Hook, and speaking of him, it sounded like this wasn't your first encounter."

"Arnie let him out once before," Jack said as he counted on his fingers. "Five years ago, I think. He thought a pirate from a children's story might be interesting and relatively harmless. But Hook is not how Arnie imagined him."

"He's a disturbing mash-up of versions," Stella said. "How is that possible?"

"I'm not sure how we're altered when we leave our stories and come here."

Stella walked toward the circulation desk, and Jack followed. "What happened between you two? If Crusoe hadn't taken his sword, I think he would have fought you."

Jack didn't respond right away. The windows illuminated with another lightning strike before going dark again. Words slithered across the tiles. **Ending. Gasp. Wail.** She rubbed her hands up and down her arms.

"What happened?" she asked again.

Jack glanced down at his hands. "Hook had been moderately tame for the first week, but then he lost his patience with this place. An annoying kid kept pestering his sister, and Hook appeared and decided to shut the kid up by choking the life out of him. Arnie yelled for me, so I snuck up behind Hook. I only meant to coerce him into letting the kid go. So I flashed my knife, but Hook lunged toward me, and I stabbed him in the gut. It killed him— Well, it sent him back early. He's obviously not dead."

Stella gasped. "You can do that? I thought if characters die in this world, they disappear everywhere."

Jack exhaled. "Not exactly. If they die near the source of the magic, they just go back into their books. Since the magic is stored in the library, the characters are, in a way, bound to the library because it's where they're brought to life. But if characters get too far away from the source and die, then—"

"Then we lose them forever," Stella finished.

Jack nodded. "But having to send someone back early is the last choice because you have to 'kill' them, and that's not something Arnie or I are keen on."

Stella grimaced. "Does it hurt them?"

"I don't know," Jack admitted, "but Hook made a big show of

'dying' before he disappeared. Then he turned to ashes, and Arnie swept him into a dustpan, and we dumped him in the garbage. We had to convince the kid it was all part of an elaborate magic show. I doubt he ever annoyed his sister again. Afterward, Arnie and I never talked about what had happened. We didn't have to. We both understood it was unintentional but also a welcome reprieve."

Stella rubbed her fists against her eyes. The idea that the characters brought out of the books could turn to ashes if they were *killed* in the library disturbed her. "Of all the characters I could choose."

"Don't be so hard on yourself. You didn't really believe me."

She rolled her eyes. "No excuse. I could have chosen Anne Shirley or a Care Bear. I'm sorry, Jack. For all of this." Thunder boomed loudly, and Stella flinched. She glanced around the library. "Should we keep looking for Hook?"

Ariel cleared her throat and startled both Stella and Jack. Stella had forgotten Ariel was still there.

"Hi, yeah, still here. So I'm following along as best as I can, which, *believe me*, feels like I've been thrown into a movie halfway through and expected to catch up without asking questions. Jack, am I clear on the fact that you *killed* a man but he didn't die and instead turned to ashes?"

"Oh, well, he didn't actually kill anyone," Stella responded. "Because that man isn't . . . or wasn't . . ."

"Uh-huh," Ariel said. "Clear as mud. Because that man is *from a book*? Are you trying to explain to me, albeit terribly, that you can bring characters out of books to roam around the library? And that roguish pirate is actually Captain Hook from *Peter Pan*? You're right, Stella, this sounds outrageous. But . . ."

"But what?" Stella asked.

"Fascinating!" Ariel said, an enormous smile breaking across her face. "How is this possible? Can I bring someone out?"

"No!" Stella and Jack said together.

Ariel held up her hands. "Okay, okay. No reason to freak out. Just so you know, I'd choose better than Captain Hook. How was he *not* going to be awful? He's a pirate who tries to kill children."

"He doesn't actually *kill* children. He swordfights them mostly," Stella argued.

Ariel smirked. "Well, that makes him a much safer option."

Stella's shoulders slumped. "I didn't think it would work."

Ariel looked at Jack. "And how do you fit into all of this, Jack?"

He made eye contact with Stella, and she shrugged, telling him to go ahead and share the truth. "I'm from one of Stella's favorite novels."

Ariel inhaled a sharp breath. "You're Jack from *Beyond the Southern Horizon*?" She pointed at Stella. "You brought out a love interest and you won't let me choose a character? Aren't there rules about personal gain and magic?"

Stella's mouth fell open, and Jack laughed before saying, "Actually Arnie brought me out before his heart attack."

"Wow," Ariel said. "This is a lot, Stella. No wonder you've been avoiding talking to me. I want to learn more about all of this, but a more pressing question is, what are y'all going to do about Hook?"

Stella glanced at the clock on the wall. It was almost nine o'clock and time to lock up the library for the night. "I can close up, and then we can make a final sweep. Ariel, why don't you go on home? It's late, and it's been a long day. We can catch up tomorrow."

"And you'll tell me everything about this library magic?"

Stella pulled Ariel into a hug. "I promise. Thank you for not freaking out."

Ariel laughed. "Oh, I'm freaking out but also handling it well. Until tomorrow." She pointed her finger at Jack. "You take care of her. No pirate mishaps."

"You have my promise," Jack said with a slight bow of his head.

Ariel waved good night to Jack, and Stella walked her to the front door. "This is kinda surreal," Ariel said.

"Tell me about it," Stella agreed.

"Are you okay, like *really* okay?" Ariel asked, studying Stella with her large eyes. "With Arnie in the hospital and those painful words that show up unannounced, and now Jack, who's clearly into you, plus a pirate on the loose."

Stella rubbed her left temple. "My life is a complete disaster. Ever since I burned that journal."

Ariel's eyebrows lifted. "That could have been the catalyst for all of this."

"That's what I believe," Stella said. "I think burning those words set loose all these other events too. Like dominoes." *More like dynamite.* "I don't know how, but burning my heartbroken words freed my heart."

Tears filled Ariel's eyes. She touched Stella's arm. "I've been wanting your heart to be free for so long."

"Me too," Stella said. "But I'm no closer to understanding what those painful words mean, and having the added complication of Jack and the library just adds to my confusion."

Ariel scrunched up her nose. "Is Jack a complication?"

"Good question," Stella said honestly. "In a way, yes, because I—"

"Because you're totally into him!" Ariel said in a dramatic whisper, glancing over Stella's shoulder to locate Jack.

"Without getting too deep into the workings of everything, what you don't know is that the people from the books can only be here for two weeks, the same amount of time you're allowed to check out a library book."

Ariel's disappointment pushed out her lips. "Jack can't stay?"

Stella shook her head with the leaden reminder.

Ariel twirled the crescent moon earring in her right ear. "Regardless, Jack and the library might be part of what leads you to understanding all of this, including yourself and the new words. Call me tomorrow."

"Be careful in this weather." Stella locked the library doors behind her. She waved through the glass as Ariel dashed into the rain.

Stella returned to the desk, her thoughts whirling. "If we find Hook, what should we do? Tie him up again?"

"That's probably our best option."

Rain slashed against the windows, and Stella watched the raging storm for a moment. "Where should we start?"

Jack slipped his hands into his pockets. "Hook likes to brood. That much I know about him. He's likely plotting revenge in a hideout somewhere, but he'll also be searching for his sword, which he won't find. There's a back corner in the archives floor where the stones are loose, and Crusoe hid it. If we can't subdue Hook, you won't like my suggestion for how to get rid of him."

Stella's expression twisted. "You don't mean turn him to ashes, do you? Because I won't be able to stab him. I'd more likely stab myself in the process."

"Leave the stabbing to me," he said. "The other option would be to buy a case of rum and let him drink himself into a stupor."

Stella groaned. "Our two options are murder or breaking not only the library rules but also the law by having *a case* of rum in a public building that's open to children. I'm not interested in jail time."

"That's a no on the rum, then?" She cut her gaze at him, and he offered her a comforting smile. "We'll get through this together. I promise."

Together. The word wrapped around her heart like a hug. Her breath stilled, and a flicker of hope appeared inside her. She wanted to tamp it down—hope was dangerous—but looking at Jack's smile, she didn't want to close herself off or push him away. She wanted to pretend for a few minutes that she was together with a handsome man who made her almost believe everything *would* work out.

With the help of Crusoe and Darcy, Stella and Jack spent the next half hour scouring every corner and opening every door. Hook was a no-show and didn't respond to threats, name calling, or insults of any kind.

At nearly ten Stella dropped into the chair behind the circulation desk. "I think we should call it a night. At this point, I'm so exhausted I don't care where he is or if he shows up as soon as I leave."

The thunder and lightning had dissipated, but the rain continued to fall in dark, fast-moving sheets.

Jack looked toward the windows. "Crusoe can keep an eye out for him, but I bet Hook will sulk a while longer. Why don't you stay at Arnie's tonight? He wouldn't care, and you won't have to drive home in this weather. After all this rain, the roads will be slick."

Jack had a point. The day had been so long and full that it felt like a week's worth of time folded into one day, leaving her weary and emotionally drained. She could run across the grass and go to bed without having to drive through the rainstorm.

"That's a great idea," she said, reaching for her purse.

With the book club disaster and then searching for Hook, Stella had forgotten what she and Jack had been doing right before Ariel and the screaming interrupted them. The memory returned as she faced Jack. He had been seconds away from *kissing* her.

"Well, good night, Jack," she said. "I'll see you in the morning?"

He nodded. "Give me a few minutes, will you? Don't leave until I get back."

Stella leaned against the counter while she waited. In an unexpected moment of foolishness, she gave herself permission to daydream about what it would be like to kiss Jack. Without much effort, her imagination took off on feathery wings. Minutes later, her eyes snapped open when she heard Jack's footsteps. She touched her fingertips to her cheeks, feeling her warm, flushed skin.

"Crusoe and Darcy will keep watch for Hook," he said.

Baby-blue words as fluffy as goose-down pillows slid out from beneath her sandals. **Don't go. Come closer. Hope.** She tried to step on them before Jack noticed.

"I'll see you tomorrow, then," she said, awkwardly riffling through her purse in search of her keys.

Jack reached out for her hand, twining his fingers with hers. "I'll walk you home."

"In this weather?" she asked in surprise, even though the idea thrilled her.

He grinned. "I'll *run* you home. Probably at a full-out sprint, but yes, I'd like to see you safely to Arnie's."

"Can you . . . leave the library?" Stella asked. Panic speared through her at the thought of something happening to him.

He squeezed her fingers gently. "There's nothing to worry about as long as I come back. Will you let me walk you home?"

Stella nodded, and happiness swelled inside her. She flipped off the library's lights, leaving the one light on over the circulation desk. She set the alarm, which would give them sixty seconds to leave, then she pushed open the back door only to have the wind slam it shut again.

"This is going to be fun," she said, pushing open the heavy door again. "I hope you know how to swim. It might be more water than land out there."

She and Jack rushed out the door and jumped down the stairs. They were soaked within seconds. The lawn between the library and Arnie's cottage was a soggy mess, as if they were hightailing it through a marsh instead of across the grass. Her sandals gave her no traction, and she slid over the ground like someone wearing roller skates.

When they reached the cottage, Stella stood beneath the sheltered side porch, wheezing and laughing. Her wet curls were plastered to her face and dripping down her back. She shoved them off her cheeks. Jack's face was shadowed in the darkness, but she could tell he was smiling. Watery words formed in the raindrops over his shoulder. **Breathless. Whisper. Come here.**

"Thanks for running me home, Jack. I really—"

He stepped toward her and pressed his mouth against hers, his lips warm and wet with rain. Desire moved through her lightning-fast, her body responding naturally to his closeness. A tingling sensation in her chest spread a slow, pins-and-needles-type burn, waking up all the parts of her that had been sleeping or hiding from intimacy for months. She pressed her palms against his chest, feeling the warmth of him through his wet shirt. He slid his hand to the back of her head and pulled her closer, then looped his other arm around her waist, holding her.

She couldn't remember the last time she'd been properly kissed. Wade had kissed her, but they'd never found a rhythm that worked well, and she'd always thought of his kisses as a desperate escape for him, always on a timer.

Jack kissed her like he could go all night, and more than that, like he *wanted* to go all night.

He let his hands slide up her sides. She felt his heat through the thin, wet fabric of her blouse.

He stopped kissing her long enough to say, "I think I should come inside. Make sure you get in safely."

"Oh, I'll be fine—"

"I'd *like* to come inside, Stella."

Stella's lips formed a small *o*, and her heart thumped a frantic beat in her chest. He wanted to come inside. "You'll be gone in a few days," she said before she could stop herself. Just saying the words swept low-grade grief through her.

"But I'm here now. I don't want to leave you yet."

Stella's heart pounded and begged her to dive into the moment. "I don't want you to leave either."

She fumbled for Arnie's key on her key ring. Then she unlocked the door, turned the knob, and looked over her shoulder at Jack as she pushed it open. He looped his arm around her waist and tugged her toward him, leaning down to kiss her as they stumbled through the open door, locked together and dripping water all over the hardwood.

Chapter 16

Stella dropped her purse on the floor as Jack closed the cottage door with his foot, then reached back to twist the lock on the doorknob, never once breaking from their kiss. He slow walked them into the living room, and they moved as one, as though they couldn't separate long enough to decide where to go.

A frenzy of longing overtook her. She couldn't keep her hands off him. Every time her fingers grazed his skin she felt the pull to him grow stronger and more intense. For the first time in a long time, Stella's thoughts were full of one person and nothing else. There wasn't enough space in her mind for anything but Jack—his kisses, his touch, his hands in her hair.

Her legs backed into the couch. Jack pulled away and looked at her. The streetlights cast a dim glow into the room, just enough to see his features.

"This is fast," he said. "Too fast?"

Stella pressed her lips together and tried to gather a response, but all she could think was how life-giving, soul-soaring it was to be kissed by him. Kissing Jack might not be the best decision, with him leaving soon, but now that she'd been close to him, she craved more. "I don't know," she said quietly.

His arms rested around her waist, and he slid one hand up to her neck and then to her cheek. "I can tell you good night. I've seen you to Arnie's safely."

She still felt the imprint of his lips pressing against hers. "I don't want you to go."

His hand warmed her skin. "I don't have to."

"Then don't," Stella said, surprised at her boldness.

Jack kissed her again. He guided their bodies down toward the couch. When Stella sat on the cushion, she hesitated and pushed them back to standing.

"We can't," she said.

Jack tensed in her arms. "Okay." He released his hold on her and took a step back.

Stella wrapped her arms around his waist. "No, I mean, we can't get on Arnie's couch. It's leather, and we're soaking wet."

His shoulders relaxed, and he chuckled. He pressed kisses up the side of her neck. "We have a few options."

Stella's eyes closed, and she leaned her head to the side to give him easier access to the sensitive skin on her neck. She slid her hands up his chest and sighed. "I'm interested in hearing them."

"There's the floor," he said, kissing along her jawline. "There's Arnie's room, but that seems inappropriate." He kissed her cheek. "There's the couch, but we'd have to lose the wet clothes. Your choice." He kissed her lips.

Stella's whole body quivered. *Is this really happening?* Then anxiety clawed at her—a bitter, familiar warning—but she forced her thoughts into the present with Jack. She wanted to enjoy this moment. Let her excitement soar. Give herself permission to feel light and blissful—emotions no longer foreign. The desire to let go and be reckless overtook her. She'd been playing it safe and disconnected for months, perhaps even years. But now she didn't want to detach herself from the hot ache searing through her body. She didn't want to push Jack away.

She lifted one side of his T-shirt and touched his bare skin. He watched her, and his mouth tugged up on one side, causing Stella's heart to thump.

"I like your choice," he said and reached for a button on her blouse, easily undoing it.

Then Jack kissed her so deeply that she fisted her hands in his shirt and held on.

✦ ✦ ✦

FRIDAY MORNING STELLA opened her eyes to 1940s music playing at low volume. She inhaled the scent of coffee and bacon cooking. Pushing up on one elbow, she glanced toward the kitchen where Jack was moving around. Was he cooking breakfast?

Discarded shoes and clothes were scattered across the floor. A Jimmy Dorsey record spun on Arnie's record player in the corner. Stella wore a white undershirt she'd pilfered from Arnie's dresser drawer. The shirt was too big for her but only fell to mid-thigh. She reached for the blanket and pulled it up to her waist, covering her bare legs. Sunlight drenched the living room with pale summer light. As her mind fully awoke, she replayed last night in her mind, and her body tingled with the memory.

"Good morning," Jack said.

She repositioned herself on the couch so she could see him. "Hey."

"Hungry?" he asked. "I made eggs and bacon. Biscuits are almost ready. Want coffee? Arnie doesn't have creamer, but there's plenty of sugar. I know you like yours sweet."

Jack stood in the kitchen wearing boxer shorts and nothing else. As if that wasn't the most distracting sight she'd ever seen. A cowlick at the back of his head caused his dark hair to stick up in one spot, which was completely adorable. Stella stared at his physique for a few seconds before answering.

"This feels like a dream," she said. He'd woken up and made breakfast. For her.

Jack grinned and returned to the stove. "'All that we see or seem is but a dream within a dream.'"

"You read Poe?" Stella asked.

"I've had a lot of time," Jack said. "If this is a dream, I'd prefer to stay asleep. Don't wake me up, okay?" He leaned over to glance at the biscuits through the glass oven door. "But being here with you feels like I'm truly awake, and the rest of my life has been a dream."

Stella stared down at her lap before getting up off the couch. "Be right back." She went to the bathroom and searched through Arnie's cabinets until she found an unopened toothbrush so she could brush her teeth. Then she wet her hair and combed her fingers through her tangled curls. In the bedroom she found a pen on Arnie's side table and used it to pin her hair up in a messy bun. When she walked out, Jack stood in the kitchen, holding a mug of coffee for her. She self-consciously pulled at the T-shirt, trying to tug it lower.

"You're a real dish, you know that?" he said sweetly.

She chuckled and walked to him. "Thank you." She grabbed the mug.

Jack kissed her cheek. "I could get used to this, seeing you first thing in the morning, making you breakfast, drinking coffee with you."

What would that life be like—a life where a handsome man *wanted* to be with her every morning? Hope rose inside her, hesitant and unpracticed, as though it wasn't sure if it was safe to stretch out. She sipped the coffee and hummed in approval as the warmth slid down her throat and filled her chest.

Jack had set the table for two, and Stella sat in one of the chairs. "Can I help you with anything?"

"No, ma'am. I have this under control." He removed the biscuits from the oven. Their buttery scent filled the kitchen, and her stomach growled in response. "How'd you sleep?"

Stella glanced at the couch. "Not bad. For a couch." She'd never slept on a couch with anyone before. She assumed it would be too uncomfortable and cramped to sleep much, but it hadn't been that bad. She'd been content to sleep pressed against Jack's side with her head on his chest. Once she'd fallen asleep, she didn't remember anything else about the night other than having a sense of peace and relaxation. "You?"

"Like a dream," he said and winked. "Like I said, I could get used to this."

While he finished making breakfast, Stella reached for a paper napkin and a pen left behind on the table. Words blew through her like a traveling breeze.

> *Your shadow on the wall quickens my pulse,*
> *the outline of your sleeping form*
> *illuminated by the starlight.*
> *The heat of you stretching across the couch,*
> *reaching me and pulling me nearer.*
> *The steady rise and fall, the calming sound*
> *of your sleepy breaths,*
> *pressing me into sleep.*

In this half dream,
if we can make promises
that we don't have to keep,
will you promise to never leave?

She folded the napkin in half and slid it to the side of the table. The song changed on the record, and Stella watched Jack, allowing herself to savor this time with him. For a brief moment she thought about the purple words from yesterday and their reference to an excruciatingly handsome man. Whose story were they telling? Hers? Would more be coming? She opened her eyes just as Jack brought over the food. Were the words connected to Jack?

"This is extravagant," Stella said. She filled her plate with scrambled eggs, pieces of bacon, and a biscuit covered with melting butter. "I can't remember the last time I had a sit-down breakfast. Maybe it was when we celebrated Arnie's birthday and went over to Grits & Gravy, the diner up the street."

Jack slathered jelly on his steaming biscuit. "My brothers couldn't be bothered with the kitchen, but I remember being fascinated by my mama cooking and baking. She'd pull a chair over to the counter when I was young, and she'd let me help her with the easy stuff—rolling out biscuits or mixing cookie dough. When I got older, I cooked a lot because I enjoyed it."

Stella swallowed a mouthful of eggs and reached for her coffee. "Your author created all that backstory?"

Jack shrugged. "No idea," he said and then chuckled. "But it's all here." He tapped the side of his head.

"I'm an awful cook, but I'm a whiz with the microwave." After a sip, she asked, "Do you know what a microwave is?"

Jack laughed. "Of course. I've been here enough to learn more about technology. As for cooking, I can teach you."

Stella almost smiled, but she instantly realized that if Jack were to teach her how to cook, he'd have to be around, and according to the time clock in her head, he would be gone in less than three days. *Gone.*

He reached over and touched her hand. "You okay?"

She breathed past the tightening in her chest. *Enjoy yourself while you can. You knew this was temporary. But life is temporary. Hold on to this moment.* She let her eyes trail over his handsome face, the straight lines of his jaw, the fullness of his lips.

"Just thinking about what a terrible time that would be for you. I'm a disaster in the kitchen. All thumbs, I think. Percy and I tried to make a cake one year for Dad's birthday, and it rose lopsided and was as grainy as dirt. It kinda tasted like pine tar, but I'm pretty sure that's because Percy used too much molasses because we didn't have brown sugar."

Jack laughed. "I doubt Percy was the best teacher for cooking."

"Definitely not. He excels at everything except cooking. Hence why I'm a whiz at the microwave." She bit into the biscuit. "This is delicious. Teach me how to make these first."

They finished breakfast and carried their dishes to the sink. Stella paused when she glanced at the calendar Arnie had pinned to the refrigerator with an *I'm a Librarian. Don't Make Me Shush You* magnet. Arnie had drawn a blue circle around Saturday's date. Stella stared at the circle trying to understand the significance of the day.

"Tomorrow is the Blue Sky Valley Festival," she blurted. "How has it gotten here so fast? I forgot to talk to Arnie about it yesterday because I was so focused on the magic."

Jack took the plate from her hands, ran it under the water, and scrubbed it clean. "What needs to be done?"

"Arnie always spearheads it. With the town committee, of course." Stella rubbed the back of her neck. "There's so much that goes on. So many vendors and people and activities. Some people use the library and others will be out on the grounds. I don't have a map or times or anything. I bet it's in one of the folders at the circulation desk. I also need to get my booth arranged for the military care packages."

Jack dried the plates and placed them back in the cabinet. "You've been his copilot for years. You can do this," he said. "Do you know where he keeps the folders?"

Stella nodded, grabbed her unfinished coffee, and drank the rest in a few gulps. She walked toward the kitchen window and stared out at the lawn between the cottage and the library. The space would be crowded with people expecting a completely functional festival tomorrow. A car pulled into the back lot and parked. The library wouldn't open for a couple hours, so they were either extremely early or using the parking lot as a temporary spot.

"You're right," Stella said, facing Jack. "He's so organized. I'll go through the folders and call the head of the committee and ask her to give me a rundown. She might already know about Arnie, but she might not. I hadn't thought to call her."

Jack grabbed Stella's hands. "First thing you should do is go home, shower, and change clothes. Call Vicki and Dan to make sure they plan to help out on Saturday. If you have time and you think he'll be awake, you can swing by the hospital and talk to Arnie about specifics. I'll clean up here and meet you in the library. Tell me where the folders are, and I'll look through them while you're gone."

The image of a silver hook flashed into her mind. "I've been so distracted, I forgot about Hook!"

Jack wiggled his eyebrows playfully at her. "A good distraction?"

Stella blushed and then sobered. "I'm serious. We can't have him running amok during the festival. What if we can't find him?"

"I'll handle it," Jack assured her.

Looking at him lessened her worry. Her expression softened.

"What?" he asked.

She kissed his lips gently. "Thank you."

"For what?"

"For making me feel like we can actually make this work," she said.

Jack reached for her. "I have no doubt that we *will* make this work. Our goal will be to make this the best festival yet."

A fist hammering on the door sounded, and Stella's heart leaped into her throat. She looked questioningly at Jack, and he appeared as surprised as she was.

She whispered, "Maybe they'll go away."

The knocking persisted.

Stella shook her head. "I can't open the door." She pointed to her bare legs.

"I can see movement in there," a man's voice called through the door. A shadowy face pressed against the wavy glass window in the door.

"Percy?" Stella said. Without thinking, she unlocked the door and flung it open.

Her older brother stood on the doorstep with a cross between a scowl and a look of bewilderment on his face. He wore a teal golf polo and pressed khakis with a pair of white loafers, looking every bit the beach preppy she expected. Percy scanned her clothes—or lack of clothing—and his dark eyebrows lifted.

"What are you doing here?" he asked.

"What are *you* doing here?" she repeated.

"Arnie had the hospital call me," Percy said and stepped into the cottage without being invited. "I took a late flight from Sarasota and got home last night, but you weren't there. I assumed you were out, but when I woke up this morning, you still weren't home. I texted, but you didn't answer, so I thought I'd check the library. It's locked. Why are you staying in here?"

Stella babbled, "Late night at the library, and the weather was bad, so—"

"Who are you?" Percy asked, catching sight of Jack. "Stella, tell me you're not shacking up with boyfriends at Arnie's."

"What? No!" Stella protested.

Percy glanced around the room at their scattered clothing and the rumpled blanket on the couch. "Stella," he said, his voice taking on a disappointed edge.

"It's not what it looks like," Stella said quickly.

"Yeah? So those aren't your clothes on the floor and nothing happened on the couch and you're not having breakfast in your morning-after pj's?" Percy asked.

"I'm Jack." He held out his hand, but Percy didn't move to shake it.

"I'm Percy. Stella's *brother*. You know this isn't her place, don't you? It belongs to the librarian who's in the hospital recovering from a heart attack." Percy's gaze lingered on Jack's face. "Do I know you?"

"Possibly," Jack said. "I know this is Arnie's home. We've been friends for a long time."

Percy cocked an eyebrow. "He doesn't mind you being in his house?"

Jack shook his head. "Nope."

"Where do I know you from? School?"

Stella stepped between them. "Percy, I'm sorry to have worried you, but you could have texted me yesterday to tell me you were coming."

"It was a last-minute decision," Percy said. "I didn't mean to interrupt your party."

"Oh, give it a rest," Stella snapped. "It's not like you've never had a girl on the couch before. I'm not a child, and I don't have time for your judgment. I'm heading to the house to get changed and ready for work. With Arnie out, the library is a lot to handle, and we're preparing for the festival this weekend. So if you don't mind, stuff your disdain for a while and find something else to do, like go visit Arnie."

Percy's shocked expression held him quiet for a few seconds. "I suppose you don't want me to mention that you're using his place for sleepovers."

Stella waved her hands in the air. "Do what you want, Percy, but I suggest you quit acting like such a brat. I'm happy to mention to Arnie that you and your friends are the ones who set fire to his favorite tree beside the cottage in high school."

"You wouldn't," Percy breathed in disbelief.

Stella opened the door and pointed. "Try me. Now go see Arnie. I'll be in the library later if you want to have a civil conversation."

Percy walked out the door, shaking his head. "What has gotten into you, Stella? You're acting like someone I don't even know."

Frustration flared hot. "This might come as a surprise to you, Percy, but honestly, you're right. You don't know me very well."

Percy's shoulders straightened. "Is this about the Miami job?"

It was way too early in the morning to have a life discussion with Percy, especially after the night she'd shared with Jack. "I don't want to do this right now," she said. "But yes, that's one indicator."

"Do *you* even know what you want?" Percy asked, his voice less harsh.

Stella gripped the edge of the door. "Actually, yes. And I'm getting there."

He scrubbed his hand through his curls. After casting a side-eye at Jack, he sighed in surrender. "I'll keep your secret if you keep mine."

Stella half smiled at Percy and closed the door. Jack stared at her with a grin of his own.

"Another plot twist. Remind me how everything is going to be okay," she said.

"After everything we've handled together so far, we've got this in the bag."

All she had to do was successfully help execute a major festival that would draw in hundreds of people, make sure Captain Hook didn't ruin the event or kidnap any unsuspecting women, explain what was happening to her best friend, keep her brother from asking too many questions, and not fall in love with Jack Mathis, who would be gone from her life in a matter of days. Easy, right?

Chapter 17

Stella stopped by the hospital and put on a show of "everything's fine at the library, including embracing the magic." Arnie was suspect of her jovial attitude, saying he sensed an undercurrent of stress. She played it off as festival worries. He asked about Jack, but she quickly diverted that topic. What could she say? That she'd spent the night in *his* cottage with Jack? Absolutely not.

Arnie briefed her about everything he could think of concerning the festival and assured her the committee would do most of the work. If she could keep the library organized and assist the inside vendors as needed, the rest of the festival would run smoothly.

The committee already knew about Arnie's hospitalization, and some of the members had even stopped by to see him. Stella called the head of the committee while she was with Arnie so they could both talk to her. Afterward, Stella's brain was so full that her temples throbbed. Could she handle this? She'd find out soon enough.

She arrived at the library half an hour before it was time to open the doors. Melanie was back from her vacation and scheduled for the afternoon-into-evening shift, but with festival prep and Arnie being unable to work, Stella confirmed with Vicki and Dan that they could assist for the day. They agreed to come in late morning.

When she parked in her usual spot, she sat in the car for a minute, gathering her confidence and trying to assuage her fears. As though the words knew what was coming, a group of shimmering gold letters flowed out of an air conditioner vent. **Hook. Keep it together. Release control.**

"Release control?" Stella asked, shooing away the words. "That sounds completely unhelpful." She got out of the car.

Jack was sitting behind the circulation desk with separate piles of papers organized on the counter. He'd changed into a light blue University of North Carolina T-shirt and a pair of shorts.

"Good morning again. How's it going here?" she asked, dropping her purse on the desk.

A light on the top corner of the desk phone blinked red, indicating messages were waiting to be listened to.

"Phone's been ringing since I got here," he said. "How's Arnie doing?"

"He's good," she said. "So much better. He thinks he'll be home soon. He gave me a rundown of the festival, and I feel mildly less concerned." She pointed to the papers on the desk. "What have you got there?"

Jack motioned her closer. "Let me show you."

Stella leaned over his shoulder as he pointed out the different piles and what each represented. There was a master list of food vendors, merchandise vendors, musical guests, speakers, children's activities, and the charity's information. Jack had a list of which booths would be set up in the library and which ones would be outdoors on the lawn or down the street in the park at the end of Main Street. He explained which groups would be there to set up this afternoon, both indoors and out, and which vendors wouldn't be able to set up until first light Saturday morning.

The music stage and dance floor would be erected during lunchtime today, and the performers would sound check right afterward. Jack shoved aside the papers and displayed maps.

"Here's a layout of where everyone will be in the library," he said. "Here's where they'll be on the lawn, and this last map is of the park down the street. The numbers on each map coordinate with a group or vendor, so it's easy to know where everyone will set up. There will be plenty of help, and here's a list of the volunteers. The committee sent all of this information out to the vendors, performers, and volunteers a month ago. Their swell organization has made it nearly impossible for us not to succeed."

Stella was grateful for the committee's meticulous approach to the festival and for Arnie's detailed paperwork. Blue Sky Valley, along with Arnie, had spent years perfecting every aspect of this summertime festival.

Stella glanced over the list of volunteers' names. "Do you think the committee took into account what to do in the event of a pirate crashing the festival?"

Jack leaned back in the chair and folded his hands behind his head. "No one saw or heard from Hook all night or this morning. Darcy and Crusoe are on high alert, so for now, the best we can do is not focus on Hook. They plan to keep a lookout for him during the festival."

"Where can he possibly be?" Stella asked, glancing around. "There aren't that many places to hide in here."

Jack sat up straighter. "You'd be surprised."

"We checked all the closets, the bathrooms, the archives, and the attic. Unless he's wedged himself into a steamer trunk, I don't know how he's stayed hidden for so long. I guess he could be slinking around just behind us and moving as we are."

"Has Arnie ever told you about the tunnels?" Jack asked.

Stella's mind couldn't make the connection between the library and underground passages. "Tunnels?"

"Old tunnel systems run below Blue Sky Valley, and some of them lead off from the archives. Most are blocked off to keep people from going in, and we've all—the characters—been warned about them."

Stella looked toward the archives door. "Are you kidding me right now? There are tunnels below the library?"

Jack nodded. "It doesn't look like Hook has used any of them, *but* he could be hiding out."

Stella rubbed her temple. "Just when I think I have all the details. There are tunnels that Hook could have snuck out of, and it's possible we've lost him from literature forever. I don't like him, but I don't want us to misplace him. Aren't you the least bit concerned that he's plotting your doom and might leap out when we aren't expecting it?"

"Focus on keeping this operation running smoothly," Jack said. "Arnie and the committee have done 90 percent of the work for us. All we have to do is direct people where to go. Let me worry about Hook." He stood and stretched before slipping his arms around her waist. "I hope we can enjoy the festival some too. I read the bio on The Ink Blots, a group that plays my kind of music—1940s big band. I can spin you around a few times on the dance floor."

Stella's heart leaped at the thought of dancing with Jack and having him hold her close again, but then she remembered why she'd skipped every school dance.

"We've talked about this. I don't dance. As in, I've never been to a dance before."

Jack brushed his lips against her cheek. "Never? Would you be willing to go with me?"

"Jack," she said, pulling away from him, "I don't know the first thing about dancing. I'd embarrass you."

"I can teach you." He kissed the side of her neck.

"Are you planning on teaching me everything?" she asked, closing her eyes.

"Not everything," he said against her neck. "In some areas you're already killer diller." Then he kissed her lips.

✦ ✦ ✦

BY LUNCHTIME THE library and grounds were full of activity. Dan and Vicki had arrived together, and Vicki sent Dan to the break room to put away their belongings so she could ask about Hook and the police. As much as it tweaked her guilt, Stella lied and said it had been taken care of. Vicki's relief washed over her, and she jumped into festival prep with a renewed sense of focus.

The local tent rental company sent workers just after the library opened, and they busied themselves setting up the ten-by-ten tents for the outdoor vendors. Tables and chairs were placed inside the tents, and vendors arrived to decorate and organize their spaces. Generators were hooked up, and extension cords were connected to allow for electricity. Stella watched the progress with anticipation, wishing Arnie were there to witness his plans becoming reality.

Once the music stage was erected, performers sound checked, and Stella took a break to linger on the back steps of the library and listen to a few songs. The day was beautiful, but the intense heat caused everyone to sweat straight through their summer clothes and gulp bottles of lukewarm water. They walked around while fanning their faces, swirling the soupy hot air. Cardinals chirped wearily from the shade of an oak tree, and no clouds marred the bright blue sky.

Stella lifted the sleeve of her T-shirt and swiped it across her face. At least the heat had dried up most of the sogginess left over from yesterday's rainstorm. The lawn still sank in places, and a few stubborn puddles remained in the parking lot, but by late afternoon the whole place would be dry and thirsty.

Back inside the library, volunteers bustled, and Vicki hurried through the foyer with a clipboard in her hands. She pointed toward the children's section.

"Puppet show booth is that way. Number fifteen," she said to a woman whose arms were full of limp cloth puppets. "There's an open area right beside your table for you to set up your backdrops and props."

"Thank you," the woman said as she hurried away.

"Everything under control?" Stella asked.

Vicki pressed the clipboard to her chest. Her round cheeks were flushed, and her fiery hair was exceptionally large because of the humidity. "I'd say in the absence of our ringleader, we are keeping this circus organized."

"Hungry?" Stella asked. "I thought I'd grab lunch for us."

Vicki nodded. "Famished."

"How about the deli? Then I'll swing by Frost Bites for desserts. We deserve a cool treat. What would you like?"

Vicki gave Stella her order, and then Stella wandered through the first floor looking for Dan and Melanie. After taking their orders, she searched for Jack and found him talking to a man setting out stacks of books on a table.

As Stella approached them, she saw that the books appeared to be historical fiction novels about World War II. Jack and the man were discussing the Battle of the Bulge. How strange was it for Jack to talk about a war he'd been part of, even if only in a novel? Did it stir up difficult memories? Could he picture the faces of the other soldiers and friends he'd lost? Did he feel like a man out of time?

Soon he *would* be out of time. A pang of sadness followed.

Jack noticed her on the periphery and a slow smile changed his face. She wanted to linger in that space of being seen by him.

"Hey, Stella," he said. "This is Thomas Linden. He's a local author with a passion for World War II."

Stella shook Thomas's hand and introduced herself. "We're happy you're here. Please let us know if you need anything or have any questions about the festival. We appreciate your support."

"Happy to be here," Thomas said.

"Please excuse us." Stella grabbed Jack's arm and pulled him aside into the privacy of an aisle between bookshelves. "Is that weird? Talking about the war?"

Jack glanced back at Thomas, who was arranging his books. "It's strange, but I'm thankful for men like Thomas who are still interested in sharing our history with others so soldiers aren't forgotten."

Her dad had said something similar, which was another reason he'd created the care packages for soldiers. She leaned her head against Jack's shoulder. "How could anyone forget you?"

Jack tucked a curl behind her ear.

Stella patted her hair, feeling the frizz creeping outward. "It's out of control today. All the humidity."

Jack grinned. "I like it. How're you holding up? From what I can tell, the setup is running smoothly."

He followed her to the circulation desk. "I'm going to the deli to grab lunch for me and the rest of the crew. Can I bring something back for you?" She grabbed her purse.

Jack hooked one finger around her purse strap. "Could I walk with you?"

Stella glanced toward the library's front doors. In the past forty-eight hours, she had broken all kinds of rules. "Arnie told me to keep everyone in the library. I know we only went to his place, but is town too far? Are we pushing the limits?"

"Arnie's let me outside a few times."

"Off the grounds?"

Jack reached for her hand. "No, but you could protect me."

Stella laughed. "From what?"

He tugged her close. "From getting lost. Come on, Stella. It'd be sweet to see the town." He placed a quick kiss on her neck, and her knees wobbled.

She rolled her eyes. "No fair." But she leaned into him. "I doubt you going into town with me would upset Arnie more than knowing that a drunken Hook tried to lure a book club member into his captain's quarters. Come on, dreamboat."

Jack's laugh filled the foyer, and Stella marveled at this new woman who was evolving inside her. She pushed open the library's front doors and nearly ran into Dana Cannon. She had a canvas bag slung over her shoulder and wore a ball cap emblazoned with the name of a local Little League team.

"Dana," Stella said as she held the door open, "I'm sorry. I wasn't paying attention."

Dana smiled as her gaze shifted toward Jack. Her expression said, *I bet I know where your attention was.*

"Looks like festival preparations are in full swing," she said. "I'm looking forward to it tomorrow. Arnie and the committee always do the best job with it. Can I return the books I checked out about Wildflower Hill?"

"Of course," Stella said. "The library isn't open for normal activities"—she glanced into the foyer—"even though it's full of activity. But I don't mind returning these for you."

Dana reached into her canvas bag. "Thank you for suggesting *Fried Green Tomatoes*. I'd forgotten how much I loved it."

Stella's chest filled with warmth. She quickly glanced at Jack, wanting to tell him that she'd called forth the words *on purpose* and helped Dana find this book.

Dana continued, "I also hoped I could talk with Arnie about the books. Do you think he'd have a few minutes to spare? I'm sure he's busy today, but it wouldn't take long."

Stella's shoulders sagged. "Arnie isn't here today." When Dana's smile slipped right off her face, Stella added, "But if he were, he would definitely take the time to talk with you. He suffered a heart attack a couple nights ago, and he's still in the hospital."

Dana gasped and covered her mouth with her hands. Her green eyes opened wide over the tops of her fingers. When she lowered her hands, her bottom lip trembled. "Is he going to be okay?"

Stella reached out to touch Dana's arm briefly. "Yes, and he promised me that he'll be right as rain ASAP. He's already feeling better, but it's customary to keep a heart attack patient in the hospital for at least a few days."

Dana dropped the novel back into her bag and then gripped the straps of her canvas bag with both hands. "Can he have visitors?"

"Yes," Stella said.

Puffy white words floated out of Dana's bag and lifted into the air. **Comfort. Chances. Kindness.** "Does he need anything? Could I bring him something?"

The warmth continued to spread through Stella at seeing Dana's words. She caught Jack's gaze before his eyes flitted to the words too. If only Arnie knew how much goodness Dana wanted to share with him. An idea popped into Stella's mind.

"He's suffering on the hospital food diet, but he loves white chocolate macadamia nut cookies. I bet if you smuggled in a few of those, you'd win his heart forever."

A lovely, hopeful smile lifted Dana's cheeks, and Stella was struck by her beauty. Dana would never be described as dainty or frilly like some women. She was capable and sturdy and strong—a marvelous fit for Arnie.

An inner joy lit her green eyes. "I have a wonderful recipe for white chocolate macadamia nut cookies from my grandma. I'll drop off my books and scurry back home. I have baking to do."

Dana said goodbye and disappeared into the crowded library, and Stella and Jack headed down the concrete stairs toward the sidewalk.

"Arnie is going to be beside himself when she shows up," Stella laughed. "He'll freak out at first and he might even babble, but then she'll distract him with the cookies, and before he realizes what's happening, they'll be having a normal conversation."

Jack slipped his hand into Stella's. "Clever of you to send her with his favorite cookies."

Stella leaned her head against Jack's arm. "He needs a little push. I guess we all do sometimes."

Jack chuckled. "Have you been pushed recently?"

"Ha! More like shoved right off a cliff," she said and stopped walking. "A few days ago I realized I've been stuck in a cycle of monotony. Not unhappy but not fulfilled. Then—*bam!*—I burn a journal, words start appearing like mad, those purple words start pushing me toward something, I learn I can command the words, Arnie has a heart attack, I meet you, I unleash a pirate and a sailor into the library—"

"Don't forget Percy catching you indecent with a man in Arnie's house."

Stella laughed. "His face, though. I wish I had a photo of how flabbergasted he was. I wasn't actively wishing for change, but maybe, like Arnie, I needed a shove. I just didn't intend for it to be so jarring."

"So what's next for Stella Parker?"

Waves of heat rippled up from the black pavement, blurring the edges of everything and giving the town a magical appearance like an image pulled from a summer dream.

"Definitely not Miami," she said. "But I might give extended education or certification serious thought." She peered at him. "The idea of writing and completing something feels exciting, using my words in a way I've been doing for years but more intentionally and focused. Now that I can call them forth, what's stopping me from creating a whole lot of things? And I can help connect readers with the perfect book. And with the magic, if Arnie allows me to use it officially, even more possibilities arise." She stopped when she noticed Jack was staring and smiling at her with a goofy grin. "What?"

"You," he said. "You look happy, Stella."

She couldn't see her expression, but she felt the truth of his words, effervescent and swirling with gratitude. Somehow she'd dropped the heaviness she'd been dragging around, and there was space for lightness and—she smiled at Jack—for falling in love. "I am happy."

A neon-pink van emblazoned with the words *Fur Real Dog Grooming* parked against the curb. Ariel waved through the window and hopped out, then hurried to join them on the sidewalk. Always a blaze of color, today she wore a set of scrubs covered in a rainbow of pawprints. Her blond hair was pulled into a high ponytail, showcasing her pink stripe.

"Where are you heading?" she asked. "I figured it would be nutso in the library today with festival setup." She leaned forward into Stella's space like someone with a secret to share. "What's the update on the pirate situation? And why are the two of you looking so glowy? Did something—"

"We're going to the deli," Stella said quickly, "and Frost Bites to get lunch for the library crew and ourselves. We haven't found Hook yet, but we have people on the lookout."

Ariel's forehead creased. "People? What people?"

Jack said, "Darcy and Crusoe."

Ariel frowned. "And they are?"

"Fictional characters," Stella said, bracing for Ariel's response.

Ariel laughed but stopped when she realized Stella wasn't joking. "Oh, you're serious. Wait. You don't mean"—she clutched Stella's arm—"*Fitzwilliam* Darcy." Stella nodded, and Ariel squealed. "Is he as dreamy as we hoped?"

Jack looked pointedly at Stella. "Are you interested in Darcy?"

Ariel scoffed. "Not a chance with you around. Can I meet him?"

Stella waffled. "Possibly."

Ariel bounced on her toes. "I wonder if he's interested in girls with pink hair. But you're ignoring the glowy comment?" Stella nodded. "Fine. We'll talk about that later. Mind if I join you? I was coming by to see if you needed anything and to check in. I'm glad I caught you." She looked at Jack directly. "How's modern life treating you?"

"Couldn't ask for anything more," Jack responded.

"How about temperatures to drop twenty degrees?" Stella teased and leaned into him as they commenced walking.

"What about sticking around longer?" Ariel said. "Is that a possibility?"

"Ariel!" Stella said.

"Aren't you curious?" Ariel asked. "Why is there a time limit?"

Jack squeezed Stella's hand. "I don't know all the intricacies of how everything works, but there's always been a time limit. In most instances, having someone around for two weeks is a welcome rule. But not in every case."

"Have you never asked Arnie about it?" Ariel asked, ignoring the "stop talking" look Stella shot in her direction.

"Of course," Jack said. "Some rules can't be broken."

"But some can," Ariel said.

"Subject change!" Stella insisted. If there was a way for Jack to stay longer, wouldn't Arnie have already figured that out? Wouldn't he have told them? Thinking about Jack leaving shortened her breath. "What was Blue Sky Valley like in your time?" Stella led them toward the deli and glanced at Ariel. "Jack grew up here."

Ariel nodded. "I remember the story."

Of course she did. How many times had Stella talked about Jack as though he were someone she knew, someone who might have been an active participant in her life? That was the thing with characters in books: They *were* real to the reader. Readers felt as though they intimately knew their favorite characters, like they were long-lost friends, best mates, and sometimes sworn enemies. Talking about characters provoked genuine emotions in readers. And now Jack was more real to her than he'd ever been.

Stella continued, "Does the downtown area look a lot different?"

Jack nodded. "The basic outline is the same, with the same streets, but there are more buildings downtown now. I remember how it looked in my time, but because Arnie has shown me pictures of the town through the years, there are all of these layers in my mind too."

As they walked, he described the storefronts that were the same and which businesses had occupied the buildings when he was younger. He pointed out places he used to visit with his parents and where he and his friends had hung out on the weekends. Frost Bites hadn't changed much through the years, but it had originally been a soda fountain shop where Jack tasted his first root beer float.

For fifteen minutes of walking and talking, Stella forgot her anxiety. She enjoyed being with Jack and Ariel and not concerning herself with anything else—not her past or future.

It wasn't until Jack said, "I could do this forever. Walk with you on a street that never ends, talking, learning, smiling," that her fears returned.

She slipped her hand out of Jack's as the three of them stepped beneath an awning that provided a rectangle of shade on the sidewalk. "It's not possible to do this forever. It would end. Everything does."

"Stella," Ariel said, a trace of sorrow in her voice.

Jack looked intently at Stella, and she squirmed beneath his gaze before averting her own down the street at the vendors setting up in the park.

He grabbed her hand. "Love is eternal. Infinite. It never ends."

Stella made the mistake of making eye contact with Ariel, who mouthed, *Love is eternal*.

Stella cleared her throat. Love might be infinite, but Jack's time with her wasn't. "You'll be gone in days. *That* is what I know. And I'll be here without you." She tried to release his hand, but he held on.

"You'll never be without me," he promised, pressing their bound hands to his chest. "I'll carry you in my heart for the rest of my days."

Stella would have swooned if she hadn't been sweating on a city sidewalk. In all her daydreams, Jack Mathis had never been as eloquent as the man standing before her. Against impossible odds, he was looking at her like he sincerely cared for her.

"I wish I had your optimism," she said.

"I have plenty to share," he replied.

"I do too," Ariel chimed in. "I've also heard it's contagious."

"We should get lunch," Jack said. "I don't want to keep you from the library for too long, not with everything going on."

He released her hand and continued walking up the sidewalk toward the deli while Stella trailed behind, watching tar-like words ripple across the pavement. **Be present. It's coming. Silver light.** Sometimes the words made sense, and other times they were a cross between a reprimand and nonsense.

Ariel leaned close to her and whispered, "What if there's a way?"

"A way for what?"

Jack crossed the street toward the diner, and Stella turned to face Ariel on the sidewalk.

Ariel's expression glowed with hope and possibility. "A way for you to be together."

If only. "Are you trying to get my hopes up and then have them smashed to smithereens? How would that even be possible?"

Jack stood on the opposite sidewalk and waved them over.

Ariel waved back and held up one finger. "Before now, did you think it was possible for book characters to come to life?" Stella shook her head. "Let's talk about what's impossible but possible. You're a girl who sees words floating around. Your vibe, by the way, is so sparkly right now, which is lovely. You've never been this way before, not even with Wade. You and Jack have something special, Stella. I've never seen you this happy."

She locked her gaze with Jack's across the street. He fired up all the nerves in her body, making her breathless and passionate. "You're right. What if it's possible? We have less than three days to figure out a way."

Ariel hooked her arm through Stella's, looked both ways down the street, and then tugged her across the road toward Jack. "We'll figure this out together."

"I don't even know where to start," Stella said. "Well, Arnie seems like the best place."

"See?" Ariel said. "You *do* know where to start."

Could they find a way to allow Jack to stay permanently? If he could stay, was she willing to take a risk on another relationship? Stella's heart flip-flopped in response, saying *yes*.

Chapter 18

After sandwiches and ice cream, Stella kept busy preparing the care package booth and gathering supplies and donations for it. She also spent a lot of time walking around the grounds and the library ensuring everyone had what they needed or fetching what they still lacked. Dwelling on Jack and discussing their future with Arnie slipped to the back of her thoughts.

As the early evening passed and the sun eased lower behind the pine trees, the sky filled with brilliant swirls the colors of orange push-up pops and strawberry sherbet. Vendors loaded empty boxes and crates into cars and trailers and drove away until tomorrow. As a precaution, a squad of Blue Sky Valley police officers had scheduled overnight shifts for guarding the grounds and the park down the street.

The last of the vendors trickled out of the library, along with the volunteers. The library would close in half an hour. She—with a truckload of helpers and the committee's top-notch organization—

might actually pull off the festival without having Arnie there to keep everything on track.

As quiet settled over the building, Stella's mind and body finally started to relax. She walked the library's second floor to check for any stragglers or messes to clean. Near the women's fiction section, she paused long enough to sit on the edge of a study table and exhale a relieved breath. A sudden stabbing pain speared through her chest. The familiar burning spread through her as though she'd fallen into a bonfire. A neon-violet gooey substance rose from the center of the study table, forming an amorphous blob on the polished surface. Trembling letters rose from the goop, dripping and revealing their dangling tendrils. Stella struggled to breathe and pressed her hands to her chest as if that would help. It didn't.

The words shimmied across the tabletop, and Stella blinked through the pain to read them out loud. "'But one built from paper and rich black ink.'"

She gasped as her lungs expanded and the fire in her chest extinguished. Leaning over the study table, she pounded her fist against the table in frustration. "Is the pain necessary?" she cried to the words.

They wiggled in response.

"Couldn't you come gently?" She pushed herself upright. "I *see* you, okay? You don't have to kill me."

The words rocketed off the table, skittered across the tiles, leaped over the balcony, and rushed toward the circulation desk where her journal was tucked away. Stella faltered the first few steps and then regained her balance as she walked toward the staircase.

A shadow lengthened across the floor in front of her. Stella turned her head just in time to see a flash of silver and black before she was snatched down an aisle. She gasped and stumbled sideways. Her cheek crushed into clothes that stank of rum. She half dangled in the man's grasp, her feet dragging behind her.

"I thought you had better taste, love. Choosing that soldier over me? Repulsive," Hook said, pulling her so tightly against him that she felt the coming bruises.

Stella kicked her legs and struggled to stand. The pirate's silver hook scraped down her arm. The skin burned as though she'd leaned up against a metal pole in the summertime. A line of blood rose to the surface through the slice.

"Your fault," Hook said. "You brought this on yourself, like all women do."

Stella stilled, staring at the blood oozing from the wound. It reminded her of the way magma pushed up from fractures in bedrock. Drops of deep red splattered onto the floor, and crimson words writhed and grew out of them. **Your fault. Another failure. Disappointment.** Her stomach rolled, and she would have pitched forward if Hook hadn't held her so tightly. Warm blood slid down her arm and across her palm.

"You'll be sorry you chose him. After what he did to me, the least I can do is take away what he seems to care about."

The world tilted beneath her, but she clenched her jaw and fought Hook. Her sudden movement startled him, and he lost his balance, which allowed Stella to gain hers. She slipped out of his grasp, and he lunged for her, slashing his hook toward her face.

Stella darted out of the way, but the hook caught on the hem of her shirt and ripped through the fabric. She scrambled away from him and ran toward the main staircase, overturning chairs behind her.

Hook leaped over the chairs and stopped to pick one up. He hurled it at her. The chair caught Stella in the back of the legs, knocking her forward. She slammed into a bookshelf and desperately tried to grip a shelf's edge for balance. She pulled herself up and yanked off books to throw at Hook.

He batted them away, until one book caught on his hook. While he tried to sling it from the sharp silver point, Stella lifted a chair as high as she could and flung it at him. One of the legs cracked against his jaw and spun him away from her.

Her gaze zeroed in on the sword hanging in his scabbard. She recognized it as one that had been encased in the archives—a mysterious sword of unknown origin discovered in Blue Sky Valley a few hundred years ago. The ruby-studded hilt caught the light, and the crimson jewels sparkled like warning lights.

Hook turned back toward her with his fist pressed against his bruised jaw. He glowered, his blue eyes menacing. He yanked the sword from its scabbard and pointed it at her. "You shouldn't have done that."

Stella ran. With her arms pumping and legs aching with effort, she sprinted toward the staircase. Within seconds she realized the pirate was much faster. He ran up an aisle parallel to hers and rounded the end of the bookshelf, wielding the stolen sword.

She lurched to a stop, nearly barreling into Hook. With his footing firm, he swung the sword at her head. She tripped over her feet as she staggered backward, arms windmilling for balance but unable to grasp anything to stop her fall.

Hook slashed the sword down at her as she struggled to crab crawl backward and away from him, pushing her shoes against the floor as hard and as fast as possible.

The sword hit the top edge of her tennis shoe and sliced off the rubber tip, scarcely missing her toes. Stella barely got to her feet before the blade whizzed past her head as she ducked to the side. She gripped the edge of the nearest shelf, panting and feeling as though her heart would crack through her rib cage any second.

Hook grinned. He was playing with her, toying with Stella like a cat batting around a helpless mouse, already knowing the battle was won. Anger and fear collided inside her, creating a desperate, uncontrollable burst of self-preservation. Fight or flight. She couldn't outrun or outfight Hook, but maybe she could outsmart him, catch him off guard.

She ran full speed at him while he raised the sword at his side. At the last second, she bent over to ram him with her shoulder and barely registered the look of surprise in his eyes before he tripped over his boots and careened out of control. He slammed into a study table and sprawled out on top of it.

The sword slipped from his grasp, its jeweled hilt glinting as it bounced against the floor.

Stella clambered for the sword as Hook pushed himself to standing with incredible speed. In a mad rush, Stella gripped the hilt with both hands, groaning as she lifted the cumbersome blade.

She faced Hook just as he dove toward her.

The silver blade shoved itself into Hook's chest, piercing him all the way through, exiting out his back. Stella stood stunned, unable to move. Then, realizing what she'd done, she released the hilt.

Hook's eyes widened as he stared down at the sword protruding from his chest. Stella's heart pounded so hard that bile rose in her throat.

Hook stumbled into the second-floor railing, and his tall body pitched backward over the balcony toward the foyer below. A few seconds later, she heard a grotesque *thump* and someone screamed. It wasn't Stella.

She slapped her hands over her mouth and gagged. Then she staggered toward the staircase saying, "Oh my God," on repeat as she ran. She almost tumbled down the steps as she took them as quickly as possible.

Hook lay on his back, one leg bent oddly and his arms splayed out beside him. His glassy eyes stared toward the ceiling. Blood pooled beneath him, oozing out from underneath his back. Deep red wetness stained his shirt in a widening circle as he blinked. The sword had propelled itself out of his body and lay off to the side.

Ariel stood near the circulation desk clutching Percy's arm. Both stared at Stella, stricken with horror. Stella gulped air and dropped to her knees beside Hook.

Her whole body trembled. She leaned over Hook and touched his shoulder. Warm blood continued to drip down her own slashed arm. "Hook, can you hear me?"

He blinked again and turned a slow gaze toward her. His blue eyes seemed unfocused. The pool of blood enlarged beneath him, staining her knees red.

"I am so sorry," Stella blubbered. She grabbed his hand, careful not to jostle him too much. "I didn't mean to."

Hook closed his eyes, and his right cheek dimpled. "Bravo, love. You're stronger than I thought. I didn't think you had it in you."

"I *don't*," Stella argued. "I'm not a killer. Don't die, okay? I can find help."

Hook surprised her by squeezing her fingers. His exhaled breath gurgled in his lungs. "Not a killer," he said, his words garbled. "You saved yourself. Well played, love." His body convulsed and he groaned.

"Hang in there, Hook," she said. "I'll get you back on your feet in no time."

He grimaced, and his body tightened as his spine stiffened before it relaxed again. His dilated pupils turned his eyes almost black. "Let go."

He inhaled one final time.

Then he exploded into ashes. When Stella opened her mouth to scream, soot coated her tongue and covered her entire body. She coughed and hacked, spitting black ash onto the tiles.

Footsteps hammered against the floor, and Stella lifted her palms to her eyes and wiped away the grime. As she blinked, Jack came into view. He dropped down beside her.

"What happened? What's this all over the floor?" he asked in quick succession. "It looks like—"

Stella burst into tears, crying hard into her dirty hands. Jack pulled her against him and held her until she could breathe normally.

"What in the hell just happened?" Percy demanded.

Ariel knelt beside Stella. "Is that man dead? Why did he explode?"

Stella cried harder. Jack lifted her into a sitting position. "Stella," he said, pushing her hair back from her face, "talk to me."

"Somebody better tell me what's going on," Percy said.

"Hook," Stella said and wiped the back of her hand across her runny nose. Then she stared down at her bloody, dirty arm. A black line of soot clung to the cut. "I-I killed him."

"What?" Jack asked as he gripped both of her shoulders and made her face him.

Percy squatted next to them. "You killed who?" Then he looked to Jack and pointed up. "A man fell from the second floor, and then he . . . disappeared."

"He didn't disappear," Ariel argued. "He exploded into dirt."

"Ashes," Stella said, sniffling. "Hook attacked me, and when I defended myself, he ran into the sword, and then he tripped, and . . ." She shuddered. "I was going to save him, but then he . . . he—"

"It's okay," Jack said, pulling her against him and rubbing her back.

"Who is Hook?" Percy asked.

Ariel huffed. "Captain Hook from *Peter Pan*," she said as though it should be obvious. "He's been terrorizing the library after he came out of his book, and now . . . I don't know what happens now. Is he dead?"

Jack shook his head. "No. He's back where he should be. This is what happens when characters die near the source." He pointed to the ashes around them.

"Ick," Ariel said, standing up and brushing Hook's remains from her knees.

"Has everyone here lost their minds?" Percy said, standing again and shoving his hands through his dark curls. "I have no idea what's happening."

"Should we tell him?" Ariel asked Stella. "Will Arnie be okay with that?"

Stella closed her eyes and hung her head. "The more the merrier."

Jack lifted Stella's arm gently. "This needs to be cleaned. Stay here." He rushed off to the bathroom and returned with two handfuls of wet paper towels.

Stella wiped her face and body. Jack removed a first-aid kit hanging on a wall nearby and pulled out supplies, then sat down beside her and cleaned the wound.

Peroxide bubbled on her skin, and Stella clenched her jaw and winced. "Is it bad? Do I need stitches?"

Jack shook his head. "Antiseptic and maybe a few bandages. It's not deep." He wadded up the soiled paper towels. Then he dabbed antiseptic ointment on the deepest sections of the cut before covering the wound with bandages and medical tape. "He's not really dead, Stella. He's gone back into his story where he will always be alive and roguish. I'm sorry you had to experience that, and I understand that it's upsetting, but you didn't really kill anyone."

Stella nodded, but she had unintentionally killed a man, fictional or not. There was a trace of comfort knowing Hook wasn't permanently dead.

Percy paced the floor. "It sure as hell looked like someone died," he said. "I've never seen a body do that. Explode into dust like that."

"That's because real people don't do that, Percy," Ariel said. She helped Stella to her feet.

Jack stood. "I'll clean up the floor." He pointed toward the sword. "And I'll clean that and return it to its case in the archives. Why don't you head on over to Arnie's? Get some rest."

"No one is going anywhere until I get some answers," Percy said. Two angry lines formed between his brows. "Speaking of *that*"—he pointed at the bloodied sword—"a man *with a sword* in his chest fell from the balcony and *died*—"

"He's not dead," Stella corrected.

Percy pointed to the second floor as though they needed clarification. "You were in a fight with him up there? And *you* stabbed him? With a *sword*?"

"Percy," Stella said in exasperation. Her temples throbbed. "If you give me a minute to clear my head, I'll explain everything. First I need to lock up the library."

Jack grabbed the sword and walked off. Percy continued to stare, seemingly uncertain what to do next.

"Tell me how I can help," Ariel said as she followed Stella to the circulation desk. While they walked, Ariel touched Stella's arm. "I want to ask if you're okay, but how could you be? Things have escalated drastically, but at least . . . at least Hook's gone." She grimaced. "Too soon?"

Stella wrapped her arms around herself. "I know it's not real, but it *feels* real," she said, her voice still quivering.

"What was he saying to you at the end?" Ariel asked. "It sounded like he was talking, but I couldn't understand him."

Stella felt the prickle of tears again. "That he was proud of me."

Ariel's mouth fell open. "For fake murdering him?"

"For standing up for myself," Stella said. "For fighting for what I want."

Ariel leaned her arms on the high desktop.

Stella continued, "It dawned on me how long it's been since I've stood up for myself and been firm about what I want. I know this is a lousy comparison because I was literally fighting for my life tonight, but before all of this"—she waved her hand through the air to mimic a windstorm—"I've done next to nothing to assert my needs or pay attention to what I truly want. But that's all going to change. I'm *already* changing."

The most recent purple words popped back into her mind. She opened the drawer in the circulation desk where she kept her purse and notebook and pulled out the latter. She flipped to the page where she'd been cataloging the violet words. She added the newest ones. Now the collected words read: *I fell in love once. Did I ever tell you that? He was excruciatingly handsome and no ordinary man, but one built from paper and rich black ink.*

She handed the journal to Ariel.

Ariel read slowly. "Definitely sounds like a story."

"I know," Stella admitted. "I've written so many stories, never finished anything, and words have been showing up for years, but never this way. Never with such intensity. The more I think about the last few days, the more I know it's all connected. Maybe this is the beginning of my first novel."

Percy walked toward them, but he kept an eye on Jack as he swept up what remained of Hook. Stella's chest tightened, and she whispered so only Ariel could hear. "Even Jack's appearance is part of what's happening to me. He can see the words, *my words*, and no one else can."

"That has to mean something," Ariel agreed. "Have you had any more thoughts about how we can make his stay permanent?"

Stella shook her head. "I'm asking Arnie as soon as I can."

Ariel glanced at how close Percy was to them and quickly added, "Careful with Percy. He's giving off a superintense vibe."

"Meaning?" Stella asked, making eye contact with her brother.

"He's as mad as a hornet."

"Fantastic," she said dryly. "Let's lock up and turn off the lights. Percy, I'll be right back."

"I expect a full explanation," he said.

"I expect you'll need a stiff drink afterward," Stella said as she walked off. Any expectations she had for getting to bed soon and resting before the festival tomorrow were becoming less and less reachable.

Chapter 19

"This needs to be stopped immediately," Percy demanded in the library foyer. His face had become blotchier and more scrunched as the minutes of explanation continued. Now Stella feared he might self-combust.

"We have it under control," she said, which wasn't a complete lie. With Hook no longer lurking and plotting doom, the remaining library inhabitants were harmless.

"This is under control?" Percy barked. "A dead, not-dead pirate tried to murder you with a sword tonight. Look at your arm! You're in way over your head. We need to tell Arnie."

"No way!" Stella argued, raising her voice for the first time that evening. "He's recovering from a heart attack. We're absolutely, 100 percent *not* telling him anything. Do you want to send him into A-fib?"

"Then send all the characters back now," Percy said. "Including Jack."

Stella inhaled sharply. Jack moved in her periphery, and Ariel's body tensed beside her. "Why would we do that?"

"Because this has gone too far, Stella," Percy said. "This whole paranormal thing you've got going on here has to stop. You don't need to be involved in something so dangerous. Tonight is a prime example. You can't handle this. What gives you the right to bring fictional characters to life?" He pointed straight-armed at Jack. "Who's next? Genghis Khan?"

"Don't be absurd, Percy," Stella said, laughing. "We'd never do that, and you can't bring out nonfiction people anyway."

"This isn't funny!" His voice pinched like that of a child on the verge of a tantrum. "This is too much power for you. Or for anyone. I can't believe Arnie has been doing this all these years. It's irresponsible and unsafe. Why would he let you, of all people, bring out a murderous pirate?"

"Well, to be fair, he didn't," Stella admitted. "I didn't think any of this was real, but"—she laughed uncomfortably—"surprise! It's all legit. Arnie would have advised against Captain Hook if he'd been here."

"So even you admit you don't have enough responsibility or the intelligence to have this kind of authority," Percy said. "Send everyone back now. Right now, Stella."

Stella stared at her brother. She didn't have the intelligence? Did he realize how offensive that sounded? He'd always been the supportive older brother, the responsible sibling looking out for her best interests. But now she saw him as someone who didn't even know who she was anymore. That was clear by his persistent urgings to sell their home and his recent insistence on her taking an accounting job *in Miami*. It was no secret she wasn't excelling at life in Blue Sky Valley, but half a dozen changes had already happened in less than a week. Her life was starting to resemble something exciting and adventurous. Working in the library had taken on new meaning and importance for her.

Percy wasn't completely wrong about how dangerous the situation with Hook had been, but with the pirate returned to the pages where he belonged, the threat of danger was doused. After experiencing Hook, Stella didn't want to bring out characters who would cause her or anyone else harm—if she ever used the ink pad again.

She frowned at Percy and said simply, "No."

Percy puffed up and his cheeks reddened, and she thought, *This is it. This is the moment Percy implodes.* His polo shirt had come untucked on one side, and his curls had gone rogue from all the times he'd shoved his hands into his hair in frustration and disbelief.

"No?" He looked and sounded so much like their father that for a moment Stella backpedaled in her mind. Was he right? Was she out of her depth? Was it time for her to give up on the idea that she and Jack could actually handle the rest of the weekend, including the festival? That all her forward momentum with the words and the library was just a fantasy and not a life she could possibly live every day?

"No," Stella repeated, more to herself. She refused to go back to the life she had before she burned the journal, before she found the magic hidden in the library, before she kissed Jack Mathis.

"I get it, Percy. You want me to be safe and you're trying to protect me. I get how shocking all of this must be for you. Believe me, I do. But I'm not sending anyone back early. Not Darcy, not Crusoe, and definitely not Jack." She slid her gaze to Jack's quickly before returning it to Percy.

Jack walked to stand near Stella. His closeness strengthened her resolve.

"Do you even know what that would mean for them?" Stella continued. "Or for me? I'd have to *kill* them. I'm guessing you don't want that job either. So unless you have something supportive to say, you should go home."

Percy stared at her. Then he walked away from the desk toward the back door. Halfway there, he turned to look at her. "You're making a mistake. Be sensible. Take the job in Miami. Start over. You can leave all of this behind. Don't you want to get your life together?"

Stella found Jack's hand and entwined their fingers. "That's what I'm finally doing. Getting my life together."

Percy shook his head and pushed open the back door, then disappeared into the darkness. Stella exhaled and leaned her head against Jack's arm.

"That was a disaster," she said.

Ariel shrugged. "He'll come around."

Stella looked at her best friend. "What makes you think that? He's furious with me."

Ariel shook her head, and her dangly star earrings twirled at her neck. "He's not furious. He's worried, and that won't last. Not once he sees you're happy, because really that's what he wants. Your happiness."

"And he thinks my happiness is in Miami?" Stella asked. "It's like he thinks he can find my happiness somewhere for me."

"He does," Ariel said. "Most people do. They think they can find your happiness for you. But if you're not satisfied in Blue Sky Valley, then you aren't going to magically find contentment in Miami." Pillowy white words puffed out from the fabric of her shirt. **Inner peace. Self-love. Resurrection.**

For the first time Stella spoke someone else's words out loud to them. "Inner peace, self-love, and resurrection. If I don't find those in myself, I won't find them anywhere else."

Ariel smiled. "Exactly! It's like you read my mind."

"I did in a way," Stella admitted. "Those words just came out of you."

Ariel looked down at her body as though she might see them herself. "Wow."

Stella hugged Ariel. "Thank you for being here tonight. I'm sorry about the whole Hook-falling-from-the-balcony bit."

"That was terrifying and horrific," Ariel admitted, "but more like watching a movie that I can turn off now. Don't worry about Percy. Give him some time." She yawned. "Time for me to skedaddle. I want to be refreshed for the festival."

"You and me both," Stella said. She walked Ariel to the back door and waited for her to climb into her car before waving good night. After Ariel drove out of the parking lot, Stella returned to Jack.

He waited for her at the circulation desk. "You're staying at Arnie's, right?"

Stella nodded. "Definitely. Percy's at the house, so I'm not going there." She reached for his hand. "Walk me home?"

He smiled. "Of course."

"Then come inside and stay awhile?"

Jack wrapped his arms around her. "You want me to stay with you?"

"I don't want to be alone tonight," she admitted. "But that's not the only reason I want you to stay with me."

Jack pulled away so he could kiss her. "As long as you need me, I'll stay."

Even though that wasn't actually possible, she liked the *idea* that it was possible. She liked the seed of a dream that was planted in her heart. What she wouldn't give to have that seed grow, steady and strong, within her. Maybe Arnie had answers to how Jack could stay indefinitely.

Until tomorrow, though, she wanted to be as close to Jack as possible and squeeze as much as she could out of the time they had left.

Chapter 20

Saturday morning dawned with a watercolor-painted sky, a horizontal rainbow of soft pastel colors. Stella stood at the bay window in Arnie's cottage with her mug of coffee while Jack finished cooking breakfast. Tomorrow, Jack would be gone. *Will he disappear Sunday morning or will I have all day? How much happiness can we fit into a day?* She wished time would slow down, perhaps start turning backward to give them more. *We'll fit in as much as possible.*

She walked to the table where her notebook sat. She opened it before taking another sip of coffee. Words darted through her mind, swooping like agile wings. She grabbed a pen and wrote.

You are the dragonflies
bursting from knee-high grass,
reflecting the light on your wings,
spreading warmth with your wind,
holding me captive.
I am like air,

shivering in your light.
I close my eyes,
open my hands for you,
as you move around me.

"Ready?" Jack called from the stove.

She closed the notebook. Her chest expanded when she looked at him. Jack was so full of life, and Ariel was right: Optimism was contagious. The woman who'd been intentionally pushing away relationships and closing herself off had been left behind.

"I could get used to this," Stella said, repeating his words from the day before. "Seeing you first thing in the morning. You making breakfast, me drinking coffee with you."

Jack pulled out his chair at the table. "I can't imagine any better way to start every day."

Stella sat and leaned her chin against her fisted hand. "Do you think that sounds too much like a fairy tale?"

Jack shrugged. "Fairy tales come from somewhere, don't they? There's a grain of truth in every story. Hans Christian Andersen said that life is the most wonderful fairy tale."

Stella reached for a piece of bacon. "It has its share of evil queens and dragons and moments when we aren't sure the hero's going to make it."

"Don't forget the handsome prince," he teased.

Stella touched his hand. "Are you referring to yourself?"

"I wouldn't say no in this story."

Stella squeezed his hand. "You're definitely made of prince material."

After breakfast, Stella left Jack at the cottage and drove to the coffee shop for pastries and then to the hospital. It was early, but she hoped Arnie would be awake so she could talk to him.

Lisa was working behind the desk, blowing pink bubbles and tapping her pen to the rhythm of a country song crooning quietly in the background. Her expression lifted when she saw Stella. "All ready for the festival? I get off at lunch, and I'm heading straight over."

Stella leaned her elbows on the high counter. "As ready as I can be. The committee's preparation makes it so much easier, and Arnie is just as organized. How's he doing? Do you know if he's awake?"

Lisa nodded. "His nurse just left a few minutes ago. He's doing well but impatient to go home, as to be expected. Go on in."

Stella knocked on the door and pushed it open when she heard Arnie call for her to enter. He was sitting up in the raised hospital bed holding a cup of coffee.

"Hey, kiddo," he said, before putting the cup on the bedside table. "I've been eager to hear about everything. Percy stopped by yesterday and surprised me. I had the nurse call him because I thought he'd want to know, but I didn't know he was coming to town."

Stella tamped down the irritation that wanted to erupt. "He surprised me too." *In more ways than one.*

"He looks good and happy," Arnie said.

"Mm-hmm." *Good thing Arnie hadn't seen Percy last night.*

Arnie clapped his hands together once. "How did festival setup go yesterday? Did everyone show up? Any problems? Any concerns?"

Stella grabbed the orange chair and slid it to the edge of the bed. "I told you not to worry. If the doctor gets wind that I've flustered you, they're going to forbid me from visiting. Do you want that? Then who will bring you breakfast pastries?" Stella shook the brown bag she'd been holding before putting it on the bedside table. "After a plateful of cookies, I figured you'd need healthy treats."

Arnie's eyes narrowed. "I *knew* you were somehow involved—sending Dana here with my favorite cookies."

Stella held up her hands in defense. "She asked if she could bring you anything, and I just told the truth." Stella sat in the chair. "So, how was it? Did you two hit it off?"

Arnie leaned his head back and sighed. "She's a lovely person."

When he didn't elaborate, she bounced her elbows on the bed until he opened his eyes again. "And?"

"And we're going to have tea or coffee or lunch when I make my jail break."

Stella smiled widely, and Arnie looked at her strangely. "Why are you looking at me like that?"

"I haven't seen you smile like that in ages," he said.

Stella sat upright, clasping her hands together in her lap. "I'm happy for you, that's all. You deserve someone nice to have conversations with. I like Dana. She seems like good people."

Arnie eyed her but continued, "She is. I should thank you for your sneakiness. Dana spent the better part of two hours here talking about all sorts of interesting topics. We could have talked for the rest of the day, but she had to go home to let out her dog. I'm looking forward to seeing her again."

"I knew once you got over the babbling bit, you'd have a great time," Stella said.

"Enough about me. Tell me about the festival, and I promise not to work myself up."

Stella explained how well the setup had gone, due to the committee's and his impeccable planning, and that there had been no issues they couldn't handle. She told him about the volunteers and the vendors and about Jack. But she purposely left out information about Hook and his untimely departure and her confrontation with Percy.

When she finished, Arnie's features relaxed. "That's what it is, then."

"That's what *what* is?"

"Jack."

Stella stilled. "What about him?"

Arnie reached over and patted her hand. "Someone has turned your light back on. You're glowing. I've missed that. I would tell you to be careful, but love is an adventure worth taking, and playing it safe isn't always worth it. Listen to an old man. Take the leap."

Stella stared at him. "I don't—"

"Don't deny yourself the pleasure of basking in it for a while." Arnie held out his hand to her, and she slipped hers into it.

Her throat tightened when she looked at him. "It's kinda terrifying, opening myself up again."

He nodded. "My two cents, kiddo? Love is always worth trying, even when it's scary. Don't let fear of the unknown keep you from living."

Stella nodded. "I hear you."

"You've only got this one life," he continued, glancing over at the machines beeping and keeping track of his vitals. "Go live it, and I suggest you love the hell out of it."

"Are you planning to take your own advice with Dana?"

Arnie grinned and rubbed his belly. "If those cookies are any indication of our future, it's going to be a sweet, fulfilling ride."

Stella released Arnie's hand. "Arnie, there's something I want to talk to you about. It's about Jack."

His expression sobered to match hers. "I'm listening."

"The ink only allows characters to visit for two weeks," Stella said.

Arnie nodded and shifted on the bed. "That's correct."

Stella inhaled a deep breath and then spoke in a rush of words on the exhale. "Have you ever, what I mean is, did you ever try or want to try to keep someone around longer? Is that a possibility?

When the Irishwoman gave you the ink, did she say there were exceptions?"

For an excruciatingly long pause, he didn't respond.

"Arnie, he's leaving tomorrow. You want me to take a leap? Not that I can stop myself at this point, but what about the fall? I'm picturing Icarus with wax wings. Why does Jack have to go? Why can't there be a way to help him stay?"

"There are rules," Arnie said.

Stella gripped the bedsheets in her fists. "Let's break them! There has to be a way. All of this is magical, so can't there be a magical solution?"

Arnie rubbed the back of his neck and looked toward the window. "If there is, I don't know it. I'm sorry, Stella."

A niggling started in Stella's gut. "What about Ruby Lou and Pearl?"

Arnie shot his gaze toward her. "What about them?"

"You brought them out, but they ran off and weren't in the library at the end of two weeks, right? Is that why their book disappeared? Because they weren't near the magic at the time they should have returned to their book? Or . . ." Stella's mind whirred. "Could they still be somewhere in the world, alive and well? Maybe the book disappeared not because something bad happened to them but because they weren't inside the library on time."

"No," Arnie said. "I *know* something happened."

"How could you possibly know? You've never seen them again. You don't know without a doubt that they"—she lowered her voice—"died."

"Yes, I do."

"But *how*? What if Jack isn't in the library when his due date comes? Could we keep him away and see what happens? Maybe keep him from the source of magic forever so he can stay here with me?"

"No," Arnie said, shaking his head. "I'm not doing that again—" He abruptly stopped.

"What do you mean *again*?"

"Drop it, Stella," Arnie said. "I've been using this magic longer than you've been alive. There are rules, and we will abide by them. Jack must return."

"Then why do this at all?" Stella asked. Her whole body began to tremble. An emotion akin to grief sprang up inside her. "Did I really need to experience someone else leaving me?"

Arnie reached for her hand, but she didn't take it. "Stella, I thought you'd like to connect with him in person, so to speak, since you have always been so fond of him. I thought it might give you courage to open up to the idea of dating again, but I didn't expect you to want to literally date Jack. I didn't know you'd fall in love with him."

"Well, I did!" she said, standing to her feet in a swell of emotion. She walked to the window and stared at the parking lot, blinking away tears.

"I'm so sorry, kiddo," Arnie said sincerely. "If I had known . . . I would have done this differently. I would have done a lot of things differently, but sometimes life is a learn-as-you-go experience."

"So that's it, then?" Stella said, fighting to control the tremble in her voice. "Jack has to leave."

Arnie nodded.

If Jack's leaving was unavoidable, she wouldn't spend her last hours with him crying and feeling sorry for herself. She wanted to enjoy his company so she could carry it in her heart for as long as possible. Jack had been supporting her and helping her since the moment she met him. He'd made her feel stable and more confident in herself. She had opened herself up to him, something she'd sworn to never do again with a man. She wouldn't ruin their final moments together being a weepy mess.

She wiped her cheeks. Sparkly words pressed through the sunlit windowpanes. **Anticipate. Create. Together.** They circled around Stella before pressing into the skin on her hands and disappearing. "I'd better get to the library. Keep resting up so you can come home soon. Everyone's been asking about you."

"Stella," he said with so much compassion. "I didn't mean to hurt you. I wouldn't have done any of this if I'd known it was going to bring you more heartache."

"You know, Arnie," she said, grabbing her purse, "this has been the best thing that has happened to me in a long time. The magic, the characters, Jack, these past few days. Jack might have 'turned my light back on,' but so much more has come to life inside me. I can see possibilities now." She hooked her purse over her shoulder and walked to the door. "I wish there was a way for him to stay longer. There's not a character we can bring out who could help us?"

Arnie closed his eyes and shook his head. "If there was, I would have resurrected that person years ago to repair lots of mistakes. I've met a few characters I wouldn't mind sharing my life with."

"Really?" Stella asked. "Who?"

Arnie waved his hand. "Never mind that. Would they have agreed?" He patted his belly. "I'm not exactly Aragorn."

A thought occurred to Stella. "I haven't asked Jack what he wants."

Arnie reached for his coffee and took a drink. "He'd definitely say yes."

Stella's brow furrowed. "How do you know that? You haven't even seen us together."

"That man would be an idiot not to want to stay with you."

She smiled at Arnie. She knew without a doubt that if he'd thought bringing Jack out for her would have harmed her, he never would have done it. For all Arnie knew, Stella and Jack could have enjoyed conversation but nothing more. "If I brought out the genie from Aladdin, could he grant me wishes?"

Arnie's laugh rattled his bedframe. "Doesn't work that way, but it's a brilliant idea."

"How do you know?" Stella asked. "Did you already try it?"

He winked at her. "What do you think?"

She grinned and waved goodbye, then rushed off to the library to spend what remaining time she had with Jack, all the while wishing for a solution to her heart's desire.

Chapter 21

When Stella parked at the library, vendors and volunteers were already arriving on the grounds. As she got out of her car, Jack walked out of Arnie's and crossed the lawn to meet her on the back steps of the library. Within an hour, a constant hum of energy and chatter filled the air. The festival didn't officially begin until ten, but dozens of people were already milling around, slapping backs, and hugging people they hadn't seen since the year before. Children chased one another around the gigantic oak tree in the parking lot and twirled in empty spots on the bright green lawn. Booths came alive with activity and the ticket takers prepared for the throng of people already lining up at the temporary gates.

Stella, Vicki, Dan, and Melanie met with the volunteers posted in the library and reviewed their jobs one final time. Then the group wandered off to find their stations.

Stella stood near the circulation desk and fanned herself. The air conditioner did its best to keep up with the summer heat, but sweat dampened the back of her shirt. "I want this to go well. Arnie's eager to hear about it later, and I want positive news for him."

Jack drank from a water bottle. "There's nothing to worry about. Did you see that line of people waiting to get in?" She nodded. "You know what you really need to do?"

She looked quizzically at him. "What?"

"Enjoy yourself." He wrapped his arm around her waist. "How could this day not be swell? I'm at a festival with you."

Stella rolled her eyes but she was smiling. "You always know what to say, don't you?"

"I ought to. I've had a hundred years of practice."

Stella's laughter sent out a surge of happy energy that spread throughout the library, and people nearby smiled wider and leaned a little closer to their friends. Crusoe and Darcy were gazing out a nearby library window that gave them a view of the grounds. She walked over to them.

"You know the rules," Stella said. "No book characters are allowed outside of the library."

Darcy peered down at her. "Yet Mr. Mathis walked with you through town. The rules don't apply to everyone, I've noticed."

"Mr. Crusoe," Stella said, "I know Mr. Darcy doesn't like strangers, but how do you feel about spending time with hundreds of people? You might be more accustomed to living without human contact since you spent so many years on your island."

Crusoe returned his attention to the window. "I overcame my despair and built a life out of what I had been given. I thanked God for a fate in which nothing I needed was missing, except friendship. As complicated as humans can be, and as barbaric, I still delight in the presence of others. I do believe I would enjoy spending time with people. Are you offering to break the rules for me? Perhaps for us?" He looked at Darcy.

"Well . . . Miss Parker is mostly right," Darcy said. "I don't dislike strangers, only being around so many of them and forced to converse." He focused on the activity outside the window. "What would I even say?"

Stella looked at Crusoe and then at Darcy. "What if you didn't have to say anything? No one's going to force you into small talk, Mr. Darcy, but you might enjoy being out in the sunshine for a while."

"I do enjoy a promenade," Darcy said.

"To feel the wind on my face," Crusoe added.

"You both must promise to be on your best behavior and come back at the end of the day. Can I trust you?"

Darcy smiled so widely that the sight momentarily stunned her. Had he ever looked so happy in his life? He practically radiated with pleasure. Then he reached out and clasped Stella's hand between both of his. "On my honor I will return at the closing of the festival."

Crusoe agreed. "You have my word. I am grateful for your faith in me."

"One more requirement," Stella said. "You can't tell anyone who you really are. If anyone asks, can you pretend to be impersonators hired by the library?" Both men nodded. "You've both done so much to help me with the mess I made. Get out there and have fun. You deserve it."

Her phone beeped in her pocket, so she excused herself. It was a text from Ariel. Heading your way. Any word from Percy? How are you holding up?

Stella replied: Haven't seen Percy. I'm doing okay for being knee-deep in a festival and trying to accept I can't keep Jack. Arnie said it's not possible.

Ariel texted back a frowning emoji followed by a shooting star and prayer hands. Stella slipped the phone back into her pocket.

"That was kind of you," Jack said. "Letting those two go free to enjoy the festival."

She leaned into his arm and wrapped her hands around his biceps. "Maybe it's irresponsible, but I'm going with my gut. I think I'll be able to tell which characters can be trusted and which ones can't handle that kind of freedom."

Jack's eyebrows lifted. "You sound like you want to be a part of this long term."

"I've been here for four years just doing a job, not knowing where I belonged. Just passing time. But now I think this *is* where I belong." She slipped her hand into Jack's. "I love it here. I love the books and helping people and being with Arnie.

"Now that I can use my gift to be of even greater service and I know about the magic, all of this feels like my purpose. I could start helping people find the right books since I can call on the words. And maybe—Arnie might completely reject this idea—but maybe we could bring out fictional characters and share them with the library patrons, just like I'm doing today. Say they're impersonators. Think how much fun the patrons would have being able to interact with their favorite characters. Who better to play them than the actual characters from the books?"

"And the new words? The purple ones?" Jack asked. "How do they fit in?"

"Another layer," Stella answered. "Rather than filling notebooks with my words and shoving them in my trunk or in a box to collect dust like I've done for years, it's time to do more with my writing. The new words are telling me a story or encouraging me to write one, to put something of my own out into the world." She glanced around the library. "Can you imagine seeing one of *my* books in here one day?"

"I'd memorize it like you've done mine," Jack said, and Stella laughed. "It'll only increase my obsession." He kissed her cheek. "I mean that in the least creepy way possible."

"You"—she poked her finger into his chest—"could never be creepy. You have too much of a Captain America vibe. Too much good guy plus the handsome hero."

"That's an honorable comparison. And you prefer the good guy to the rogue pirate?"

Stella scoffed. "Any day, all day." She leaned into him and sighed. "I'm going to miss you."

"Hey," he said, lifting her chin so she looked at him. "I'm still here."

Arnie believed Jack would want to stay permanently, even though that wasn't an option, but Stella was curious. "Would you stay longer than two weeks if you could?"

Jack's smile slipped. "That's not possible, unless . . ." Hope flashed through his eyes.

Stella shook her head. "No, according to Arnie it's not. I asked."

"You did?" Jack questioned. "You want me to stay longer?"

"Of course I do."

Jack wrapped his arms around her and pressed his face into her neck. "I'd stay for a hundred more years if I could. What I wouldn't give for a life with you."

"I wish there was a way," Stella admitted. "But I'll enjoy these last days with you, and then next year . . . next year you can come back." Did it sound pitiful that she was willing to wait an entire year to see someone she adored again?

"It won't get here fast enough," Jack said.

She shifted away. "What will it be like for you when you go back into your book? Will you remember all of this? Will you remember me?"

Jack rubbed the back of his fingers across her cheek. "I'll remember you when I return. It's difficult to explain what it's like when I'm not here. It's a state of being, but it's like being in my whole life all at once, like everything happens simultaneously. It's not controlled by time like life is here, and it's not like a movie on replay as though I'm reliving my life from start to finish indefinitely. The awareness of daily life and timekeeping . . . they just aren't something that's perceived."

While he struggled to explain, a line formed between his dark brows.

"That's mostly confusing," Stella said, "but it almost makes sense."

"There's no equivalent I can use as an example. The closest I can imagine is inner stillness, or heaven, but that's still too much for the human mind to completely grasp. It just *is*. All things, all time, all connected, forever."

Stella grinned. "Yeah, that clears it up. When Arnie brings you back, do you remember all the times you've been here before?"

Jack nodded. "That returns instantly. The easiest way to explain is that it's similar to downloading a file on a computer. All of my moments here are downloaded immediately into my mind as soon as I arrive."

Stella moved closer to him. "How strange that must be. It sounds like waking up after a dream." She entwined her hands with his. "Does it feel like a dream for you? Being here now?"

Jack shook his head. "No. Being here with you feels more like reality to me. Nothing has felt more real." He leaned down and kissed her.

Stella pressed into him, tumbling into the exquisite moment of kissing Jack. A tingling sensation started in her chest and then increased tenfold, shooting blasts of heat through her veins. She thought it must be the power of the kiss, but when Jack inhaled sharply, she realized it was much more than that.

Violet words pulsed from her shirt in rhythm with her beating heart. But bright purple words also erupted from Jack's T-shirt, arcing toward Stella's words until the two sets formed a bridge between their bodies. Then in a smooth motion, the words lifted into the air between them, pulling away from their bodies. Jack and Stella stepped away from each other.

Heat continued to course through Stella's veins, but unlike the times before, she wasn't in pain. This experience was more like being dropped into a hot tub, surrounded by warmth and flowing water. Instead of rootlike tendrils hanging from the words, they sprouted wings. In awe, Stella spoke them aloud. "'He talked about eternity and love as if the two were impossibly entwined.'"

The words acknowledged her voice, flapped hard enough to send blasts of wind over them, and flew high into the arched foyer ceiling. Then they dive-bombed the circulation desk and shot right through the countertop, disappearing into the wood. Stella didn't realize she was trembling until Jack rubbed his hand up her arm.

"What just happened?" he asked.

A wild storm of thoughts bombarded her, rendering her incapable of answering immediately. Stella opened a bottom drawer of the desk and reached for her journal. She found the page where she'd been cataloging the violet words and wrote down the new ones. The collection now read: *I fell in love once. Did I ever tell you that? He was excruciatingly handsome and no ordinary man, but one built from paper and rich black ink. He talked about eternity and love as if the two were impossibly entwined.* Stella looked up, her wide eyes finding Jack's.

"What?" he asked.

The last time the painful words appeared, Stella had asked them to come gently. They'd obeyed her. This instance had filled her with a sense of profound love.

Jack touched her arm again. "What is it, Stella?"

She closed the journal and returned it to the drawer. "The words aren't *happening* to me, making me a helpless victim of their whims. We're more like partners, working together."

"They looked different this time," Jack said.

Stella placed her hand over her heart where it beat in a synchronized rhythm. "I asked them to change after the last time, to not be so painful."

"And they obeyed," Jack said, sounding amazed.

"I also think the words are about you," she said, finally connecting the various pieces together.

"Me?"

Stella nodded again. "You can see them, and this last set, they came *out of you*."

He pointed to her. "And you."

"Both of us," Stella agreed. "Reading them all together now, it sounds like I'm talking about you. About us. The beginning of a story."

Jack smiled. "That's a story I'd like to read."

"Stella," Vicki called, coming up a nearby aisle. "One of the indoor vendors has requested power even though they didn't originally sign up for it. Can we get power to them?"

"We might be able to," Stella said. "It depends on if we have an open space to hook them up to it." She looked at Jack. "We'll continue this later?" Jack nodded, and they both joined Vicki to check the library's power grid.

Food trucks arrived soon after and parked in designated spots. They prepped their menu items, and soon the summer breeze carried the scents of vanilla waffle cones, melting chocolate, funnel cakes, spiced nuts, hamburgers, french fries, and tacos. And those were just a few of the offerings.

The line to get into the festival stretched down the sidewalk. At promptly ten o'clock the gates opened and a flood of people flowed in, eyes bright and faces eager. The first band kicked off its opening number, and Stella held her clipboard of maps and information against her chest as she stood on the lawn.

"Here we go," she said to Jack. "I know you want to help me keep everything under control, but I think you should enjoy yourself too. Wander around and be free for a day. You could dress up in your uniform and give people a proper history lesson."

"Do you need help at your booth with the care packages and receiving donations?" he asked.

She poked her finger into his chest. "Go enjoy the festival. I have volunteers working the donation booth. I'll pop in and check on them, but I have complete confidence in them."

"I'll be around if you need anything," Jack said. "I'll find you in a couple hours, and we can grab a snack at the food trucks. Remember, you owe me a dance or two later."

Stella wanted to spend the day with Jack, but most of her attention belonged to the festival. "I'll keep this ship on course."

✦ ✦ ✦

AROUND LUNCHTIME, ARIEL found Stella making her rounds outside on the library grounds. Ariel had a sun painted on one cheek and a rainbow on the other. She wore her hair in a high ponytail, and crescent moon earrings dangled from her lobes.

"I hope you're proud of yourself," Ariel said. "The festival is fantastic."

Stella grinned. "The committee and Arnie did 99 percent of the work. I'm just overseeing the library vendors and problem-solving as needed. I see you've been enjoying yourself."

Ariel puffed out her cheeks and glanced down at them as though she could see the colorful designs. "It was either this or a dragon face. I figured this would be slightly more acceptable for someone my age."

"Pfft," Stella said. "Who cares? We're never too old to enjoy ourselves."

"I like this happy version of you," Ariel said as a kid ran by with a balloon shaped like a dog.

"Me too."

"Anything more happening with those new words?" Ariel asked. "The ones that are kinda scary?"

Stella placed a hand on her chest. "Yes. I've received a lot more. Just this morning the purple words came out of me *and* Jack." Using her fingers, she drew an arcing bridge in the air. "They joined up, grew wings, and flew away."

"Well, that's not the weirdest thing you've ever told me," Ariel said, "but it ranks pretty high. What do you think it means?"

"It feels like a story about Jack and me," Stella said.

"Not to be a downer, but Arnie said it's not possible to prolong Jack's stay. What exactly did he say?"

Stella stared off into the crowd of happy faces. "He said there are rules, and we have to follow them."

Ariel's sunshine and rainbow wilted when her lips did. "That's it? No details? No explanation as to *why*?"

Stella nodded but stopped. "Hmm, well, now that you mention it, when I asked him about extending a character's stay, he said he wasn't doing that 'again.'"

Ariel's lips parted in a look of surprise. "Do you think he tried to keep someone here before?"

Was Arnie adamant about not allowing Stella to try because he'd tried and failed? Who would Arnie have wanted to stay? "I'll have to ask him. He wouldn't say more this morning."

Ariel touched Stella's arm. "I'm sorry, though. I was hopeful you could get more time with Jack."

Stella sighed. "I'm trying to enjoy the time we have left."

Ariel grinned. "Are you now?" she said playfully. "In what ways are you enjoying it?"

"Lots of ways." Stella laughed as Ariel clapped with delight. "I didn't tell you that Percy surprised us at Arnie's cottage."

"No, he didn't!" Ariel exclaimed. "He didn't surprise you in the middle of—"

"Good heavens, no!" Stella said, and they both giggled. "That would have been awful. He showed up yesterday morning, and we were still in our pajamas."

Ariel put her hand over her heart. "Poor Percy. He can't handle you growing up and making your own decisions. Have you seen him today?"

She hadn't been intentionally looking for her brother, but she'd spotted a face in the crowd a few times and thought it was him. "If he's here, he's probably avoiding me or concocting a plan to redirect my life."

They both scanned the throng of people around them. Ariel grabbed Stella's arm and stiffened beside her.

"What?" Stella asked. "Do you see him?"

"Yes," Ariel said.

"Where?"

Ariel motioned with her head. "Over by the lemonade stand."

Stella followed Ariel's line of vision but didn't see Percy. At the stand she saw a woman dressed in a flowery sundress and a man with a German shepherd on a short leash. "I don't see Percy."

"Not Percy," Ariel whispered. "Liam."

"Who's Liam?" Stella asked. Rose petal–pink words rose from

the rainbow painted on Ariel's cheek. **Ask me. Romantic. Sunset walk.** "Wait, is this your client with the dog named Scout?"

Ariel nodded.

Stella nudged her with her elbow. "Go talk to him."

"I can't," Ariel said. "What would I say?"

"Hello?"

Ariel laughed and then stopped and stared at Liam as he ordered a drink from the vendor. "What am I scared of?" Ariel asked, sounding like she was talking to herself. "You're taking a chance on love with someone you *know* can't stay forever, and I'm too afraid to take a chance on a guy I don't even know. And there *could* be a chance for something special. You're right. I'm going to walk over there and say hello." Then she winced. "Do I look ridiculous with my face painted?"

"You look adorable, and if Liam doesn't think so, he can beat it. You don't need to be with anyone who doesn't embrace all of you."

Joy stretched Ariel's smile. "Wow, Stella, you *have* changed. Thank you for the encouragement. Wish me luck!"

"Good luck! But you don't need it."

Ariel bounced over toward Liam. As soon as Scout saw Ariel, her tail wagged, and Ariel bent down to pet her, causing Liam to engage with her immediately. Within less than a minute, they were both smiling and chatting like two people who'd planned to meet at the lemonade stand. As they walked off together, Stella squeezed the clipboard against her chest and felt buoyant with hope for everyone, including herself.

The day went much smoother than Stella had imagined. By afternoon, there had only been a few minor issues that were easy to fix. Although she remained on alert for problems, the festivalgoers and vendors sailed through the afternoon on a sea of enjoyment. She'd even seen Darcy and Crusoe a few times. To her surprise,

Darcy had been playing a game of croquet with a trio of ladies who looked enraptured by his attention. Crusoe had been engaged in a lawn game of giant Jenga and appeared to be winning.

Later in the day Stella stopped by the donation tent for the charity her dad had started. The sight of all the contributions amazed her. "There's so much," she said.

Esther, one of the volunteers, agreed. "Twice as much as last year. You should have enough to create at least fifty care packages."

Stella walked through the boxes of goods given by festivalgoers. "More than that," she said. Her dad would have been thrilled by all the kindness shown to a cause he loved. "Thank you for all your help today."

"My pleasure," Esther said. "And we'll make sure this is all sorted for you. Stack it in the same library room as last year?"

"Yes, thank you."

After leaving the donation booth, Stella saw Darcy coming out of a photo booth with a woman dressed in Regency attire. They were both laughing while looking at the black-and-white photos. Crusoe had won an oversize teddy bear at a game of ring the bottle, and in the late afternoon when she saw them returning into the library with their hands full of food, she was thankful she'd broken the rules for them.

She'd caught sight of Jack a few times, but each time he'd been deeply engaged in conversation, and similarly to how she felt about giving Darcy and Crusoe their freedom, she experienced a squeeze of gratefulness for not monopolizing Jack's last days in Blue Sky Valley.

The Ink Blots took the stage at 7:30 p.m., and Jack found Stella helping a young girl tie off a yellow water balloon. As he approached, Stella shielded her eyes from the setting sun. The girl ran off with her balloon, calling out to someone who should "run for their life."

"They're playing our song," Jack said, holding out his hand for Stella.

She wiped her wet hands on her shorts. "We have a song?"

"If I'm honest, any song that will get you to dance with me can be our song."

She hesitated before taking his hand. "I meant it when I said I don't know how to dance."

"I plan on taking it slow."

Jack led her to the dance floor, which was crowded with couples swaying to a 1940s ballad. He wrapped one arm around her waist and held up his other hand so she could slide her fingers through his. He swayed their bodies back and forth in rhythm, and she exhaled, willing herself to relax. By the time the second song started, Stella was more at ease and rested her head on his shoulder.

She had skipped every dance her middle school and high school had hosted to avoid embarrassing herself by being clumsy while on display. She also hadn't wanted to suffer the sting of no one asking her to a dance, since she'd adamantly sworn to anyone within earshot that she had no interest in going. But she'd been curious and more than once wished some boy would have asked her anyway. Now she understood what she'd been missing.

"I like this," she said, closing her eyes and resting her head on his chest.

"I *love* this," he said.

When the next song started with a quick tempo, Stella tugged Jack off the dance floor. "I don't think I'm ready for the jitterbug or swing dancing."

He pulled her against him. "I can teach you."

Stella laughed. "Not right now. I'm just getting used to the idea that I can dance to the slow ones. Thank you for bringing me out here. I'm glad my first dance was with you. It was really nice."

Jack pressed his cheek against her hair. "'Really nice' is an understatement. I could dance with you until the stars come out and the sun rises and then—"

She laughed again and playfully pushed him away. "Are you sweet-talking me? Trying to woo me?"

Mischief glinted in his eyes. "Is it working?"

Stella pressed her hands against his chest. "Jack, I need to be honest with you."

His playful expression disappeared. "Let's hear it."

"Everything you do works for me."

He covered her hands with his. "I know just what you mean."

✦ ✦ ✦

BY 8:30 P.M. the festival started winding down, and the crowd thinned as people found their way to their cars. Vendors packed up, and the food trucks sold the last of their goods to late-night eaters. Everyone would be gone in less than two hours, so Stella headed inside the library to make sure vendors had help packing up if they needed it. More than half of the indoor booths had already been dismantled, and volunteers helped vendors carry boxes and supplies out to their vehicles.

Stella took the stairs up to the second floor and looked around. It was empty except for a scattering of left-behind papers and to-go cups. She gathered the trash and carried it to a trash bin. When she reached across a table to scoop up a few stray pencils, someone walked up behind her.

Stella glanced over her shoulder with a smile, assuming it was Jack, but her stomach plummeted. Wade Haynes—handsome and confident—stood there grinning at her.

Chapter 22

"Hey there," Wade said, still grinning at Stella as though they'd planned this encounter, as though he hadn't been gone and silent for months.

She stared at him. She tried to inhale a slow breath that might control her heart as it galloped out of control, but her lungs didn't respond. She gripped the pencils in her hand. One snapped.

"No hello? No hey, how are you?" Wade said, moving closer, his shadow like a menace inching toward her.

Thoughts slammed around in her mind like trapped, angry wasps. Where had he come from? After all this time, why was he here? He'd never been in the library before. Seeing him standing in her favorite place felt all kinds of wrong. The back of Stella's neck burned. "What are you doing here?"

"We brought the kids to the festival," he said. "Great job with it. Myles brought his girlfriend, so he didn't spend as much time with us, but she's a nice girl. Hannah and Christian had a blast with all the activities. There was plenty for the older kids to do this year, even more than last year, I'd say."

He stepped closer, and Stella took a step backward.

"I saw you out on the dance floor with a guy," he continued. "Who is he? I haven't seen him before. Seemed like you two know each other pretty well."

There was no mistaking the jealousy in Wade's voice. He sounded like a man hinting at someone invading his territory. Stella dropped the pencils on the table, and her empty hands balled into fists. What right did he have to care who she was with?

"Not that it's any of your business, but he's not from around here."

When she didn't offer any more conversation, he said, "Vague on the details. But you look good, Stella. Beautiful as ever. I've missed you. Every day I've thought about you. Every. Day."

Disbelief washed over her. He expected her to believe that? Anger crackled in her veins. "You haven't contacted me for months. You might as well be a stranger to me."

Wade smirked. "That's a little dramatic, don't you think? We've never been strangers."

He walked toward her. She caught a whiff of his soap and remembered how his scent lingered on her hands. He spoke to her in that unguarded voice he used when they were alone. "You know me better than anyone."

In an instant, she recalled Wade disappearing without a word. Tumbling backward into the past created a hollow inside her, and the emptiness expanded.

"The man I thought you were wouldn't have ghosted me. He would have answered at least *one* of my messages. But somehow you've thought about me *every day*?" Stella pointed toward the exit, wishing her hand wasn't trembling. "You should go. You don't get to show up and act like everything that happened is okay. Don't act like we're friends. My heart *starved* in your silence."

"Still my favorite wordsmith," he said as though she wasn't serious. "Can you honestly say you haven't thought of me? That you haven't missed me?"

Stella backed herself against the table. "How was it so easy for you not to contact me day after day?"

Wade frowned. "You knew how stressful life was for me. You knew the pressure I was under. Temporary changes had to be made."

A sickly feeling slithered through Stella. Old wounds struggled to remain closed, but the woman she had been had burned up in the flames alongside the journal. That woman was ash, fertile ground for someone new to be reborn.

Stella clenched her jaw. Why hadn't she seen how *temporary* she was back then? Why had it taken her so long to realize the truth? At least clarity was with her now. Her insides trembled so hard that she felt herself visibly shaking.

"When you left I felt sick with grief and confusion. I actually believed in us. I believed you wanted a future with me, but it's so clear to me now that was never your intention. You were happy to drag me along indefinitely so you could have it all."

Wade reached for her hand, and for a moment, she let him intertwine his fingers with hers. His cold fingers sent a shiver up her arm.

"Stella, baby," he said. "I never stopped thinking about you or loving you. I don't have anyone in my life like you. I miss us. I miss *you*. We had a lot of fun. We had a good thing, didn't we?"

Stella pulled her hand away. "No. We had a broken thing, a mess of a relationship where you came and went when you had time. If something had to give or be pushed aside, it was me. I was always the expendable one." She walked past him. If he wouldn't leave, she would.

But Wade grabbed her arm.

"Stella, I never pushed you aside in my heart. You're still there. You're still my favorite girl."

Bright blue words sneaked across the books behind Wade. **I miss you. I love you. You were my escape.** Wade slid his hand up her arm, across her shoulder, and up her neck. "I still love you." His hand crept down her arm. "I will always love you."

Stella shuddered and stepped away. Any lingering desire she might have had for Wade had vanished. She wanted nothing to do with him anymore. He'd come to the festival with *his wife* and kids. Nothing was different from when they first started seeing each other. "And what has changed?"

His brow wrinkled. "What do you mean?"

Fury tore through her. She'd wasted too many days on Wade already. "What have you changed in your life that would make our situation any different? Would I not be the *other woman* now? Would I not be second? Or third or fourth or fifth? Maybe sixth if you place me behind your job as well? Would you have *more* time for me because you'd be free to spend time with me without either of us feeling ashamed of what we're doing?"

Wade stared at her.

Stella shook her head. His lack of response said it all. "I think the answer you're searching for is *nothing*. Nothing has changed because you were never going to change anything about your life for me." She clenched and unclenched her hands. "Your silence and your leaving broke my heart. But your leaving was the greatest gift you could have given me. There's no place for you in my life anymore, and even if there was, I don't want you in it. I've always deserved more than you were willing to offer." She turned and walked away.

Wade didn't speak. A few seconds later, he called her name just as she reached the staircase. She sprinted down them as though he might pursue her and ran to a broom closet on the first floor where she closed herself inside.

She leaned her back against the far wall and slid down, pushed a mop bucket out of the way, and pressed her knees into her chest. Then she hugged her arms around her legs, touched her forehead to her knees, and let hot, furious tears roll down her cheeks, releasing the last traces of emotional garbage she'd been carrying around in her heart since Wade left. An awareness of deliverance broke the surface, and for the first time since Wade had left, Stella felt truly free.

✦ ✦ ✦

SOME TIME LATER Jack opened the closet door and filled the small space with light. Stella blinked in the harshness of it.

"I'm going to assume you're not rearranging shelves or searching for the perfect broom." He stepped inside and held out his hand. Stella grabbed it and let Jack pull her to her feet.

She wiped at her cheeks. "How did you know I was in here?"

"I didn't, although not for lack of searching. Darcy said he heard crying. Then I recognized Wade from the photograph you showed me. He was walking out of the library looking like a survivor of a great war."

She'd never seen Wade upset about anything, not in any heartbroken capacity. Had she actually upset him? She assumed his heart was closed off and unaffected. How else could a man who professed to love her ghost her for months?

"No," Jack said, as though reading her mind. "Don't you dare feel sorry for that man. He made his bed. Let him lie in it. *Without* you." Jack's gaze held a questioning look. "You *did* tell him no, didn't you?"

"Of course," Stella said, miffed that he'd question her desire for Wade. "I don't want anything to do with him."

Jack's gaze softened. "Come here." He folded her into his embrace.

New tears formed, but the intensity of her sadness had faded. These tears filled her with relief. She'd never stood up for herself when it came to Wade. She'd let him do whatever he wanted whenever he wanted, always putting her own needs to the side. Not anymore.

"How's your heart?" Jack asked while rubbing her back.

She sniffled against his chest. "Good. Strong." She leaned away from him to meet his gaze. "I imagined his return so many times in a million different ways. I imagined how my heart would react, everything I would say, and even how he might explain his absence in a way that would make his leaving less hurtful. But when the moment finally arrived, I was angry and indignant on my own behalf. He doesn't get to waltz back into my life like he's the returning hero. He doesn't get access to me anymore. He gave that up. Willingly. I thought I'd feel guilty for telling him to get lost, but I don't. I *want* him to get lost."

Jack held her. "It's important that you take care of yourself. I hope you know that."

Vicki called her name from the foyer, and Stella released Jack. Vicki held two white paper plates with funnel cakes dusted in a thick layer of powdered sugar. "I brought dessert to celebrate the success of the festival! Arnie will be so proud of us. Oh, I didn't realize Jack was still here. Well, we can share— Hey, are you okay?"

Stella touched her fingertips to her wet cheeks. "Just stress relieving."

Vicki put the plates on the circulation desk. "I get that. There were a few touch-and-go moments when I thought I might lose it, but I think we did the library proud. I received hundreds of compliments. The only thing people complained about was the heat, and that's out of our control. Get over here, and let's celebrate a job well done, and thank the heavens we don't have to do this again for another year."

Stella appreciated the distraction. She, Jack, and Vicki finished off the funnel cakes and chatted about the day's events. It was late, but she called Arnie because she'd promised to update him. His relief and pleasure traveled through the phone and filled Stella with satisfaction and gratitude.

When she finished talking with Arnie, she, Jack, and the rest of the library crew walked the grounds outside the library while the remaining volunteers made sure the park was empty. At nearly ten thirty Stella locked the rear door to the library and waved goodbye to everyone. She sat on the back steps and stared at the empty lawn. Jack sat down beside her.

In the soupy evening air, a sprinkle of lightning bugs flashed as they weaved above the grass. A crescent moon peaked over the pine trees in the distance. Crickets eased out in the silence, making sure the coast was clear, and then chirped a summertime song. Stella's shoulders sagged forward as she propped her elbows on her knees. Jack's warmth felt strong and solid beside her. She leaned her head back and looked up at the stars.

Stella was proud of herself for standing up to Wade and happy for the festival's success. She should be content with how her life was changing, guiding her toward a better path, but all she could think about was that Jack would be gone in less than a day.

"So . . . tomorrow," she said, trying to pretend the conversation was easy.

Jack reached for her hand and pressed it between both of his. "It normally happens around sunset or just after. There's no definite time, but around then seems to be the case more often than not."

Stella closed her eyes, the starlight imprinting on the inside of her eyelids. She had let hope loose like a wild thing with no chance of catching it again. A quiver started in her heart and then spread out like a shock wave. She dropped his hand and stood.

"I'm going to take a walk, get some air." She stepped off the back stoop and trudged across the grass with no destination in mind. Tears stung her eyes, and she clenched her jaw to keep the threatening sob at bay. After a long, exhausting day, plus the encounter with Wade, she was overly worn down, which meant she was also overly emotional.

"Stella," Jack called.

His shoes slapped the soft earth as he hurried to catch up with her, but she didn't stop. She *couldn't* stop because then she would have to face him. She would have to look in his eyes and know she'd have to say goodbye soon.

"Stella," he said, taking hold of her arm and slowing her forward motion. "Hey, look at me."

Stella stopped walking, but she didn't turn her head. She didn't trust herself to keep her composure. "No."

"Why not?"

"Because I-I'm about two seconds away from making a blubbering, embarrassing mess of myself."

Jack stepped in front of her. "Tell me why you're upset."

"Is that a joke?" she asked, her voice breaking with sadness. "You *know* why I'm upset. You're leaving. Tomorrow. And then what? What about me? What am I supposed to do with that?"

"I can't tell you how to feel, but I can tell you how I feel. I'm thankful."

"That you're leaving?" Stella glared at Jack and shoved him out of the way. But he hooked her arm and spun her around.

"No, because of the time we've had. This is the best thing that has ever happened to me," Jack said. "*You* are the best thing that's ever happened to me. I know it's been only a few days, but these have been the most wonderful days. Because of *you*. And I don't regret a second of our time together. I don't want to waste our last hours together feeling sad. I want to enjoy every moment with you."

Tears filled her eyes. "I can't pretend that you're not leaving."

Jack touched her face. "I'm not asking you to pretend. I'm suggesting that we both try to enjoy the time we have left. No, I can't stay here forever, and yes, we knew this was temporary, but I wouldn't change anything. Look what's happened to you in just a few days. Your heart has opened back up. You're *happy*, Stella."

She opened her eyes and pressed her finger into his chest. Warm tears slid down her cheeks. "Because of *you*."

"Don't give me all the credit. You're the reason your heart opened, but if I can help keep it open, then there's hope that someone else can too."

Stella's bottom lip quivered. "I don't want someone else. I want you."

Jack cupped her face in his hands and wiped away her tears with his thumbs. "And I want you. Tonight we still have each other."

He pressed his mouth against hers, and she responded, melting against him. It was so easy to let go of her anxiety and sadness when he was kissing her, when he erased everything from her mind except for the feel of him. She gripped the back of his shirt and pressed him as close as possible.

Lightning bugs danced around their bodies, and Stella sighed against Jack's lips. He filled her with the kind of happiness that made her buoyant. Without his arms around her, anchoring her to the earth, she would have lifted off the ground. She could hold herself together for one more night.

Before they disappeared into Arnie's cottage, she noticed the lightning bugs left behind trails of flickering words.

Hang on.
Come through.
Have faith.

Chapter 23

Early the next morning Stella woke up with her arm and leg draped over Jack. Faint sunlight drifted through the slats in the blinds. Something had woken her. *A noise?* Jack shifted beneath her, and when he spoke, his voice rumbled in the ear she had pressed against his chest.

"Your phone," he said. Then he stretched his arm off the couch and reached for her cell phone on the chair, tapping it with his fingertips until the phone slid over far enough for him to grab. He handed it to her.

Arnie had texted her, which he had *never* done for as long as she'd known him. She had no idea his phone was even capable of texting. He believed texting was a passive-aggressive mode of communication that gave people a way of talking about serious topics without having to actually *talk* to the other person. Arnie believed talking in person was vital for a solid, healthy relationship. So the idea that he had just texted her made her smile. Did he think he was betraying himself even while he did it?

She read the message and pushed herself up on one arm. "Arnie wants to come home this morning. He didn't want to call this early because he thought I would still be sleeping. He probably thought I'd snooze right through the text alert."

"He *wants* to come home or he's being discharged?" Jack asked.

Stella leaned over him and put her phone on the floor beside the couch. She lay back down on his chest and inhaled. "I'm going to assume they told him he can go home or he's pestered them enough to consent to his will. But I want to lie here for another few minutes, and then I'll get up and call him."

Jack put his arm around her and held her against him. Then he rubbed his hand against her hair, slow and gentle. When the thought of his leaving popped into her mind, she shoved it aside. *Just a little while longer.*

Her peace lasted for approximately five more minutes, and then her throat tightened and her stomach responded in kind. Thoughts of the future crept in and robbed her of the last slivers of stillness.

Jack kissed the top of her head. "Right now, in this moment, I would give anything for this to go on and on."

She wanted to clutch him as tightly as possible. *Why did I do this? Didn't I know it would end? Why did I think this was worth it—worth hurting myself?* Another voice in her head whispered, *Love—real love—is always worth it.*

"Hey," Jack said. "You okay?"

"Yeah." She was surprised her voice didn't crack. She'd been acting like she was okay for so long, the lie came out easier than it should have. But this time, the lie made her uneasy. "Why?"

"You were holding your breath," he said, shifting beneath her. He sat up on the couch and lifted her with him, forcing her into a sitting position. "You don't look okay. What's wrong?"

She swung her legs off the couch and hopped up. "I need coffee."

"Stella," he said, grabbing her hand.

She sighed. "I stink at living in the present. I stink at appreciating this moment right now because I'm so caught up in the fact that you'll be gone in hours. I *want* to be present and here and feel a spirit of thankfulness, but this empty, sick emotion is growing because I can't stop reminding myself that you're leaving. I've had the best days ever with you, and I'm . . ." She struggled to control her emotions. When she opened her eyes, feathery words flapped in the sunlight. **Sad. Leaving. Goodbye.** "And I'm sad."

Jack stood beside her. He opened his mouth to say something, but she shook her head.

"I don't want to talk about it. Nothing we can say will change what's going to happen. Let's have coffee, and I'll swallow this. I'll save my falling apart until you're gone." She walked into the kitchen and grabbed the carafe from the coffee maker. "Talk about something else."

"I don't want you to fall apart," Jack said, following her into the kitchen. "I don't want that for you."

Stella filled the carafe with water and lifted the back of the coffee maker and poured it in. Jack took the carafe from her and placed it on the counter.

"Hey," he said gently. "Look at me."

Sadness reflected in his eyes, mirroring her own. She touched his cheek. "What's wrong?"

"What's *wrong?*" he asked incredulously. "I'm leaving you, and I don't want to." He pulled Stella close, and she wrapped her arms around him. "*This* is the kind of love I was looking for, I guess you could say my whole life. Now I've found it, and I have to leave, and, Stella, I don't *want* to leave you, and I don't want you to fall apart or be sad, but I'm sad too."

Stella held him tightly and squeezed. "We're a miserable pair," she said, trying to regain her composure.

"At least we're together," he said.

"For now," she added.

Jack put both hands on her cheeks and kissed her lightly. "I'll take it." He pressed her head against his chest.

Simple bright white words coasted over Jack's shoulder and shimmied up her arm. **Be here now.** His gaze followed the words until they disappeared into the fabric of her sleeve.

"Okay, I see you," she said out loud to the words. "Let's have coffee and you can tell me a story," she said to Jack.

"What kind of story?"

"Something hopeful."

Jack grabbed the can of coffee and placed a filter in the pot. Then he spooned in a few tablespoons of the dark ground beans. She turned on the machine, then grabbed two mugs out of the cabinet and placed them on the counter. Stella retrieved the half-and-half from the refrigerator and placed it beside their mugs. Then she opened the silverware drawer and took out a spoon.

"A hopeful story? How about the story of us, my favorite story?" Jack said, slipping his arms around her. "And I can't keep my hands off you."

She allowed herself a smile. "So don't."

✦ ✦ ✦

TWO HOURS LATER Stella helped Arnie into the passenger seat of her car and made sure he was buckled in before she closed the door. They drove in silence for a few minutes while Arnie closed his eyes and turned his face toward the warm sunlight flooding in through the car window.

After a long, slow exhale, he said, "You forget how much you love and need the sunshine when you're stuck indoors for so long. You know you love it, and you know it's a blessing, but you almost forget how *good* it feels on your face. The warmth, the feeling of peace in knowing that it's still rising and setting and right now it's warming you with its light. I've missed that. It came through my windows every day, but being outside reminds me of how much I like being alive."

Stella glanced over at him before returning her gaze to the road. She wondered what it would feel like to know that her time in the sun was limited, that she might be confined to the hospital and never feel the sun's warmth on her face again. Would she be anxious? Sad? Accepting? As soon as she was free again, she imagined herself standing in the sun, arms stretched open wide, face turned toward the sky and smiling.

"I like you being alive too," she said.

She felt Arnie's gaze turn toward her. "Thanks, kiddo. It's good to be going home. Want to tell me what's going on with you?"

Stella shot a look at him and then focused on driving again. "What do you mean?"

Arnie turned slightly in his seat to face her. "I'm not one to pry too much into your personal life, but I've known you a long time, and I think that gives me a pass when it comes to prying."

"Agreed," Stella said, knowing where Arnie's questioning would go.

"You were lit up like a lantern the last time I saw you, but now it's dim. This is about Jack leaving?"

Stella used her turn signal and turned toward the library. "I feel like my whole world opened up, like Dorothy must have felt when she stepped into Oz. Technicolor overload. Kansas was black and white, but Oz . . . Oz was beautiful and magical and brilliant. It was the adventure of a lifetime. But then she couldn't stay. She had to go back home, where the world was black and white."

Arnie stared ahead at the street, at the pine trees lining the sides of the road. "I hear what you're saying, but not everything is black and white."

Stella's grip tightened on the wheel. "No, not everything. The magic is real, and my words have led me toward a new path."

"Your words?" Arnie asked.

"Later," Stella said, waving a hand through the air. "But yes, most of this gloom and doom is about Jack. I don't want him to go, Arnie. How am I supposed to be okay with him leaving?"

"Letting go of something that brought you joy will *seem* as though it might take the life out of you, and it can for a while, but it won't forever. And Dorothy carried the dream and beauty of Oz in her heart forever."

"That's garbage, Arnie."

"Stella!"

"What? Maybe it's not garbage, but right now I'm sad and disappointed and frustrated. Can't you understand that?"

"Do you regret that it happened?" he asked. "Are you sorry that you've allowed yourself to feel something again? To be happy?"

She pulled the car into Arnie's driveway and parked behind his convertible. "Mostly no." She pressed both hands to her chest. "I have loved the feeling I've had with him. But I have regret because I'm afraid of how much it's going to hurt when he's gone."

Arnie reached over and grabbed her hand. "I am so sorry, Stella. I never would have brought him here if I'd known. I thought I was finally ready to tell you the truth about the magic and you'd get a kick out of talking to him. I didn't know you'd get so attached."

"To my childhood crush?" she argued. "Why wouldn't I have gone all googly-eyed for him?"

"You're not a child anymore, kiddo," Arnie said. "I didn't know you'd still be harboring feelings for him."

"Have you *seen* him?" Stella asked, exasperated.

"I'm sorry," Arnie said again, and the pained look on his face caused Stella to lean over briefly and lay her head on his shoulder. He laid his hand on her cheek. "I'd never hurt you on purpose."

"I know." She turned off the engine. "You're *sure* there's no way to let him stay?" She couldn't stop the tears that pooled in her eyes.

"I wish I had all the answers for you," Arnie said. "I wish I could help in some cure-all way. But the magic is powerful, and there are rules for a reason. Rules we shouldn't break."

Stella met his gaze. "Again?"

Arnie's face paled. "What do you mean?"

A tear slipped down her cheek, and she wiped it away. "In the hospital you mentioned that we couldn't try to keep someone away from the source of the magic *again*."

Arnie averted his gaze. "The babblings of an old man."

Stella leaned against the seat and dropped her head back, releasing a loud exhale. "Love is a wonderful, terrible thing."

"More wonderful than terrible, I hope," Arnie said.

Stella looked over at him, wiped at her tears, and nodded. "Me too." She cleared her throat and inhaled. "Let's get inside before we start sweating. It's gonna be as hot as a two-dollar pistol today."

✦ ✦ ✦

AFTER SETTLING ARNIE back into his cottage and starting a load of laundry, Stella felt calm enough to walk over to the library. She checked in with Melanie and Dan and updated them on Arnie. She also found Jack and asked if he'd like to eat lunch with them at the cottage.

"I told Arnie about us," she admitted.

Jack gawked at her. "What did you tell him?" His gaze drifted toward Arnie's cottage.

"Don't be absurd," she said, understanding the panic on his face. "I didn't tell him everything, just about my feelings for you and how I want you to stay and I'm sad and blah blah blah."

Jack grabbed Stella's hand, causing her heart to wobble. "What did he say?"

"He's mostly upset with himself for bringing you out. He assumed we'd have a nice chat and that would be the end of our story."

"How could anyone have a nice chat with you and want that to be the end of the story?" Jack asked.

Warmth tingled over her body, and she snuggled up to him. "That's kinda what I said about you." She smiled. "Lunch?"

Jack hesitated. "Is he angry with me?"

"Not at all," she said. "Give me your order for the deli, because I *want* you to join us." He leaned over and kissed her. When he pulled away, she asked, "Is that a yes?" He kissed her again, and she laughed against his lips.

✦ ✦ ✦

STELLA, JACK, AND Arnie sat around the small kitchen table and ate salads and sandwiches, making small talk until Arnie asked about the magic.

"Darcy's still here, isn't he?" Arnie glanced between Stella and Jack. "He knows the rules, but without me around to keep everyone accounted for . . . is everything still okay in the library? No mishaps?"

Jack caught Stella's eyes, and their shared gaze was enough to alert Arnie.

He wiped his mouth slowly with a napkin. "What's going on? Did something happen to Darcy?"

"No, nothing happened to Darcy," Stella assured him. "He's safe and sound in the library."

"What is it, then?" Arnie asked. "What aren't you telling me?"

Jack nodded his encouragement. Stella took a drink of her Pepsi before speaking. "A few things actually."

Arnie shifted in his chair.

"Percy and Ariel know."

Arnie's bushy eyebrows lifted. "Why would you tell—"

"I used the magic and brought out Captain Hook," she blurted. "They saw Hook fall from the balcony, but that was only after I stabbed him by accident. I also brought out Robinson Crusoe, but he was helpful—he and Darcy both—and the reason I had to tell Ariel and Percy about the magic was because they saw Hook die. I mean, Hook's not dead, of course, but he *died* in the fictional way."

Jack had stopped eating and gaped at her.

"Percy is extremely unhappy with me," Stella continued. "He thinks this is too dangerous and I'm irresponsible and incapable of using the magic. He also demanded I send all the characters back early, including Jack. And, Arnie, it was horrible watching Hook die. I can't do that again, and I don't want to."

Arnie lifted his water, and the liquid quaked inside the glass. He drank but said nothing.

Stella's stomach twisted. "Well . . . say something."

Arnie cleared his throat. "It was bound to happen, I guess, other people finding out. We'll have to swear them to secrecy. Ariel seems the trustworthy type—"

"She is!" Stella agreed.

"Percy won't tell anyone because they'll think he's lost his mind," Arnie said. "And he cares too much about what other people think." His gaze went to Jack. "You didn't caution her first?"

"I did!" Jack said.

Stella placed her hand on Jack's. "He did, Arnie. I ignored his warning because I didn't believe him, and by the time you explained things to me, it was too late. I'd already brought out Hook and Crusoe, except I didn't know it at the time. Not until I got back to the library and things were . . . We handled it."

Arnie cleared his throat again. "You handled it, did you? Before or after it was bedlam?"

Stella glanced away, and Arnie's laugh surprised her.

"Did you tell her about the time I brought out the White Witch?" Arnie asked, still chuckling.

"You did not!" Stella exclaimed.

Jack and Arnie both shuddered. "That was a lesson I could have lived without. Was Hook surprised to see you?" he asked Jack.

Jack smirked. "He was. Righteously angry too."

Arnie chuckled, and then he returned to seriousness. "I'll talk to Percy."

"Are you mad?" Stella asked.

"Mad?" Arnie shook his head. "We all make mistakes, Stella. The magic comes with rules, but . . . we don't always follow them as closely as we should. We can't see how our decisions will ripple into the future or create consequences we aren't prepared for."

Stella relaxed against the chair back. "I'm sorry I used the magic foolishly. Thanks for not being furious."

"I'd be a hypocrite if I was," Arnie said, folding the parchment paper over the unfinished half of his sandwich. "There's something else I haven't told you. I've wanted to tell you for years, but I kept putting off revealing the magic, and if I didn't tell you that, this other thing wouldn't make sense. I still don't know if you're better off not knowing."

Stella looked at Jack. He shrugged.

"What is it?" Stella asked.

Arnie clasped his hands together on the table. "I'm assuming you found my copy of Jack's book beneath the hidden panel in the desk drawer."

Jack touched Stella's thigh beneath the table. "I showed her."

Arnie nodded. "Did you notice the other book with it?"

Stella scanned her memory and recalled there had been a second book. "A green one."

"*The Unraveling of Mrs. Russo*," Arnie said. "I need you to go get it and bring it back here."

"Now?" Stella asked.

Arnie nodded.

Stella pushed away from the table, rushed out the door, and ran across the yard between the cottage and library. When she arrived at the circulation desk, she was grateful no one was there. A quick scan of the library revealed that Melanie was talking with someone in the children's section, and she heard Dan's voice upstairs.

Stella yanked open the drawer as quickly as possible and removed the extraneous items, then grabbed *The Unraveling of Mrs. Russo*, which rested below Jack's book and the ink pad and stamp. She assembled everything back into place and hurried out of the library.

She flung open Arnie's door, out of breath and sweaty. Jack looked at her from the table, his expression curious, but Arnie appeared pale and unwell. Stella sat back down and placed the emerald-green book on the table between them.

"Open it to the back," Arnie said.

Stella flipped open the back cover. The library due date card was still tucked into its sleeve. She pulled out the card and saw that the date stamped on it was from more than thirty years ago. A prickly sensation started in her fingers. Words resembling a child's crayon scribblings wiggled out of the sleeve. **Disappeared. Why? Come back.**

Jack frowned at the words as they wobbled off the table.

"What is this?" Stella asked, her mouth dry.

Arnie inhaled slowly and exhaled before speaking. "It's the story of Mrs. Russo. I found it years ago when I first moved to Blue Sky Valley. At the time, it hadn't been checked out in years, and the author had already passed away. But it's about a woman born to Italian immigrants in New York City in the 1920s. While she's still a young woman, she dreams of stardom on Broadway but is trapped in a loveless marriage and an unfulfilling life with a man her parents insisted she marry. She tries to assert her independence and reclaim her dreams, but she has her own personal demons to overcome first."

Stella didn't speak, so Arnie continued.

"I was drawn to her, so I brought Mrs. Russo out years ago," he said. "Her story fascinated me for some reason. I imagined she was beautiful, a passionate woman. I thought bringing her here would give her a way to see the world without feeling oppressed. It wouldn't be as fancy as Broadway, but it would be a chance for her to relax and laugh and talk about her dreams."

Stella's hands started shaking. She flipped to the front of the book. The opening line of the novel read: *Every night, as Maria lay beside her husband in their cramped apartment in Little Italy, she closed her eyes and stepped onto a Broadway stage, a world away from the life she had never chosen.*

"Maria?" Stella whispered.

Arnie continued, "Your father came into the library two days after she arrived, and he was smitten. Maria had never experienced a man so doting and generous. She begged me to let her stay. She wanted to get married, have a family. I didn't know she would leave you."

Stella's eyes widened. "But she couldn't have stayed. You said . . . you said—"

"I know what I said!" Arnie barked. He inhaled a noisy breath

THE CHARMED LIBRARY

and held it before releasing it. He reached for the book. "You were right. The magic is tied to the place because the source is there. If I bring out characters in the library, when it's time for their return and they're in the library, they return to their books."

Jack sat rigidly in his chair. "And if they're *not* in the library when it's time for them to return?"

Silence stretched between them for a few moments.

Arnie sighed. "I wasn't sure at first. Ruby Lou and Pearl went missing years ago, and their book completely disappeared. I thought the same would happen with Maria's."

Stella slapped her palm flat against the table, and the men flinched. "My mother is from a book? My *mother* is fictional?"

Arnie lowered his gaze. "You know firsthand that characters are *very* real when they're here."

Stella covered her mouth with her hand. Nearly a lifetime of unanswered questions about her mother swirled within her. She lowered her hand. "If Ruby Lou and Pearl's book went missing, why is hers still here? Why didn't you bring her back out? Why didn't you *make* her stay and be our mother?" Furious tears stung Stella's eyes.

"Don't you think I thought of that?" Arnie said, raising his voice again. "Don't you think I tried to bring her back out? Nothing happened, Stella, because she's *not* in her book. Even the date stamps I applied immediately disappeared."

"Why didn't her book vanish?" Jack asked.

"Because she's not dead," Stella said and shoved back from the table and stomped into the living room, her curls dancing wild around her head.

"Are you sure?" Jack asked.

Arnie got up from the table and walked into his room. The sound of rustling followed and then he returned with a postcard. He handed it to Stella.

The front photo was of the Statue of Liberty, and the date stamp was from twenty-four years ago. The cursive writing was sloppy and hurried, written in fading blue ink. The message had been addressed to Arnie.

> Tell them I'm sorry. Forgive me for leaving, Arnie, but I must pursue my dreams to find my true self. My family has been a great joy, and I hope they understand my journey one day.
>
> Love, Maria

The postcard trembled in Stella's hand, and the words blurred with her tears.

"If she'd died, the book would have disappeared," Arnie said, looking at Jack. "Every last copy of her story would be gone, like with Ruby Lou and Pearl. That's how I know Maria's still alive and they aren't."

Stella's arm fell to her side, dangling the postcard from her hand. Nausea swept through her. "All these years she's been alive? She just never *wanted* to come back." Stella's dad had lived the rest of his life thinking he'd somehow failed at marriage, never knowing his troubled wife was from a fictional story. Never knowing Maria had escaped a miserable marriage. Never knowing her dreams, whether fictional or real, were always taking her to Broadway.

"I'm sorry I didn't tell you sooner," Arnie said.

Stella wiped at her tears. "I wouldn't have believed you." She wrapped her arms around her middle and doubled over with an ache so deep it seemed entangled with her very core. Then a rogue thought popped into her head, and she straightened. "Is that why I can see words?"

"What words?" Arnie asked.

Jack stood from the table and walked closer. "Because you're—"

"Half fictional?" Stella's laugh sounded cynical, tempestuous.

"What words?" Arnie asked again.

"Don't you remember years ago when I asked you about Stella and the words around her?"

Stella waved her hands through the air as though sprinkling fairy dust. "I see words *everywhere*," she said. "And I don't mean on a page or printed in books. I mean, alive and three-dimensional. Jack can see them, and Maria knew about them. In fact, she encouraged me to write them down, saying it would guide me to my dreams." She placed her palm against her forehead. "She wasn't wrong, but this is too much."

"Why didn't you tell me?" Arnie asked.

"Seriously?" Stella asked. "Are you the pot or the kettle?" Another wild thought bolted into her mind. "What if when it's time for Jack to go back, we're not in the library?"

Jack reached for her hand and swung his gaze toward Arnie. "Is that possible?"

"Of course it is," Stella answered. "We'd just need to keep you away from the library. We can move. Anywhere!" She squeezed Jack's hand. "If Maria can stay away and survive all this time, then why can't you?"

"There's something else you don't know," Arnie said. He grabbed Maria's book off the table and carried it to Stella. "Flip through it."

Stella took the offered book and thumbed through the pages. Three-quarters of them were blank.

"At first, nothing happened to the book," Arnie said. "Then a few years after she left, pages started going blank, starting in the back. Just one or two every couple years. But in the last few months, they've been disappearing faster. I worry the entire story will be gone in a matter of weeks, maybe less."

Stella squeezed the book. "What does that mean? Is she . . . dying?"

Arnie shrugged. "I don't know."

Anxiety clenched Stella's body. "But you have a guess."

Arnie nodded. "I assume she's been away from the magic too long, and now it's reclaiming her."

Stella reopened the book and flipped through the pages. "But her story is disappearing."

"Which means she can never come back, even if she wants to," Jack said.

"That's my belief too," Arnie said.

"Is the magic reclaiming her? Is she dying?" Stella asked.

Arnie shook his head. "Could be either. Or both."

Jack shook his head. "Then I can't stay away from the library."

Stella's head jerked up and she gaped at Jack. "Why not?"

He pointed at Maria's book. "Because I'll disappear. Forever."

Stella *knew* he was right, but she refused to agree. "Not right away. Maria's been gone twenty-four years."

"There's no way to know how fast *I'd* go," Jack argued. "I don't want to lose you forever. Coming out once a year is safer."

"But even if I bring you out once a year, I'll grow older and you won't!" Stella yelled. Then she threw Maria's book across the room, and it slammed into the lower kitchen cabinets. "This isn't fair! My awful fictional mother gets to spend the last twenty-four years chasing her ridiculous dream in New York, but I can't have mine?"

"Stella," Jack said, reaching for her hand.

Stella jerked away. "I need some air."

Arnie pulled her into a quick hug, and she stiffened in his arms. Stella released him and flung open the front door, then slammed it behind her. She stomped across the library grounds, trapped between the urge to cry and the desire to rip something to shreds. She walked, sweating profusely in the heat, until her erratic emotions settled to something almost tamable.

If Jack refused to leave the library, to move *anywhere else* with her, what were their other options? She imagined all sorts of ridiculous scenarios: holding on to Jack when he started to disappear, sprinkling the glittering potion over her head like a baptism, even stamping Arnie's copy of *Beyond the Southern Horizon* again with the magic ink just to see if it would extend Jack's stay. None of her ideas seemed plausible, but she was willing to give any—or all—of them a try.

✦ ✦ ✦

A HALF HOUR later Jack found Stella on the library grounds. At first they walked in silence while Jack held her hand and led her into the shade scattered around the wide lawn. Still her mind labored over harebrained ideas that might allow Jack to stay—or could she go with him? Could she mix the potion into milk and cocoa powder like an enchanted hot chocolate or drink it straight like Alice did in Wonderland? The ideas grew increasingly absurd in her rising desperation.

Stella sensed the awareness of time so profoundly that it felt like another person following her around all day, reminding her, whispering in her ear, counting down the hours, minutes, seconds until Jack would be gone.

Finally, after they'd walked the day away, the sun dipped low, turning the sky the color of pink cotton candy. Stella stood at the long windows inside the library with Jack as they stared at the sunset. He reached over and grabbed her hand, and she stepped closer to him, leaning her head against his arm. She tried to etch every second with him into her mind—the way it felt to be near him, his warmth, the way his cheek dimpled when he smiled at her.

He leaned down and kissed the top of her head. "I wish I could bring you with me to my Blue Sky Valley," he said.

She closed her eyes and nodded against his arm. A bolt of electricity exploded from her heart, traveling all the way to her feet. She gasped and dropped Jack's hand.

"What's wrong?" he asked.

Tangled midnight-blue words floated all around Jack before circling him, faster and faster, until she and Jack were enclosed in a tornado of phrases. Stella couldn't read all of them, and when she opened her mouth to speak, nothing would come out. It was as if all the words she wanted to say were flying around them. She reached out her hand and four words crashed into her palm. **This is your life.** She and Jack both looked at the crumpled words in her hand. Stella closed her fingers, and the words melted into her skin.

"I need to talk to Arnie," she said, grabbing Jack's hand and pulling him behind her while she ran toward the back entrance of the library.

Stella shoved both hands against the door, slamming it open, and jumped down the stairs. Then she ran across the lawn toward Arnie's cottage with Jack close behind. She knocked on the back door and waited a few seconds before calling Arnie's name and knocking again.

Arnie opened the door, looking slightly disheveled and sleepy. He gazed at her with a confused expression marred with worry. "What's wrong?"

"The extra magical potion," Stella said, sucking in gulps of air.

She squeezed a cramp in her side. "Where is it? You said it was in the archives somewhere. But where?"

Arnie pushed his glasses up on his nose. He glanced between her and Jack. "Why?"

Stella bounced on her toes. "Where is it?"

"It's in a box behind the first four books on Blue Sky Valley's earliest history, those leather-bound monsters held together by goodwill and deteriorating threads."

"Thanks," she said as she turned and leaped off the back stoop.

"Stella!" Arnie called.

She stopped and looked up at him and Jack, who remained on the steps.

"What's going on?" Arnie asked.

Stella knew she looked as reckless as the idea that had formed in her mind. "I have an idea I'd like to test."

Arnie crossed his arms over his chest. "Why do I feel queasy? What are you up to?"

She glanced over her shoulder at the setting sun, and a tidal wave of panic hit her, pushing her back toward Arnie and Jack.

"Hear me out," she said. She looked at Jack. "You don't want to go away with me—"

Jack's posture stiffened. "It's not that I don't *want* to—"

"So I have another idea," she continued. "I'm going to drink a little bit of the magical liquid, and then I'm going to . . . Well, I don't know because I haven't figured it out yet, but I think I'm going to hold Jack's hand, and when he starts to disappear into his light and warmth thing, I'm going to see if I can go with him."

"What?" Arnie and Jack exclaimed at the same time.

"Absolutely not," Arnie argued. "You have no idea what that would do to you, what *drinking* the liquid might do. What if it kills you?"

"What if it doesn't?" Stella said.

Jack shook his head. "Stella, I'm not willing to take that chance. I can't let you do that."

Stella frowned. "What if it's a chance *I'm* willing to take?" She stepped closer to them. "I don't want my life to be like it used to be. I want something different. I want to take a new path."

Jack's features set with determination. "So much has changed for you in the last few days. You're finding yourself and your purpose, Stella."

"You're right. I can see a way forward," she agreed. "My words and my writing—all of that I can bring with me."

"You don't know that," Arnie said.

"What about the library?" Jack asked. "You love it here. You said you feel like this *is* where you're supposed to be. Don't throw all that aside for a whim."

"A whim?" Stella asked. "Is that what we are? Some silly little fling?"

Jack's expression changed to indignation. "Absolutely not," he said. "I love you, Stella Parker, which is why I don't want you to do this."

His words pumped passion through her heart. "You love me?"

"How could I not?" he asked, his voice quiet and grave.

"What if this can be *our* story?" she asked him. "What if we could, at some point, get married and have a family and all those things you've wanted?"

Jack stepped off the porch and walked to her. He touched her arm. "I don't know if I can have those things in my story. You know how it ends. But what do *you* want, Stella?"

"I want all those things too," she said honestly. "With you."

Jack slid his hand down her arm. "You have no idea what might happen to you."

"I've never met anyone like you before, and I won't ever meet anyone like you again."

"Stella," Jack said, his voice gentle, "remember what I told you about how returning to my book feels? It's not a life lived the way you live here."

"I don't care!" But Jack's caution made sense. How could she stop the war, stop him from leaving for active duty, if his world was everything all at once? What did that even mean? How would she find her own way in a world unlike anything she'd ever experienced?

But what if she could find a way to live her life and also have Jack as part of it? "I want to try," she said, determined.

"You'll be leaving your home," Jack said. "We have no idea what might happen over there, wherever *there* is to you. What if it's nothing? What if it's a void? What if we can't find each other?"

She reached for his hand. "What if we can?"

Arnie shook his head. "No. I don't like this at all. Stella, you're asking me—no, *both* of us—to let you try something that might harm you, that might take you away from us. Permanently. You can't expect us to be okay with this."

"What about Ariel and Percy?" Jack added. "Don't you think they want you to stay?"

Ariel would want Stella to follow her heart, but that didn't mean she'd be excited for Stella to jump into a book and disappear forever. Percy, even though he was so focused on what he thought was best for her life, would be upset too. There was a slim-to-none chance that he would support her taking this risk.

"You have a life here, and I don't want to take that from you," Jack continued. "There are so many opportunities still waiting for you." He smoothed his hand down her hair. "I can't even imagine what's waiting around the corner for you here, the amazing things you'll do and the people who will be drawn to you. Think about all the people you can help find the perfect story. What about the stories you'll write? We'll find them on the library shelves, and they'll change people's lives."

Stella pressed her hands against her heart. Electricity zinged through her still, causing her fingers and toes to tingle. "I have a feeling about this, an overpowering sense that everything will be okay. I promise."

Arnie removed his glasses and cleaned the lenses. "You'll be the death of me. I've been trying to keep you safe since you were a little girl, and this goes against my good judgment, but let me get changed and put my shoes on. You're not going to do this without me."

"Hurry," Stella urged. "I don't know how much time we have left. Jack, come with me. Arnie, we'll meet you in the archives." She grabbed Jack's hand, and they hurried across the lawn, sending up bright green words from the grass with every step. Stella glanced over her shoulder and watched the words soar into the air like hundreds of launched rockets. A few were grander and more vibrant as they raced skyward.

Rush. Start over. Your choice.

Chapter 24

Down in the archives, Stella pulled on a pair of white gloves and removed the first four volumes detailing the history of Blue Sky Valley off the shelf. She carefully placed them on the closest table. The leather-bound books looked as though they'd survived a few million sunsets. Brittle yellowed pages barely held on their spines with fragile, flaking glue and dangling threads. Arnie had been talking about enclosing them in glass cases for years, but so far, nothing had been done to create safer housing. She laid the gloves across the top of a book.

Behind where the books had been sat a wooden box about the size of a quart of milk. Stella gently removed the box from its hiding place. A triquetrum, an ancient Celtic symbol, was engraved on the lid. Stella traced her fingers over the grooved, curving lines. She placed the box on the table and unlatched it.

A clear glass bottle with a cork stopper was nestled in a space carved to its exact size. Just as Arnie had described it, the cobalt-blue liquid inside the bottle sparkled and shifted like a living entity.

A fading label affixed to the front of the bottle read *anáil na beatha*. The beauty of its glow mesmerized her.

Jack went to the kitchenette to grab a can of Pepsi at Stella's request. She thought she might want something to chase the magical liquid once she drank it. Movement in the shadows pulled her attention away from the bottle, and Crusoe and Darcy stepped into the dim light.

"I spent a lot of time alone on that island," Crusoe said. "I daydreamed that someone would rescue me and relieve my despair. My misery created a hole, and I wallowed. I thought of never facing the world again. Then I understood that I couldn't depend on someone else for my happiness, not on humanity or even on a single person. Humans will disappoint you, Stella. They can't help it. We're all flawed. But you have the power to live on your own terms. Live the life *you* want because *you* chose it, not because someone else influenced it."

How could a castaway like Robinson Crusoe speak such profound words? "I'm living my life on my own terms," she said.

"Are you?" Crusoe asked. "Are you making the best decision for you?"

Stella knew what he was hinting at, so she said, "I'm kinda busy here, and I don't see how that is—"

"Relevant?" Crusoe interrupted. "Excuse my presumption, but I believe you were desperate for an escape, just waiting for someone to pull you out of your misery." He pointed to the gleaming bottle.

Darcy nodded and stepped closer to the bottle. "Wouldn't you agree that you've been finding your way back to yourself? And yet here you are, looking for an easy fix."

"Easy?" Stella asked. Irritation combined with her nervousness. "Nothing about any of this has been *easy*."

"I agree," Darcy said. "But are you not considering upending your life for yet another man?"

"You have no idea what you're talking about," Stella argued, even as her stomach lurched in response.

"I admire the lengths you are willing to go to for love," Darcy said.

"Then you understand," Stella said.

Darcy nodded. "I understand you could lose everything. Not only your life here but also Jack. Have you considered your own words, that you belong here, that your life is meant to be lived *here*?"

"It is difficult to let people go," Crusoe said. "But there are times when we must so we can move on to greatness."

Stella stared at him and then at Darcy before returning her gaze to the magical liquid. "I don't want to let Jack go," she whispered.

The men looked toward the sound of Jack returning, and they disappeared into the shadows.

Jack approached, holding a plastic bottle of Pepsi. "Were you talking to someone?"

Stella stared at the spot where Crusoe and Darcy had disappeared and shook her head. Shadowy words fluttered out of the darkness. **Look ahead. Move forward. Trust your heart.** "Do you think it will work?" she asked, staring at the liquid.

Jack shook his head. "Not really."

Stella lifted the bottle from its resting place and popped off the cork. She poked her pinky finger into the bottle and tilted it, allowing the glowing liquid to touch her fingertip. A current of power zapped her finger, then raced through the palm of her hand and up her arm. She stumbled backward a step and almost dropped the bottle.

"Ow!" She shook out her arm.

Jack grabbed for her.

"I'm okay," she said. She put down the bottle, and the liquid moved in agitation.

Jack rubbed his hand down her arm and entwined their fingers. "I'm against this."

Stella looked at him. Uncertainty bubbled within her. Crusoe's and Darcy's words churned in her mind. Was leaving with Jack an escape, an easy way out of a life she hadn't truly been present for in months?

"I'm not telling you no because I don't want to be with you," Jack said. "But going back to my story, that's my life, not yours. You aren't even *in* my story, and—"

"I understand," she said, and she did. "I'm not part of the original story, and if I go with you, I might not *be* anywhere." She touched his cheek. "But what if the story is rewritten to include me?"

Jack sighed. "Say it is, but you know how my story ends, Stella."

The moment bridged them in silence.

"I die," he said. "Every time. Every ending. Do you want to relive that on repeat?"

Stella's throat tightened. "But I would live part of a life with you. Isn't that better than a life without you?"

On impulse, she kissed him. A burning, not entirely unpleasant sensation blossomed in her chest as Jack held her close and kissed her like this was possibly the very last time. At least for another year. The burning increased, and Stella broke away.

Violet words bubbled inside the bottle, rising from the blue liquid. The words pushed their way out of the glass and landed on the table where they quivered and then lifted on lavender wings.

Stella whispered the words. "'Timeless. And he was right.'"

The blazing trail within her released its hold, and she heard Jack take in a deep breath. The glowing purple words flapped their wings, zoomed across the archives, and disappeared into the darkness.

"What if I could go with you and write—no, *change*—our story?" Stella said. "What if *my* words could somehow change everything?"

Jack didn't respond.

Footsteps sounded on the archives' staircase, and Arnie called out to Stella and Jack.

"We're down here," she answered.

Arnie appeared a second later, puffing up an aisle and looking determined. Ariel and Percy followed him.

"I see you found the stash," Arnie said.

Stella looked only at Percy. "What are you doing here?"

"What am *I* doing here?" Percy asked. "What are *you* doing here?"

"Arnie texted us," Ariel said. "He said you're going to—"

"Take a leap into the unknown to be with Jack," Percy interrupted. "How can you stand by and let her do this?" he asked Jack.

"Back off, Percy," Stella said.

Jack placed his hand on Stella's arm, attempting to calm her, then he stepped toward Percy. "I stand by Stella and support her in any way I can. I don't believe I can or should force my ideas on her. However, for the sake of this argument, Stella knows my concerns."

Percy's chest puffed up. "Excuse me? Are you insinuating that I'm forcing my ideas on Stella? I would never do that."

Ariel cleared her throat. "I'm not sure that's accurate, Percy. What about Miami?"

"Miami is a great opportunity," Percy said. "Is it wrong to want something more for her? You, of all people, have seen how much she's been struggling."

"I get your desire to help, but Miami isn't a great opportunity for Stella," Ariel said. "She loves the library. Shouldn't she do what she loves? How can you possibly think Miami is a good fit for her?"

"Hello?" Stella said with an eye roll. "I'm standing right here."

Percy continued without acknowledging her. He looked at Arnie. "She's proven she can't handle this." He gestured wildly around them.

"I'm guessing they didn't tell you about Hook and his swan-dive exit from the second-floor balcony?"

"What is wrong with you?" Stella asked. "Why are you so adamant that I do what *you* want?"

"Because . . ." Percy started and then paused, rubbing the back of his neck. "Because I can't lose you. You're all I have, Stella. You and me. Mom and Dad are gone. It's just us, and you're not like me. I don't know what to do with you. I don't know how to help you or understand what's best for you. If you love the library so much, why are you so willing to disappear from it? From *me*?"

Stella blinked at him in the silence that followed. No one spoke.

Percy continued, "Listen, Stella, I'm sorry I've been coming across as an overbearing jerk. But is there any way I can convince you not to do this? No offense to you, Jack, because I'm guessing you're a stand-up guy, and I bet if you were real, you might be great for Stella. I know Dad would approve." Percy looked at Stella. "But leaving here, if that's even possible, for some unknown place that might not even accept you because you're . . . not of their time, I don't know what will happen, and I don't—I don't want to lose you."

Stella's throat burned, and she felt the familiar salty sting in her eyes. She hugged Percy. "I would have been long gone without you all these years. You kept me sane." She squeezed her eyes shut. "You and Arnie and Ariel."

Arnie swiped at his cheek. Was he crying? "Don't give us all the credit. You're a lot stronger than you think. You've been keeping us on track too. You've been my daughter."

"And my partner in crime," Percy said.

"And my best friend," Ariel said. "Accepting all my weirdness with love."

"I couldn't have loved you more if you were my own child," Arnie said. "I've been rooting for you since you were riding that tricycle down the sidewalk with those pink and purple streamers. And I think you've done me the biggest kindness yet—sending a wonderful woman to me with a plate of cookies. Completely devious yet appreciated. If this does work . . . I'm going to miss you sorely."

"We all are," Percy agreed.

Stella wiped at her tears. "You're going to let me go?"

Percy shrugged. "Not that I could ever stop you. For the record and everyone present, I think this is a terrible idea."

"Noted," Stella said with a slight smile. She looked at Arnie. "You can bring us back, though, right?"

Arnie sighed. "I don't know, Stella. Jack is in his book, but you're not. You don't exist there. I have no idea what's going to happen."

Stella returned to the bottle. She stretched her arms over her head and leaned her neck from side to side. Then she shook her arms out at her sides and bounced on her toes. She twisted open the bottle of Pepsi and listened to the pop of bubbles rising to the top of the dark liquid. "Here goes. Everybody ready?"

"No," everyone said at the same time, causing Stella to release a nervous laugh.

She picked up the bottle. The magical liquid churned inside, swirling wildly like a storm brewing. All she had to do was lift the bottle to her lips and drink.

A throbbing started deep in her heart. Thinking about leaving Arnie, Percy, and Ariel, of never seeing them or the library again, created a fracture inside her. What if their fears were valid? What if she was lost forever? Clarity reverberated through her, and she trembled with the awareness.

She lowered the bottle.

Stella looked at Jack, willing her bottom lip to stop trembling. "I can't." She corked the bottle. "I can't go with you."

Chapter 25

Stella's chest seared as if she'd swallowed a Roman candle. She wanted to wrap her arms around Jack, to explain why she couldn't go, but she didn't trust herself to speak. Instead, he closed the space between them and grabbed her hands.

"There is no one I'd rather have near me than you. But you'd have to change your whole life to make that happen. You'd have to live according to what *I* need, and I have nothing to offer you but a life of uncertainty. And me allowing you to take this risk was selfish." He crushed Stella against him. "I almost let you give up your life just for the slim chance that I could be with you in *my* world. I'm no different from Wade."

Stella pushed away from him. "You are *nothing* like Wade."

"Aren't I?" he asked.

"I've been avoiding my life for years. Leaving with you is so tempting, but I don't belong in your world. My life is here. In the library, writing, chasing words." Stella wrapped her arms around him. "Thank you, Jack. For being you, for *seeing* me, for making me feel special, for helping me believe in love again. I'm going to miss you terribly."

Jack squeezed her against him and kissed the top of her head. "You're one in a gazillion, Stella. You deserve all the love in the world."

Ariel gasped, staring wide-eyed at Jack and Stella.

"It's happening," Stella said, stepping away from Jack. His body illuminated as though he were made of starlight. "You're glowing."

Arnie approached them. "You take care of yourself, Jack."

Jack nodded. "You take care of her." Then he smiled at Stella as he placed his hands over his heart. His eyes turned the golden color of a summer sun. "I will never forget how wonderful my time with you has been. Never."

"Never ever," she said.

A windstorm of air and light swirled around them. Within seconds, Jack was gone.

Stella pressed her hands over her mouth, closed her eyes, and cried.

Chapter 26

The next day Stella showed up for work at the library and engaged as little as possible with anyone. Arnie wasn't allowed to return to work, but he stopped by that morning to check in. He tried to talk with Stella, to check on her, but what was there to say? She wasn't fine. She understood she *should* be fine with her decision not to drink the magical liquid, with her decision not to escape her life again. She didn't exactly regret her decision, but she also wasn't overflowing with joy. She needed time to process the last few days.

Both Percy and Ariel texted a few times during the day, so by the afternoon she finally silenced her phone and tossed it into her purse in a desk drawer. Before closing the drawer, Stella noticed her journal and remembered she hadn't written down the last set of violet words—the ones that came out of the bottle of magical liquid. She flipped to the page and wrote.

> *I fell in love once. Did I ever tell you that?*
> *He was excruciatingly handsome and no*

ordinary man, but one built from paper and rich black ink. He talked about eternity and love as if the two were impossibly entwined. Timeless. And he was right.

These words were about Jack. Her mind created a blank sheet of paper, then a full sheet of paper filled with her handwriting, then page after page of her written words. Enough pages to fill a book. *The story of us*, she heard Jack's voice say in her head. Was that her next step in this new life? To write a story about the time she fell in love with Jack Mathis, a man built from paper and ink?

The familiar swirl of sorrow orbited her. How could she wait an entire year to see him again? Was that preposterous? Waiting an entire year for someone, only to spend two weeks together before he was gone again? She couldn't devote the rest of her life to following that pattern. She would age and Jack wouldn't. She couldn't trap herself in an impossible relationship. For the millionth time, she wished for a way to alter that part of their story.

Stella riffled through the desk drawer where Arnie hid the box containing the ink pad and stamp. Huddled with the box was Arnie's personal copy of *Beyond the Southern Horizon*. He hadn't returned Maria's book, and she hadn't asked about it. Eventually she would. Whether that would happen before or after all the pages were blank, she didn't know.

Stella pulled out Jack's book and flipped it to the library due date card in the back. She slid out the card. Her gaze wandered over the years Jack had been to Blue Sky Valley. He couldn't return until next summer, which sounded like a lifetime away, and in a way, it was. Who would she be in another year? She returned the box to its concealed spot but left Jack's book on the desk like a friend she wasn't ready to part with.

The rest of the afternoon and evening passed uneventfully. Stella eventually texted both Ariel and Percy and told them she needed time to herself. Percy was flying back to Florida the next day and asked if Stella would be home later so they could talk before he left. She reluctantly agreed to make time if he promised not to offer life advice. Percy's response was an emoji with zipped lips. Ariel agreed to give Stella space, but only until the morning.

After closing down the library that evening, Stella turned off the lights except the one hanging high above the circulation desk. She grabbed her purse and journal, and as she dug around for her keys, illuminated words lifted from the cover of Jack's book. **One more try. Believe. Reborn.** Stella picked up the book, and the words faded back into the cover. She tucked the book beneath her arm and locked up the library's main entrance.

She set the alarm, then closed and locked the library's back door behind her. As she descended the back stairs, a firework of heat exploded inside the area behind her rib cage. Stella stumbled into the handrail. Out of a pavement crack, glowing violet words emerged. They soared upward like magical creatures emerging from the bowels of the earth.

Against the star-filled backdrop of the night sky, Stella read them aloud. "'Dazzled by the power of love and moonlight, I called to him and asked him to stay. He said yes.'" The words rippled as though windblown and then shot toward her purse.

Stella sank onto the concrete step and inhaled deep breaths while her heart beat erratically. With shaking hands, she pulled out her journal and wrote down this new set of words. Then she read all of them out loud.

"'I fell in love once. Did I ever tell you that? He was excruciatingly handsome and no ordinary man, but one built from paper and rich black ink. He talked about eternity and love as if the two were impossibly entwined. Timeless. And he was right. Dazzled by the power of love and moonlight, I called to him and asked him to stay. He said yes.'"

Stella laid her hand on the journal page and gazed up at the waxing moon suspended above Blue Sky Valley. "If only it were that simple," she whispered to the listening moon. She reached for Jack's book and flipped it open to the back cover where the dates were listed. "I would stamp you again and again and hold you in the sunlight so you could come back to me."

Her fingers warmed on the pages. The stamped dates began to shimmer and take on a silvery outline. She glanced up at the moonlight, then back to the now-glistening dates.

"Love and moonlight." She reached out her hand to catch moonbeams in her palm. "Sunlight brings you here, but what is moonlight doing? Could it . . . ?" Stella raised the book so the moonlight covered it. Feeling foolish, but doing it anyway, she asked, "Jack, would you like to stay?" Tingles and goose bumps rushed over her entire body.

An illuminated figure appeared in the darkened parking lot. A form made of silver moonlight and shooting stars approached her. Stella scrambled to her feet. The book dropped to the ground. The closer the figure got to her, the more fully formed it became.

Stella covered her mouth with her hand. Jack Mathis continued closing the distance between them, then stopped a few feet away. His silvery eyes sparkled before shifting into the hazel she knew. She lowered her hand. "Jack?"

"Yes," he said. "I'd like to stay."

Stella leaped off the steps and into his arms. A windstorm of air and starlight swirled around them, and Stella laughed into the curve of his neck.

"How?" Jack asked.

Stella pulled away enough to talk but not to release her hold on him. "The words told me. The purple ones I've been collecting for days. The last few lines were about moonlight, and I wondered if sunlight brings you to life, what if moonlight gives you a chance to stay? And . . . here you are."

Jack held her against him. "Any doubts you had about not belonging here with the library and the magic should be gone."

Stella smiled into his chest. "Only I had the power to do this. Only I can see the words that revealed this. But"—she released her arms from around him—"is this okay? I've taken you from your story and brought you into my world."

"It's more than okay, Stella," Jack said, cupping his hands on her face. "You've given me the chance at a different life, and more than that, a life with *you*. I'll be around for more than two weeks. Are *you* okay with that?"

Stella lifted on her toes to kiss him. "I'm hoping for two weeks and two weeks and two weeks to infinity." Jack smiled against her lips before wrapping her in his arms.

Epilogue

ONE MONTH LATER

A cardinal chirped from a windowsill outside the library. Stella walked toward the window, gazing at the library's back parking lot. Arnie and Dana climbed into his BMW with the top down, and Stella watched for a moment longer as Dana leaned back her head and laughed. Arnie smiled over at Dana and reversed out of his driveway. They were on their way to a weekend getaway in Wild Dunes, South Carolina.

Sunlight warmed her cheeks, and she sighed. Arnie and Dana being together and happy *felt* right and good and perfect. Their joy spread to her.

She returned to the circulation desk just as Jack walked through the library's front doors and across the foyer. He placed a to-go bag from the deli behind the high desk and pulled a small black object out of his front pocket. "Look what I did!"

"You got a cell phone?" Stella said with a laugh. "Took you long enough."

He drew her into a quick hug. "Some technology is too *out there*, but you badgered me long enough."

Stella poked her finger into his arm. "*Badgered* is a strong word. *Encouraged* is the one I'd prefer. Besides, most people understand almost zero about how high-tech gadgets work. I just know they work and that's enough for me." She pointed to printouts on the desktop. "Any more life decisions?"

Jack picked up the papers, a mix of job descriptions, job applications, and college forms he'd printed out earlier in the week. "A few are rising to the top."

"Which ones?" Stella asked.

Jack shuffled the papers and handed her two of them. "Licensed practical nurse and massage therapist."

Stella smirked. "My vote is definitely for massage therapist. I'd willingly be a practice client."

Jack leaned over and nuzzled her neck. "So noble. Sure you aren't slanting your opinion for selfish reasons?"

"Never!" Stella teased.

Ariel pushed through the library doors with Liam and his German shepherd, Scout, in tow. Ariel waved dramatically in her canary-yellow scrubs. Her rainbow Crocs squeaked across the polished tile. "I told Liam it was okay to bring in Scout since she's so well behaved."

Liam carried another to-go bag from the deli and lifted it in lieu of a wave. He gave Stella a questioning glance, asking with his eyes if it was okay for Scout to be in the library.

"As long as she's okay with small dogs," Stella said. Ariel's face scrunched in confusion. "Toto's here today." Stella pointed toward the story time room, which was presently packed with nearly thirty kids.

"Toto?" Liam asked.

Stella's smile widened. "Dorothy, the Tin Man, Scarecrow, the Cowardly Lion, and Toto are visiting today." Stella leaned over the desk toward Ariel and whispered, "And the kids *love* it."

"Ahh," Ariel said in recognition. "The *impersonators*." She glanced toward the story time room. "How could they not love being entertained by real-life characters from *The Wonderful Wizard of Oz*? Would you mind if I skipped lunch and hung out with the kids instead?"

Liam faked disappointment. "What will I tell Scout? She's been excited about this outing all day."

Ariel leaned down and rubbed Scout's ears. "Who's my best girl? You are! I'd never skip out on lunch with you. If it was just your dad, maybe. But never you!"

"Hey!" Liam protested.

Ariel laughed and leaned into Liam's shoulder. She tossed a gaze at Stella. "Y'all ready?"

Stella nodded. "Let me tell Vicki I'm leaving. She hasn't come out of the story time room yet, but I can't blame her. Those characters are perfect." She winked at Ariel.

Stella eased open the door so she wouldn't disturb the entertainment inside. She was once again amazed by the electrical buzz that passed over her skin as soon as she saw the fictional characters come to life before her.

After talking through the magic with Arnie, who'd unofficially passed the baton to her, Stella had decided she wanted to use the magic not just for her own curiosity but for the patrons. If she brought out some of the most beloved fictional characters and let people experience interacting with them, how much more would kids and adults enjoy the library? Books had the ability to transport readers to other worlds and times and experiences. Bringing out characters only elevated their enjoyment, creating lasting memories.

Stella's first experiment was to bring out characters from *The Wonderful Wizard of Oz*. Once they arrived, she explained her plan and her ideas for how they'd mingle with the patrons. So far, it had been a smashing success. Both the characters and the people reveled in their moments together. A bonus for Stella was that she could talk with the characters after the library closed for as long as she wanted. Being a book lover herself, this new life felt like a dream come true. She already had a list of all the characters she wanted to meet. A very long list.

Vicki saw Stella and walked over. "Sorry, I got mesmerized. How on earth did you find such a young girl who stays in character like a pro? She's amazing! They all are. And that lion, seriously, he's downright real-looking."

"He is," Stella agreed. "I'm going on lunch break. You okay to watch the desk?"

Vicki sighed. "No, but yes. Think they do private parties? I'd like to hire them for myself so we can chat about Oz more."

Stella laughed. "Anything is possible. I'll be back in a bit."

She returned to the circulation desk and opened the bottom drawer, then grabbed her purse and notebook. Words continued to pop up everywhere and at any time, and Stella didn't want to miss a single one. She kept and respected each one, from the swarming, agitated words to the fluffy, downy-soft ones. Her current notebook was almost full, and another blank journal waited patiently to be filled.

Arnie's copy of Jack's book, *Beyond the Southern Horizon*, was in the drawer too. They no longer hid his book with the library stamp and ink pad. Somehow the magic formed that evening in the moonlight had encased Jack's book and his life. Ruby Lou and Pearl's book had disappeared when their lives were lost. Maria's story had started disappearing when she hadn't returned to the source of the magic. But so far Jack's book and fictional story hadn't vanished even though he was now permanently part of the real world. People could still check out *Beyond the Southern Horizon* anytime they wanted. Jack said it made him feel like a celebrity even though no one had connected him to the character in the book yet.

The moonlight magic had overridden the ink's sunlight magic, and Stella never went a day without being grateful to have found a way to bend the magical rules. Jack, Arnie, and Ariel were the only ones who knew *how* Jack was able to return and stay.

She hadn't told Percy. She also hadn't told him about Maria, and the more days that slipped by, the less she felt sure that telling him offered any benefit. Percy lived a comfortable life in Florida, a long way away from the magic and from having to think about it on a daily basis. Keeping him as oblivious as possible seemed like the kindest option, especially given the state of Maria's book.

When Stella finally asked about it last week, Arnie said there was only one chapter remaining. After more than twenty years, Stella couldn't stir up any emotions other than disbelief, anger, and scanty acceptance that she would never know Maria and didn't really want to know her now.

Ariel caught sight of the notebook. "How's the story going?"

Stella exhaled a trapped breath. Thinking of Maria did that to her every time. She grabbed Jack's hand and walked around the desk to join Ariel, Liam, and Scout. They crossed the foyer in a group. "I've never written so quickly in my life. I'm about fifty thousand words in, and I finally settled on a title."

Liam held open the library doors and handed Scout's leash to Ariel. "Thank you," she said and looked at Stella. "Don't keep me in suspense! What's the title? Can I add it to my TBR?"

Stella glanced at Jack, who was smiling at her. "*The Charmed Library*."

Ariel shivered and bounced down the stairs. "I have chills! That means it's the right title."

"It's perfect," Stella agreed as they stepped fully into the sunlight together. Jack squeezed her hand, and the four of them, plus Scout, walked down the sidewalk toward the park. Silvery words floated by on a breeze that offered relief from the summer heat.

Live life. Laugh often. Love more.

Author's Note

The first spark for *The Charmed Library* lit in my imagination many years ago when I asked myself a whimsical, wishful question: What if I could magic fictional characters out of their books and spend time with them in the real world? Not just by rereading the same cherished pages or imagining new adventures in my head, but in an actual, tangible way. What if I could talk to them, share a cup of tea, ask them the questions that have lived in my heart since I first met them? What if I could spend the night in a library—and not just read the books, but live among the stories?

That daydream never truly left me. It nestled somewhere inside me like a warm ember, and over time it began to glow brighter, drawing other questions toward it: What makes a character stay with us forever? What if the stories we love could love us back? And most poignantly: What if stories could help us find our way when we feel lost?

As for many book lovers, libraries have always been a place of wonder and enchantment for me. Libraries were my retreat, my hiding place, my treasure chest. They offered the comfort of silence, the thrill of discovery, and the gentle kind of belonging that doesn't ask you to be anything but exactly who you are.

When I left home for college, I found myself in a new place

AUTHOR'S NOTE

that was foreign and unfamiliar. In college, making friends felt about as easy as running a marathon in high heels. I felt like a bumbling awkward kid who didn't know much of anything, but I *did* know how to find a library. The university library became a sanctuary. I went there to do homework, yes—but also to feel tethered to something quiet and kind. Even when I didn't realize I needed comfort, the library offered it, like an old friend quietly sliding into the seat beside me, just to be near.

And that's the thing about libraries, isn't it? They're always open in spirit, even when their doors are closed. They say, *You're welcome here. Come as you are. Stay as long as you like. And when you leave, take a piece of the magic with you.*

That feeling—that blend of safety, wonder, and possibility—is at the heart of *The Charmed Library*. I knew this would be a book that honored not only my love of libraries, but also the healing power of words and stories and the people who create and care for them. I knew this book would whisper, *You're not stuck. You're just paused. There's more life ahead than you can see right now.*

Stella's story is about what it means to be caught in the in-between, in that liminal space where you know the life you had no longer fits, but the new shape hasn't yet formed. It's a story about grief and growth and the quiet courage it takes to start again. Through Stella, I wanted to explore the way stories help us shift perspective, imagine new futures, and even reckon with our pasts. Sometimes a fictional character says the exact thing we didn't know we needed to hear. Sometimes a line of dialogue or a single sentence can reorient an entire worldview. Books, words, libraries—they are doorways.

And as readers, we are so lucky. We get to walk through those doorways again and again, meeting new friends, exploring new lands, falling in love, falling apart, healing, and beginning again. I

AUTHOR'S NOTE

am endlessly grateful for the authors who have created fantastical, enchanting, beloved, and even feared fictional characters whom I still love—and will love all my life. Their stories made me who I am. Their words lit the way forward when I couldn't quite see the path. And it is my greatest joy and deepest honor to now offer my own stories in return.

To every reader who picks up *The Charmed Library*, thank you. I hope this book feels like a cozy nook and a spark of wonder. I hope it reminds you that stories are alive, and that sometimes they reach out to hold us when we need them most. And above all, I hope it leaves you believing that magic—*real magic*—lives in the spaces we share, the words we write, and the stories we carry home.

Acknowledgments

Writing *The Charmed Library* felt like stepping into a cozy, enchanted world—one built from book whispers, childlike wonder, and the wild belief that stories can change lives. This kind of enchantment only appears when your heart is wide open. This book stretched me, healed me, and reminded me that sometimes stories choose us.

Writing is often called a solitary act, but that's never how it feels to me. When I'm immersed in a story, I'm never alone—I'm surrounded by characters who chatter, charm, and challenge me, and by a circle of real-life magic-makers who believe in the power of stories and in me.

Heaps of thank-yous to Jason Steffens, who's been listening to me talk about stories for what feels like forever (and probably has been!) and who always responds with the same calm, thoughtful steadiness. You listened to the earliest ideas for *The Charmed Library* and said, without hesitation, "You can write this. You *have* to." Thank you for being you—exactly the puzzle piece that fits with mine. Your presence in my life is grounding, encouraging, and everything I need and more on this life adventure.

To Ami McConnell, my brilliant, radiant agent—thank you for choosing me. I will never get over the joy of being on your team.

ACKNOWLEDGMENTS

Your belief in story, in beauty, in goodness, and in heart is a gift to this world. I am endlessly inspired by your guidance, your vision, and your fierce advocacy for the magic of the written word. Thank you for helping me expand not only my career but also my capacity for dreaming bigger and bolder.

To N. P. Conti, my soul sister in every way—what would I do without our cosmic conversations, our dream-weaving afternoons, and our endless text threads that somehow solve everything? You see my heart and help me listen to it. Thank you for walking beside me in all dimensions. You hold my dreams like they're your own. There's no magic quite like ours, and I cherish it with my whole heart.

Rea Frey, you are a champion for creativity, for following your own path, and for facing challenges head-on. Thank you for your endless encouragement during stormy seasons, for being a cheerleader through every win and wobble, and for not only believing in me but also truly seeing me. I treasure your friendship more than words can express. You are a warrior and an inspiration.

To Kathie and Roy Bennett and Magic Time Literary—what a stroke of serendipity to have found you. You are a force of nature and a heart-led guide. Thank you for believing in my stories and for lighting the way with grace, joy, and sparkle. You add so much goodness, fun, and travel to my author journey. I feel so blessed that you said yes to me!

To Lizzie Poteet, thank you for bringing such clear vision, care, and insight to this story. Your guidance helped shape this book into something I'm deeply proud of. To Laura Wheeler, thank you for bringing the book across the finish line with grace and precision. I'm so grateful for your brilliance and your incredible support of my writing and my voice.

To Harper Muse, thank you for being a dream team. Amanda Bostic, thank you for making space for my voice and for nurturing every

ACKNOWLEDGMENTS

step of this journey with thoughtful care. Taylor Ward, Savannah Breedlove, Natalie Underwood, Jere Warren, Kerri Potts, Colleen Lacy, Margaret Kercher—you bring beauty, strategy, and creative joy to every part of this process. Thank you, thank you, thank you. And to HarperCollins—thank you for helping me share stories that come from the deepest parts of my heart.

To Jackie, thank you for being my earliest reader, for sharing your honest feedback and your dazzling intelligence, and for bringing your entire heart to my words. Your brilliance is rivaled only by your kindness. Thank you for helping me shape the early draft into something I truly believed in—I adore every chance we get to work together.

To my forever-amazing family, thank you for your never-ending encouragement, your love, and your laughter. You make all of this so much more interesting, hilarious, and fun. The things we've done and seen seem so much wilder than anything I could create in fiction. Thank you for sticking with me whether I was thorns or rainbows or a mix of both.

To every library, bookstore, book club, and reading group who has welcomed me with open arms—thank you. You are the soul of this reading world. Your warmth, curiosity, and kindness make this work feel so deeply human. It is a true honor to be invited into your spaces and your conversations. You are magic. Pure and simple.

And finally, to my incredible readers. Thank you for returning to my stories again and again, for letting me whisper a little magic into your world. May this book find you at just the right moment and remind you that wonder lives everywhere—especially in the quiet corners and forgotten shelves of a charmed library.

With love and stardust,
Jennifer

Discussion Questions

1. If you could bring one fictional character to life like Stella does, who would it be—and why?

2. *The Charmed Library* is, at its heart, a love letter to books. What book changed your life the way Stella's favorite novel changed hers?

3. What does the story say about the power of imagination? How does Stella's ability to see words give her deeper insight into the world?

4. How do you think the presence of fictional characters in real life might impact society—or our own lives—if it were truly possible?

5. Stella finds safety, magic, and discovery in the Blue Sky Valley library. What has a library meant to you during different chapters of your life?

6. How does *The Charmed Library* remind us of the importance of libraries—not just for books, but for community, healing, and belonging?

DISCUSSION QUESTIONS

7. Stella is grieving multiple things: the death of her father, a breakup, and her struggle to regain a sense of direction. How do her losses affect her ability to move forward?

8. The burning of Stella's journal acts as a turning point in the story. Have you ever experienced a moment when releasing something opened the door to unexpected transformation?

9. Jack was Stella's childhood book crush. What does the story suggest about the nature of fictional love versus real-life connection?

10. What do you think the changing colors, fonts, and behaviors of the words symbolize in Stella's journey?

11. Stella feels "stuck" in her life. What role do stories—both fictional and our own—play in helping us discover our path or calling?

12. If you were to write the next chapter in your own life, what would the first line be?

LOOKING FOR MORE GREAT READS? LOOK NO FURTHER!

Illuminating minds and captivating hearts through story.

Visit us online to learn more:
harpermuse.com

Or scan the below code and sign up to receive email updates on new releases, giveaways, book deals, and more:

@harpermusebooks

About the Author

Photo by Matt Andrews

Jennifer Moorman is the *USA TODAY* bestselling author of six novels, including *The Charmed Library*, *The Vanishing of Josephine Reynolds*, *The Magic All Around*, and the Mystic Water series. Her creative works also include a collection of folklore retellings and Strawberry Shortcake children's books.

Jennifer is a graduate of Middle Tennessee State University from the Recording Industry and English programs, and her writing has appeared in numerous publications, including *People*, *Parade*, *Writer's Digest*, *The Nerd Daily*, *Women's World*, *Hollywood Weekly*, and many more. She holds degrees with concentrations in mass communications, linguistics, and fiction writing, reflecting her diverse background in storytelling and communication.

She put together a band and toured the United States as an accomplished professional singer for five years. She also worked many years as a senior editor for HarperCollins, guiding authors through the writing, editing, and publishing processes.

Jennifer is the cocreator and cohost of the podcast *One Happy Thing* with fellow bestselling authors Kerry Schafer and Maddie Dawson.

When she's not writing, you can find her testing a new recipe, chasing rainbows, or stargazing. Jennifer lives in a magic house in Nashville, Tennessee.

Connect with Jennifer at jennifermoorman.com
Instagram: @jenniferrmoorman
Facebook: @jennifermoormanbooks
BookBub: @JenniferMoorman